Damaged

Eric Horridge

(Writing as Saul Friedmann)

Front Cover Design: Michael Horridge

Cover photos: Public Domain, Royalty Free

Book design by Eric Horridge

Eric Horridge

DEDICATION

This book is dedicated to every person who has ever looked up to the stars, sought inspiration, and received it.

Damaged

Damage

Word forms: *plural, 3rd person singular present tense* **damages**, *present participle* **damaging**, *past tense, past participle* **damaged**

----

1. VERB

To ***damage*** *an object means to break it, spoil it physically, or stop it from working properly.*

Synonyms: *spoil, hurt, injure, smash*

2. UNCOUNTABLE NOUN

Damage *is physical harm that is caused to an object.*

3. UNCOUNTABLE NOUN

Damage *consists of the unpleasant effects that something has on a person, situation, or type of activity.*

(Collins Dictionary)

"No matter where we each stand, together we can look upon the same sun, the same moon, and the same sky, so we are forever one."

(unknown...extracted from Kristin McCarthy article 92 Quotes... – as amended)

Prologue

15th April 1912

The screams had grown louder since midnight. The panic increased as it became evident that there were not enough lifeboats. The order to abandon ship had been slow in coming and many passengers on board believed that it was only a drill. They decided to stay where it was warm and not venture out into the cold. It was a mistake and would cost many their lives.
He had been lucky and had gone to the right place. The ship was listing slightly to port, but they had been able to launch a few of the lifeboats from both sides of the ship. Many had already moved away packed with those lucky enough to get on board while some had been launched with empty seats. The man found himself near the front of the queue, people were pushing, shoving, clawing, and shouting to be let onto the next craft to launch. It was now a quarter to two in the morning, the icy water was filled with those who had jumped from the many decks of the great ship. The superstructure was a sad silhouette against the moonlit sky, the lights from its many portholes and windows reflecting on the disturbed water.
"Get in," shouted the officer, "hurry or someone else will take your spot!"
The man stood for a second, the injury to his head still bled and fear seemed to keep him rooted to the spot. "Hurry up!" the officer repeated, his breath like steam as the cold air took his words and threw them into the night sky. The man was in shock, taking a long look around him, confused by what was happening. It had been unthinkable just a few hours before. "Yes Sir," the man replied finally, "but what about you?"
"I'll be alright, son," the officer said, and then in what appeared to be an afterthought he removed his wedding ring and passed him a small silver locket. "Here take these, give them to my wife…tell her I…."
The officer's words were lost to him as the lifeboat lurched with the sudden movement of the large ship. An explosion from deep within its bowels shook the skin and tore a hole in one of the bulkheads. Icy seawater poured deeper and further into the vessel's corridors and

passageways. The officer fell backward, and the lifeboat lurched again, the lines holding it steady, failing, and it dropped towards the waiting sea, smashing into the waves sending water spraying in all directions and drenching many of those on board. The man had just managed to clamber aboard falling heavily, hitting his head against the side of the boat, and breaking ribs on one of the oars as his body jackknifed and spasmed. Shouts of "move away," and "row," brought the man to his senses. All around him the cacophony of screams, people falling from great heights, jumping and flailing in the air as they accelerated down towards the black water, assaulted his consciousness. Tears flowed down his cheeks as the boat moved steadily away from the large bulk that was beginning to yaw back to starboard. The sound of screeching metal as the ship began to break up filled the air. The sight of the mighty ship dying would stay with him forever. Others in the boat with him watched in horror, noticing heads and arms bobbing in the freezing water, some passengers were already dead, some desperately hanging on for a few more moments of life, their cries lost in the noise and chaos. Those in the overflowing lifeboat could only watch as they slowly drifted away from danger. They were the lucky ones, and he was one of them. He should not have been there, but it was fate that had allowed him to find his way to that specific deck. He had only left his position after it became obvious that nothing more could be done. Most of his mates and fellow crew members had already abandoned their positions, some knocking him over, trampling him in their eagerness to escape. It was every man for himself and yet despite being left behind in the blackness of the ailing ship, and being partially concussed, he had somehow managed to find his way out of the darkness.
His confused thoughts turned to the officer, the man's bravery and trust. The young crewman felt the locket and the ring against his wet thigh, while tears continued to sting his eyes. He began to row purposefully but painfully, only lifting his head when some of those in the boat screamed in horror as they observed what was happening in front of them. He noticed some of those in the boat were praying. Some sat silently, the shock of what had happened too much to comprehend. The cold had numbed his hands and feet, yet he continued to row despite having no feeling in his fingers. He found himself shivering violently, his entire body racked with fear, guilt, and anger.

Guilt…
Why was he in this boat when so many others were dying?
It was a fleeting thought, but one that remained with him…..forever.

CHAPTER 1

The wall and the trees surrounding the graveyard kept him from being seen. That, and the pitch-black night. He guessed he wasn't the only one taking advantage of the stillness. He had noticed a few cars parked close by, in some of the quieter spots. Areas used by lovers and others that frequented the remoter parts of the cemetery. The places furthest from the Chapel but still within the trees of the Common.

It was just above freezing and there was very little cloud in the night sky, the only mist to be seen was that expelled from the crouching figure's mouth. There was a new moon, the stage in the cycle when there is no moon to be seen at all. This ensured the depth of the darkness. The figure crept slowly through the weeds taking care to find a firm foothold with each step. It was slow going but there was no rush. Time was of no concern. As he continued searching he turned on a small torch that he could conceal within his hand, allowing his fingers some control over the beam and giving him just enough light to see the headstones that surrounded him. He didn't care that Southampton Old Cemetery had become overgrown in places or that the dead lying there were associated with many of the country's most significant conflicts. The Boer War, the Charge of the Light Brigade, and the Battle of Waterloo, amongst others. He had a conflict of his own and nothing outside of that mattered. He continued with his slow walk, shining the light on the occasional slanting edifice, finding some had weathered to the extent that it was impossible to read any of the inscriptions written upon them. Fortunately, he knew which grave he was looking for and where it was situated. As he continued, his feet brushed through the now frost-covered grasses which crunched underfoot. Suddenly and without warning a screech split the silent air. He flinched, bending at the waist, his coat brushing the ground. He anticipated being attacked but no blow came. He was puzzled for a second but kept a low profile, his breathing rapid, his heart rate accelerating. He listened carefully but could only hear the faint sound of a few cars that passed along Hill Lane on the Western side of the graveyard and Cemetery Road to the East. He remained still for almost a minute allowing himself to gather his senses and understand what had happened. An owl, or something similar, he concluded. He would not let his friends know that he had been scared, all they needed to see was his handiwork. Tagging a headstone was part of the game. He felt the reassuring weight of the tins that he had bought that morning. The material of the backpack was light and though he had added padding to prevent the tins from rattling together, there was no weight to think of. He looked at his watch, the green dial showed him that it was nearly three-thirty. He needed to keep going, so he continued his slow walk. His eyes had now grown accustomed to the dark but occasionally the low beam of the torch impacted his ability to see clearly. He tripped, falling over a low stone base, landing awkwardly, his shins and ribs cracking against opposite sides of the oblong outline of the grave.

"Shit!" he exclaimed. It was an automatic response, unintended but louder than he had wanted. Slowly he lifted himself up, then immediately felt the effects of the bruises and the grazes he had acquired. The pain was less than the indignity suffered but as there was no one there to see what had happened he would let his friends know that the soiled knees of his jeans, the knicks on his hands, and the stain on his parka elbows were the result of something else, rather than admitting to a fall. He pushed on, snapping a twig that startled a fox. He caught a glimpse of it as the animal ran into the undergrowth, away to his right, disappearing as quickly as it had shown itself. He was sweating now. At eighteen he was fit but slight, and the nervous energy he had used as a result of the fall had affected his confidence. He felt as though he had aged, that his youthful exuberance and no-care attitude had been affected. This was harder than he thought it would be. His willingness to continue was being impacted by his nervousness but he needed to prove that he could do it. He carried on, finally finding what he was looking for. He dropped into a squatting position and began to remove the bag from his back. He placed the torch on the ground facing the headstone, lighting up part of the inscription. As he did so a gloved hand seemingly from nowhere covered his mouth. He felt himself being pulled over, falling backward, and bumping against the leg of someone, preventing him from hitting the ground. A blade glinted briefly in the torch light. The boy's eyes bulged indicating the panic he felt inside. The blade sliced across his throat. A wound deep and raw opened and blood spurted, splattering down his neck and onto the ground. The hand remained where it was, holding the boy's mouth closed. The sound of death gurgled between the fingers of the attacker who remained silent, unknown, holding the boy partially upright. The struggle for life ended quickly. The boy's coat was covered with a sticky mess, almost invisible in the poor light. The attacker let the body drop, walking away silently, leaving behind the boy to rest where many already were.

CHAPTER 2

"Who is he?" he asked. It was a predictable question, and he received a predictable answer.
"We don't know," DS Barry White replied, "nothing was found on the body that we can use to identify him."
The man nodded, then stood up to his full height, his knees cracking as he did so. He gently pulled the blue blanket back over the top half of the body. It had been placed there a while earlier by an ambulance driver, one of the first on the scene after the authorities had been notified. Detective Inspector James 'Jim' Brierly, ex-Royal Navy, known as *'The Gnome'* to all his colleagues, looked around him but stayed completely still. The cold of the night had remained even as the sun had risen. There was no warmth in the rays as they filtered through the trees surrounding the body.
"Do we know who found him?" he questioned.
"Yes, a man walking his dog."
"What, through here?"
Brierly moved his head but not his feet. He was conscious of the need not to disturb the scene. The Forensics team was on its way but had been delayed. "Staff cuts and illness", was what he had been told. He pointed at the weeds and trees, the way they stood covered in frost and ice. Some looked like accusing fingers pointing at the two policemen. It was as if they were finding the two men guilty of what had happened overnight.
"Yes Jim," White continued eventually, in answer to Brierly's question. The lack of formality was a sign of the men's relationship. They had worked together for several years now, and they were good friends as well as colleagues. White, stockily built, bald as a coot, and a gym junkie of sorts was dressed in a bottle-green chore coat, with only the bottom two buttons fastened. It seemed to Brierly that White didn't feel the cold as much as he did. Brierly's grey Peacoat was fully done up and under which he wore a knitted dark blue jumper. Black slacks completed his look, while White was satisfied with his jeans. Brierly was glad he was wearing thermals too, given the temperature. He looked down at the body, noting the still-open eyes which exacerbated the surprise etched on the boy's face.
"The poor sod," Brierly said, nodding in the boy's direction. "Why

the hell was he here? What was he doing all alone in the middle of the night?" he queried rhetorically, knowing that White would have no immediate answer to his questions. "Did the dog walker find anything else?" he asked.
"From what he told PC Weatherall, the answer to that is no, Jim."
"Nothing at all?"
"No."
"Do we have his name, the man who found the body?"
"Yes," White replied, "A Terence Silver," he added, looking at his notes. White had arrived at the scene a quarter of an hour before Brierly who had been in a meeting when Constable Weatherall had called in to report the finding of the body. The PC had been in his patrol car when the 999-call made by Silver had been passed on. Having been shown the body of the young boy, he had called for an ambulance before contacting CID at the Southampton Central Police station.
"Where is he now?" Brierly asked.
"According to Weatherall, he's been taken home….in the ambulance. The paramedics said that Silver was suffering slightly from shock but didn't think he needed to go to the hospital."
"And I assume they decided not to stick around because they had other jobs to do?"
"Yes. There's no need. Until Forensics get here, we can't move the body and the mortuary is where this kid is going to end up for now anyway…plus the ambulance was needed elsewhere."
"Bloody funding cuts!" Brierly said. The Police, the NHS the Fire Brigades, and many other essential services were all being affected in the same way. It had started while he was still in the navy. More was being demanded with less. Funding had now been a part of the landscape for years. Budgets were continuously slashed, yet crime was still expected to be brought down. Cases required to be solved more speedily. Brierly wasn't political but he knew that whoever was in power in Downing Street, the Left or the Right, Labour or Conservatives, money or lack thereof, was always an issue.
White didn't react to Brierly's outburst, remaining silent even though he agreed with his boss. It wasn't the time or the place. Maybe in the Duke of Wellington later? Brierly looked around, the crushed grass that surrounded the body showed several partial footprints. Brierly guessed they were of the boy, the killer, the dog walker, and likely

those of PC Weatherall as well. He and White had tried to be careful of the environs so it would be interesting to see what the scientific boys came up with once they had surveyed the area.
"We'll need to speak to Mr. Silver," Brierly said, looking at the boy's shoes. They were quite new and expensive, a trend he was made aware of from the requirements of his sons. "How much do you think they cost?" he asked, pointing at the yellow, blue, and slightly dirty branded runners: Nike.
"No idea, Jim," White replied. His only daughter now lived with his ex-wife up in Derby and had done so for quite some time now. She was nearly fifteen and her focus was on beauty products, clothes, and proper shoes, not runners.
"A hundred quid?" he added.
"More like five hundred plus."
"Bloody hell!"
"Exactly," Brierly replied. "How does someone as young as this afford to buy them?"
"Buggered if I know," White answered. "Maybe a rich father?"
Brierly nodded imperceptibly. He was thinking of something more nefarious. "Once we get a name, then I guess we'll find out," he said. "In the meantime, get Weatherall here, we need to go and have a chat with Mr. Silver....and call Ops, to find out where that bloody Forensics team is."
White took out his mobile phone and made the call. Brierly took another look around before slowly making his way back through the graveyard toward his car. As he reached Cemetery Road and a strip of parking spaces he looked back to see PC Weatherall walking in the general direction of where the body of the boy was lying. He unlocked his car just as the Forensics team turned off Northlands Road and drove towards the cemetery gates. They would likely spend most of the day doing what they needed to do. Brierly would give Gemma Atkins a call later, to arrange for them to meet in the next day or so.
"Jump in," he said to White, who had found his way back to the car, "you have his address?"
"Yes, Jim. It's Kineton Road, just off Hill Street, literally just a couple of minute's drive away."
Brierly started the car, cranking up the temperature of the car's heater. He hadn't noticed how cold his feet were until now. The weak

sun was already heading down, and it would set just after five. It wasn't his favourite time of year; Winter. Even worse was that it had been a poor summer, seemingly colder and wetter than usual, particularly in this part of the country. He noticed it was only seven degrees now and wouldn't be getting any higher.
"You navigate," he said to White. He didn't see the point of using the car's GPS for such a short trip.

CHAPTER 3

The house on Kineton Road was a typical semi-detached, with a pebble-dash exterior, bay windows under a faux Elizabethan parapet, and a red tile roof. The whole street seemed to be made up of houses made from the same mould, even down to the single red garage doors. Brierly found a spot to park his car a few houses down from that of Silver. He was fortunate as the street was almost full of parked vehicles.

"I guess people are still mostly working from home," he said. "It's a pretty busy street for a Tuesday."

White agreed, nodding as he walked slightly ahead of his boss, before rapping his knuckles on the front door of Terence Silver's home. Initially, there was no response until White knocked again a little firmer. They could hear someone call out that they were on their way. Brierly took a step back and looked up to the bedroom window. It was covered with lace, but he thought he saw the curtain twitch just as he lifted his head. He was about to give White a gentle nudge when the front door opened. A woman in her early forties, dressed in jeans with upturned hems, a plain black tee-shirt, and an open grey cardigan stood in the doorway. She was slim, with short auburn hair that was cut around her ears and with a jagged fringe just above her eyebrows. An attractive woman, Brierly thought, noticing the white runners on her feet. They could feel the warmth of the house from behind her, which contrasted with the cold they were standing in. Somewhere from the back of the house a dog barked.

"Yes, can I help you?" she said.

Brierly and White showed her their police identification.

"Mrs. Silver?" White asked, introducing himself and his boss, "Is your husband here? We need to ask him a few questions if we can."

"Oh, is it about the body he found on his walk earlier?"

"Yes. Could we come in, please?" Brierly said, taking over from White.

"Of course," she answered, calling out to the man who then suddenly appeared at the top of the stairs. She moved to her left allowing the two policemen inside the house. "Oh, and it's Ms.," she added as they entered the hallway. "Grovedale, Christine Grovedale. Terence and I are not married."

Brierly smiled an affirmation of understanding. The formal relationship of the couple was of no importance for now, though he found it strange that she mentioned it when she did. Terence Silver met them at the bottom of the stairs. After completing introductions, he requested that the policemen should follow him into a formal lounge that was just off the passageway. He was a man of a similar age to Christine Grovedale, though he was a few inches taller than her. Brierly estimated the man was around five feet ten, with a normal build. He was also dressed casually in jeans and a light grey jumper. A light blue work shirt and loafers finished off the ensemble.
"I'm working from home," he said, almost apologetically, but with a smile. "Mostly having meetings via my computer or on the phone....upstairs, in my study," he added, pointing at the ceiling. Christine Grovedale who had remained standing just inside the door to the room while the three men had sat down, offered them a drink. Brierly and Silver asked for tea, but White declined. She turned and left them alone to talk.
"So, I suppose you have come to ask me about this morning?" Silver said, leaning forward on his chair. Brierly studied the man briefly. He had dark grey hair, seemingly premature given the man's apparent age, with clear blue eyes, a strong tan that seemed out of place given the time of year, and an open face. Brierly got the impression that he must smile a lot given the laughter lines around his mouth. He was also clean-shaven and smelt of a good cologne.
"Yes, that's correct," Brierly responded. "Perhaps you can fill us in, starting with what you saw."
Silver leant back and crossed his feet, placing his arms on either side of the high-back chair he was sitting on. "I'm not sure I can add much to what I've already told the Constable," he answered. "I was walking my dog through the graveyard, and we came across the body. A young boy, a teenager maybe? I got such a shock at first, then I called the police. That's about it."
"What time was this?" White asked.
"Oh, about ten to seven… it was just getting light."
"Do you always walk that way…every morning?"
"Not every morning, no. On the weekends I sometimes give it a miss and have a sleep-in until later. Then I'll walk a different way….the opposite way, towards the Ornamental Lake, rather than towards the Chapel as was the case this morning."

"But usually it's into the graveyard, via the common?" Brierly asked.
"Yes, I go down our road, cross Hill Lane, and then onto the common itself."
"Did you see anyone on your walk? Anyone acting suspiciously, in the graveyard itself or anywhere else?"
"No, I'm sorry Inspector, I didn't. As I explained to the Constable when he arrived, it was just getting light when I found the body. In fact, it was the dog that saw him before I did." Silver pointed over his shoulder to where they could hear a dog barking again. "He's a bit excited," he added, just as Christine Grovedale entered with a tray containing cups, saucers, milk, sugar, and a stainless-steel teapot. While she poured the drinks, Brierly looked around the room. It was nicely decorated using modern wallpaper with splashes of random colours on a predominantly white base. The furniture in the room was expensive, a real leather couch and two individual recliner chairs; light grey. They matched perfectly with the darker grey carpet which covered the entire floor. There were no loose cushions anywhere and no curtains either. Brierly recognized the incongruity with the lace over the upstairs windows that he had seen earlier. The windows were covered with blinds. Roman blinds without cords. They appeared to be motorized. The room had no TV either, just a three-sectioned wall unit filled with books. It was obvious that there had been money spent on the room. To give an impression, Brierly queried? Once everyone had what they needed to drink, Grovedale left them again, letting the three men continue their conversation.
"What do you do, Mr. Silver....for a living, I mean?" Brierly asked, noting White already had his notebook in hand.
"I'm a partner in a medium-size engineering firm, EL Bradman. We do surveying, design, and management of different projects, such as new housing estates, roads, and bridges, that sort of thing."
"And you do this from home?"
"Mostly, yes. Since the Covid pandemic however, my partners and I have realized the need for office space is not as it used to be. We encourage those that can, to split their week, two days at home and three in the office. The following week the staff do the opposite. Since we introduced the policy we've reduced our office footprint by fifty percent, and it's saved us a lot of money."
"So, you do have an office then," Brierly affirmed.
"Yes, in the Centurion Office Park, just off the A3204, on the other

side of the Northam bridge."
"Not very far then, Sir?" White said.
"No. It takes about ten minutes in the car, subject to the traffic of course."
"It hardly seems worth staying at home," White said to himself under his breath. Silver ignored the comment which had been said a little too loudly. Brierly asked for the address of the office which White began to note down, but Silver stood up and took a business card from a small cardholder that he had in his back pocket.
"It has my phone number and email details on it as well, if you need them," Silver said, pointing to the card. Brierly took a brief glance at it, before handing it over to White to pocket. Ever the salesman, Brierly thought as Silver sat down again.
"Getting back to this morning," Brierly continued. "Is the route you took the same one you normally take when walking your dog?"
"More or less. The dog sometimes goes off in unusual directions, but when I call him, he usually returns to me quickly enough."
"So, he goes off lead?"
"Once on the common, I take him off, yes. He goes snuffling around and I walk on, mostly on the paths. Occasionally I'll follow him if he's insistent. Sometimes he may see a fox or a rabbit and he gives chase, but he's a Labrador so he can't run very fast." The two policemen smiled along with Silver at the very thought of such a large dog trying to chase a rabbit. Their host continued. "This morning he wouldn't come when I called him, and he started barking. I went to find out what the problem was and came across the poor boy. That's when I put the dog on the leash and called 999."
"And there was nothing else that you could see? Just the body?" Brierly asked again, wanting to validate that there were no possessions of the victim anywhere nearby.
"That's right. The body was fully clothed, but there was blood everywhere. There was nothing else that I could see."
Given that Forensics had not been to the site by the time he and White had left the scene, it was too soon to conclude that there were none of the boy's possessions scattered around somewhere. Brierly found it odd that the body had no ID on it at all and a wider search of the area would likely be needed, particularly given the overgrown nature of the body's immediate surroundings. There was no obvious reason why the boy was in the graveyard, and certainly not in that

particular spot, but it was clear from the blood on the ground and on his clothes that he had been killed there. He may have just been passing through, on his way to somewhere else, but where? Until they identified him, any connection with the graveyard itself was a moot point.

Brierly realized that Silver could contribute little more to the investigation than he had done already, but he expected that they may need to talk with him again at some future point. "Can I ask that you come into the Central Police station tomorrow and give a formal statement?" Brierly asked. "We'll make the necessary arrangements for someone to be available to take it."

Silver agreed, "No problem," he said, "Is there a specific time?"

"No, but perhaps after ten would be best. It allows us time to clear out any 'overnighters' and get the paperwork done and out of the way," White said, smiling at the very thought. His sarcastic dig at the red tape a policeman had to endure, was less than subtle. "We don't want you having to waste your time waiting around until we have cleared the decks," he added. This latter comment was for Brierly's benefit. However, the use of nautical terms always amused Brierly when his team tried to be clever, given his own Royal Navy background. His time in the armed forces and what role he played during his time was well known.

A nod of understanding from Silver effectively concluded their conversation, however, Brierly had one more question to ask. "Tell me Mr. Silver, where were you and Ms. Grovedale last night, say between the hours of eight and midnight?"

Without hesitation, Silver answered, "We were here Inspector at home. We had a couple of glasses of wine, watched a bit of TV, and then went to bed. We have a routine, and we are normally asleep by about eleven. We go to bed about ten-thirty."

"Every night?" Brierly queried.

"Yes…more or less. If there is something we want to watch on TV or have something to do, we may stay up a little later, but not beyond midnight, I can assure you."

Brierly nodded, his face giving nothing away, then he stood and shook Silvers' hand. White did likewise. As they walked towards the door, Brierly pulled out a card of his own. With a smile, he asked Silver to give some thought to the scene he had come across. "I know it's upsetting, but if you can think of anything that comes to

mind, anything that might be relevant, no matter how immaterial, please don't hesitate to contact me."
He pointed at the card being spun around between Silvers' fingers. "It has my phone and email details on it," he added, with a dead-flat tone, a flat bat. White knew that his boss was also being sarcastic, but remained silent, keeping his face statue-like.
"I will," Silver replied, non-plussed.
The three men shook hands again Silver opened the front door and cold air rushed inwards. As they were about to leave, Brierly looked backward from the threshold and down along the passageway, just in time to see Christine Grovedale step back into what he guessed was the kitchen. Had she been listening to their conversation? Brierly wondered if she saw him glance at her, and questioned why she was standing there.

CHAPTER 4

The report on the radio and the story in the local paper, the Daily Echo, which they noticed on the newsagent's rack frightened them both. They had met up before their lectures and the two young men were now standing just outside the coffee shop/cafe on the campus of Solent University.
"I think we'd better go to the police," the one said in a hushed tone, as other students passed by walking into and out of the café.
Peter Damson suggested that they should move to a quieter spot, under a tree, about twenty yards away from where they were standing.
"Okay," he said eventually, a slight reluctance in his voice which his friend Sam Klein picked up on, "but let's do it at lunchtime, after lectures, say about one-thirty. We don't have anything on this afternoon until four o'clock when we have to attend our lab."
Klein nodded. He was pleased that Damson had agreed. His friend was bigger than himself in every way and exerted significant influence over the friendship group that they had created at the university. Klein as his name suggested in both Dutch and German was small. At around five feet two he was dwarfed by Damson, who stood just over six feet, and who had been the initiator of the graveyard stunt. Klein had been unsure how his friend would react to his suggestion. Standing under the tree which still seemed frozen, its branches bare and black, a silhouette of spiky fingers against the grey muddy sky, they drank their just acquired hot drinks. Gloved hands held the polystyrene cups tightly. They drank in silence for a while, both contemplating what they had gone through just over thirty hours prior and how it had impacted them both since. Dressed against the cold, they wore similar clothes. Jeans, knee-length puffer jacket coats, Damson in blue, Klein in black, beanies on their head, and runners on their feet. They had met when the study year began just ten weeks ago, both registered in courses related to Computer games. Damson was doing a B.Sc in Games Design, while Klein was reading for a B.Sc in Games Technology. Their mutual interest along with that of their friend Dave Crossley who had also been studying Games Design meant that they were almost bosom buddies from the start. A kind of collective. Their love of online gaming led them to start

playing together as a team. Games like *Overwatch, Counterstrike, Smite, Halo*, and others, had sparked an easy friendship and with that a taste for risk-taking. The graveyard episode was one such example. Being out during the early hours of the morning on a day when they had lectures to attend was dumb and they knew it, but they did it anyway. Now they were faced with the unknown. Their friend was dead. Crossley had come down from Dundee and had been staying with his divorced Aunt who welcomed both the company and the small rent that her nephew paid her. Damson and Klein were both local and had been able to slip in and out of their own homes at any time of the day or night. Students working late in university libraries or laboratories was not unusual and they used that fact to hide some of the antics that they had been getting up to. They were mostly engaged in innocent fun in their eyes, but not everyone would agree with them. Graffitiing old headstones or tagging bus stops was an expression of art to them. They didn't see the harm in it. What they were doing was capable of being washed off anyway, as far as they were concerned. They didn't see that what they were doing was permanently damaging property. Now, however, given what had happened, they realized just how much trouble they could be in. They didn't yet know if Crossley had been named as the victim, the newspaper story had said that the body had not been identified and that the police were hoping someone would be able to advise them once an appropriate picture was ready to be published in the press and on social media.

To ease their conscience, the decision was made to get in first and answer the necessary questions that would inevitably follow. The two students hoped it would be the right one. With coffee finished they walked towards their building readying themselves for the day. Both felt unsettled by what they had experienced. The conversation with the police wouldn't be as simple as they would like, but they hoped that after a ten-minute walk from the East Park Terrace campus and a three-minute bus ride, via the Central Bus station, they would be ready.

The morning lectures would test their powers of concentration.

CHAPTER 5

Brierly had assembled his team just outside his office. He was sitting on the edge of a desk. White had cleared it for him, giving him ample room on which his boss could perch. Usually, they would meet in a conference room a level above their floor, but there were renovations underway, and the entire area was off-limits. Burst radiator pipes some weeks before had flooded several offices often used as situation rooms and apart from the fixes, there was a need to replace carpets which had rotted from the fetid water. The burst had occurred over a weekend and the station had been unusually quiet, no one noticing the water leak until the early hours of the Sunday morning. It had been running for over fifteen hours, disrupting some of the backroom staff as well at the start of their working week. The radiators were replaced or restored to working order within a week, but the carpets were still to be delivered. Furniture was piled up on top of each other ready for the laying of the replacement, but it was still expected to be another ten days before things would start moving. Brierly looked around him. Apart from White he still had DC Bryn Hughes, but he had lost DC Wendy Davids. The recent death of their colleague DC Lindsey who had been hiding his involvement in the murders of several women in the local area had shaken her very badly. Lindsey had been able to keep his private life along with his deteriorating mental condition secret. This he was able to do while working on the investigation into the murders alongside Brierly and the rest of the team. The case had been a difficult one and had affected Davids's sense of purpose. A career in the police force, especially in CID, had been her dream. Lindsey, however, had shattered that illusion and after being given time off to consider her future as a police detective she had decided to resign. Davids had a daughter who was now ten and a husband to look after, so she had decided to revert to her other love which was teaching. She knew that she would need to go back to college for a while but she hoped that in the long run, she would be happier than investigating the deaths and killings that she had been exposed to in recent years. Brierly missed her, but in her stead, he had found able replacements for both her and Lindsey in DC Clive Proctor and DC Evan Track. Proctor was originally from Cheltenham in Gloucestershire and was a big rugby union fan, something that he was able to discuss ad nauseum with DC Hughes. Brierly had originally expected Proctor to be into horse racing given his hometown, but it soon became evident that it was not the case. "I may be from Cheltenham but I'm not much into jumps racing," he had said to Brierly's surprise. A big man, at twenty-two years of age, Proctor was six feet four tall. Solidly built, a second-row lock in a rugby union scrum if ever there was one, with cauliflower ears to match. He played for Southampton RFC in the first team. Despite being so tall, he was also very good-looking. He had constant stubble on his face making him seem older than he was, but also more rugged. Except for his ears, his face was unmarked despite the occasional raking with a boot he received when at the bottom of a tackle or a ruck. With his physique and wide smile, he was a hit with the ladies and always received plenty of attention from those working in the police station. DC Track however was a somewhat different proposition, and it was how Brierly liked it. He needed people on his team who could think differently, independently yet sensibly. Track was originally from York and had graduated some years prior from the University of Bournemouth, completing his Law degree under the Professional Policing Degree scheme. He was relatively small in comparison to Proctor, standing at an inch below six feet, but he had a very good intellect and Brierly admired that. It wasn't a case of brains or brawn that distinguished between the two recruits into his team, it was rather, as Brierly described things, as "bodies *with* brains".

With just the five of them gathered together, Brierly laid out what they had so learnt far. Describing what he and White had seen of the body in the cemetery and what they had discussed with Terence Silver and Christine Grovedale. "So, we need to find out who this boy is," he said, "there must be someone who knows. It's doubtful that he was in the cemetery without anyone being aware of what he was doing."

"Sir," Hughes asked, taking a lead over the others, "Is it possible that he was just wanting to vandalize the headstones? Graffiti or tag them perhaps? We seem to be seeing a lot of that at the moment."

"Anything is possible, Hughes, so you may well be right, but I'd suggest that what occurred was a case of the boy being in the wrong place at the wrong time."

"Why do you say that Sir?" Track asked. "Isn't it just possible that the killer was waiting for a victim…and he was lucky enough to find one on the night?"

Brierly smiled at his relatively new DC. "As I said, anything is possible, but someone waiting around the graveyard in the freezing cold, just on the off chance that a victim will come along…well, I think it's highly unlikely don't you? No, I think there is something else behind it."

"Any ideas, Sir?" Track asked again.

Brierly looked directly into the Constable's face, before saying with conviction words that surprised the team as to their candour. "Absolutely none, Constable, and that's why we need to find out who this boy is in the first instance! Someone knows something," he added, his hand slapping his knee to emphasize his point, "and we need to find that someone." Turning to DS White, he said, "Let's get the kid's picture out, get the appeal going for any information anyone may have. Check on CCTV from the area. If and when necessary we'll issue an appeal via Crimestoppers, but not just yet. The murder has already been splashed on the radio and in the *Echo*, but no descriptions have been given, as we requested, so at least the public is aware that there has been a body found, but that's all. We just need to catch the bastard before they strike again."

"Do you think we need to set up a patrol, Sir?" Proctor asked, speaking for the first time. He had heard what had been said so far but given his naturally robust nature, he was always keen to get physical if needed.

"You mean around the immediate area?" Brierly answered, "Around the common and the cemetery?"

"Yes, Sir."

Brierly looked at White before answering. "If we need to set up an operation to catch the person responsible, we most certainly will, Proctor. However, given we are not sure if this is an opportunistic killing or something else, we'll need to keep our powder dry for now."

DC Proctor nodded but seemed unsure of where Brierly was going with his comments. He raised a hand midway through Brierly's reply, intending to seek clarity, but then lowered it as Brierly continued. "It's not often that we have people murdered in this area, as I'm sure it's the same in and around Gloucester. We're not like London or Manchester or any of the other big cities, but when it does happen it's quite often related to a domestic matter or drug-related, gang-related. Random killings are rare. Being the size of the community that we are, gives us an advantage of sorts that other cities don't always have."

"So, DC Proctor, DC Track," White jumped in, "what DI Brierly means is that the person who did this is likely a local, though not guaranteed obviously. If we can find out the victim's name, where they live, and what their personal circumstances are, we can use our local knowledge and our known local crim-base as a good starting point in the investigation."

"Keeping it low-key for now then?" Proctor asked.

"Yes," Brierly replied. "We'll have more success that way in my opinion, than if we started panicking the community." He knew from experience that over-reacting would only cause the police and public echelons to get in the way and cause more logjams during the investigation. If there were leads provided that were without substance, it could cause their focus to go down unnecessary rabbit holes. Brierly liked order and process, not dysfunction. Random links within a case, with arms that stretched nowhere and everywhere, tended to drain his limited resources. It had happened in the past and because of that people died…young girls, unnecessarily. He didn't want to experience that again.

The room had gone quiet. DC Hughes and DS White knew where Brierly was coming from, Proctor and Track however still had some way to go before they fully understood their boss.

"Right!" Brierly said, getting to his feet. "DS White, can I leave the organization to you with regards to who is doing what?" White nodded in response. "Good, then I'll see you in an hour," he added turning towards his office door. "Oh, by the way, I'm due to see DCI Hammond in five minutes, so can you contact Gemma Atkins at the University mortuary and let her know if she can send us her autopsy report on the boy as soon as possible? I would appreciate it."

White gave a brief flick of his chin indicating to Brierly that he had heard what his boss had said, but he was unsure if Brierly noticed. It was clear that with nothing having been said during the meeting about additional resources for the investigation that things were tight and that budgets were likely on the agenda for Brierly's meeting with his own boss. Perhaps that was the reason why things were being maintained at such a low key?

CHAPTER 6

"So, Jim, do you have anything to go on as yet?" DCI Hammond asked as he sat forward on his chair. He had both hands clasped together as if in prayer, resting on his desk. Brierly looked at his boss, considering how to answer. He liked the man and they got on well together, both understood the foibles of the police force as it was today and the limitations it possessed. The public hardly knew anything about the way the institution worked nowadays. The days of youngsters marching into police stations and asking questions to satisfy school project requirements about *Sir Robert Peel, the Peelers* and *Bobbies* had all gone. Now everything was online and information about the past could be Googled. It seemed to both men that the only time any young person made their way to a police station today was to trash it, to protest, or because of them having been arrested. The police were now the enemy, a force used by the State to control the public. This was particularly evident during the Covid-19 pandemic, which coupled with ongoing climate change rallies only seemed to exacerbate the problem. The element of trust across the community had been broken. It was another reason why Brierly was cautious in how he approached any investigation. Information the police had, needed, or requested was often used, abused, and twisted to create a narrative of thought. A lack of resourcing, and the ability to resolve crimes quickly, was never allowed to get in the way of a good story as far as those with an agenda were concerned.

"No Sir, nothing concrete anyway," Brierly answered, "though it's still early in the investigation. I've kicked off the process and I've asked for Gemma's report, which I hope to get in the next twenty-four hours or so, but…."

"But…?" Hammond queried, raising an eyebrow at Brierly's hesitation.

"Well something is bothering me about the murder, and I'm not sure why or what it is."

"Go on," Hammond encouraged.

"I'm not sure I can, Sir, but there is something unusual about it that I just can't seem to put my finger on just yet. I have to give it more thought."

Hammond sat back in his chair, sighing loudly, expelling the tension

that Brierly's comments had started to build up inside his chest. He had expected something more. Now, he felt deflated like a balloon that had just popped. It was as if Brierly had already worked out what had happened in the cemetery, but anti-climactically had refused to share his findings. Hammond knew that this wasn't the case. He knew that Brierly was not the type of copper who kept things from his boss, so he offered his full support, telling Brierly that he would do everything he could to help the team. "Except I can't give you any more officers," he said, "no additional feet on the ground…at least for now. You know how it is."
"What about admin staff?" Brierly asked, "those we need to man the phones, do the paperwork, capture data? What about them?"
Hammond sighed again. It was the part of his job that he hated. He picked up a printed spreadsheet that had been lying on the right-hand side of his desk, pointing towards a series of numbers. "Those are the redundancies," he said, highlighting several names and amounts that seemed to stretch beyond just a handful. "I'm showing you this in confidence," he added, "just so you know what's going on around here."
Brierly was shocked, not having been aware, even via the rumour mill that cuts were coming. Cuts he now understood were deep and wide. He was simultaneously concerned and angry. "How are we to do our jobs if we keep on doing this, Dave..Sir? How the hell can we protect the community when we don't have people to do the work?" he continued, his voice rising. "And what about my new DCs, Proctor, and Track, what message is this…this…sending?" he added, pointing at the spreadsheet.
"What do you mean?" Hammond queried.
Brierly took a deep breath. He was as angry with himself for showing so much emotion as he was with what he was hearing. "Look, Dave, you know as well as I do that recruits of today are not like we were. They need to see themselves going places and having opportunities. If we limit their chance of developing because we keep cutting the roles or levels they can grow into, they'll just pack it in, go elsewhere, do something else."
"I know that Jim," Hammond replied, sympathetically, "but what can I do? These cuts have come from the very top. We all have to do more with less."
"Even at the expense of operational policing?"

"Yes."
Brierly looked downcast. He was annoyed at the implication, yet he knew he needed to keep a brave face for his team's sake. He didn't blame Hammond, but he did want to let him know the likely outcome.
"You don't need to tell me," Hammond said, raising a hand and nodding in anticipation of what he expected Brierly to say. Brierly commented anyway. "Slower case resolution, less diligence with regards to paperwork, staff morale declining, crimes unsolved, more violence…."
"Okay, okay, I get it!" Hammond replied, his temper flaring, something both men rarely saw in each other. Brierly remained quiet, waiting for his boss to speak again, noting how red with anger Hammond's face had become. He recognized that Hammond felt as he did and knew that they both faced the same challenges going forward. It was this unspoken shared understanding that resulted in mutual respect, despite the difficulties they both faced. "I'll see what I can do but I can't promise anything," Hammond said eventually, slowly purging himself of his frustration. "In the meantime, your investigating unit will need to share admin staff with DI Robins and his team, and if necessary one of Track or Proctor may need to assist Robins' group as well."
"What?"
"You heard me, Jim," Hammond replied, hoping that there were not going to be any further outbursts. "You've seen the picture," he pointed again at the spreadsheet. "This is happening in the next few days, and you need to be ready for the fallout. So, keep the team focused, get on with finding out who killed that boy, and just accept what I've told you as being something shared in confidence. It's going to happen whether we like it or not."
Brierly stood up, readying to leave. He knew that he had little option but to accept what he had been told. He would keep it quiet until any announcements were made. He wasn't sure how he would break the news to his team when it came, though he knew what to say to his boss now. It was very simple.
"I don't fucking like it!" he snapped, slamming the door as he made his way back to his office.

CHAPTER 7

She stopped in her tracks. She had only walked a few paces when she noticed them lying at the door. It was dark already and the few steps she had taken from the garage along the pathway had taken her less than a few seconds. The lights of a passing car had illuminated the front step as it had driven up the street towards the roundabout, someone taking a shortcut perhaps? She looked around and across the road at the houses on the opposite side of the road. The dimmed lighting behind already curtained windows seemed to mock her. There was insufficient brightness to illuminate their gardens, let alone provide enough light for her to see what else there may be lying on the ground. She was wary. Suddenly, she turned around at the sound of her garage door clanging against its metal frame, the chilly breeze that had irritated many during the day, was beginning to strengthen.
Why were they there, she thought? Who had left them? Was it a mistake? Picking up the bouquet she quickly opened the front door and along with her computer bag, the mysterious flowers, and a carrier bag containing milk and her evening easy meal, she fell into the hallway, before pushing her back hard against the door to close it. She took a deep breath, then switched on the hall light with her elbow, placing everything in her hands onto a small hall table. She then removed her coat, throwing it onto one of a series of hooks attached to the hallway wall. After pushing a few loose strands of hair back into place and taking a quick peek into the letterbox attached to the door, (in which there was nothing), she kicked off her short-heeled boots and looked again at the flowers. Lillies! Grasping the small bouquet from the table, and being careful not to damage anything, she walked towards a small kitchen while admiring the colours. White, beige, and fine red stripes filtered delicately throughout the petals. She was looking for an attached card but there was none. It was the second time that it had happened. She guessed that it was a mistake, that someone had got the wrong house again, but somehow that didn't make sense. With no details and no card, it was unlikely that they could have been left by a courier. Without any specific information, it would be pure coincidence that someone had arranged for a drop-off of the flowers at the same house, twice! No, she thought, these had been left deliberately by someone. The

obvious question was by whom? She could ask her neighbours but she doubted any would know who had delivered them unless she was extremely lucky. Most were out at work during the day, and it was not a neighbourhood with lots of cameras, if any, especially any attached to homes. This was Oaktree Road, Bitterne Park, in Southampton, not Hollywood!

She walked into her kitchen, opened a cupboard door, and from the top shelf extricated a glass vase. She half-filled it with cold water and then placed it on one side of a small countertop. She then opened her fridge door taking out a full bottle of wine, Pinot Gris. She found herself a wineglass from behind another cupboard door and after opening the bottle, filled it to just below the brim. Replacing the screw cap she sat the bottle back down on the countertop.

"To me…to you, whoever you are!" she said, toasting the air and taking a large swig. After taking a second sip of her wine, she looked at herself in the reflection from the glass splashback sitting behind the low-level cooker. Mary Owen thought that she wasn't a perfect ten, but she didn't think she would be a bad catch for anyone who might be interested. Having just turned thirty she knew that time was against her to have a family of her own, but the way she felt now, she was happy in her skin and she didn't need anyone or anything to ruin her life for her…including a man. The flowers were nice, and she tried to think who they may have been sent by, dropped off by, especially if they were intended for her. Could it be Keith in accounts, she thought? Or perhaps, Brendan in sales? Or it could be someone else? She would try and find out as soon as she could, but that was tomorrow's problem. She took another sip of wine then putting her glass down walked up to her bedroom. She ascended the short flight of stairs with ease. She was relatively fit, a benefit of her gym and pilates classes that she attended each week. At five feet four with a slim figure to match, she was occasionally mistaken for a late teen, something that was a curse at times. She had clear skin with no wrinkles, no laugh lines, and no crows feet around her green eyes. Her deep red auburn hair encircled a face that many would suggest had been created to shine, even though she was self-critical and thought her nose was off-centre and too large, giving her a slightly awkward look. Not quite Cyrano de Bergerac but sometimes she felt that way. Her smile though was her best feature. It was warm and genuine. With an almost meticulous dress sense, people usually looked at her styling first and foremost. She was wearing black jeans, her boots now lying in the hallway where she had kicked them off before making her way upstairs. Her sky-blue buttoned top under the hip-length jacket completed the ensemble.

She was eager to change into something more comfortable. It had been a difficult day. Meetings and arguments about unnecessary issues had frustrated her. Being responsible for the overall Quality Assurance function at her workplace, was something she enjoyed but it was also very stressful. The long hours also impacted her social life, which was very limited anyway. The wine helped her to unwind, as did the opportunity to take long baths if and when she wanted to. Tonight, was such a time. Being single, she had no one to rush home to, no one seeking dinner at a set time or requesting a specific meal. No one demanding washing and ironing of their clothes, no one even seeking sex (though at times she would have been happy to address that specific problem), no one to please but herself.

She smiled at the thought as she began to run the water for her bath. She added a few oils as steam began to fill the air, the grey/white vapour beginning to limit her visibility inside the small room. As the water continued to rise, she opened a frosted window above the bath by a few inches, allowing the cold air outside to replace that of the warm misty interior. She would close it when the bath was full and she was ready to step in. Sitting on the rim, she slowly lowered her hand into the water to check the temperature, aware that she needed to be careful not to scald herself.

"Perfect," she said to herself, before turning off the taps and listening to the last drops of water as they fell into the now full bath. She walked back into her bedroom and began undressing, searching as she did so for her wine glass before realizing that she had left it in the kitchen. With a mild curse, she finished undressing, then made her way to the bathroom, climbing into the warm water and sliding down until she was completely submerged. It was a ritual she regularly performed, one which she believed was paramount to how her skin felt, keeping it soft. She also felt that submerging herself completely, energized her, and reinvigorated her, similar to those who loved to dunk themselves in icy rivers. She had been under the water for just a few seconds when she thought she heard something. She sat up quickly, water splashed over the edge of the bath and onto the tiled floor. She rubbed a hand quickly across her face and her still-closed eyes. Yes, she was right…she had heard something. For a second she was unsure what. She listened again….. It was her mobile phone. Like the wine, she had left it downstairs in the kitchen along with her bag and the flowers. She decided to ignore the call. It could always be a crank call or a scam, the latter of which seemed to be occurring daily. If it's serious or genuine, they'll leave a message, she thought, before sliding back below the water, sensing the tension she had been feeling within her, slowly beginning to fade away.

It took her a few moments to realize that the water was cold. She awoke with a start, a distant noise having pierced her consciousness for the second time. After resurfacing from the water, she had placed her head onto a small towel that she had folded into a square on the side of the bath and had allowed the warm liquid to ease the tension out of her, eventually falling asleep.
The noise, the sound, what was it? She listened again, shivering in that instant between needing to know what had woken her and deciding to get out of the water. There it was, soft, insistent….the phone. Her mobile again. She quickly scrambled out of the cold water, and stepped onto a damp bathmat, grabbing at a beige-coloured bath towel hanging on a hook behind the bathroom door and wrapping it around herself. She took one step out of the bathroom before hearing the phone stop ringing. "Shit!" she said, angry at herself for missing the call. She didn't expect it was work-related, but then again. She decided to dry herself off before making her way downstairs, suddenly realizing that she still hadn't eaten, her stomach rumbling in response to the thought. As she finished climbing into a light blue tracksuit she looked at her watch, checking the time. It was nearly eight-thirty and she had been home over two hours now and she had done nothing. She blamed the wine for making her drowsy even though she had barely touched it. Making her way downstairs she guessed that if the recent call was from her sister or her father, they would leave a message for her, but was it either of them that called a second time? If so, why? It was rare that either would do so more than once in an evening, and that would only happen if something serious had happened, like the time their mother passed away suddenly from a heart attack, nine years ago. As she got to the bottom of the stairs, she noticed that she had left the lights on in the kitchen and hallway and had forgotten to close the

curtains and blinds, to any of the downstairs windows. Finding her phone, she checked the screen to see where the missed calls had come from. They were both from her sister, Gretchen, and she had left two short voicemail messages.
Mary Owen listened to the frantic voice of her big sister, asking her to call her back urgently. It was obvious that she was very upset, and was crying. The words on the voicemail were scattered with emotional pauses. Despite the obvious, there was no detail left about why Gretchen was so upset, she just asked Mary to call her. Had something happened to their father? Or Tom, Gretchen's husband? Or was it one of the kids, Trish or Robert? All these thoughts raced through Mary's mind. Having listened to the first message she decided not to bother listening to the second and called her distraught sibling straight away.
"What is it, Gretch? What's happened?" she said, without any attempt at any greeting as the phone was answered
"Where the hell were you?" Gretchen Millwright replied, her anger clear and her chastisement intended. "I've tried a couple of times to call you! I've…."
"I know, I know," Mary interrupted, "I'm sorry…I…I…," she stumbled, "anyway it's irrelevant, what's happened?"
For a second there was silence, with just a sob and a sniffle echoing down the line. "It's dad," Gretchen wailed, "he's..he's…"
"He's what?! What's going on?!" Mary pleaded, now desperate to get to the heart of the issue. She was losing patience with her bigger sister. It had always been this way. Gretchen was a procrastinator, and could never make decisions, often figuratively sitting on her hands when things went wrong and actions needed to be taken. If it wasn't for Tom, their house in the village of Westbourne, ten miles northeast of the centre of Portsmouth would still be needing repairs. It was just as well that he was good with his hands otherwise nothing would have happened with the renovations they had needed to do when they first moved into their current house. That was a couple of years after their mother's passing and the reconstruction took three years to complete. The irony of the phone call was not lost on Mary. On the one hand, she had been shouted at for not being available when Gretchen called, yet now, trying to get any detail out of her sister was almost like trying to extract hens' teeth. Despite being filled with dread about what may have happened to initiate the frantic calls,

until Gretchen told her, she was none the wiser. She wondered where Tom was and why he hadn't taken over from Gretchen. Why he hadn't made the second call himself as he normally would, taking over, taking charge. It was only a fleeting thought before she spoke again, trying to sound conciliatory. "Gretch, calm down….tell me what's happened…. take your time."
"As I said, it's dad. He's been in an accident."
"When? Where? Is he okay?"
"At the Asda Havant supercentre..in the car park there."
Mary knew the place that Gretchen was referring to. It was a popular retail park, just off the A3 in Bedhampton. "Is he okay? Is he hurt?"
"No."
Mary's heart which had been beating like a snare drum suddenly started to lessen its intensity. Her chest which had been feeling tight with sudden emotional stress began to ease. She processed what she had heard and then found herself feeling a little confused. If their father was okay, then what was so urgent? "Is the car, okay?" she inquired.
"Sort of."
Mary closed her eyes. The conversation was beginning to annoy her. "What do you mean sort of? What kind of accident was it then? What about the other driver?"
"There wasn't one."
"I'm sorry Gretch, but I'm not getting this. You said dad had an accident but there was no other car involved. He's okay and his car is sort of okay…so what's the problem?"
The time it took for Mary to receive the response seemed like an eternity. The time to process what was said seemed even longer. She would never forget the words.
"He knocked down a child and he's been arrested."
It seemed like the world was spinning, Mary felt weak and collapsed onto a chair. Speechless, she stared at the reflection of herself in the still uncovered window. The darkness outside seemed ready to reach through it and grab her. She shivered involuntarily.
"What…?" she managed to say, her voice cracking, dry with fear. Every sinew in her body tensed up again, the benefit of the warm bath suddenly forgotten.
Gretchen knew that Mary was in shock. It was unusual for her young sister to be so quiet for any length of time. "Look, let's meet up

tomorrow morning if you can…at my place," she said, "Dad needs to make a formal statement at the police station in the city. After that, he could be charged."
"He's not in Havant police station then?"
"No, they don't have any proper facilities to hold anyone in custody anymore, and they are even closed tomorrow, can you believe it?"
Mary grunted a reply, still trying to process what it all meant.
"Waterlooville police station is apparently still open, but they don't have the right staff available, either. That's why he's been taken to Portsmouth."
"What do mean? And what's he being charged with? You said it was an accident." Mary questioned. Her mind was slowly clearing, her attitude becoming more resolute and she was beginning to think of all the implications.
"That's all he said when he called me after it happened."
"Then I don't understand why he was arrested. Surely they investigate by getting witness statements, and…..," Mary's voice drifted away, a sudden realization dawning on her…., "Oh my God! Was he drinking?"
"No…it seems it was a genuine accident. From what he said, the kid ran into the road between two parked cars as he was driving by. The mother had dropped her shopping bag and the kid got away from her."
"So why the arrest?"
"Because of what the police found in his car!" Gretchen cried without warning.
"What was that?"
"A bloody gun!"
Mary dropped the phone. In an instant, all thoughts of the unexpected bouquet sitting on her doorstep, and the unfinished wine were immediately forgotten.

CHAPTER 8

It had been a long journey that she had put him on. Now that she was gone however it hardly seemed worth all the effort, particularly the years of searching. Despite the frustration, he was glad that she had suggested it. It had taken some time and while he had begun to act on what he had found; it had been more lip service rather than doing anything concrete…until now. He had more reason today, something more compelling, something he could no longer ignore. The years of inaction, despite all the resentment and fury that he had been carrying within him were now beginning to eat away at him. He realized that he should have listened to his gut when he had originally discovered the terrible truth. Sitting in the room, alone, he stared again at the pictures that he had stuck onto the wall, ignoring those photographs that had fallen to the floor from his lap. Outside it was dark, cold, and quiet. The pandemic had created a new-normal and many people still preferred to stay inside their homes once they had returned from work.

The small lamp that stood at one end of the large wooden desk provided just enough light for him to see. He stared at the long-gone faces. He knew their names and he knew some of their stories. He had used several sources on the internet and various paid subscriptions had helped with his searches. In addition, he had spoken with those that had known some of them. He had travelled extensively across the country to verify things that were unclear, vague, or incomplete. He was confident now that he had found what he had been looking for.

The drawing of the tree that lay in front of him, flat against the mahogany desk, was extensive. It covered the complete page. Branches went in all directions and the roots curved and twisted. Some were thicker than others, and some were dying out ending just a short distance from the trunk itself.

The anger inside him had been building ever since he had found the source. It had sparked within him the need to act upon them after years of suppressing his emotions. The final ugly piece which completed the picture confirmed the story. The myth was now verified by the facts. It meant that he could wait no longer. The puzzle was solved a few weeks ago and he had already started the process to address what needed to be done, already laying down a few markers. He wasn't sure if his approach lacked subtlety or had been too provocative, but he would watch and see what happened. He would be patient if he needed to be. The secret, their cover-up would soon be exposed. It was just a matter of time.

CHAPTER 9

The two students seemed smaller to the Desk Sergeant than they were. They had slipped into the police station, walking through the glass front door as if trying not to be seen. They had no idea of the recording made of their arrival by the CCTV camera hidden in the forecourt ceiling as well as behind the charge desk. It was nearly two pm and a new shift was about to start. The Sergeant was hoping to leave a little early, but his spirit sank when Damson and Klein advised him why they were there.

"You're telling me you know about the murder of the young lad found in the old cemetery?"

"Yes," Damson replied, answering for them both. Taking the lead as he usually did.

"Wait a second for me, I just need...actually, take a seat...over there," the Sergeant said, pointing at a group of four unoccupied blue fabric-covered chairs. "I'll get someone to come and see you." The two students did as instructed, waiting nervously. They had rehearsed their story several times as they made their way from the university. They realized that they may be questioned separately so wanted to ensure that each knew what to say and what not to say. It was doubtful that they would be back in time for their lab session but thought it best to get things out of the way once and for all.

While they waited, looking down at their phones, they failed to see the man approaching. A shadow loomed over them and suddenly realizing he was there, they both looked up at the massive bulk of DC Proctor. He introduced himself, stuck out a hand, and told them to follow him. Slightly intimidated, they did as requested. Proctor nodded to the Desk Sergeant who was happy to have the boys off his hands and led the visitors through a small maze of passages to a small interview room, which had no windows and was just large enough for six people to be seated. A table approximately three metres in length and a metre wide was surrounded by five chairs. Damson and Klein sat on one side of the table and watched as Proctor left the room, telling them that someone would be along to take their statements. This was a lie. Statements would be taken later if what the boys had to say was relevant to the murdered body found in the old cemetery. Brierly's team didn't have time to waste on chancers. They would be interviewed first.

They kept the boys waiting. Long enough to know that they would be uncomfortable. If they were wasting his time, Brierly would not be happy. He wasn't in the best of moods as it was. The discussion about resources with Hammond was still playing on his mind. White and Brierly entered the room after applying a faint knock on the door and introduced themselves. They noticed that Klein was very nervous, but Damson appeared much more in control of himself.
"Right, gentleman," Brierly said, "I understand you have some information for us, about the murder, the killing of a young lad found in the old cemetery yesterday?"
"Yes," Damson answered, his voice a little croaky, looking towards Klein. Nerves thought Brierly. It suggested that the boy opposite him was not as self-assured as he had initially tried to convey. "A friend of yours was he?" he asked.
The directness of the question threw Damson, it was as if Brierly could read his mind. Klein answered this time.
"Yes...he was."
"Do you have his name?"
"Dave Crossley."
White wrote down the name on a writing pad inside a brown leather-bound A6 size cover that he had brought into the room with him.
"Do you have an address?"
"Yes. He stayed with his aunt. We can give it to you."
"Good," Brierly said, a smile on his face, trying to ease the boys into the conversation. He hoped to get everything they knew from the pair, though he still had some doubts.
"Can you tell me what happened?"
"Not really. We didn't specifically see anything."
"But you were in the cemetery?" White questioned.
"Yes," Damson replied, feeling more confident. The questions they had been asked so far seemed less invasive, factual, non-threatening, and non-judgemental.
"Why?" Brierly asked, his tone changing slightly.
"Why what?" Damson queried.
"Why were you there? What were you up to?"

"We ...Errr...we were messing about," Damson responded, trying not to say too much. Their earlier discussion about telling the police what happened had them agreeing with each other to be as vague as possible, but still trying to show a willingness to cooperate.
"Doing what?" Brierly asked. He sensed that the boys were trying to deflect, obfuscate, telling them as little as they could get away with.
"Not much," Damson answered, shrugging his shoulders.
"In the middle of a freezing cold night?!" Brierly said, his voice indicating an element of annoyance. He decided to be a little more aggressive. "Come off it.....was it drugs then? Were you dealing?" he asked.
"No!" Damson replied, shouting at Brierly, suddenly realizing their predicament, the trap that Brierly had set. After a short pause, he answered the question. "We were tagging a specific headstone. The oldest we could find."
"Why?"
"Because. It was a game, just a bit of fun."
"And your friend, Dave Crossley?" Brierly enquired, checking the name on Whites' notepad, "Why him?"
"It was something he wanted to do, a sort of informal initiation for each of us," Damson said, looking at Klein who remained silent, a deadpan look upon his face. "We set each other challenges."
"Like what?" Brierly asked, folding his arms across his chest.
"Different things....tagging the outside of a double-decker bus near the top, or a railway carriage or even climbing to the top of a flagpole on a large building at night, like the ones down at Saint Marys."
The mention of Brierly's beloved Southampton football team caused a stir. University students doing things like vandalizing property and acting recklessly was something that he thought had gone out years ago when the whole rag-week scene had become focused on doing charitable work rather than acting stupidly. "And?" he asked, seeking more information about what 'different things' implied.
"And what?" Damson said, a little confused at the question.
"Look don't mess with me, what did you see?"
"Nothing...we didn't see anything at all. That's the truth. Dave left us just inside the trees near the car park on Cemetery Road when he went off on his own. We waited, but he never came back. We didn't know what had happened. We thought he'd gone home as a joke....leaving us standing in the cold while he buggered off to a

warm bed. It was only when Dave didn't meet us at Uni as he usually does every morning, and we saw the report in the paper that we worked out what had happened."
"Did anyone see you in the cemetery?"
"Not that we know of," Klein said, speaking in a soft voice, almost as if talking to himself.
"Not that you know of….? What is that supposed to mean?" Brierly enquired, more forcibly than he intended. "And likewise, did you see anyone in the vicinity of where you were?"
Brierly noticed Damson make a subtle shake of his head as if to indicate to Klein to stop talking. He decided to put a bit of pressure on the two boys. "Look," he said, "if you boys know something, you'd better advise us now. If you don't, and we find out later that you knew something but didn't tell us, then it's likely we'll be charging you with withholding information pertinent to a murder. The implication as you'd gather is serious. I doubt that's your intention but I think you'd better consider your position. If you know something, then you should tell us now….for the sake of your friend."
White looked at Brierly who winked back in return. During the conversation, the answers the boys had given had the effect of confirming Brierly's view that they knew more than they were willing to share. His commentary about charging them had some factual basis, but it was more of a subtle threat to get them to open up, their conversation was still off the record. Until things were formalized with recordings and legal support for the boys, the police had nothing to charge them with at this stage. The boys had come voluntarily.
The room fell silent for a few seconds. The tactic of letting your opponent crack first by speaking first while silence reigned, was one that Brierly was exceptionally good at. Surprisingly it was Damson who filled the void.
"We saw a couple," he said, "in a car."
"When?"
"It was just a few minutes after Dave left us. So about quarter past three."
"What happened?"
"Sam and I were freezing our arses off, stamping our feet while hidden in the trees as we waited for Dave to come back. We heard a

car turn left into Cemetery Road from Northlands Road, and we expected to see it drive by us, but it didn't."

"Go on," Brierly said, his voice offering encouragement to the bigger of the two students to tell his story. Damson obliged. "The driver had turned the headlights off almost immediately, as soon as they had turned off Northlands Road."

"Which was an odd thing to do, even on a small road like that, going into the cemetery grounds," Brierly said.

"Yes, we both thought so too."

"So what happened next?"

"The driver stopped the car under the canopy of trees. It was as if the driver knew where to park. Far enough away from the official parking area so that the cameras there couldn't pick them up."

"And what did you do?"

"Nothing," Damson said.

Brierly could tell that the boy was lying. He decided to wait before he drew any conclusions. He wanted to hear more. "Really? You did nothing?" he queried, "Weren't you curious? Didn't you wonder what was going on?"

He stared at them as both boys contemplated what to do next. Brierly had seen this so many times before. People preparing for questioning, trying to get a story straight. It hardly ever worked. Now it was as if their obvious rehearsal had not considered where things could lead. Maybe they had hoped that they could get away with just talking about the reason for being in the cemetery and nothing else. Brierly knew that he had gotten them to a place where they now needed to explain something that they had hoped they would never have to. With hesitation in his voice, Damson finally answered Brierly's question.

"We watched," he said.

"Watched? What do you mean…watched?"

"We watched them have sex. In the car."

Brierly whistled through his teeth. He knew that there were various places used around the city for illicit trysts and where some prostitutes took their clients, but he wasn't aware of the area around the cemetery being used. For a second something didn't seem right, so he asked curiously, "How could you see what was going on in the car from where you were, in the trees?"

"We crept up on them. After we saw the windows begin to steam up

a bit." Klein said, appearing to be uncomfortable and embarrassed.
"Did anyone in the car see you? Either of you?"
"I don't think so," Klein replied, looking to Damson who shook his head in agreement.
"How close did you get to the car? Would you recognize anyone inside it?"
With a brief cough to clear a dry throat, Damson said, "We were able to watch through the back window, but at one point we went around the front. We saw nearly everything, though mostly they looked like silhouettes If they did see us though, it didn't seem to bother them, they just kept at it."
"But you didn't see the participant's faces?"
"No..."
Brierly guessed that there was more to the story and pursued another line of inquiry. "While you were...watching...did you think about your mate...Dave?'
The question had its effect. Both Damson and Klein looked embarrassed.
"No," Damson admitted, looking down at the table.
"No," echoed Klein, following his friend's lead.
"So, you just watched, then left to go home. Is that correct?"
"And you saw no one else?" White asked.
"No," Damson replied.
Brierly rubbed his chin, pretending to think. White waited, knowing what his boss was doing. By staying silent, Brierly knew that the boys would become unsettled, possibly wondering whether there was something that they could be charged with, as had been outlined earlier to them both: Property damage, Vandalizing a gravestone, amongst other things were just a couple of examples that he hoped were going through their heads. Eventually having thought about his own two sons, Brierly asked, "Everyone has a phone nowadays. Did you use it?"
Klein was the first to register the implication behind the question, gasping slightly. Brierly smiled inwardly, pleased that he had hit a nerve.
"Do you know it's a crime to film someone having sex without their consent? You can be charged with voyeurism under the sexual offences act of 2003."
The reference to legal proceedings was enough to open the

floodgates, Klein speaking first.
"Yes, we used our phones and took some videos plus a couple of photos....both of us did, but they are not of much use as it was too dark to be able to see anything."
"We only did it for a laugh," Damson pleaded. "We weren't intending to do anything with it."
"I should bloody well hope not," White said. "We'll want to see those recordings. I assume you have your phones with you?"
The question was answered with a vague nodding of heads.
"Okay," Brierly said, "once we've finished here, DS White will arrange for you to see our Tech team and have your phones checked over and the film and photos we think we need will be copied, then permanently removed."
"But we..." began Damson.
"Can you pass them over now, please," Brierly continued, holding out his hand and ignoring Damson's interruption.
The two students reluctantly took out each of their phones. Damson from his jacket and Klein from a jeans pocket. They passed them to White who sealed them inside a small plastic bag. Brierly continued with his questions.
"Now, after you finished filming, what did you do? What happened to the car? Did you see it leave? Did the occupants ever get out of the car? Are you sure you didn't see anyone else?"
The rapid-fire questions were designed to show the seriousness of the situation. Violence in the county occurred regularly. Road rage, domestic incidents, burglary, and robbery, but murders were much rarer than most imagined.
Still unsettled as a result of their phones being confiscated Damson asked, "When are we likely to get our mobiles back, Inspector," acknowledging Brierly formally for the first time. "I, we, need them. We have our Uni diary and calendar and other things on there....plus all sorts of private stuff. Our emails, our apps!"
"I understand," Brierly replied, softening his tone slightly. "I expect it will only take a few hours. If you are prepared to wait, you can take them with you. The team here works until six."
Brierly suddenly had a thought about his earlier conversation with Hammond. Here he was trying to solve a murder and the team he needs that can extract information from a couple of phones, only work to a set of rigid hours...all because of resourcing. How can

crimes be solved if the resources needed are not available? He kept the thought to himself, but he planned to raise it again at some point. The fleeting diversion gone, he noticed that Klein and Damson were talking in tandem.

"....finished filming, we left. We walked across the common, keeping to the trees and we caught an Uber on Northlands Road. You can check the ride on the phone..." Klein said, pointing to the sealed package sitting on the table.

"We saw the car leave. It went past us with its headlights still off," Damson added, "and just at the junction of Cemetery Road and the Avenue the lights went on."

"And you are absolutely sure you saw no one else around?"

"Yes, as we said before," Damson replied.

"There was something a little strange about the car though...when it left, when it turned into the Avenue," Klein said, his voice sounding as if he had suddenly recalled some detail not previously shared.

"Which was?" White asked.

"There was only one person in the car."

"Are you sure?"

"Yes, I'm positive."

White looked at Brierly. They both connected the dots, but it would need to be checked. Was the missing individual the killer? Had that person murdered Dave Crossley after leaving the car? If so, why?

"We need to view that film," Brierly said urgently. "DS White will take you to Reception....in a second." He looked at both of the boys in turn. They began to stand but he remained seated himself. Noticing Brierly sitting immobile, tucked up like the gnome he was known for, the boys sat down again fearing that they had been presumptuous in readying to leave. Brierly waited a few seconds before telling them what he was thinking.

"As you came in today of your own accord and have been open about what you witnessed, *and* because it is still early in the investigation, I will hold off taking any action against both of you at this stage." Despite sensing a sigh of relief ripple through each of the two boys, he added a warning, "If however, I find out later that there is more information that you have on the matter that you could have shared with us today, but haven't, then believe me, when I do, I'll be down on you both like a ton of bricks."

The boys nodded in unison. The point was noted. Their contrition

was absolute. Standing up, Brierly said, “Okay…dismissed!”
White smiled inwardly at the last comment, the issuing of an order. Despite the passing years, he knew that his boss still couldn’t get the navy out of his system.

CHAPTER 10

She didn't want to make a scene, but she did want to know what was going on. Mary was impatient, she wanted to see their father immediately. However, after arriving at the police station, she and Gretchen had been required to wait. Eventually, they were met by the Duty Solicitor assigned to assist him.
"Guy Fawkner," he had said when introducing himself and holding out a hand. Mary immediately linked the man to the famous leader of the gunpowder plot in 1605, but sadly he didn't seem that adventurous. His speech was slow and concise as befitted his stature and profession. A short man, less than five feet six inches tall, slightly taller than Mary, but nearly as wide around the girth. With ruddy cheeks, that suggested rosacea rather than rosé. His short pug nose and slightly misaligned brown eyes made him look almost elvish.
It was nearly eleven in the morning, and the drive down to Portsmouth had been tense. Mary and Gretchen had argued, with Mary seeking answers that Gretchen had been unable to give. "I have no idea," she had said, the moment Mary had walked through her front door, demanding to know what was going on. It was just as well that her sister was on her own. Tom had left for work and had already taken the kids to school. Mary seldom used profanity but her questions aimed at her big sister included enough to make her cry.
"The only thing I know is what I told you last night."
"So, what's with the gun? Where the fuck would he get that from, and why did he need it anyway?" Mary asked.
"I told you, I don't know!" Gretchen had replied, her voice rising and her emotions getting the better of her.
"And the child?"
Tears in her eyes, Gretchen had again let Mary know that she had nothing further to add. She was as much in the dark as her sibling.
Now having been taken into a small interview room and seated on either side of a small desk cum table, Fawkner cleared his throat, and opened a small folder, passing a copy of their father's statement about the accident to each of them. He waited in silence while they read. Mary was the first to finish and began to make observations and ask questions before Gretchen had read beyond halfway. Pointing at

the page she had placed back on the tabletop, she said, "He says here that he had no chance to avoid the kid. That the child just ran out into the road, between two cars."
"That's right,"
"So, what's the problem?"
"Concerning the accident specifically, it seems pretty straightforward. Nonetheless, there will be a police investigation into the particular circumstances. Witnesses will be spoken with and depending on whether the child comes out of the coma or not, the coroner will likely call an inquest. At the moment though the doctors are fighting to save the little girl's life. Time will tell what happens next," Fawkner advised. "With regards to the firearm found in your father's car, however, that's a different matter."
"Can we see him?" Gretchen interjected, her voice trembling, tears beginning to stream down her face.
"Soon," Fawkner advised, his voice expressing the applicable amount of sympathy.
"How soon is soon?" Mary replied, passing her sister a tissue. She felt herself getting more agitated, impatient to find out where things stood. The gun in her father's car was incompatible with everything she knew about him. He was a pacifist if ever there was one. She looked at her watch, it was nearly midday. She had been on the go for five hours already and she still didn't have the answers to anything yet. She knew that she was fortunate that Bill Tiley, her boss, had given her the day off, "to sort things out." He had told her that the business would continue to function without her, and she need not worry. The staff at the office were a great bunch of people and she did not doubt that her team would step up to the plate while she was out of action. The call that had felt necessary to make to Tiley, after she and Gretchen had finished their conversation, had caught him by surprise. It had been after ten and he was about to turn off his phone for the night. He had provided a sympathetic ear and a level of understanding about the matter that had touched her and she had thanked him profusely for it. After finishing her wine she went to bed expecting to be unable to settle, her mind was racing. However, despite feeling on edge, she had quickly fallen into a deep sleep, only waking with fright when her alarm went off.
Fawkner shook his head in reply to Mary's query, indicating that he didn't know how long things would take. As she was about to

chastise the man, the door to the room opened. Along with their father, another man entered. He was of average build, around five feet nine, mid-forties with receding blond hair, cut short.
"Detective Inspector Phil Sutton," he said trying to introduce himself. He wasn't sure however if any of the two women in the room heard him. They had immediately jumped from their chairs, wrapping their arms around their father, mobbing him like a group of rugby players in a scrum. Mary started asking questions while her face was still deep in his chest, while Gretchen cried on his shoulder. As he tried to calm his daughters down, Trevor Owen, noticed Sutton whisper into Fawkner's ear. After a few seconds, the Detective let them know that he would give the three of them ten minutes to talk privately, after which he required the two women to wait in the police reception area while he discussed the next steps with their father. While tears were still being wiped across faces, Sutton and Fawkner left the room, the former repeating that he would return after the allotted time. For a second there was silence between the three family members as they stood together, unsure how to use the time available to them. A small camera hidden away in the ceiling recorded the moment. It would continue to do the same until Sutton turned it off. They sat down at the table and Mary asked the obvious question. Gretchen stayed quiet keeping hold of her father's hand. Her grip was so tight, it was as if she never wanted to let go of his hand again.
"Dad, what's going on? What's this about a gun?"
"I drove over a child…," Owen replied, ignoring Mary's specific question. His voice was soft and contrite. He seemed to be reliving the event in his mind. Mary noticed that his eyes were bloodshot, which she assumed was from lack of sleep. His clothes were creased, and she guessed that they were the same ones he had been wearing the previous day. His disheveled look upset her. He had always been a man who was proud of his appearance. A legacy of his past. A tall man of above-average height who sported a full head of grey hair. The abundant follicles were usually the butt of family jokes, the way he cared for them. He had kept the same style for years and he always carried a comb with him, "to keep it in place" he always said. Somehow that was not the case now, Mary thought, noticing that his face was drawn and his pallor grey. Lines that she hadn't seen before suddenly seemed to have found their way across it. He seemed a shattered and damaged man, much older than he was. He had been

lucky to retire at fifty-nine and in his daughter's eyes he hadn't aged in the seven years since. Until now. Almost overnight, he had suddenly become old.
"Dad, Dad!," Mary exclaimed, her voice reflecting her concern, her impatience getting the better of her. She was trying to get him to focus. She wanted, she needed, to get an answer from him…even if only for her sanity. "Dad, we only have a few minutes. What the hell is going on?! This gun thing…..?!" she asked.
The tone and directness of her question finally produced a reaction.
"What about it?" he replied.
"Is it true? Is it yours? Why would you need it and what's it doing in your car?" The avalanche of questions began to upset Gretchen who put her hand on Mary's arm, who shrugged it off contemptuously.
With no further response from her father as she would have expected, Mary raised her voice. Her intense anger at the situation they faced was becoming more evident.
"Dad, for fucks sake we…," He stopped her mid-sentence, holding up his hand, palm facing her, just as he always did when he had needed to discipline them as children.
"I nearly killed a child," he repeated, "isn't that more important? Isn't that what we should concentrate on? There is a family out there scared that they might lose her. That she might never recover." His face indicated his inner turmoil. Mary sensed there was something more going on, but she knew that she needed to show more compassion towards him, despite her impatience to get the answers to her questions.
"Dad, you're right, I'm sorry." She looked at Gretchen who smiled wanly, accepting the change of tone in Mary's voice. However, the calm only lasted just a few seconds as Mary continued with her quest for answers. "What happened yesterday as you've stated in this, this, document…" she pointed at his statement, "clearly indicates was an accident. Terrible that it was. But in your own words, it was just that…an accident!"
Trevor Owen nodded, his mind returning to the incident. In his heart, he knew that he had done all he could to avoid hitting the child, but she was in front of the car before he even saw her. Milliseconds between life and death. However, the reliving of the scene in his mind over and over seemed to be creating a mental image, a recurring scar on his brain, that he would have to endure for

the rest of his life. It was an image that he couldn't get rid of.
"I know it was an accident," he replied eventually, trying to accept the reality of what had happened, "but..."
He fell silent again, holding his head in his hands, sobbing quietly.
Mary looked at her watch, they had already wasted half of the agreed time available to them.
"So, what happens now?" Gretchen asked, speaking for the first time since they were alone, beginning to chew her bottom lip.
Realizing the need to provide his daughters an answer of sorts, at least to give them something to hold on to, he replied to her in a thin monotone. "I suppose Mr. Fawkner has told you that the police will investigate the accident?"
"Yes," Mary replied, relieved that he was talking. She needed it for herself and her sister.
"And that it's unlikely I'll be charged with anything? Though that could change if the child dies?"
"Yes, he intimated that," Mary replied again, anxious to get to the real reason they were stuck inside the police station. She didn't want to seem insensitive, but it appeared that everyone agreed that the running over of the young girl was an accident. With that behind them, she wanted more. She could tell that he was procrastinating, it was where Gretchen got the trait from and it irritated her more.
"What about the gun though? Tell us about that," she insisted.
"That's a bit more complicated."
"What? Why?" she replied incredulously, becoming annoyed at his continued obfuscation.
Sighing loudly, he looked from one daughter to the other. He didn't want to frighten them but knew he needed to explain.
"I needed it...for...protection." Both women looked confused. They didn't know what he was referring to. He resided in a good area, safe and with little crime. He was a quiet man who lived alone. Someone who tended to his garden most days, seldom going out except for groceries. He had no enemies that they knew of and certainly none that required a firearm. His comment made no sense.
"Protection? From whom?" Mary asked.
He responded hesitantly. "I don't know."
"You don't know?! But you have a gun anyway?"
"Yes."
Mary threw her hands into the air, exhaling a gasp of frustration, her

jaw clenching with anger. She sat back in her chair, barely stopping herself from getting up and walking out. She crossed her arms furiously, noting on her watch that their ten minutes were already up. There were so many questions to ask but just getting a simple answer out of him was infuriating her. She stared at him. For a few moments he stared back, then his eyes softened, and he dropped his gaze. "I know this may not help," he said quietly, "but I have told the police the reason already. They want more details before they decide to charge me or not, but…"
"But what?" Mary interrupted, her face showing her continued annoyance.
"But I don't think they will."
"That's very presumptuous of you Dad. I read on the way here on Google that having a gun without a license has a minimum sentence of five years, maybe more, and you can be fined as well."
"That may be true, but as I …"
Not wanting to hear anymore, Mary cut across him, "No buts Dad, please! Just tell us why you had a gun in your possession. Why in the car for God's sake?!"
As the words left her mouth, Mary could hear the door behind them opening. Sutton and Fawkner were returning as expected. Before they crossed the threshold, Trevor Owen leant forward and whispered, "Someone was threatening to kill me. That's why I had the gun."

CHAPTER 11

He was nearly home after the tests, just a few minute's walk away when he noticed the article in the newspaper as he passed by the newsagent. He had gone inside and bought it. It was unusual for him to do so as he preferred getting his news online, but he couldn't wait until he got home. The headline had stood out against the competing multicoloured advertisement for Aldi, which covered a third of the same page.

Child in coma: knocked down by an aged driver in Asda car park

As he walked back home while reading the story, he noticed the irony between the headline and the advertising on the front page, However, in reading the article which was supported by the obligatory photograph on page three of the vehicle with its registration plate easily readable, as well as the driver's face, it confirmed his suspicions. Now safe in his room, his face was contorted with disgust. His anger, quick to rise, took hold of him. He tore up the entire paper with a viciousness that those who knew him would have said was of someone else. With a scream he threw the remnants across the room, scattering a multitude of newsprint into the air, across his desk, and onto the floor. His rage seemed excessive given that the incident had no direct bearing on himself. However, his mind was in overdrive.

He acknowledged to himself that his fixation, his desire for justice was getting worse, affecting him in ways he could never have expected, and he needed it to be over soon. To keep his sanity.

As his breathing slowly returned to normal, his chest no longer rising and falling apace, his jaw ached. He realized that he had been clenching his teeth again. He looked around him. He didn't see the chaos that he had created, the tiny pieces of paper lying everywhere, a mess that he would need to clean up himself. He only saw the torn paper as a metaphor for his thoughts. Clutter, confusion, disarray.

He needed to take his time and consider what steps to take next, for despite his exasperation he needed to be careful, acting irrationally would only hurt his cause.

CHAPTER 12

The IT department had done the best they could. The video taken on the cameras was grainy and despite using the sophisticated tools at their disposal the vision wasn't exactly clear. Brierly chastised them for taking as long as they did to provide him with what he wanted. It was obvious that the titillation factor had meant that the footage was viewed more times than it should have been before it was passed over to him having been burnt onto a DVD. Having his own copy would help when they began their further inquiries. The original video downloaded from the phones was being kept in storage, specifically 'in the cloud' the geeks told him. It was maintained there for safekeeping should it be needed as evidence in the future.

His team gazed at the screen, crunched together, almost shoulder to shoulder. They were all assembled outside his office, a TV and a DVD player having been brought in and placed on a spare desk. The restorations in the building were still underway and their usual situation room was still out of bounds. Brierly sat on a chair just to one side facing the screen at an angle.

"So what do we see," he asked, "apart from the obvious?"

There was no immediate response, heads were angled, and eyes were moving rapidly trying to follow the erratic movement of the film. Brierly had deliberately kept the volume down. He didn't want the cackle of Damson and Klein to take away their attention from making observations. The film lasted just a few minutes and it was obvious that it had been spliced together from the two different phones. When it had finished and the screen went black, he said, "I'm going to play it again in a minute but any immediate observations?"

DC Track was the first to answer. "I couldn't see any faces, just heads, Sir."

"And the film is so dark, it's almost impossible to see inside the car. All you can see is movement," Proctor added, with a smile.

"The steamed-up windows don't help either," Track added, "the hands on the windows and the silhouettes are the only clues to what's going on inside."

Hughes joined Proctor in a smile, Brierly guessed the comments were

typical of club rugby humour. "What about the car itself? he asked, "Is it possible to see what type it is? I couldn't make it out, and IT told me that this is the best they could do with the film."
"Play it again Jim," White suggested, "perhaps frame by frame?"
Brierly had no idea how to do that, so he asked his Sergeant to take over the remote control, despite offers from all the others to help. As White collected the device from him Brierly suddenly felt older. He kept his feelings from showing, deciding to get more up-to-date with the use of technology whenever he could. White pressed a few buttons and the team watched the footage again. At times it was almost impossible to guess what they were observing, particularly at such a slow pace, single frame by single frame. Occasionally White would speed the video up. At one point Brierly asked for the blinds on the windows to be pulled down, cutting out the little light there was from the muddy grey sky outside. It made little difference until near the end. One of the boys must have moved away from the car possibly to cross from one side to the other, his phone still filming. As he had done so and for the briefest of seconds a shot taken while looking through the windscreen at the two bodies had recorded the bonnet of the car. Inside the car, one could just make out the dark image of somebody's back and the top of a head.
"Stop!" Brierly said, "Go back!"
White looked at his boss, then pressed the relevant buttons. The video ran backward for a few seconds before Brierly told White to stop the "tape" and go forwards again, keeping to one frame at a time. Someone groaned but Brierly ignored the outburst concentrating on the screen. "Next," he said, repeating his request after each frame had been reviewed. It took nearly three minutes before two seconds of the video had been played.
"There!" Proctor suddenly exclaimed, pointing at the screen, even before Brierly had processed the picture. "Sir, there!" he repeated, taking a few steps towards the TV, pointing at the very bottom of the screen. The others stared, each looking at different parts of the frozen image. "There! There!" He tapped the screen again with his fingers. Brierly had seen what Proctor was looking at with the first run-through, and it had burnt into his subconscious, but he now realized that Proctor had noticed it a few moments before he did. He stood up and joined Proctor in front of the TV, the Constable towering above him. "Do you see it now?" he asked the team, with a

nod towards where Proctor was still pointing. A smile creased White's face then Hughes and Track did likewise. "Yes, exactly," Brierly said, thankful that his team now had something to work with. On the TV, the vision still paused on the single frame, there right at the very bottom of the screen was the car's registration number. While they had no idea who the occupants of the car were, they now had two things to work with. One, they could find out the owner of the car, and secondly, they knew from the interview with Damson and Klein, that the car left the area with only the driver inside. The obvious question therefore, was whether the second person, whoever that was, had murdered Dave Crossley. Suddenly the room was energized.

"Let's check who this car is registered to and be quick smart about it," Brierly said, pointing at Track, making him responsible to find out. He turned to Hughes asking him to see if the IT boys could take a second look at the film, wondering if they could improve it in any way. He was looking in particular for a face. He was doubtful that they would be able to give him what he needed, based on their earlier feedback, but he wanted them to give it a try. "If you don't ask...," he said. He was trying to pre-empt what the owner of the car, once found, might say when questioned, and he wanted something in his back pocket just in case he needed it. Turning to his 2-I-C he asked White to meet him in his office once Track had the detail of the car's legal owner. With access through the PNC (Police National Computer) to the DVLA (Driver and Vehicle Licensing Agency) database or the PNID (Police National Intelligence Database), they would have the owner's details in minutes, even knowing if the vehicle was stolen.

It wasn't long before they had what they needed, a name and address.

CHAPTER 13

Trevor Owen had been pleased to see his daughters. He suspected that they were still sitting in the reception area of the police station even though he had told them not to wait. It had been a long day and he guessed that it was already dark outside. Sunset was a few minutes after five and it was already past six. He was sitting with Fawkner, just the two of them. DI Sutton and a colleague DS Alex Supto had left the room together, over half an hour ago. Sutton had said he would be back as soon as possible after what Owen had told them. Fawkner had observed the conversation as it had unfolded, giving Owen advice where necessary. Afterward, once the interview had been suspended he told Owen that the discussion had gone well. He then advised his client that he expected Sutton to release him without charge.

"I think you'll be 'RUI', Released Under Investigation," he stated, "but it's likely to be subject to some conditions." Owen stayed quiet, listening to every word that Fawkner said. He just wanted to go home. "The law was introduced in 2017 to address situations where individuals found themselves in positions such as yours. It allowed for people to be released from custody without bail being posted, while an investigation continues."

"What type of conditions would apply? I told Sutton all I know."

"Which is why I think you'll be free to go."

"But there could still be some conditions attached?"

"In all probability, yes"

"Like what?"

"Surrender of your passport perhaps? The need to provide further evidence if required."

"But I was the one being threatened," Owen said, feeling aggrieved.

"That's still to be verified, Mr. Owen. They can't take your word alone, they need evidence. In addition, the owning of an unlicensed gun is an offence."

"But…"

"You were lucky that you are a clean-skin, someone without any history of trouble with the police," Fawkner said. "Your willingness to provide as much information as you could, such as where you acquired the gun also helped. Though I must say I think it was incredibly stupid to acquire a firearm from the street."

"I realize that now, but I couldn't…."

Before Owen could complete the sentence, Sutton and DS Supto came into the room. There was no tap on the door in advance of its opening. It was obvious who was in charge. Owen knew that Sutton wanted to make a statement about the investigation. His demeanour made it very clear as he sat down across the table from the old man.

"Right Mr. Owen," he said, his voice firm. He stared at the man sitting directly opposite him, looking into his eyes, his soul. "Here's the deal, and remember there are two issues here. Both serious."

Owen nodded, he held his breath, and his body stiffened. He needed his freedom. He needed his daughters. He hoped that Fawkner was right. Sutton took his time, opening a folder, taking out a piece of paper, and holding it up so that neither of those on the other side of the table could read any of it.

"Regarding the car accident, we are not going to charge you for that. Our investigation and the witness statements we have received, including your own, confirm that the incident was an unfortunate accident."

Owen sighed audibly. "However," Sutton went on, "we may need to talk with you again, should the child die and the coroner decide to hold an inquiry seeking additional detail. We don't think this is likely, but it is a possibility. Do you understand this Mr.Owen?"

"Yes."

Sutton placed the sheet back into the folder, taking out a second page. Before referring to it, he said, "Just as a matter of information, there is still the potential for the parents of the child to take civil action against you, which would be the remit of the courts to address. That would be the parent's decision, not that of the police."

"But I…" Owen tried to protest.

"…told us that it was an accident?"

"Yes, and you seem to agree."

"I understand that Mr. Owen. The police will provide the witness statements we have to assist the court with its decision-making process should that be required. However, I am just advising you of that possibility."

"Thank you," Owen responded, happy that Fawkner was right. He prayed that he would be right again, with the other charge that had kept him locked up since the accident in the Asda car park.

"Now, about the gun....," Sutton took a deliberate pause before continuing, again looking at the second piece of paper as if seeing it for the first time. "Despite the reason you gave for its purchase, because you gave us the information you did about where you acquired the firearm and noting your clean record to date, I have decided to release you without any conditions concerning your person. However," he continued, "as with any investigation, the firearm you had is now to be held in our possession as evidence, only to be returned to you should we deem it no longer useful in our inquiries, and, you have the necessary license to own such a firearm."
"I understand," Owen replied.
"Good, glad to hear it."
"But what about the threat...to me...who is going to look into that? Where do I get protection from?"
"As I mentioned in our... err ... interview, your concerns will be looked into. However, with no hard evidence to suggest that you are in any immediate danger, I don't have the resources to waste time on a 'possible' threat. However, I strongly recommend that you keep us abreast should you receive any more communication or encounter anything more substantive."
"But I ..."
"As I said before Mr. Owen," Sutton said emphatically, "I only have your word for why you wanted to own a gun in the first place, but having one without a license as I have told you, and I am repeating myself here, is illegal. So, it is difficult for us to help you at this stage I'm afraid. Remember this though, I am taking you on trust and that's why I am letting you go for now....so please...don't disappoint me."
Fawkner leant across to his left, whispering into his client's ear, letting him know to quit when he was ahead. Owen got the message, which was effectively, "don't push it." Having received a nod of understanding from the old man, Sutton said, "You are free to go Mr. Owen. We'll be in touch." With that Sutton stood up from his chair, turned away from the table, and left the room, followed swiftly by Supto, who had stayed silent throughout the entire interview. Owen was relieved. He sat quietly for a few seconds while Fawkner filled his briefcase with his files, folders, and other loose papers. "You'll need to sign a form when you leave to get all your personal belongings back," the lawyer said. "I'll come with you."
The hugs and kisses Owen received from his daughters when he

walked into the reception area were akin to fans mobbing their idols at a rock concert. Squeals, sighs, and tears rent the air causing the Desk Sergeant to ask Mary and Gretchen to tone things down a bit before they were arrested for their behaviour in a public place. Finally, once the cacophony of noise had abated Owen, with Fawkner's help, did what was necessary; the signing of forms and the recovery of his wallet and house keys. Once the paperwork was completed Owen and his daughters finally left the police station, walking out into the night. In their excitement, they failed to see that they were being watched. They also failed to see the car that followed them, all the way back to Southampton.

CHAPTER 14

They were standing just outside a two-storey house in a recently completed development, Argosy Cresent in Eastleigh. The humming sounds from Southampton airport, its terminal just a three-minute drive away could be heard on the other side of the A335 and the railway tracks of the Southwest Main Line from Waterloo. The homes were nearly all the same in look. Redbrick, white window frames containing double glazing, and a dark grey roof. The only difference between one house and the next was that the front door differed in colour from its attached neighbour. When they had first driven into the estate, Brierly had noted how the area had grown. "Almost like mushrooms overnight," he had said. White agreed.

Jill Tucker was an attractive woman. White almost whistled through his teeth when she finally answered the door. He had pressed the doorbell several times before they had seen movement behind an oblong-shaped frosted glass window wedged in the middle of it.

"Can I help you?" Tucker said, her voice expressing some caution. She was slim, her lithesome body showed that she looked after herself. Around five feet five, she was dressed casually. Dark blue jeans wrapped tightly around her legs, following every contour. A beige woollen jumper, a white blouse with a slight gold tint on the collar, and new white runners completed her ensemble. However, it was her hairstyle and face that White had noticed first. Short jet-black hair cut around her ears like a young boy, and a fringe that seemed to sweep across her forehead. She had clear skin, almost white. It seemed translucent in the subtle mid-morning light, accentuating her almost black eyes and her smallish mouth.

Noticing White staring, seemingly bewitched, Brierly introduced himself and his Sergeant then asked if they could go inside. She remained at the door, her long fingers on the door frame. She gave the impression that she needed more information before allowing them to cross the threshold.

"What is this about?" she asked, "I'm a little busy right now. I have work to do."

"We need to ask you some questions," Brierly replied. "About your whereabouts over the past few days."

"Why?" she replied.

Brierly sighed inwardly before saying, "It's in connection with a murder and…"
"A murder? What's that got to do with me?"
"If you let us explain…inside, then I'm sure you'll be able to get back to your work quicker than if we ask you to accompany us to the police station."
He let his words sink in, knowing that she would likely acquiesce, that she would eventually waver. It was a ploy that rarely failed. Most people wanted to get the police out of their lives, not in it, and especially inside their homes.
"Okay," she said after a few seconds, moving away from the door, "Come in."
They were taken through a narrow hallway, with black and white posters on the wall. Brierly glanced at each as they walked by. Audrey Hepburn, Bob Dylan, Jane Fonda, and Steve McQueen, all classic photographs from the 1960s. White kept his eyes on Tucker's backside and took a heavy nudge from Brierly just at the point she turned around asking them to take a seat in a small but brightly lit conservatory with free-standing lamps chasing away the outside gloom. Brierly looked through the glass wall at the neat postage stamp garden outside. There was a small patch of grass, recently mowed and the obligatory fencing guarded the border between the house next door, but there was nothing else. No flower beds, no children's toys lying around, nothing. The sun was predominantly stuck behind a low cloud that now persisted over the southern counties, having moved in overnight and threatened to remain. Fortunately, there was little rain forecast over the next twenty-four hours, at least that was the hope. The temperature however remained below double figures, hence why the two heaters situated around the room were necessary.
"Would you like some tea?" Tucker asked as they both sat down, her voice seemingly sincere. Both men declined, so she shrugged her shoulders and sat on a peacock-back wicker chair with a teal-colored cushion directly opposite Brierly, crossing her legs as she did so. Brierly looked around taking in the rest of the room's furnishings. The easy chairs that he and White were sitting on were made of light wood, with faded sand-colored cushions and occasional throw blankets, also teal, which provided colour to the lack of any elsewhere. The teak wooden floor shone in the lamplight, a single

beige rug lay in the middle of the room, it was an expensive setup.
"So, how can I help you gentleman?" she said, her tone now relaxed, the initial reaction to Brierly's murder inquiry statement no longer appearing to concern her.
Brierly sat forward, the design of the chair making him bend his back. White noticed that he was sitting in his gnome-like posture again and smiled to himself.
"I didn't notice a car outside the front of your house," he said, "I believe you own an Audi A4?"
"Yes," she replied, "so what?"
"Can you confirm the registration number for me?"
"Yes, of course," she replied, spelling out the applicable details. White looked at his notebook while trying not to stare at her. When she had finished White gave a subtle nod in Brierly's direction. "Look what is this all about?" she complained. "You said you were here about a murder. I can assure you that I have nothing to do with any such thing."
"Can I ask what you do?" Brierly enquired, "For a job," he added, clarifying his comment.
"I'm a Designer. An Interior Designer, for homes, not offices. I can be more specific if you'd like me to. Why?"
"I just wondered…" he said, raising an arm and pointing at different pieces in the room, commenting about the hallway posters.
"I'm relatively new to the game, compared to others," she admitted, "I've been on my own for the past few years, building my business, ever since my partner committed suicide."
"I'm sorry," Brierly replied in response. He looked into her face, noticing a certain sadness behind her eyes.
"No matter," she continued, shrugging her shoulders again. It was a habit that he noticed she did quite frequently. "Can we get on with it, I have a zoom call with a client in about half an hour."
Brierly took a few seconds before asking, "The car, your car, can you tell me where it is?"
"Easy, it's parked just two doors up and around the back in its official parking bay, number sixteen to be precise."
With a smile, Brierly asked, "Is it always parked there at night? Overnight?"
"If I'm at home, yes, of course. Which is most of the time as I mainly work from home anyway."

"Do you visit your clients, visit their homes?"
"Yes, when necessary."
"And then…?"
"I use my car…unless I'm flying. In which case I'll leave the car here especially when I'm using the local airport. Most times however I'll drive to the client. Anyway, I don't see how what I do ties in with murder. You still haven't told me where I fit in with your inquiries."
It was obvious that she was beginning to feel unnerved. The questions she was being asked didn't seem connected in any way to the matter of murder. Brierly decided that it was the right time to ask the question he needed an answer to. "OK Mrs. Tucker, can you tell me why your car was parked on Cemetery Road, the night before last? Particularly at three in the morning?" Raising an eyebrow, he waited for her reply. He watched her body language. She slowly raised both feet in front of her, pulling her knees up into her chest, her runners resting on the edge of the chair. It was as if she was trying to hide behind herself. The silence that ensued was deafening. Seconds passed before she spoke, and her cheeks glowed with embarrassment, a contrast to her unspoiled face a few minutes earlier.
"It's private," she answered, hoping that her response was enough.
"Private?" Brierly queried.
"Yes."
"I'm sure you know that it's not illegal to have sex in a car, it is however a potential offence when conducted in a public area, specifically a public car park."
"What?" she answered incredulously, untangling herself and sitting forward, "what is this?" she demanded. "Has someone been spying on us, err, me?"
Brierly had gotten the reaction he wanted. He wasn't interested in what went on inside her car, but he wanted to know who else was there. Was that person the killer of Dave Crossley?
"Us?" he enquired, deflecting the implied query as to how the police knew of the liaison. Jill Tucker stared back at Brierly and then sought out White, looking for some form of sympathetic understanding, but the latter remained statue-like his notepad resting on his knee. She bowed her head, shaking it slightly but did not answer the question.
"Ms. Tucker," Brierly continued, "what you did in that car is none of my business. What is important however is whether the person you were with, has brutally murdered someone."

With obvious concern, Tucker responded, "What? What are you talking about…why…?" Her voice fell silent, whatever she was feeling appeared to suggest that the other person in the car could not possibly be a killer.
"Look Ms. Tucker, a young boy was killed the other night, brutally murdered. We have no idea as to why, but we need to know who was in the area around that time and we know that you were with someone and that you left without them. So can you please tell me who was with you?"
Jill Tucker clenched her jaw, her defiance evident. Brierly guessed that she was torn between protecting her lover and protecting her privacy. She tried to protect both. "Tell me how you know I was where you say I was…at that time," she said.
"You deny it?"
"I'm not saying anything just yet. I'm trying to understand how you know?"
"We have a couple of witnesses," White said, looking at his boss, trying to take some of the heat out of a growing conflict of wills. Tucker stared back at the Sergeant. "A couple of perverts, more likely," she said. "What were they doing, filming us?"
"I'm not going to comment on that," Brierly replied, getting annoyed at her lack of acceptance that the police knew she was in the car park at that time. He was tired of her game-playing.
"So, somebody was filming us," she stated, continuing with her attack. "Isn't that illegal?"
Brierly ignored the question. "Look, Ms. Tucker, this is a murder inquiry, and I am seeking your cooperation. I am trying to eliminate people from our inquiries here, so unless you are willing to help me, I'm afraid I will need to arrest you as a potential accessory to that murder. So, I'll ask you one last time, who were you with, in your car the other night?"
Brierly waited, his impatience nearly getting the better of him. He watched Tucker wrestle with her thoughts, her eyes giving away her internal struggle.
Eventually, she gave him the name. When she spoke, both he and White were stunned into silence.

CHAPTER 15

His plan was working. He had watched them all the way, keeping them in sight. He had been able to park his car around the corner after they had driven into the driveway. After following them to confirm their intent, he had continued past the house, driving up the old man's road and then taken the first right turn, then right again at the next two streets. He was three-quarters through completing a square before pulling over just before he arrived again at the street where the old man lived. By almost completing a loop, he knew that they couldn't see where he had stopped. He then left his vehicle. Now, he was crouching in the garden opposite the house. The lights of the building behind him were off, the occupants were either out or had gone away. It had been dark for quite a while and despite the low scudding cloud, blown by a north-westerly wind, he didn't feel the cold. How could he when he thought of what *they* had experienced years ago? He continued to watch, pleased with himself at what he saw through the open curtains. The interior light was shining onto the small, unfenced lawn, and the picture window framed the gesticulating arms of the inhabitants, coupled with the robust conversation taking place inside.

CHAPTER 16

Brierly had just put the phone down on his desk. Hammond had cancelled their regular morning meeting as he had been summoned by his boss Chief Constable Olivia Pinkerton to an urgent meeting.
"Nothing serious I hope, Dave?" Brierly had enquired.
"Not sure, Jim. You never know with those upstairs. I think it's another cost-cutting meeting."
"Bloody hell, how are we…?"
"Don't go there, Jim," Hammond had interrupted, conscious of the recent spat the two men had endured. "Let's just see what happens. Maybe she'll surprise me and offer us all a bonus."
The sarcasm was evident in Hammond's tone, leaving Brierly to consider what his boss had just imparted to him without ceremony once he had terminated the call. For a second Brierly didn't hear the tap on his door. It was DC Proctor, his bulk framing the opening, blocking out most of the light from the outside office.
"Yes?" Brierly asked, trying not to show his junior officer how he was feeling.
"Sir, if I may interrupt you for a second?"
"Of course, what is it, Proctor?"
The use of a policeman's surname always seemed to put his team on edge whenever he used it, but Brierly couldn't understand why. It was in his DNA, drummed into him from his time at sea, a tradition within the Forces. Name first, Rank next.
He knew that it was a sign of the times today, the use of Christian names becoming the norm, but he couldn't get used to it when dealing with those who worked for him. There was a contradiction in his thinking however especially when he was speaking to his superiors. It was something that he still struggled with though. He normally used the term 'Sir' when he was doing so, except when he was angry.
He offered Proctor a seat, one of two on the opposite side of his desk, but the Constable remained standing. "Sir," he repeated, which Brierly smiled at inwardly. "I've just had a conversation with one of our temporary call-takers who was put through to the team after they had received a 999 call."
"That's a bit unusual. Why isn't the applicable station handling it?

Don't tell me it's because of the cutbacks. What is it, vandals again? Did you let DS White know?"
"No Sir. They came through to me directly because someone found a body. I couldn't find DS White, he's been away from his desk for a while."
"Where's the body?"
"In the Hollybrook cemetery. In the bushes not far from the chapel near Tremona Road."
"Shit!"
"Sir?"
Brierly had stood up quickly, knocking his knee on the underside of his desk, a howl of painful indignation escaping from his lips. Before he could even talk, the pain still rippling through him, White appeared at the door. "Jim, Jim, what the hell happened?" he said, noting Proctor trying not to laugh at Brierly's discomfort. Rubbing his injury, Brierly repeated what Proctor had told him. "And anyway, where were you? I could have saved myself a bloody bruising if.."
"I was in the toilet, Jim, if you must know. A man's gotta do what a.."
"Alright I've got it," Brierly conceded, rubbing his knee again, before sitting back in his chair, feeling slightly worse for wear. Pointing at Proctor he said, "Get a patrol car out there, asap. Have Hughes get hold of Forensics, and get Track started on setting up a situation room, but not one on this floor. Tell him that I'm insisting on a proper room, I'm not making do with what we have endured so far, no matter what renovations are going on. After that, you can come with me to the cemetery."
"Sir!" Proctor replied officiously.
"Oh, and by the way, stop bloody grinning like a Cheshire cat," Brierly added, a brief smile across his face. "Now get on with it."
White tutted as Proctor left the office, glad to see that his boss had accepted his own stupidity with a little grace. "I'll see what support staff I can get, Jim, I suspect we may be needing a few, and I only hope that this isn't what I think it is. First the old cemetery, now Hollybrook."
Brierly looked up from the lump he could feel now growing just above his knee. In his mind, he had a strange feeling and he doubted the words that he was about to share in response to White's comment, but he relayed them anyway. He guessed that White would

likely doubt them as well.
"I hope so too, DS White, I really do."

The body was draped across the grave. It was an unnamed plot, someone who had died without a name.
"Thank God it's not on the Benny Hill grave," Brierly said to Proctor, "though I doubt you know who he was?"
"My mum and dad used to rave about him," Proctor replied, though it was a bit before my time yes, Sir."
"I guess so, though we've had a few incidents over the years where his grave has been vandalized, though there has never been a murder near it. It's such a shame that people nowadays seem to have no respect. Not even for the dead." Brierly pointed in the direction of where the late comedian had been laid to rest in 1992. Changing the subject, Brierly knelt to observe the body now beginning to stiffen from the overnight cold and the early beginnings of rigor mortis. He winced slightly at the way his own knee creaked. When Brierly and Proctor had arrived, the first officers in the closest patrol car sent by police despatch had been at the scene for a while and had begun to seal off the area with the obligatory red tape close to the body itself, and blue tape to cordon off the wider area. The Forensics team had not arrived as yet, but fortunately, Brierly had been provided shoe protectors and plastic gloves by the enterprising DC Proctor. Brierly made a mental note of the Constable's forward-thinking. Observing the body, the first thing they noticed was the apparent age of the deceased as well as how poorly he was dressed. "A ragged black knee-length coat, holes at the elbows, a frayed collar on the shirt, well-worn shoes with loose soles. Looks like he's been sleeping rough too," Brierly said aloud, pointing at the man's grey stubble and pockmarks on the upper cheeks, and small veins on the nose. Standing up again, his knee cracking, he looked around for a discarded bottle. "Over there," he said to Proctor, noticing a small brown paper bag, crunched at the top, lying a few feet away from the body. "I suspect there is something inside that packet that was keeping him warm overnight. We'll let Forensics handle that, but in the meantime what do you see as to the apparent cause of death?"
Proctor looked down at the body, the blood-stained clothes and the pool of dried brown sticky liquid now congealed in the stone and

grass around the grave. "Looks like he's had his throat cut, Sir," he answered, pointing to a deep gash from ear to ear across the victim's neck, exposing a mess of flesh and sinew. It was an ugly sight.
"Anything else?"
Proctor scanned the body, looking for anything obvious that Brierly could be referring to. "Nothing that I can see, Sir."
"Look at his hands. I know it may be difficult to see given some of the blood, but do you notice anything?"
Proctor looked closer but couldn't see what Brierly could be referring to. He wasn't sure if he was being tested so decided to answer as he saw it. "No, Sir. I can't see anything unusual."
"Good, that's exactly what I noticed."
"Sir?"
"No obvious defensive cuts," Brierly stated, noting that the pathologist who would do the necessary PM, would likely confirm that fact. "It was as if whoever attacked him had the element of surprise. In all probability came from behind, slashed the throat, held him upright for a while, maybe to stay away from any of the blood splatter, and then dropped him straight onto this grave."
Proctor nodded, realizing that Brierly was indicating a pattern. The same M.O. as with the Dave Crossley murder. It was a different cemetery but two killings in quick succession suggested something neither wanted to consider. If it wasn't a copycat, and how could that be, when the details of the Crossley murder had not been made public, then a serial killer was on the loose.
"Unfortunately, there isn't any CCTV inside the Cemetery," Brierly advised, "so it will be difficult to know how this happened. Was it someone just waiting around hoping to find a victim or was the murder a result of something else?"
"Like a drug deal, Sir?"
"Maybe…or an execution," Brierly replied without emotion. "You can see that the victim looks like a tramp, a homeless person. It wouldn't surprise me if the killer found an easy target and took advantage. The question is why here?" The two men looked around, moving their feet gingerly as they scoured the immediate area, conscious of the need not to damage any footprints, crush grass, or impact any other detail that may become useful in the future. On the face of it, they couldn't see much, but Brierly knew that the Forensics team would have the tools and the skills to find any trace evidence,

maybe even some DNA, of either the killer or the victim should it be present.
After a minute or so of careful inspection, scouring the immediate vicinity at a snail's pace, they heard voices of people approaching. Brierly realized that it was the Forensics team talking with the PCs from the patrol car, getting clearance to enter the inner area. Within seconds a three-man team could be seen, their white paper suits contrasting with the darkened bark and overhanging canopy of the Hornbeam or Ironwood trees of the cemetery as they made their way through to where the body lay. Upon reaching the clearing where the rows of graves began, Brierly recognized the senior Forensics man. He was talking to the others about setting up their equipment and the necessary scene of the crime tent used to protect the immediate environment around the body. The tent the other men had carried with them was a blue lightweight concertina shelter that expanded as required.
"Bob!" Brierly called, referring to Robert Tankowski, a Polish immigrant who had lived in the UK for three decades but who still kept the faintest of accents from his motherland. He and Brierly had worked together on a recently solved case, it was one of several over the years that they had partnered on. Tankowski looked toward Brierly then at Proctor, before telling his team to continue with the process of setting up the tent and organizing their equipment. The two men nodded and silently began their task. Without them shaking hands, Brierly introduced him to DC Proctor before asking where Tankowski's relatively new 2-1-C, Peter Francis was.
"He's on a course, over in Holland," came the reply. "He should have been on it a few years ago, but the pandemic didn't help. Everything had to be postponed until recently. I expect him back in the next few weeks."
"A long course?" Brierly enquired.
"Three months."
Brierly nodded an understanding. "What do you think of this?" he asked, pointing towards where the body was lying about ten feet away from where they stood, slowly being engulfed by the blue material of the Forensics tent.
"Looks messy," Tankowski said, noticing the throat of the victim, just as the body disappeared from view.
"I agree," Brierly replied. "Look, Bob, we haven't had a chance to

look into the victim's pockets, so I don't know what you'll find. There may be some ID, maybe a phone or a wallet, though I doubt there will be much money in it even if there is one. But anything you do find I'm sure will be useful to us...."

"You'll be the first to know after Gemma and I have had a discussion about anything we do find," the Forensics man said, turning away slightly to check on whether his team was ready to start work. Gemma Atkins was the lead pathologist at the Southampton General Hospital. She would be the one to determine the cause of death, conclusively, though both men could see almost instantly what the cause was. Tankowski looked upwards at the low leaden sky. It was a mishmash of swirling greys but fortunately, it was remaining dry, a godsend when searching for evidence in an open area.

"We'll leave it to you then," Brierly said, realizing that he and Proctor could do no more than they had already. They received little response except for a brief acknowledgement of their departure. The wait for the report from Tankowski and the follow-up with Atkins was all they could hope for. The name of the victim would be useful, but there was no guarantee that they would get it. The pieces of the puzzle relating to the two cemetery killings were just the beginning, but how many more would they need before they had the answers they required? Brierly hated to speculate.

CHAPTER 17

It had been difficult trying to get any answers from him, and Mary was frustrated. She was sitting at her desk in her office, lost in her thoughts, the computer screen showing the same spreadsheet that she had started looking at some twenty minutes before. Her mind was stuck on the conversation she and Gretchen had shared with him after they had managed to get him to focus, once they had settled down with cups of tea taken in his front room, the lounge.

She had been gentle at first before her impatience had gotten the better of her. She had asked the same questions while they were in the car on the way home, but she had been rebuffed. She had found herself talking with a raised voice at times but had been met with stony silence. Gretchen had been of little help. She had sided with their father telling Mary that she needed to calm down and that their father was traumatized by the entire episode.
Once they were in his house, however, she had insisted that he told her what was going on. Eventually, after much cajoling he left the room with a sigh, returning a few minutes later with a birthday card. On the blue outside of the card was a white stork carrying a cartoon baby in a white cloth bundle. On the inside was a typed date: April 16th, 1953. There were no other markings.
"What does it mean?" Gretchen had asked without thinking.
"Is there anything else?" Mary questioned, ignoring her sister's comment.
"What do you mean?" Trevor Owen replied, feigning ignorance.
"Look don't be stupid Dad, or rather don't treat me that way. I know that *this*," she had pointed at the card, "is hardly something to get excited about, to buy a gun over, and especially without going through a license application, is it? There is something more going on, so what is it?"
While he considered what to say next, Mary had noticed the confused look on her sister's face. "The date, on the card," she said, "it's Dad's birthday."
"Oh," Gretchen had replied, not immediately sure of the dates' relevance.
"I received it a few weeks ago," Trevor Owen said. "It didn't make

sense at first until I remembered that I had another card dropped through the letterbox a month or so earlier."
"From whom?" Mary asked, her concern rising.
"I don't know. It was a card like this one, but it had a different date on the inside of it."
"Did you keep the envelope? We can check the postmark on the stamp, and see where it was posted from."
"There wasn't any stamp on it. Just like the envelope that this card came in. It was just pushed through the letterbox."
"So not by the postman then?"
"No."
"Were you here at the time, Dad?" Mary asked. "You hardly ever go out. Did you see anyone at the door or see them through the front window?"
"No. I found it on the floor when I got up that morning. Just like this one." He said, holding up the card in his hand. "It must have been pushed through the door overnight."
"Bloody hell, Dad," Mary retorted, "why haven't you said anything or told anyone?"
Trevor Owen looked downcast. The stress of the last twenty-four hours was starting to tell on him. The constant questioning and the need to justify himself were becoming an ever-increasing burden on his already frail shoulders.
"Because I didn't want to make a fuss," he answered, "I'm not even sure if I am not imagining things."
"But you went and sourced a gun. Illegally!" Mary responded. Her voice tinged with bitterness. She crossed her arms, showing him her continued displeasure, her face set hard. Looking at Gretchen she noticed a faraway gaze in her sister's eyes whose bravado of the previous day had been displaced with confusion.
"I had to," he continued, speaking sadly.
"Why?"
Trevor Owen stood, then walked out of the room for a second time. The two sisters looked at each other and waited. He was gone less than a minute, returning with a shoebox, which he placed on a small side table. Removing the lid, he took out a second card. It was like the first one that he had shown them. The same size, the same picture on the front, and the same card type. Inside was another date 11th October 1924.

Gretchen spoke again for the first time since her earlier question and reaction to the date on the initial card. "Does this have any relevance to you Dad?"
"Yes."
"What? What does it mean?" Mary interjected, cutting across her sister.
"It was *my* mother's birthday."
"But...but...," Gretchen stammered, "how would anyone know these dates? And besides, what does it all mean, these cards? I'm so confused."
Mary stared at her father. She knew that something was missing. No one would try to arm themselves with a gun just because a couple of random cards with birth dates on them had been pushed through a letter box. "What else was there, Dad?" she asked. "You said that you were being threatened, but these cards hardly suggest anything serious, despite what's typed inside, so what else has been going on?"
Owen turned slowly, reaching for the shoebox. Removing the lid for a second time, he took out a small clear plastic bag, roughly ten centimetres square. Inside were what appeared to be bullets, four of them. The metal casings clanged together as he placed them on the small table. He put the shoebox on the floor next to his feet. Without saying anything, he pointed at the transparent package, waiting for a comment from either of his daughters. None was forthcoming.
"These arrived on the same day as the first envelope. They were in a separate little cartridge box."
"One used for bullets?" Mary said, eventually.
"Yes."
"And apart from these and the cards, anything else?"
"Just a short, typed note."
"For fucks sake Dad," Mary howled. "How many more surprises have you got for us? Where is the note now?" she continued.
"I threw it away."
"I don't believe you."
"Mary!" Gretchen shouted, annoyed at the temerity of her younger sister, and of accusing their father of lying.
Mary ignored her. "Dad," she said, her voice slowly rising as she searched for answers, "something in that note caused you enough concern to go out and find a gun. I can't believe that you would have

kept these cards but not a note that came with the bullets. I know you well enough. So, tell us what the note said!"
After a short intake of breath, and a slow running of a hand across his scalp and through his still uncombed grey hair, Trevor Owen replied to his daughter's question. "Firstly, just so you know. I wasn't lying. I did throw the note away, but only after I got myself the gun."
"And…what did it say?" Mary said, forcing the issue, trying to get the answers she was seeking.
"It was just a list of birthdates. Mine as you've seen in the card. Gretchen's, plus yours Mary and Tom's."
"How the..?" Gretchen blurted out, thinking of how or why her husband could be involved in what was going on.
"Was that it?" Mary queried again. There still seemed to be some other driver that made her father act as he had done. She needed to find out what it was.
"No. It also contained a threat."
"What kind of threat?" Gretchen asked, her concern having increased as soon as she had become aware of her husband being in danger.
"It wasn't overly specific," Owen answered.
"Yet it frightened you enough to get a gun?" Mary questioned.
"Yes, I suppose so."
"You suppose so?!" Mary shouted her anger now to the fore. "Look, Dad, I'm sick of all this pissing about. Just tell us what the note said! Please!"
Reluctantly the words spilled from the old man's mouth. "All it had written on it were a few lines."
"And what did they say?"
"It was a riddle, a rhyme of sorts. It was something like: The dead had woken, they had finally spoken, and the line that remained would soon be broken."
"What the hell does that mean?" Gretchen exclaimed.
"That someone wants to kill us," Mary said, understanding for the first time what had driven their father to act so desperately.
"But why would they?" Gretchen asked innocently.
"I don't know, but I don't think that it was the first note you received, was it, Dad?"
With eyes now beginning to shimmer with tears, Trevor Owen answered the only way he could. He wouldn't be able to hide behind the silence of the past anymore. "No, it wasn't."

"Go on then," Mary insisted, pressing her advantage over him, now that he was opening up, "tell us everything."
"I received a note a few years ago, and before that, one just after your mum died. They were almost six or seven years apart, so I just ignored them, at least until this latest one, which I took more seriously."
"Why?"
"Because this one as you heard said some very threatening things."
"But I still don't understand. Why now? What is so different with this note than with the others."
"The bullets."
"And?"
"The one thing I haven't told you yet. What was also written in the note."
"Which was?" Mary asked, afraid to hear the answer.
"That all of us would be dead before my seventieth birthday, starting with me. That's in just over five months!"

CHAPTER 18

She had told him what she had found so far. There were very few signs of defensive cuts on the body other than a few nicks that crisscrossed the inside of the finger on the left hand, between the ring and little fingers. This she surmised was possibly due to the hand trying to grab the knife in the instant of the attack. Brierly nodded an understanding however the details she offered of the grime around the deceased's neck and under the nails, the state of the clothing, the content of the stomach, and other technical detail went over his head.
"So, you are saying that there are two killers?" he asked in reply, speaking into the microphone from the viewing area where Gemma Atkins preferred all visitors to stay while she conducted her examination.
"Not necessarily," she answered, the microphone attached to her gown lapel picking up her comment and expelling it out from the speaker at the back of the viewing room. She had her back turned to him as she continued with her work. Brierly and DC Proctor continued to watch from behind the glass window roughly ten feet above her. Her assistant had begun the messy job of placing the organs Atkins had removed into large silver bowls, readying them for further analysis. After which they would be returned and placed inside the deceased's body. Brierly could never understand why it was necessary to do this when it was so obvious as to the cause of death. In the case of the body now on the steel slab, it was the throat that had been slashed. Carotid arteries and jugular spliced in two resulting in death within seconds.
"What do you mean?" Brierly asked in response to Atkins' comment, looking sideways at Proctor, whom he had invited to the autopsy, to see how Atkins worked. The young Constable seemed reasonably relaxed, unfazed, at the scene below him. The metallic smell of the blood and the stench of death were fortunately kept away due to the glass barrier that separated them. Brierly was impressed. Sometimes even experienced policemen would struggle when exposed to the charms of the morgue and the butchery of the forensic pathologist. Atkins stopped her fingers from probing for a few seconds and turned her face upwards to look at where Brierly was standing. They had a good relationship, so she was able to say what she thought. She

wasn't interested in the reasons why people killed others, she left that to the police to address and solve. What she was interested in however was how they were killed and who the victims themselves were. She pointed a large scalpel toward the victim's chin and neck. It was an instrument longer in size than one used in normal hospital operations. It allowed her to make deeper cuts into a body, but as if to emphasize her point she placed the end of the scalpel in a position where he needed to look at a monitor above his head which mirrored what she herself could see. A small camera was attached to a plastic headband placed around her skull leaving her hands free to film the operation as she was conducting it.

"You see these edges on the cutting line?" she said, the camera highlighting the now cleanly swabbed area of the throat. Brierly wasn't squeamish but he never liked this part of the job. He noticed that Proctor seemed fascinated by what Atkins was showing them.

"Yes," he replied, the gaping wound which would be stitched together later seemed to grow in size as Atkins leaned in closer, the picture on the monitor getting larger. "What about them?"

"They are thin, clean."

"And?"

"They are different to those of the first killing, that of David Crossley."

"In what way?" Brierly asked, his interest piqued as to her observations.

Atkins continued pointing the scalpel at the wound. "This one was done with what looks like a Stanley knife or something similar."

"Like a hunting knife?"

"Yes, something like that."

"But Crossley was killed with something else?"

"Yes," she replied. "I'm not sure if you have had the chance to read my report yet, but that young man was killed using a serrated knife of sorts."

"Such as?" Brierly queried.

"A bread knife, or a steak knife, something similar."

"Can't you tell at this stage?"

"We will be a hundred percent sure in a couple of days," she replied, "the chromatographic and spectroscopy analysis of both victims is currently underway. We'll know soon enough if my theory is right."

Conscious of the implication, Brierly said, "Could the killings still be

done by the same person?"
"Yes, that's possible."
"Any ideas?"
"What?" she answered, sounding slightly annoyed, almost flippant. "Do you want to know if the killer is a man or woman? Whether they are right or left-handed? Their size? Their weight? The colour of their eyes?"
"Whoa, whoa," Brierly said, putting up his hand and looking away from the monitor. He looked at the scene below. Atkins was now alone with the body of the unknown man, her assistant had left the laboratory a few seconds earlier. Brierly noticed that her eyes were moist when she looked up at him. It wasn't like her to show such emotion. He didn't know why, but he could guess. He would try to find out later if necessary. "I was just wondering…" his voice trailed off, after giving due consideration to her comments.
She filled the short silence between them, but her tone still suggested that she was annoyed. "It's not like the movies, Jim. Not like Hollywood. As you know, things take time. Results are not instantaneous even if my observations are, and even then depending on what we find, I may not be able to give you too much that is useful."
Brierly nodded. He understood what she was saying. One killer. Two killers. In the end, there were two bodies, both with similar wounds that appeared to suggest an obvious cause of death. Why they were killed, was his problem. It always was. As always he was impatient, and Atkins knew this. However, she and her team were not the exclusive property of the police. She had other stakeholders. The families of crash victims and suicides also wanted answers. The loved ones of those who died suddenly, on an operating table, in an aged care facility, or even on an industrial site. The stream of bodies seemed endless, and it was obvious to Brierly that something had touched her emotionally to exact the response he had. The problem for him and his team however was to find the killer or killers roaming the streets of Southampton before anyone else was attacked. The task was difficult enough when there was just one individual involved, but when there could be two or more, that frightened him. It concerned him because his resources were always under review. Other cases could potentially swallow up some of his team at any time, which was why he needed to know more about the latest killing and whether

there was any link to that of young Dave Crossley. Time was always against him even when there was just one murder being investigated. With two, it would stretch his capacity. He could see a few arguments coming with Hammond. Sighing inwardly, he asked Proctor if he had any questions of Atkins, given what he had seen. "No, Sir," was the reply.

Brierly likewise had nothing else to add. He thought it sensible and judicious of them to let her finish her work and wait until the morning for her initial report. The toxicology and other detailed analysis would arrive when it was ready. He thanked her and suggested that they catch up as soon as possible for a coffee. They had been good friends and colleagues for several years and her behaviour earlier seemed out of character. With a half-smile and a brief wave of a hand, in which she still held the long scalpel, she accepted Brierly's invitation. As he reached the room's exit he looked back at her, but she was focused on her job, talking silently to her assistant who had just returned. Her microphone was now turned off. Brierly knew that Atkins was very good at her job. It was now up to him and his team to be better at theirs.

He was uneasy with what he had heard from Atkins, and he had relayed what she had said to his team. Two murders. Two cemeteries. Two murder weapons…two killers?

They were all sitting outside Brierly's office. DS Track had been successful in arranging a space for them to use, a situation room, but it would only be available the following day. The cramped conditions were annoying Brierly as he sat hunched up in a borrowed chair, his posture showing why his nickname of the gnome was appropriate. Despite the limited space, he had decided to show some leadership and be patient, tomorrow would come soon enough. He and Proctor had returned to the station an hour or so earlier, and he had sought an update on Crossley and anything the team had found out about the second victim. Unfortunately, despite their inquiries so far they had made little progress on the latter. The only good news was that Crossley's family had been contacted by the local constabulary in Dundee and his mother was on her way down from Scotland to meet up with Crossley's aunt. A local community officer had been appointed to coordinate the formalities between the hospital morgue, the coroner, and the police regarding Crossley's body. It was a task that needed to be done and Brierly was glad that the arrangements had been made. At some point someone from his team may need to talk with the family but investigating the murder of the boy and the circumstances around his death was the priority. Only once the killer was caught, charged, and sentenced could justice be served. They were a long way off.

"Has anyone been reported missing in the last day or so?" he asked again. "No one at all?" Brierly queried into the deafening silence. He turned towards White with a raised eyebrow.

Eventually, his Sergeant responded. "No, Jim…Sir, though we've put the word out on the street already. It seems pretty obvious that our victim was a homeless man, so I'm hoping someone will come forward. However, as you know, street people don't always like getting involved with the police."

"That's true DS White," Brierly replied while surveying the rest of the team, "but surely someone knows who he is? He can't have been on the streets around here without meeting up with others. How could he survive otherwise?" he asked, the questions tumbling out of him. "Did we get anything from the Day Centre in Cranbury Avenue? I'm assuming that he may have been there at some point, maybe to get a meal and a bed for the night, given the recent nighttime temperatures?"

"DS Hughes and I were out there while you were with Doctor Atkins," White answered. "We don't have a photograph available to use as yet, but we asked around, describing him to those we did meet but we got no response from any of the 'guests'."

"Did Phil Boothby know him?"

"No," White replied, recalling the brief conversation with the Patron of the facility. Boothby was a former city councillor who was now retired, but who had volunteered several years before to mentor a team of paid employees to run the homeless shelter, and he still assisted the staff when needed. A well-respected man, tireless in his quest to ensure that those who found themselves homeless in the city could find refuge from the streets if they wanted it. With the shelter being a short distance from the Royal South Hampshire Hospital, medical support was also something the centre offered. Sadly, with many on the streets having poor diets, and using drugs and alcohol,

the conga line of those who passed through the facility meant that some came and went within hours and were never seen again. Consequently, finding information about a regular or someone transient and just passing through, from those who managed or frequented the facility was like searching for the proverbial needle. "It seems our victim never set foot inside the place," White added.
Brierly rubbed his chin, making a mental note to arrange a catch-up with the ex-councillor. "Thank you, DS White, I guess that means we need to revert to plan B?" Despite their years of working together Brierly still struggled to shake the casual way of communicating used in modern-day policing. He continued to address his officers by their rank and surname as opposed to their Christian names. White had accepted it a long time ago, smiling to himself at his boss's old-fashioned formality. Occasionally however he thought that the Royal Navy had a lot to answer for.
"Plan B, Sir?" Track enquired.
"CCTV," White said, reacting first, and beating Brierly to the punch. A groan filled the air. Searching through CCTV was the bane of a detective's life. The need to spend hours looking through selected footage from around the city was both mind-numbing and often ineffective, and everyone on the team knew it. They waited to hear who would be assigned the responsibility. Each one of them prayed that it would be someone else.
With a smile on his face, and in an attempt to create a little bit of levity and lighten the mood, White spoke, using a poor copy of Donald Ducks' voice, saying, "DC Track, DC Proctor, in that order, you have the privilege…." The response was immediate. A groan and a sudden restlessness erupted from the team. Brierly instantly put up his hand to quell the noise, taking several seconds before eventually achieving his aim. "Look, I know that looking through CCTV footage is not that exciting, but unless we can find out who our victim is, and why he was where he was when he was murdered, we'll have no chance of finding the killer. Is that understood?" He looked at the faces of his team, focusing on each for a split second, looking into their eyes, searching for commitment.
Once satisfied that he had what he needed, he said simply, "Thank you. Now let's get down to business." The team slowly dispersed back to their desks. Brierly knew that it had not been necessary to say anything else. He was aware that the work to be done would be

arduous and soul-destroying at times, but he also believed that all of his team including the admin support, who would begin work the next day, would give everything they could to find whoever was roaming the Southampton community and had already killed two innocent people. Standing up, relieved, he placed a hand on White's shoulder. "I think we'll be alright here, Sergeant," he smiled, looking at how the team was already busying themselves for the long slog ahead. "Let's leave them to it as I need you to come with me. However, before we go, I just need to make a quick phone call."

CHAPTER 19

He had been distracted all day by an endless stream of patients that never seemed to end. He was obligated to give each of them ten minutes, but in most cases that was way too short for a consultation. Even a basic flu diagnosis would require far more than just a simple observation. Doctor Alan Boothby, MBBS, DRCOG, DFFP, MRCGP, had always enjoyed his job. His shared practice along with nine other doctors, six of whom were his partners in the Johnson Street surgery which stood in the shadow of Saint Mary's, Southampton FC's home ground, had been overrun in recent times. He wasn't sure why, but even during Covid, they didn't have the same number of appointments as there were currently. He wasn't sure if the previous e-consulting arrangements that he had gotten used to, were part of it, or whether the country was about to be hit by a storm of influenza cases and what was happening now was just the start. As far as the practice statistics were concerned, there had been no uptick in any specific type of illness that would have spawned so many more patients.
Now, he was sitting in the front room of his home; his wife Carol had gone out for the evening to the Hollywood Bowl bowling alley on Harbour Parade, situated in the Westquay Centre. She was a member of a team that played in a league, every Thursday night. He was alone with a glass of wine, trying to settle his mind while aimlessly watching a Europa League game, Leicester City against Basel. He stared at the screen but wasn't focused on what he was seeing, his mind was churning with his own problems. His daughter Patricia, from his first marriage, had been giving him a hard time. She was now seventeen and had been living with his ex-wife since his divorce nearly five years prior. Unfortunately, she had somehow 'gone astray', fallen off the rails. Skipping school, drinking, staying out at night, and eventually falling into the nightmare of drug addiction. Over the past two years, he had tried to work with his ex, Anneline, to get Patricia the help she needed. Mental health support, Counselling, Homecare, but without a lot of success. Anneline had blamed him for what had happened to their daughter and that as a

doctor he should have been able to help her, to pull some strings, and rehabilitate her. He had done all he could, even secretly dispensing her drugs from within the practice, something he knew was illegal. He had thought that by doing so, he would keep her out of the system, and she would remain under the radar of the Health authorities. He had hoped that he could wean her off her dependency. Unfortunately, the opposite happened. She had seen the opportunity to use him as a supplier and the problem had worsened. So much so, that her spiral down had seen her in hospital on several occasions recently, almost killing herself by overdosing. Having been discharged for the third time only a month ago, Boothby had not heard from her again until a few days prior. She was back on the hunt for drugs. He had rebuffed her request and had refused to do anymore for her, setting her adrift. In response, she had threatened to go to the relevant authorities and tell them what he had done. How he had abused his position as a doctor and had stolen for her.

She was putting his career and reputation on the line, but he had pushed back, suggesting that she should go ahead and do what she wanted to do. He had told her that he had done all he could and that it was up to her to decide the next steps. Since their argument, he had not heard anything at all from her. He took comfort from that fact, hoping that she had gotten the message and had returned home to her mother, though he wasn't fully convinced it had happened….yet.

On the TV the half-time whistle blew, and the commentator's voice aroused him from his thoughts. He took a last sip of wine, deciding it was time for another, and was about to stand up from his chair when his mobile phone began ringing. He reached over to a side table situated to his left upon which he had left the phone and the TV remote. Using the remote he silenced the ads now playing on the television, placed his glass down on the same table, and picked up the mobile phone, checking who the caller was before answering.

"Dad," he said, "how are you? It's a bit late to be calling, is everything alright?" Without any attempt at a greeting, Philip Boothby answered the question with a pained voice, "I'm sorry but I just wanted to ask if you have heard about the murder in the Hollybrook cemetery? It occurred last night or possibly during the early hours of this morning."

"What? How do you know that? I haven't seen or heard anything about it," Alan Boothby responded.

"It was reported on the news on Radio Solent at lunchtime, plus I had a visit from the police this afternoon."
"The police? Why? What does it have to do with you?"
"Nothing directly, but they were wondering if I, or any of the team or even any of the guests at the centre, knew the person killed."
"And did you?" Alan Boothby asked.
"No. I had never seen him there, and neither had anyone else. At least that's what's being said by those who would normally know or may have come across him."
The younger man picked up on his father's words. They were subtle, and truthful, but implied something else. He decided to bite his tongue, asking a different question to his initial reaction, which was to respond to the hidden meaning in his father's words. "Is there any reason you are telling me this, Dad? I'm not sure of the relevance."
"Patricia! Pat," Phil Boothby replied.
Alan Boothby's blood ran cold at the mention of his daughter's name. In that instant, he felt that he was suddenly being choked. He began to perspire, sweat forming almost immediately at his temples, his heart racing. He felt dizzy. Instinctively he knew that his physiological reaction was not brought on by a medical condition but was a psychological response. The fear of what his daughter may have told his father. Trying to calm his voice, he said, "Dad, do the police think that Pat is somehow involved in this man's death?"
"Not that I'm aware of," was the reply, to which Alan Boothby let out a silent prayer, his eyes looking upwards as if thanking his God.
"But….," the elder man said, pausing for a second and unsettling his son, "it's just that the dead man, who the police believe was homeless was probably killed where he had been sleeping, and it made me think of her."
"What, sleeping in the cemetery, in this weather?"
"Yes…"
"Bloody hell, I'm surprised he didn't freeze to death."
"Me too, and that brings me to why I mentioned Pat."
Alan Boothby felt a further chill run down his spine. His daughter's indiscretions were a steady constant in his life. Wherever she went, he half expected a complaint to come his way soon after. "What about her, Dad?" he asked, to what he hoped was a friendly ear.
"Have you heard from her?"
"Not recently," he lied. "Why?"

"As her grandfather, I am worried about her. The streets are not safe anymore and if there is a killer around then she could be in danger. If she is spending time hanging around with …"
The inference within Philip Boothby's comment was obvious and it received the reaction expected.
"Dad! She's not!" the younger Boothby replied forcefully, interrupting his father and hoping to shut the matter down. "She's back with Anneline, in Eastleigh. I spoke to her this morning, and by the way, if she was on the streets wouldn't somebody be letting you know? You of all people, with all your contacts!" It was a reasonable assertion and for a few seconds, he could only hear steady breathing while his father ruminated over the response. Philip Boothby, an ex-army captain, and former city councillor, was a man who knew Southampton. His long history, going back many years, of working with the area's homeless people was his claim to fame. He knew the streets like the back of his hand, and he knew the people, the characters, living in them. Now having thought the matter through, he agreed with his son. If Patricia was on the streets, he would have been told. Realizing his overreaction, he apologized but re-iterated that the recent killing in Hollybrook cemetery suggested that there could be someone out in the community murdering innocent people, particularly the vulnerable, those who were sleeping rough.
"I'm sure the police will get to the bottom of it," Alan said, relieved that the conversation had moved away from where Patricia could be, even though he had no idea himself of her whereabouts. As his father continued talking, he noticed that a panel of ex-professional footballers was back on the TV screen. In their muted state, he saw them having their say before the second half began. They were analyzing what they had seen of the game so far. Highlights were being shown, interspersed silently with their expert observations.
"And how is Carol…?" he heard his father say somewhat derisively, causing him to refocus on what was being asked of him. His wife wasn't the older man's favourite female and every time the two men spoke, whenever her name was mentioned, it was like raising a red rag to a bull. Often there were huge arguments, other times phone conversations were terminated with immediate effect. The reason was simple. Alan had left Anneline for Carol. She was fifteen years younger than his ex-wife and twelve years younger than himself. Philip Boothby had not approved of what his son had done and

while the long process of divorce had taken its time, it had also taken its toll. Jeanette Boothby, Philip's wife, had died of a heart attack while Alan and Carol had been living together, awaiting the final divorce, the *decree absolute*. Philip believed that the stress of the divorce had impacted Jeanette's health, adding stress to a heart that was already broken by her son's indiscretions. Likewise, when Patricia had begun to show signs of rebelling after her father had moved from the family home, Philip, like Anneline, again held Alan responsible. "A father no more," was how he addressed his son for several years.

It was an unfair accusation as far as Alan was concerned. In his mind, he had done all he could to keep Patricia on the straight and narrow. A debate could always be held about how to be a good father or a good husband, but it was pointless. His own happiness versus his parental responsibility was a subject that never seemed to go away. It was a constant thorn in his side. When Anneline struggled to look after herself and Patricia, and continuously tried to drag him into helping her with every problem she had, it lead him to be accused repeatedly of abandoning his wife and child in their time of need. His father's words, subtle though they were, were tinged with bitterness.

"She's well," Alan replied eventually, keeping his answer short, not wanting a discussion.

"Is she about?"

"She's out bowling."

"Umm, nothing unusual there then!" Philip Boothby replied, disgustedly. He had no time for his new daughter-in-law. He saw her as selfish, and self-centered. Someone who took and never gave back. Someone who took advantage of his son.

"Look Dad, is that all you can say?"

"No, I...."

"Okay then. So, if there is nothing else, goodnight and goodbye!" With his tone angry, Alan Boothby terminated the call, his breathing had begun to shorten and his blood pressure was beginning to rise again. He moved his right hand to grab his left wrist searching for his pulse. He could feel the blood rushing through his veins. He took a couple of deep breaths just as the game on the TV began the second half. He closed his eyes, disappointed with himself that the conversation had turned out so badly, so quickly. Perhaps he needed to be more considerate next time, he thought, before dismissing the notion as fanciful. He knew that Carol would never be accepted by his father. The faults that his father saw in her, were brought up as regularly as clockwork. The bitterness that had developed between them since Alan's marriage to Carol was unhealthy, but neither man was prepared to go the extra mile and suggest a way forward, to reach a détente. The entire issue angered him, exacerbating how he felt toward his daughter. He knew that he had hurt her as much as he had hurt his ex-wife but if he had stayed in the marriage who knows how Anneline's clinginess and continual need for reassurance about herself would have impacted him? They had fought verbally but never physically, and he knew she was clinically depressed and lived with the black dog constantly snapping at her heels, but he had been unable to live with it anymore. He had tried to help her, but she had shunned it…shunned him. Sighing, he put the memories away and turned his attention to his daughter. Where was she? Was she back on the streets? Was she with Anneline as he had told his father? He looked at the time, it was just after 9:15 pm. Carol was only expected around ten. She was catching a taxi home as she usually did on her bowling nights, so he had a little bit of time. He decided to make a call. He was sorry that he did.

CHAPTER 20

They had agreed to meet in the Bellemoor Tavern, the closest practical place to the school that she taught at, the Richard Taunton sixth form college on Hill Lane. Brierly's call had unsettled her, but she had kept a straight face when she had excused herself from the common room, having told the Deputy Headmaster that she would be back before school finished for the day. She had eased the man's concern before he even asked, explaining that her first two periods after the lunch break had been covered by one of the other teachers.
"Very well," the Deputy Head had said, believing that her sudden disappearance was related to a medical appointment. He was afraid to ask for specifics noting his need to respect her privacy, so he left the question he wanted to ask, unsaid.
They were now seated in the pub's dining room. A large screen TV, no more than ten feet away, was attached to the wall above the already-lit fire. The sound was muted but even at one pm UK time there was still some sport to be watched. Golfers at the Euston open in Texas had just teed off at the start of their second round and several customers at different tables seemed glued to the screen. Brierly and DS White had decided not to order food, but both had drinks in front of them. White, a coca-cola, and Brierly his usual cup of tea. Christine Grovedale had arrived a few minutes late, taking her seat next to White but opposite Brierly. She had declined Brierly's offer of a drink or anything to eat, preferring to take her time to look around at the people seated at some of the small wooden tables spaced around the room. Brierly guessed that she was checking the faces, trying to see if she recognized any of them. Once satisfied with what she had observed around her, she turned her attention back to Brierly, showing a calm exterior that he guessed was hiding a thumping heart within. She placed her hands on the table, fingers entwined, and sat comfortably, seemingly relaxed. She was dressed for her job at school. Dark navy slacks, sensible shoes, and a white knitted jumper with a high collar. In addition, she wore an unzipped sleeveless grey puffer jacket which made her seem a little tomboyish, much different from their first meeting.
Brierly thanked her for agreeing to meet them, which she acknowledged by telling him that she had a limited amount of time

before she needed to head back to the school.
"I understand," Brierly said, smiling.
"So, what is this about?" she inquired, "you weren't very specific when you called me earlier."
Brierly had been diplomatic on the phone, only asking her for her time concerning a "delicate matter". He wasn't yet sure if anyone else was aware of what he assumed was her secret, so he tried to be circumspect …for now. He didn't care about what people did in their personal lives, but he did care about murder, particularly one that was as perplexing as the one he and his team were now investigating.
"I wanted to speak with you, to see if you were able to help us," he said.
"About what?" she replied, "If it's about the dead body that Terence found the other day, then I'm sorry I don't know anything at all about that."
White looked at Brierly, keeping his face deadpan. It was what they had expected to hear from her.
"Perhaps," Brierly replied.
"Sorry?"
Brierly sighed inwardly and looked directly into her face, their eyes meeting in a stare that she broke almost immediately. "We had a chat with Jill Tucker," he said, his voice with enough emphasis to imply what he knew would unsettle her. "I believe you know her?"
He watched as Christine Grovedale's face immediately changed from being open and friendly to one of embarrassment and shock. It took her a few seconds to gather her thoughts in order to respond to the question.
"Yes, I do," she answered confidently. "She's a friend."
"Ms. Grovedale," Brierly replied, a slight tinge of annoyance in his voice, "I think you need to be a bit more honest with me. Ms. Tucker is more than a friend isn't she?"
Grovedale looked at White sitting alongside her, then back to Brierly. She knew that the police knew something, but she wasn't sure what or how much they knew. She tried to play a dead bat. "How do you mean?"
Annoyed but trying to stay calm, Brierly arched his fingers together on the table, saying, "Ms. Grovedale, please don't treat us as stupid."
"I'm not," she interjected, "I…"
Ignoring her Brierly said, "We know that you and Ms. Tucker were

together in the early hours, on the day your partner Terence Silver, found the body of the young boy in the old cemetery. We now know that as a fact."
"But how....?" she replied running a hand through her hair and looking around to see if anyone was listening to their conversation. "We were so ...."
"Careful?" Brierly asked, filling in the missing word for her.
With a silent nod, she sat back in her chair, defeated, crossing her arms, her eyes beginning to moisten. White looked across the table at his boss, he knew what would happen next. Brierly continued exactly as predicted.
"Ms. Grovedale, as I told you on the phone, this conversation will be kept private and is nothing more than an attempt to find out any information about a case we are investigating. It is not in any way trying to suggest you have broken any law. What you do in your private life is none of our concern. We..."
"You won't tell Terence will you?" she interjected, her eyes pleading with him for understanding. She began to bite her bottom lip.
"No. As I said, we are only trying to establish some detail about the night in question."
"So how..?"
"I won't go into the specifics but let me say that we have evidence about your whereabouts and at this stage that's all I'm prepared to share."
"So, Jill told you?"
Brierly ignored the question, instead asking her if she had seen anybody before, during, or after she and Jill Tucker had met that night.
"Not that I can recall," she answered, "though I do remember thinking that someone was watching us when we were talking after......" Her voice trailed off, the memory of that night, her relationship with her lover, and the situation she now faced were causing conflicting emotions.
"After you had sex?" White stated, speaking for the first time and filling in Grovedale's missing words.
She turned to look at him, then speaking quietly, she spoke a single word, "Yes."
Brierly knew that he was on delicate ground and that he needed to be careful in his follow-up questions. He needed her cooperation; he

didn't want her to clam up. "Ms. Grovedale, Christine," he said gently, "As I said before if you and Jill Tucker are lovers, that's no concern of mine. And I can assure you that unless relevant to the investigation I have no intention of informing Mr. Silver of the relationship between you and her. What is important to me, is the death of a young man, killed in the vicinity of where you and Ms. Tucker met that night. So if you can recall anything, anything at all, that may help in our investigation then we really need to hear it."

"Tell us about that night," White encouraged, "what you think you saw or felt."

While she took a glance at her watch, Brierly drank some of his now cold tea, placing the cup back down on the table just as Grovedale began talking. Her voice was low, almost a whisper. "We've known each other for nearly two years now," she declared. "We met when Jill came to help us decorate our house." Brierly nodded in response. What happened in the past was irrelevant to him, but he let her speak, hoping that she might fill in some of the gaps he still had in his own mind. Whether what she was saying was to justify the relationship or not, he couldn't guess, but he understood where she was coming from.

"It was instant mutual attraction," she said, remembering the moment. A quick smile briefly removed the frown from her face. White silently concurred, recalling his own reaction to Tucker when he and Brierly had visited her at her home.

"We became lovers shortly afterwards," Grovedale continued.

"And you often met at the cemetery?"

"When we could, yes. It's not very far from the house. I walked…."

"And Mr. Silver has no idea about the relationship?" Brierly asked.

"No, and I want to keep it that way," she said, adding, "I love him."

Brierly hadn't expected the last comment and was concerned that her admission about her and Jill Tucker's liaison could take the conversation away from where he wanted to focus his questions.

"Tell me about the sense you had of being watched. When was that?"

"Shortly after I got into the car. Jill had turned it around so that the bonnet was facing the way she would drive off. The boot of the car was facing the woods. She had left the car engine running, with all the lights off to keep the heater going. It was only for a couple of minutes. Anyway, we were talking, and I thought someone was behind the car, in the trees. It was only for a second. I sensed something move, but Jill said it was probably just the trees moving in the breeze."

Damson and Klein? Brierly thought. "What time was that?" he queried.

"About two-thirty."

He was still confused, trying to test himself on why he couldn't see what was perhaps obvious to others. "I'm sorry, but I need to check something. When we spoke with Mr. Silver the other day, he said that you had both gone to bed around ten-thirty. That it was your routine."

"Yes," she replied, "that's true."

"Yet, you were able to get up in the middle of the night and leave the house to meet with Jill Tucker, without him knowing?" he asked incredulously.

"Yes," she replied.

"Can you explain?"

"We don't always go to bed together," she stated. "We have separate bedrooms."

"Excuse me?" Brierly queried. He was trying to comprehend her statement. His relationship with his wife being more 'traditional' as he would describe it, meant that they slept together in the same bed, every night.

"It may sound strange," she said, "but because Terence is a partner in his firm and it is so close to home, he often has to be available at short notice for meetings at the office, or on a construction site, or even to open the building in the morning....so it's quite disruptive at times."

"And?"

"We sleep in separate rooms, separate beds. Even more so since the pandemic." She looked at Brierly sensing he was still unconvinced. "Terence's firm has projects all over the world. Since Covid hit, a lot of meetings were held virtually. He needed to talk with people outside of normal business hours, especially if they were in other countries. He is often on the phone late at night or early in the morning and sometimes even has zoom meetings while he's in bed. When he knows it's a possibility he lets me know and I use another room to sleep in."

"And to slink out from," Brierly said, immediately regretting his forthrightness and realizing his barb was insensitive, despite being true.

"Yes," she answered, looking downcast.
"So, is that when you would let Jill Tucker know when to meet you? When you knew you would be in separate bedrooms?"
"Yes," she replied, "though it wasn't every time. Sometimes Jill couldn't make it, and sometimes Terence and I would sleep together anyway."
"You mean, have sex?" White said.
"Make love…yes," she corrected him.
For a few seconds, there was silence between the three of them. Grovedale looked at her watch indicating that it was time for her to leave.
"Just one final question," Brierly stated. "Did you ever consider it to be dangerous to be walking through the cemetery in the dark, alone at that time of night?"
"Of course," she replied, "but it was the only way we could meet. During the day I'm at school until at least five-thirty. Jill has her business to look after and things just worked out the way they did. I was always careful. I had my phone, and a personal alarm on my keyring….police approved I might add, and as I said before we would only meet there occasionally. When we felt it safe to do so."
The way she answered the question seemed innocuous enough, almost nonchalant. Brierly however shook his head slightly, he guessed that there must have been other places the pair had met in addition to the cemetery, particularly if Silver was travelling somewhere. Again that was irrelevant to the investigation. He was glad however that he and his wife, June, had never had to face such issues. He did understand that his conventional mindset around the subject of marriage and relationships may have coloured his view about what went on between Grovedale and Silver and that there was still some personal deceit involved, but who was he to judge? He decided not to pursue that line of inquiry any further. She had told him all he needed to know.
He thanked her for her time and offered to drive her back to the school. "No thank you," she said in response to his offer, "I'm happy to walk, despite the time," pointing to her watch as she left the table and headed towards the exit. White watched as she walked away from them, her demeanour seemed more upbeat than when she had first arrived. As she walked outside the door of the pub and into the cold, White turned to look at Brierly who seemed to be contemplating

something, his eyes looking upwards as if for divine intervention. His face was full of concentration.
"Jim? Jim?" White questioned, ignoring the normal formality of 'Sir' that Brierly would have preferred. "Jim, what's on your mind?" he asked again, trying to get his boss's attention.
With a slight grimace on his face, Brierly answered his Sergeant, "I'm not sure," he declared, "but something still doesn't seem right about the Dave Crossley killing. I'm not sure what it is that's bothering me but I have a feeling that we are missing something. Something very important."

CHAPTER 21

Mary Owen was livid. She was sitting at her office desk, staring at a large monitor. The screen was filled with numbers on a spreadsheet that she was trying to verify. Directly in front of her, and to her right were papers stacked on top of each other, technical drawings supported by estimates of cost. Checking the calculations required attention to detail but her mind was elsewhere. She didn't even notice the soft patter of rain against the large window which overlooked the company car park two stores below. As she casually scanned the rows and columns, she heard a tapping on the open door to her left.
"Are you free?" Sophie Mead asked.
Mary looked up at the young personal assistant standing at the opening, a light-grey overcoat to protect her from the cold outside was already fastened around her waist. She was a pretty woman, not yet thirty, with a large smile and long legs. She was also Mary's friend and one of the partners' secretaries. Blond, slim, and a flirt, exactly what her boss had been looking for. The fact that she could manage his diary and type the odd letter was a bonus to his self-esteem.
"Oh, is it lunchtime already?" Mary said, knowing instinctively what the time was.
"Yes, it's just after one. Are you coming?"
Mary pointed at the PC screen. "I'm sorry Soph, but I need to finish checking these costings. Can I take a rain check? Maybe we can do it tomorrow?" she asked, mouthing a sad pout.
"I guess I have no choice," Sophie responded.
"If it helps, it will be my shout."
"You're on."
"That's great," Mary replied, relieved at the extra time she would gain to work on the spreadsheet. Better than losing it at a lunch, she thought.
"Can I get you anything then? A salad, a sandwich?" Sophie asked, her kindness bringing a smile to Mary's face.
"No thanks. I'll be fine," Mary replied, and with that Sophie nodded an acknowledgement, turned on her heel, and departed.
Sitting back in the chair, Mary let out an expletive. She had so much to do, but her anger was eating at her insides, and she felt that she was out of control. She couldn't concentrate. Her mind was twirling

and jumping with questions, finding the wrong answers and then questioning everything again. Her father had been less than forthcoming when she had quizzed him. Why did someone want to kill him? Why Mary, Gretchen, and Tom? What did they have to do with anything? There were so many things that they needed answers to, yet he had stayed silent, unmoved. She opened a drawer on the right-hand side of the desk, taking out her mobile phone. Pressing a couple of buttons, she put the phone to her ear just as it was answered.

"It's me," she said.

"Oh," Gretchen replied, with concern in her voice. "Is everything okay?"

"I was going to ask you if you've spoken to Dad since the row we had with him the other night?"

"No, I haven't," Gretchen replied, the tone of her voice indicating how she was feeling. She had been angry at both her father and Mary, but more so with her sister for continuously pushing the old man for answers. Gretchen wanted him to speak freely, but with all the questioning by Mary, he had clammed up, refusing to answer, and had left them hanging.

"Have you told Tom about the threat?"

"No," Gretchen replied, her tone more combative than usual.

"Any reason?"

"Because…."

Given such a vague response, Mary decided to leave Gretchen to her own devices. She would let her decide when and how to inform her husband of the potential threat to his life. If Gretchen didn't believe it to be real, then….

"Okay. That's fine," she said. "I'm going to call Dad now to try and see if I can go around to his place tonight."

"Why?" Gretchen replied. "Should we not just leave it for now?"

"Leave it?!" Mary responded, increasingly annoyed at her sister's lack of urgency to find out what was going on with their father. She still suspected that he was hiding something.

"Yes, leave it. Give him some air…he'll tell us in…"

"His own sweet time?" Mary cut in, standing and walking to her office door, closing it softly and hoping to keep her raised voice away from the staff sitting outside. "Are you bloody stupid, Gretch?" she asked as she sat down again.

"What?"
"Don't you want to know? Don't you wonder why dad is being threatened? Why we are too?"
"Of course, I do."
"And why dad didn't tell the police about the bullets?" Mary continued.
"Yes," Gretchen replied. "Yes, Mary! Yes! Yes! What more do you want from me?" she shouted angrily. Mary's persistence was beginning to wear her down, and she began crying.
Mary let a few seconds pass silently between them before telling her older sister that she would call her again later. Terminating the connection, she realized that Gretchen was scared. It was the first time that the threat to them all had hit home. When they had left their father, they were mostly concerned about him and his state of mind. Now, after stewing on the issue overnight, both of Trevor Owens' daughters had reached a different conclusion regarding the position they found themselves in. It was obvious to Mary that they faced the matter with very different attitudes. Gretchen had closed her eyes to the problem and was hoping the matter would go away. To her the issue was merely a fantasy, it wasn't real, and it was if she refused to accept it. For Mary, the threat was genuine and needed to be met head-on. Not ignored like an ostrich burying its head in the sand. She had no idea about the motivation behind the threat, but it needed to be understood and challenged. Did someone really plan to kill them all in just five months?!
Aware of her work schedule and with a meeting to attend in twenty minutes, she made a call to her father. It was answered on the second ring.
"Dad, it's me," she said, trying to sound unfazed.
Without offering any greeting, Trevor Owen asked, "Are you calling to admonish me again? Because if you are, I….."
"Dad," she interrupted, "no, I'm not, and I'm sorry about last night. I just…I just couldn't get my head around what you told us. It doesn't seem real."
"Well, it is."
"I understand….sort of."
"Sort of?"
"Yes."
"What don't you get?' he asked.

"Well, the first thing is why you didn't tell the police about the bullets? Surely that would add weight to you asking for and receiving protection?"
"Maybe," he replied, almost offhandedly.
"Dad…" she persisted.
"Look, Mary, I tried….don't you remember what DI Sutton told me? He needed hard evidence before the police would do anything, and besides, I was in a difficult situation, remember? They wanted to charge me with possession of a gun, while at the same time I was under investigation into the accident I had which nearly killed that child. I was hardly in a strong position to get them to do me any favours, was I?"
"That's true Dad, but still…"
"Look, Mary, maybe this is just a sick joke. Maybe I overreacted last night? Maybe….," Owen said, his voice trailed off, a sense of resignation in his tone.
"You can't be serious dad, surely there is a reason for….?"
With what sounded like the weight of the world on his shoulders, Trevor Owen chastised his daughter, his voice breaking under the stress, "Mary, please!"
She didn't react immediately, the sound of her father pleading with her, caused her to reconsider what she wanted, needed, to know. The question she still sought an answer to. Finally, despite her concern as to how he would respond, she asked it anyway. "Okay, dad, I'll drop it, but before I do just answer me one last thing. That riddle you told us about, was that all of it? Nothing else?"
"Yes."
"Honestly?"
"Yes," he insisted.
"So, on that basis alone, you went out and somehow got yourself a gun?"
"Yes," he repeated. "It's amazing what you can buy on the internet nowadays," he added sarcastically.
His attempt at deflecting the question and adding a touch of humour to their conversation didn't detract her.
"I don't believe you. There has to be something more," Mary queried.
Trevor Owen sighed loudly. He realized that she wasn't going to let things go. He had tried his best to keep what he knew from her and

Gretchen, but it was clear that Mary had seen through him. He knew he had no choice but to tell her.

"There was something else written in the second note I received," he admitted. "It was years ago, now, and I'd forgotten all about it. It didn't make sense then and it still doesn't now."

"But it still bothered you."

"Not really, but put together with the latest one, then yes, I became concerned."

"Enough to buy the gun."

"Yes…but could you please stop with the holier-than-thou attitude, Mary?"

"Fuck off, Dad!" she replied, then instantly regretted her outburst. The conversation had turned into a shouting match, something she had hoped to avoid. Despite her anger and frustration, she took a few deep breaths and tried to calm herself down. She needed answers. "Just tell me why you got that bloody gun, Dad. Please!" she said.

Reluctantly, and with trepidation, he told her what he knew.

CHAPTER 22

Tom Millwright had finished work for the day. He was on his way back to Westbourne, but he needed to make a stop before he finally went home. It was already dark and just after 4:30 pm. The weather had been relatively good during the day. Now it was becoming cold and blustery but because he had been working inside, he had hardly noticed the change which began as he was leaving the building site just outside the village of Rownhams. He was engaged in a project through which a dozen townhouse units were being built and had been successful in tendering for the electrical, painting, and decorating pieces of the pie. Once he had been awarded the job he immediately sub-contracted the painting and decorating components, allowing him to make money yet not have the physical responsibility of doing the work himself. He was happy with his partner's workmanship and had said so during the earlier part of the day. Now as he drove through the gloom of a gentle mist and steadily increasing rain, he thought about the warning that Gretchen had made him aware of. He was trying to understand why he was being threatened as well. By whom and for what reason? Why was he included in the same riddle as his wife, sister-in-law, and father-in-law? From what he had been told by Gretchen, there was a reference to a line being broken. He had no idea as to the relevance of the statement for himself or indeed the overall meaning. As far as he was concerned there was nothing in his relationship with his wife that would tie in with such a crazy comment. It was a ridiculous notion.... A line!? He decided to ignore the inference as noise.

She was waiting for him when he arrived at their designated meeting place. It had been a longer drive than he had expected. The usual twenty minutes had turned into at least double that, and he still had another half hour to go after they finished, before he would get home. The traffic had been moving much slower than normal due to the rain. Some drivers had been reckless and impatient and he had nearly been involved in two accidents during the trip so far. At times he cursed the way some people drove. Some were too slow, and others just had a total disregard for the road rules, leaving him in a very unhappy mood. When he arrived at Saint Mary's stadium, she was hopping from one leg to another, trying to keep dry and warm. She was hiding in the shadows of the stand, on the corner of Marine Parade and Melbourne Street just outside the now-closed merchandise shop. Her knee-length puffer coat with faux fur was doing its best to keep out the rain as she slid into the seat beside him. Without a word, he began to drive off indicating with a nod of his head to a small brown paper bag in the footwell directly behind him, just between the back seat and that of his own. Snatching at the bag with an apparent hunger for its contents she took out the small pellets.

"Is this stuff any good?" she asked.

"Only the best," he replied, keeping his eyes on the road.

She sniffed the rolls of white masking tape that encircled the three packets, each the size of a small sausage. Smiling she put them back into the bag and then pocketed the entire package inside her coat.

"Where should I drop you?" he asked, as she placed the required notes into the centre console of the car, alongside the gear lever. He didn't need to count the notes yet as he knew that she would not try to shortchange him. She wouldn't dare. He also didn't care where she found the money to pay him either. That was her business. He had been her supplier for several months now and their understanding of the price he wanted, for what he offered her, was well-understood.

"Drop me off on the corner of Northlands Road, near where it meets Cemetery Road. I need to see someone there a bit later tonight," she said.

"What, near the old cemetery?"

"Yes."

"In this weather?" he asked, peering through the deepening gloom as the rain began to attack the windscreen and the wipers struggled to provide a clear view of the road. She stayed silent, not answering his question. Millwright kept his thoughts to himself. It was her problem if she decided to walk in the rain and the dark. Within minutes she told him to turn off Northlands Road and pull the car into a parking spot on the now quiet strip of tarmac that led to the old cemetery grounds. The few lampposts that stood at attention and stretched away from where he parked gave the area an eerie feel, the light from each catching the rain as it rushed by.

"I'll call you soon," she said as she opened the car door, pushing it hard against the wind that now seemed to come in gusts, swirling and dancing, rattling the branches of the trees that marked the start of the common. She didn't wait for his reply, and he had none to give anyway. The business had been done and within seconds she was gone, the car door slamming as the wind again made its presence felt. For a second, he tried to see which direction she had taken, but he couldn't see her at all. The colour of her coat acted like camouflage on such a dreary night. He put the car back into gear and pressed the accelerator. Before he got home, he would pocket the money and hide it away where Gretchen would not be able to find it, even if she looked.

Less than thirty minutes later he pulled into his driveway, surprised at seeing the house was in total darkness. He had expected Gretchen to be home as she had not said anything to the contrary. He turned off the ignition having parked in front of his garage, then reached for the cash still in the console and put it into his back pocket. As he clambered out of the car, he pressed the fob on his keyring and locked it, running the few metres to the front door. The rain almost immediately soaked his hair and back as he splashed his way along the short path to the entrance. Feeling for the right door key, his head down, he suddenly noticed that the door itself wasn't closed, but sat slightly ajar. It was as if the lock had not caught properly. He cursed Gretchen under his breath for being so careless, intending to have a serious chat with her when she got home. Guessing that she was out somewhere, he pushed the door open and reached for the light switch that was just on the inside wall to the right, pressing it as he did so. A gust of wind coming from inside the house and along the passageway slammed the door shut and total darkness wrapped itself around him. He pressed the switch again but nothing happened. He was in total darkness.
"Shit!" he said, his outburst indicating his frustration and sense of foreboding. He tried the light switch again but had no success. He called out in the hope that Gretchen or any of his children was actually in the house somewhere, but he received no reply. He began to think that there was an electrical fault in the house as he hadn't noticed any of the neighbour's places on either side also being in the dark. Indeed, despite the rain and his keeping his gaze low, he was

sure that he had seen some lights on there. He took a step forward and caught a glimpse from out of his peripheral vision, of light burning from the next-door neighbour's house and into his lounge window. At least that was one issue sorted, he thought.
“Typical,” he then muttered to himself, angry that Gretchen hadn’t even closed the lounge curtains despite her knowing that she would be out when night fell. Keeping them open for anyone to look in, at all hours of the night, was something that irritated him continuously. He would need to have a chat with her about it later. As he sloped along the tiled floor of the hallway, feeling his way along the walls while his eyes grew accustomed to the dark, he almost fell as his foot slipped beneath him. He telescoped his arms outwards to save himself, holding the walls on either side of the passageway. Stopping for a second to regain his balance he called out into the dark, “Gretch, are you here?! Gretch!” he shouted, expecting a response. Then it dawned on him. If his wife was indeed out then she was highly unlikely to answer him, would she? He was again greeted by an eerie silence. A sense of panic mixed with anger began to stir inside him. He wasn’t sure what to think now. Had she left him? Did she know what he had been doing? Had she gone with the kids for takeaways?
The thoughts were instant, transient, then gone as he suddenly realized that his feet were sticking to the tiles. He couldn’t see what he was standing in, but he could feel it. He lifted his right leg and touched the sole of his shoe. Whatever it was, felt wet, gooey, and thick. He placed a finger under his nose. The odour wasn’t something from the dog, he thought, but he had smelt something similar before. He briefly put a finger to the tip of his tongue and gagged. He knew what the metallic taste was. “Gretch!!” he screamed again, as he began to hurtle towards the rear of the house, to where the kitchen was. As he ran he crashed to the floor, tripping over something lying on the ground. Initially, he thought it was an overturned chair, but it dawned on him very quickly that whatever it was, seemed both hard and soft at the same time, like a bundle of rags on a November Guy Fawkes doll. Still prone, he reached out behind him, his eyes slowly able to pick out shapes. He cursed the irony of his wife having closed the blinds in the kitchen at the back of the house but not at the front. The kitchen doorway was now only a few yards away, but the room itself was black as night. He scrambled to his knees and almost

launched himself at the bundle on the floor. As he fell across it, he knew instantly what he had found, the blood-soaked clothes of his wife wrapped around her still-warm body. Flinching and screaming, his hands covered in unseen sticky liquid he crab-walked backwards, his hands slipping on the tiled floor as he retreated from the horror. Getting to his feet, he turned and raced to the front door, his hands smearing the hallway walls as he tried to escape what his eyes couldn't see but his mind imagined. As he hit the door with his shoulder, the force caused him to bounce off it and he hit his head against the wall. Regaining his balance, he reached for the door handle, hands slipping across it in his panic. Eventually, he was able to twist it enough for the door to open and he escaped into the cold, wet, garden. He fell to his knees, retching, the dampness of the grass and the rain in the air lost to him. Tears and pain mixed as he roared with agony, the sound causing his neighbour from the house to his right to come out and see what was happening. A casual passer-by had also heard the screams and had made his way towards the sound, finding Millwright kneeling, prostrate, his forehead touching the cold wet grass.

"What's happening?" the neighbour called, across the fence as Millwright howled again. The haunting, unsettling sound continuing to pierce the relative calm of the almost empty street. The passer-by, a youngster in his late teens, wearing a green anorak and jeans reached the still screaming stranger, "Are you okay?" he asked, putting a hand on Millwright's wet shoulder. For a second there was no response, then the screaming stopped, and the hand was brushed away, blood and rain staining the boy's coat. Millwright suddenly realizing the implications of what he had experienced, tried to stand, ignoring the young boy's offer of help. It was as if he was in a trance.

"The kids!" he shouted, "where are my kids?" He started to make his way towards the front door again, ignoring the offers of assistance from the youngster, nor noticing the now-soaked clothes that stuck to him like limpets on a ship's hull. "Trisha! Robert!" he shouted as he disappeared back into the darkened hallway, leaving the youngster and the neighbour standing together.

"Call the police," the neighbour, Frank Butler, said to the younger man, who by now had taken out his mobile phone from a jacket pocket. Butler noticed that the boy was shaking as he dialled 999. From inside the house, they could hear Millwright screaming for his children and crashing about in the dark. Behind them, a small crowd had started to gather on the pavement and across the road. Curious residents from houses further up the street had been roused by the noise. Some had brought umbrellas with them, while others had put coats over their pyjamas. As soon as the boy's call had been answered, Butler took the phone from him and gave the operator the details of who he was, what they had seen, and the address where they were. He also requested an ambulance. The teenager was happy to let Butler take the lead, taking his phone back once the conversation had finished. In the forty or so seconds the call had taken, the roaring from inside the house had stopped. It was now deathly quiet except for the chatter of the ever-increasing group of on-lookers and the continuing rain which had now turned to soft cold sleet.

"What should we do?" the young man asked, still shaking.

"Let's get out of the rain for a start," Butler said, walking towards the front door and the slight overhang above it which provided them some small cover. As they reached the opening, which seemed like a dark gaping hole into hell, Millwright unexpectedly appeared from the shadows within, frightening them. He was carrying the lifeless body of his wife, her head and legs falling limply on either side of his arms. He walked like a fictional Frankenstein, as he bore the weight of the lifeless Gretchen. He was crying, whimpering, and drooling, while continuously repeating, "They're not here, they're not here, where are they? Where are they?"

The two men had no answers, unsure as to what Millwright was referring but they moved aside letting him walk past them before he slowly lowered Gretchen onto the soaked lawn. Despite the darkness, Butler noticed the deep gash across Gretchen's throat. It looked as if her head was going to separate itself from her lower neck, and despite the shadows all around them, Butler noticed how the night failed to hide the dark stain across her chest, now mirrored on her husband's clothes. It was a mass of sticky liquid. He turned the teenager away, telling him not to look. In that instant, however, something triggered in his mind. The kids, he thought. It was why Millwright was asking, *where they were*. As a neighbour, he knew the family relatively well but they were never in each other's pockets. He and his wife had occasionally acted as babysitters when the children were much younger, but the last time was several years before.

Without another thought Butler ran into the house, leaving the teenager standing alone, just as blue and red flashing lights entered the street. A police patrol car and an ambulance arrived simultaneously, coming to a halt in front of the house, blocking the road and impacting the view of the onlookers, much to their disappointment. As a young constable, one of two policemen in the car, made his way towards the still kneeling Millwright, the teenager tried to explain what he and Butler had seen. "Where is the other man now?" the policeman asked, just as a paramedic began to approach Millwright who was now trying to stand.
"Inside," the youngster said, pointing towards the open door, drops of water falling from his sleeve. The policeman thanked the boy, just as Butler reappeared from within the bowels of the house. "They're not here," he said to no one in particular. "The kids, they've gone!" Millwright turned to look at Butler, whose own face was set in a grimace. As he processed Butler's comments, his mind began to reel. His wife was dead, and his children were missing. The enormity of the situation he faced and a sense of guilt suddenly surged through him. It was too much to bear and without any warning he crashed to the ground, falling in a heap like a discarded sack of potatoes.

CHAPTER 23

"So, did she see someone else lurking in the bushes, or was it one of Damson or Klein?" Brierly asked.
"Or Crossley himself, Sir?" DC Proctor suggested.
Sitting in their newly commandeered situation room they were all looking towards the case/suspect wall. Brierly had let White bring the team up to date regarding their conversation with Christine Grovedale, while he and DCI Hammond had discussed the cemetery killings as they were now being described. Hammond then took Brierly through the ongoing funding challenges they were facing. Brierly tried to be balanced and less critical of the financial situation and the resource challenges being forced upon him and his team, but it had taken all his patience to be polite and diplomatic. He knew that his concerns were beginning to affect him personally and particularly at home He had apologized to June for being less attentive than he should have been when she had tried to talk with him the previous evening. It was something he had tried to correct over breakfast, but he wasn't sure if he had succeeded. It was still on his mind as he considered Proctor's response. He had always taken his job seriously and his approach to it was unquestionable, but he knew, as did the hierarchy, that he was just part of a team. Being a leader didn't mean that you knew everything or could do everything yourself. It meant that to be successful, one needed teamwork, but without a complete team, the expectation to achieve success was a contradiction. Resourcing, tools, and good old-fashioned thinking were all components that made up his recipe for success. It had worked in the navy, and it had always worked for him in the police. He had asked his boss for more admin support, but it had been denied. "You'll have to make do," was how Hammond had closed down the discussion. Brierly now shifted in his chair, his eyes moving from the case wall to Proctor and back again. He was trying to figure out which of his resources would be best to stay in the office doing support work while the others were out in the field. It was White who spoke interrupting his thoughts.
"Hang on," White said, "something just struck me. Something that I think gives us the answer. At least a possible answer anyway."
"Go on," Brierly encouraged.

"Remember what Grovedale told us?"
"What specifically?"
"The feeling she had about being watched," White continued, looking at the brief notes he had taken when sitting next to Grovedale in the Bellemoor Tavern.
"Yes, she thought there was somebody in the trees behind them."
"That's right, but she also said the car was backed into the parking bay. Jill Tucker had reversed it so that she could drive straight out afterwards."
"So, the car was facing south, in the direction of the old chapel, and *towards* the graves where Crossley was found! Yes, I get it," Brierly said.
"And we know that before they started filming, Damson and Klein were in the trees, waiting for Crossley on the south side of Cemetery Road.
"Which means someone else was definitely on the north side."
"Exactly!" White replied, pleased at his use of logic.
"So, the question is, who, if anyone, was in the trees that night, and why?" Brierly queried.
"Sir?" Track asked, wanting to make a point about what had been suggested so far. "What if Christine Grovedale was wrong? What if her feeling is just that, a feeling? Something without merit. Particularly given her likely sense of guilt by cheating on Silver."
Brierly liked Track, he was smart and questioned most things in an investigation. Until there was proof confirming any proposition, Track always wanted to see the damning evidence. He was their doubting Thomas. While Brierly considered it a good trait to have, he also knew that policing came with an occasional need to go with one's gut. Sometimes a hunch was enough to break open a case. He expected that Track would learn this in time, but he had to agree the conclusion drawn was far from watertight. "I agree DC Track, we could, if you excuse the pun, be on the wrong track, but I tend to concur with DS White on this one. I suggest that given what we know so far, someone else, other than those students, was in those trees that night. I suspect that person is Dave Crossley's killer."
As the murmurs died down after Brierly's attempted joke, which had received groans and a few chuckles, Track asked another question. It was evident that he still had his doubts. "But Sir, why would someone be waiting in those trees? Just on the off chance that

someone would come along in the dead of night. It hardly makes sense does it?"
"That's true, DS Track," Brierly replied, "though I suspect whoever it was knows that the area is frequented by those involved in drug deals, prostitution, secret liaisons, etcetera. As we know those who sleep on the streets also use the place at times. It's not as if we haven't had complaints in the past about what goes on down there, but this is the first time we've had a murder in that part of town. Certainly, in my time anyway."
"So, it was a random killing?" DC Hughes asked, adding his own question into the mix.
"It would appear that way."
"But what would be the motive, Sir?" Proctor said, completing the triumvirate of questions by the team of DCs.
"That's what we need to find out, DC Proctor."
"As well as the who," White added, stating the obvious.
"So," Brierly continued, spelling out the next steps, "we need to see if there is any CCTV footage available from within and also around the area that may be useful. I'd guess the hours from midnight to dawn on that day would be a good starting point. We need to be mindful that the killer could have been hiding in the vicinity for a while, even before dark, in which case that might be a problem. Having said that I suspect he or she would have left the area and disappeared soon after the murder so there may be some vision, particularly during the early hours."
He pointed towards one of the team, "Hughes can I leave that job with you?"
"Yes, Sir," Hughes replied, slightly disappointed with being desk-bound and stuck with the prospect of reviewing hours of video.
Brierly continued issuing instructions. "DC Track, I'd like you to come with me later. I think we need to have another chat with Damson and Klein. I want to know a bit more about Dave Crossley."
Track smiled in response. Being asked to accompany Brierly when he met with the two students made him feel that he was to play a much bigger part in the investigation than he had expected to, being the junior DC. Being at such interviews would help him learn more about on-the-job investigative techniques and he was hungry to do so. He was pleased that Brierly had realized his desire to do more and had been willing to support the idea, seconded by DS White, who

was also happy to take a temporary sit for a while.
"Good," Brierly said, "we'll leave for the campus after lunch. In the interim, here are their phone numbers." He passed over the details taken from the file that he had placed on the table earlier. "Give both of them a call but set up separate meetings. I don't want to talk to them collectively, I want to hear their stories individually. Hopefully, they will have some time available this afternoon. If not, then get them to make some."
"Yes, Sir," Track said for a second time, "I'll see what I can arrange."
"Good, so unless there are any further questions, let's get on with things shall we?"
Within minutes the room was cleared, jobs had been allocated and the investigation was beginning to get into overdrive. On his way to his office, Brierly was intercepted by Hammond, as he walked along the corridor. His boss appeared flustered. Brierly had just exited from the stairwell and noticed his boss heading in his direction making a gesture that indicated they should step to one side while other staff moved past them in both directions.
"I was wondering where you were, Jim. I've been looking all over for you," Hammond said, his cheeks red, and his breathing slightly laboured. Brierly hadn't seen him this anxious for quite some time, his immediate thoughts turning to more budget cuts, given the folder his boss had in his hand. Hammond was known for using folders as props, tapping them whenever he wanted to convey to someone the need to talk urgently. Brierly guessed that the folder contents were likely requiring another discussion about budgets.
"I've been upstairs," Brierly said, "in our situation meeting. Remember, the room we were able to have allocated....eventually?" he added sarcastically. He asked why Hammond needed to find him so urgently. They could have met in either of their offices. Hammond just needed to have him paged through the internal communications system. As he hadn't, Brierly guessed that the matter must be particularly important for his boss to seek him out in person."
"Oh, yes, sorry I forgot," Hammond said.
"You could have rung me as well if you needed to Sir. Anyway, what's the problem...more cuts?"
Hammond looked around, noticing that they were alone, the corridor, empty except for the two of them. That scenario wouldn't last long. He ignored Brierly's question. "I had a call just a few

minutes ago from DCI Bill Nicholls down in Portsmouth. They had an incident down there last night that they think relates to the case/cases that you are looking into. Given what he told me, I thought it best that I find you myself so that I can fill you in."
"What? He thinks the matter relates to the cemetery killings?"
"Yes."
"Bloody hell, how so?"
"The victim," Hammond replied, "a woman by the name of Gretchen Millwright, was killed by having her throat cut. The MO seems to be similar to your two victims, plus she had some marks, on the inside of her ring finger, just like your second victim."
"How can they be sure that it isn't just a coincidence?"
"They're not, at least not completely, but the investigating officer, DI Phil Sutton, seems to think there is a definite link between their case and yours. It seems he connected the dots from the PNC. It's not every day that we get murders in this part of the world, especially when there are three victims found within such a short timeframe and all of them with their throats cut."
"Did he say if there was anything else?"
"No, but the victim was the daughter of an elderly man who they arrested recently for having an illegal firearm on him."
"And?" Brierly queried.
"It seems that he was being threatened. Anyway overnight he and his son-in-law were interviewed by Sutton. The old man, whose name is Trevor Owen, had previously told Sutton that the threats he had been receiving indicated that it was not only him that was in danger but also his two daughters and his son-in-law. Now one of them is dead."
"Does he have any idea why or who could be behind it?"
"No. Until recently, Owen kept the threat against his extended family to himself. It seems he didn't want to frighten them, and he didn't think they needed to be told."
"But he got himself a gun?"
"He claimed it was for his protection."
Brierly smiled to himself. It seemed strange that a man would go to the trouble of getting a gun but not tell his children why. Now it appeared that such lack of warning had resulted in something unnecessarily tragic. The initial query in Brierly's mind was why did Owen only inform his daughters about the threat after he was

arrested? He guessed that the man knew more about than he was letting on, but had decided to remain silent about it, even to his own flesh and blood. At least that's how things appeared to suggest based on Hammond's outline.

"Okay, well let me give Sutton a call," Brierly said, "I'll need to find out why he thinks what he does. If there is a link to our cemetery killings, then maybe I'll need to get down there at some point and see what evidence Sutton has. I presume he has something else that supports his theory?"

"Perhaps," Hammond replied, "but it's their case for now. We just need to verify or eliminate any linkage to ours and then we can then decide what action to take if any. Once we know whether we have a killer stalking a wider area other than inner city Southampton, then we'll need to see how to coordinate our two teams."

"Okay."

"Good. There is another complication though," Hammond said, lowering his voice as a female officer walked along the passage and entered the ladies' toilets, ten yards away from where they were standing. Brierly was intrigued at Hammond's nuance, his *sotto voce* piqued his interest. It wasn't often that his boss was so circumspect. He waited for Hammond to continue. "Sutton has asked us to keep some details about Gretchen Millwright's murder out of our daily media release that's due out later today. I've agreed with him as we don't want to panic people. We need to be a little sensitive about things for the moment."

"Keep what out?" Brierly asked.

"The murder victim's kids. Two of them. They are missing."

"Shit," Brierly said, realizing the implication.

"It's possible that they've been taken by the killer."

"So, they weren't staying with friends? Could they not turn up somewhere perhaps?"

"It would seem not. The husband of the victim, Tom Millwright, the poor man who found his wife's body, told Sutton that they should have been at home with his wife when he arrived home. They always were, every day. It is school term after all."

"Is it possible that they could be being held for ransom somewhere?" Brierly asked.

"Anything's possible, Jim, but it's not as if the Millwrights are multi-millionaires. It's highly unlikely that money is what the killer wants."

"Okay, then there must be another reason behind this, especially if the killer has taken them somewhere."
"One would assume so. As you said, kidnapping is a possibility, though I think it's doubtful."
Brierly rubbed a hand across his chin. If his own two cases did have a link to that of Sutton then given the circumstances he may need to prioritize the Millwright matter over his own. When there was life to be protected, as with the two missing children, then it was necessary to save them above all else. The two dead bodies he had on his hands currently would likely reveal their secrets in time. They always did. He made a decision.
"Okay, I'm just on my way out but I'll call Sutton from the car. He and I can then prioritize what to do once we've had a chance to chat. I was about to leave to catch up with the two students who were with Dave Crossley the night he was killed. I need to talk with them separately. There is something about the case that I still need to understand."
Hammond smiled and thanked Brierly again for agreeing to follow up with Sutton. He handed over the folder that he had been carrying with him. "Here is the detail that we have so far on the Millwright murder. It's not complete by any means, but it's all I have for now."
Brierly thanked his boss and briefly opened the cover to see what was inside the folder. There were a few pieces of paper, including notes made by Sutton, a copied statement from Tom Millwright (with further comments noted by the DI), a statement by Millwright's father-in-law, Trevor Owen, and those of two witnesses that had helped Millwright before he had been taken into the back of an ambulance. Brierly noticed another document, an assessment by a paramedic, indicating that Millwright hadn't needed any treatment for shock despite him having fainted, and becoming unconscious for a short while on the night of the murders. This surprised Brierly, as given everything that must have happened Millwright had, according to the ambulanceman, become instantly calm once he had been told that he would be taken in the ambulance to the hospital. The body of his wife was to remain in situ until approval to move her was given. The man's concern about his children being missing had been highlighted by Sutton with a marker pen. The Detective had immediately started the ball rolling to try to find them. His team was already hard at work. Time was of the essence and Sutton had wasted

none.
Closing the folder, Brierly made his way to meet Track and then continued to read through the various statements while the Constable drove them the short distance to the university, where they were to meet with Damson and Klein. As he did so, Brierly tried to guess how Tom Millwright would be feeling. Brierly's sons were much older and much more independent now than they were just a few short years ago, but if something ever happened to them he had no idea how he would react. Glancing through the pages again, he saw that Sutton had detailed in his own hand what Millwright had experienced. The man's statement showed that he had reiterated several times that there was no reason why his children would not have been at home on the night of the murder. In which case the question was what had happened to them? Where were they? Millwright's concern was obvious and extreme, indeed his written statement appeared to border on the hysterical at times. Again, Brierly could understand why. Sutton's notes also showed that he had briefly investigated the scene on the night, trying to limit the possibility of disturbing any potential evidence before the forensics team arrived. Once he had established what had happened he had given the order for the crime scene to be locked down…it was to remain that way for a while.

CHAPTER 24

The three of them Brierly, Track, and Damson, had sat in the coffee shop in the student union building. The Solent University campus was just off St. Andrews Road. Track had done well, by arranging separate meetings with the two students. Brierly had wanted to check the individual stories concerning Crossley. The police had enough information about the night he was killed but little about Crossley himself. Brierly felt that he needed to get a better understanding of the relationship between the three students and spent quite a bit of time asking specific questions of Damson. By the time they had finished, the area had begun to fill up as lunchtime crept up on them. What had been a quiet spot originally was now bustling with people, students, staff, and visitors. Brierly thanked Damson for his time, noting that the young man had seemed closed, willing to say little more than the absolute minimum in answer to his questions. Was he hiding something, Brierly thought? The discussion hadn't revealed very much about Crossley that he didn't already know. He hoped that Klein would be more forthcoming when they were to meet an hour later. Brierly wasn't sure if the two students had coordinated with each other about how they would respond to his questions, but he would soon find out.
"A sandwich?" he said, nodding towards the counter, suggesting to Track that they have lunch of their own while they waited for Damson to arrive.
"Good idea, Sir," Track said, closing the notebook he had used to record the discussion they had just concluded. "What can I get you?"
Brierly looked around to check what was on offer in the glass display cabinet then turned to decipher the squiggles on the specials boards positioned on one of the walls. He decided on a small portion of lasagne that was still available and some tea. He then sat back in his chair while Track went to place the order. Within minutes, they were both eating, Track having ordered roast chicken with mashed potatoes, vegetables and gravy. "Hungry?" Brierly questioned, nodding towards the constable's plate.
"Sort of, Sir. I've got an evening class later, French. I won't have time to eat again before then, so I need something that will get me

through the rest of the day. Once I get home I'll have something small before bed."

Brierly smiled, finishing his tea before swallowing the remainder of his food. He was glad that he had chosen a relatively small portion compared to that of his Constable. It meant that he would be able to enjoy whatever June would have ready for him later that evening.

Once they were finished, and the plates and cutlery removed, they waited another twenty minutes for Klein to arrive. While they did so, Brierly reflected on his earlier conversation with DI Sutton which he had while in the car on the way to the University. He tried to see what link if any, there was with the Crossley killing. Nothing they had learnt seemed to tie the two cases together.

Eventually, Klein appeared at the coffee shop door. He looked around within the now quieter cafe and gave a small wave of acknowledgement once he noticed Brierly. He walked over to the table and was introduced to Track. Almost immediately, Klein seemed a little intimidated by the two policemen. It wasn't what Brierly had expected, but the noticeably small weakness in Klein's character could be exploited and when the time was right, he would take the opportunity. With no Damson to hide behind, perhaps Klein would be more open to providing some answers to Brierly's questions.

"Can I get you anything?" Brierly asked, pointing towards the counter, where a couple of the staff were wiping down some of the glass surfaces.

"No, thanks, I've eaten already," Klein replied, "a pie...between lectures...earlier."

Brierly picked up on the way the boy was talking, his eyes repeatedly darting between Track and himself. It was obvious that he was nervous about something. Brierly allowed an unnerving silence to grow between them for a few seconds, keeping his gaze on the boy, while pretending to be thinking. He already knew what he wanted to say but stretched out his act for as long as he possibly could. Klein shifted in his seat before Brierly finally spoke again. "You seem pretty well dressed for a student," he said, pointing at the boy's clothes. There seemed to be brand names on almost every piece of apparel Klein was wearing. "How can you afford it?"

Klein looked down, theatrically using a hand to brush away a piece of loose cotton from his lapel. He was wearing an unbuttoned black

trench coat with a grey scarf around his neck. Underneath was a grey polo-neck jersey that suited his designer jeans and shiny black boots.
"Fakes," he replied. "Cheap knock-offs at the market."
Brierly wasn't convinced but smiled in response. "Is that where Dave Crossley got his clothes as well?"
Klein didn't answer immediately. Despite being nervous, he was still very wary. The lack of support he would normally have by being alongside Damson was playing on his mind. He wasn't sure where Brierly was going with the questions. He had hoped that the police would have moved on by now. That the evidence he and Damson had given about the night their friend was killed would mean that their focus would be on finding the killer rather than reinterviewing the two of them. He believed that he had told Brierly all he knew about that night and was beginning to find the conversation uncomfortable. "I believe so, yes," he said, in answer to Brierly's query.
"You believe so, or you know so?"
"I belie…I know so."
"Because………?" Brierly added, stretching out the inference.
"Because he and I, along with Pete, would go together. To the markets…"
Brierly rubbed his chin and frowned. It was a gesture he had used many times before. A trick. A pretense designed to suggest that something said did not tie up with something already known.
"Do you have any receipts? To prove where you bought all this gear?" Brierly asked, waving a hand up and down slightly, indicating Klein's attire. Track watched, remaining silent. He was sitting directly in front of the student. He admired Brierly's questioning technique. It was something he would continue to learn from. He watched the way Brierly was able to peel away at the layers of a story to get to the answers he was seeking.
"No," Klien said eventually. "It's a bloody market, not Harrods or John Lewis. And in any event, I bought these ages ago, last year in fact. Can't you tell?" Brierly wasn't particularly fashion conscious, despite his sons often asking for money from him for new clothes. It never seemed to end. He was aware of the term FOMO and his boys seemed to be affected by it just as much as every other student. However, he wasn't aware of what was 'in' nowadays. All he could recall was that most of the students he came into contact with, either

directly through his job or indirectly through the friends of his sons, Simon and Warwick, always seemed to wear jeans and fancy running shoes, everything else was potluck! Turning to Track, he said sarcastically, "What do you think Constable? Is Mr. Klein so out of date in his fashion choice?" Track had no idea where the specific question was leading, so he answered Brierly in the only way he knew, honestly.
"I'm not sure, Sir. Everything looks very new to me."
Klein stared back at Track, a lump in his throat, unsure how to respond. Sweat began to form at the boy's temples, and he subconsciously pulled at the collar of his polo neck. Brierly decided that it was time to go a bit harder. Klein was obviously uncomfortable and vulnerable while flying solo.
"Do you do drugs?" Brierly asked, the question catching the student off guard.
"What?"
"It's a simple question, Mr. Klein…Sam. Do you take drugs?"
"No!"
Brierly looked away from the student, noticing the remaining few patrons inside the coffee shop briefly ceasing their own hushed conversations after Klein's outburst. He smiled at a couple of mature male students who had been discussing a subject related to a large-volume book sitting between them on their table. He mouthed a silent apology. The two men appeared to shrug and began their deliberations again. Brierly posed another question.
"Did Dave Crossley…do drugs?"
"No!"
"Are you sure?"
"Yes."
"How much did those boots cost?" Brierly asked. The question was totally out of left field. It was unexpected. Even Track was caught off guard.
"What do mean?" Klein queried, somewhat hesitatingly.
"The boots…on your feet," Brierly said, pointing downwards.
"I don't know. I can't recall how…"
"…How much you paid for them. Yes…," Brierly interjected.
"So why…?"
"Do I want to know?"
"Yes…what's the relevance?" Klein asked.

Brierly took a deep breath, smiling inwardly. He suspected that he was close to the answer he wanted. He just needed to twist the knife in a little deeper. "The question is relevant because I don't believe you."

"What?"

A bastardised version of the line from Shakespeare's Hamlet spoken by Queen Gertrude, *"the lady doth protest too much, methinks"* but used in today's vernacular as 'one does protest too much,' had already crossed Brierly's mind during the conversation. It was how he felt about Klein's reactions. He guessed that his questions were getting close to the mark and that was why Klein was reacting as strongly as he was. "As I said," he went on, "I don't believe you."

"I'm confused," Klein said, starting to stand up, "what is it that don't you believe, Inspector?" It was the first time that Brierly's rank had been mentioned and there was an implication in Klein's tone that the conversation was becoming too formal than he was comfortable with. Brierly suspected that Klein was about to leave and potentially seek legal advice. He had hoped to keep things casual but businesslike. Having no evidence yet as to who killed Crossley, he was trying to establish a motive, the why, after which they could move on to the who. He looked up into Klein's face who was beginning to pick up a computer bag he had brought with him, lifting the strap ready to place it across a shoulder.

"Sit down, Mr. Klein. I don't think we are finished yet," Brierly said quietly. His calm demeanour was supported by the steeple he had created with his fingers. He had put both hands together almost prayer-like, his chin resting on top. He watched Klein hesitate, sensing a fight or flight response spinning through the boy's mind. Slowly the student put his bag back onto the floor and sat down again.

"Thank you," Brierly said. Klein rolled his eyes in response, suggesting that the policeman get on with what he wanted to say. He obliged.

"You said that you don't do drugs."

"Yes, that's right."

"And neither did Dave Crossley?"

"Yes."

"What about Peter Damson?"

"He doesn't either."

Brierly shrugged. "So where did you get the money from?"
"What money? What are you talking about?"
"I'll ask you again. Your boots and Dave Crossley's shoes. Where did the money come from?"
Brierly had learnt over the years that the public, be they suspect or victim, never knew what the police themselves knew whenever conversations or interrogations were conducted. Accordingly with knowledge being power, knowing just a little more than what one's opponent knew was always the best position to be in. When the postmortem was conducted on Crossley one of the items mentioned in the pathologist's report was that there was no trace of any drugs in the boy's system. This has sparked Brierly's memory about the shoes he had noticed on Crossley's body, the morning he had been found. It had raised a question in his mind, and he had made inquiries about them. They were the genuine article and were worth a pretty penny, Nike Road Warriors, which cost over a thousand pounds a pair. Money for those did not come from a student grant!
Klein remained silent, waiting for Brierly to carry on.
"Did you deal?"
"What?"
Brierly's patience was being stretched and he made it clear. "Let's stop playing games, Mr. Klein. What I'm asking is a simple question. Did you deal drugs?"
"No!"
"Did Dave Crossley?"
"I don't know."
"Oh, come off it, Mr. Klein. I'm not stupid…and neither are you, so let's stop messing around here," Brierly said, raising his voice slightly. "I know that you have the real answer to my question, and it isn't what you have given me so far, is it?"
Brierly's statement was itself a lie, but he gambled that Klein did not know that. He suspected that the boy knew what Dave Crossley was really up to and he believed that if he pressed hard enough then Klein would eventually fold. It was a gamble, but a risk worth taking as far as he was concerned. The shoes were the clue. After a pause of several seconds, Klein opened up.
"Dave was a dealer yes," he said. "But let me assure you Inspector, neither Pete nor I ever got involved with him, either taking drugs or selling them."

Brierly eyed the boy, unsure whether to believe him or not. "So, is that why you were in the cemetery the night he was killed? To meet a customer?"
"Pete and I went with him yes. He was our friend."
"And you owed him, didn't you?"
"Sorry?"
"You owed him…the boots," Brierly nodded again at the floor. "He bought them for you, didn't he?"
"He was very generous," Klein replied. "To his closest friends anyway, especially when he had money. So, when he asked us to go with him that night, we did."
"I'm sure," Brierly replied, glancing briefly at Track who seemed mesmerized at how his boss had got to the answer he wanted. He would tell Track later about the running shoes found on Crossley's body, and his inquiry into their worth. From there it had been easy to conclude how unlikely it was that a student could afford such luxuries without an obvious income. On a student campus, the likely link was drugs. The question he still need an answer to, however, was who Crossley was meeting with that night? Was it a customer? Was it another dealer? Was it his supplier? Whoever it was, Crossley had ended up dead. At least they now had a possible motive. A dispute over money? An argument over supply, over quality or quantity? There were so many questions, but at least there was an avenue of inquiry to follow. Brierly looked at Klein. He seemed downtrodden, spent.
"Thank you for your time, Mr. Klein," Brierly said sympathetically. "You can go now. We'll be in touch as required."

CHAPTER 25

The call to Mary Owen had surprised her. She had not expected to hear from him, and it took a few seconds to realize that she couldn't understand any of the words he was saying. He was speaking too fast. She had been busy with one of her spreadsheets when the mobile phone began vibrating. She always kept it on silent mode if she was in a meeting or didn't want to be disturbed. Initially, she had ignored it, after all, she could always call him back. Seeing his number again for the third time in less than two minutes however and noting that he had not left any messages at his previous attempts convinced her eventually to answer him.
"Slow down, Tom," she said, trying to get him to stop his rapid rattle of gibberish, "what's this about Gretchen?"
"She was attacked last night, in the house, and the kids are gone and....," he replied, his words tumbling out of his mouth like rapids on a river and the pitch of his voice increasing to a high timbre. She heard the most important words as he continued to ramble on, "...the police are..."
'Stop!" she exclaimed. "You said that Gretchen was attacked? How? When? What happened? Where are you anyway?" she asked, noticing her questions were becoming just like his own.
Tom Millwright took a deep intake of breath, trying to keep calm and wanting to give the details to his sister-in-law without causing her to overreact. He was struggling with what had happened himself. "I'm here at the police station in Portsmouth. I've just finished a second interview with DI Sutton, the Detective who your dad was interviewed by when he was arrested the other day. I spent most of the night at the Queen Alexandra hospital."
"Is Gretch with you? Is she okay?"
"No, that's what I just tried to tell you. She's dead!"
The words hit her like a hammer. She may have heard him say them earlier, but it hadn't registered if he had. She sat wordlessly for a few seconds. Her face seemed to freeze, and her eyes could not focus on anything in front of her. The mobile was against her ear, but she didn't hear him talking. Her world seemed to be spinning around her. Suddenly she heard him ask, "Are you there, Mary? Mary, can you

hear me?" It was as if the last ten seconds of her life never happened. It felt as if her heart had stopped. She felt a surge of emotions begin to course through her. Frustration, despair, fear, and anger.
"Tell me what happened?" she said, her voice a monotone, robotic statement.
"I don't know," he said, "I came home and..." She listened as he gave her a description of the events of the previous evening. As he spoke, she seemed to be floating out of her body. When he eventually finished, she asked, "And the kids? Where are they?"
"That's why I'm here...with Sutton. The police are trying to find them."
"What does that mean?"
"Mary, they've been taken. Whoever killed Mary has taken the kids."
"Are you sure?" she questioned. A feeling of utter concern for the safety of her niece and nephew was uppermost in her mind.
"Yes, and the police are too," Millwright answered.
"My God," she replied, suddenly realizing the implication of what he was suggesting. "What do the police have to say for themselves?"
"They've started investigating, but they won't tell me much. They just said it's too early, but they will keep me informed."
"Do they have any ideas, any leads?"
"I don't know," he replied, his voice cracking, "but Mary, I'm scared for the kids."
"I understand," she replied, feeling sick to her stomach. She couldn't imagine how they could be feeling if indeed they were alive to feel anything. She tried to sound optimistic, though not feeling it herself, saying, "I'm sure the police will find them. It's just a matter of time."
"I bloody well hope so!" Millwright exclaimed with a forcefulness that surprised her.
Suddenly a thought struck her. "Have you told dad yet?"
"I tried to call him earlier, but I guess he was sleeping. It was a good few hours ago. I even tried last night but I didn't get an answer then either."
"Okay, leave it with me, I'll call him," she said, the very thought of how her father would react already filling her with dread. During their last conversation, he had repeated his concern about the threats against him and the rest of the family. He had been adamant about the danger. Was the killing of her sister related to the threat? It seemed too coincidental to be otherwise. Mary thought back to what

he had revealed to her. Perhaps now he will accept that he should have told the police what he had shared with her. Unfortunately, she speculated, it may be much too late for that.
Mary and her brother-in-law spoke for a few minutes longer. It was as if they were in limbo. Waiting. Not knowing what to do next. He talked about his house being off-limits, his concern for the children, and where Mary's body was being kept. Thereafter, once they had exhausted each other's questions, their thoughts, and some guesswork as to who was behind the attack, she agreed with him that he could stay with her while his house remained a crime scene.
When she eventually put down the phone she noticed that her hands were shaking. She held them together tightly to try and stop the tiny tremors. She felt sick. While she waited for her hands to settle and ready herself to make the call she didn't want to make, she suddenly felt a wave of emotion for her older sister surge through her. She began to well up. Tears streamed down her cheeks, and she started to wail. She needed the release, and she could not hold back any longer. Feeling naked and exposed she quickly locked her office door before letting the floodgates completely open.

"Did he tell them anything?" he asked.
"I don't know dad. I don't think he knows much more than I do," she answered. They were sitting at the dining room table in his house. She had left work the moment she had finished speaking with him. It had been nearly four o'clock that afternoon before he had answered her call. When she finally left the office, it was already dark, and the weather had turned for the worse. The rain which had been steadily falling on and off for most of the day had now been joined by an icy wind that had strengthened in intensity as darkness fell. It brought flurries of sleet and rain across the south of the country which meant that it had taken longer than usual to drive to his house, the traffic having been bumper-to-bumper due to the worsening driving conditions. Outside, the rain smashed against the uncovered windows, the mood inside was sombre and unsettled. A silence gripped them. Steam rose from hot mugs of tea, untouched since they were placed on the table. Mary and Trevor Owen grieved

together while fearing for the safety of Gretchen's children. They struggled to decide what to do next.
"Where is he now?" Trevor Owen asked of his son-in-law.
"I think he's gone to stay in a hotel for now," she replied. "I'm not sure which, he only sent me a text to tell me to be careful, and that he was going to be interviewed again by the police regarding the kids. We've agreed that he can stay with me from tomorrow."
Trevor Owen looked into his daughter's face, the lines under and around his eyes showed how stressed he was. The redness inside the sclera, the white of his eye, indicated how long and how deeply he had wept over his daughter's death.
"I hope to God they find them soon," he said, referring to his grandchildren. "This is all my fault!"
Mary reached over and took his arm firmly in her hand. "No, it isn't," she insisted. "You can't blame yourself for any of this. You don't even know whether Gretchen's murder had anything to do with those threats!" Angrily, he pulled his arm away, swiping his cup from the table, sending tea and blue ceramic scattering and then shattering onto the kitchen floor.
"Fuck!" he shouted. "Fuck!" He began to stand but Mary told him to sit back down. Reluctantly he did so. Mary then left the table to find a dry cloth and a dustpan to fix the damage. Alone, he broke down and wailed, his body convulsing as he sobbed, even continuing when she returned to clean up the mess. By the time she had finished her task, he had quietened down, eventually resting his head on his arms. It was obvious that he was extremely tired, and he had exhausted himself. Soon she realized that he had fallen asleep. She decided to let him rest for a while. It was not yet eight o'clock so it was too early for him to go to bed. While he dozed, she made a few phone calls from the lounge, sitting on one of the settees. The large window with the still-open curtains was immediately behind her. The rain continued to bounce off it, little rivulets appearing and then disappearing like tiny swollen streams. After speaking with Bill Tiley and asking for a few days off, she made a call to the Portsmouth police station where she tried to get hold of DI Sutton. She was unsuccessful. She was told that she could not have his mobile number due to privacy reasons but that she could leave a message for him if she wanted to. She took up the offer, asking Sutton to call her when he was able. Finally, she called Tom and after a few seconds, he

answered the phone. She told him where she was and pressed him as much as she could for answers. By the time they had finished their conversation, she was finally able to get a better understanding from him of what had happened the night before.

"Dad?" she said softly, touching him gently on the shoulder. "Dad, are you okay?" Owen raised his head slowly, blinking for a second in the light shining above him.
"What time is it?" he asked.
"It's just before ten. You've been asleep for a couple of hours."
"Why didn't you wake me up?" he asked, stretching his arms outwards, then standing to click his back. She noticed that he was a little unsteady on his feet, not yet fully compus mentis, and she made to help him before stopping herself from doing so. It was possible that he might lash out again. "I thought it best that you take it easy for a while," she answered, a sad smile on her face.
He looked at her for a second, before accepting her rationale.
"I think it's time for bed," he continued.
"Do you want me to stay?" she asked.
"No, it's okay. I'll be fine. There's not much we can do tonight anyway. We just need the police to do their job."
"You're right," Mary replied, her voice soft, almost a whisper, her tone understanding.
It took them a few minutes to agree on how to handle the next few days. They understood that some of the time would be spent waiting and hoping for news about Trish and Robert, Gretchen's children. Some would be spent mourning and thinking about how best to celebrate Gretchen's life.
Some would be spent contemplating what to do next. What to tell and what to keep secret. As Mary drove away from the house, she knew that she had lied to her father. She knew that she needed to do more than just sit around. She would be following up with DI Sutton as soon as she could. She had things to tell him and it was obvious from her earlier call with Tom that he hadn't shared anything with the police that they didn't know already. It was true that Tom knew less than she did, and Mary felt that it was about time that she told Sutton everything she had gleaned from her father. It was in her interest as well. She was also a target and she was scared. With her

mind focused on the morning and the hazardous drive home through the continuing heavy rain, she failed to notice the car behind her, following her every turn. The headlights that stayed at a steady distance behind her car were like two eyes of some unknown creature that hunted its prey in the dead of night. The occupant smiled: there was no hurry.

When she had gone, Trevor Owen went up to his bedroom. He turned on the light before also switching on a bedside lamp sitting on a small chest of drawers to the right of the bed. He moved to the end of the bed before kneeling, reaching underneath the base. He found what he was looking for, extracting a white shoebox with a navy-blue lid. Elastic bands held it together tightly like those wrapped around an ancient Egyptian mummy. He put the box on the bed, then sat next to it for a few seconds before removing the bands, lifting the lid, and putting the cover next to him. He then removed some photographs from the box, looking at each briefly. They were pictures of his family. Random photographs over the years. Various holidays and multiple barbecues and picnics. Mary, Gretchen, Tom, his grandchildren, and his long-dead wife Barbara. He placed the photos on top of the lid, then took out the gun that had been hidden underneath. He felt the weight of it, a Ruger SR911 semi-automatic. Available legally for sale in Northern Ireland, with a license. Available if you knew someone, who knew someone, in England, without one. He checked that the gun was loaded and that the safety switch was on. He placed it on the bedside table before returning the shoebox with all its contents back under the bed. When he finally turned out the light he felt a little safer, though his mind was still unsettled. He had lied to Mary, and he wasn't sure if she had noticed or if she had seen through him. Time would tell. When he eventually drifted off to sleep, the limbs of the bare trees outside his bedroom threw grotesque silhouettes on the windowpane, occasionally brushing against the glass as the rain and wind outside battered them with strong gusts. Inside his bedroom, the scraping on the glass sounded like the nails of a thousand dead souls trying to tear their way into the room. Trevor Owen slept fitfully. During the night the face of Gretchen appeared to him. Then she disappeared, before coming to see him again. Her visit repeated itself. He woke up breathing heavily, sweating profusely, his dream had turned into a horrible reoccurring nightmare.

CHAPTER 26

He was still awake despite the lateness of the hour. It had been a long day and while the surgery officially closed at six pm, there had been a sizeable queue of patients waiting in reception when the doors were closed to any more patients. He had seen his last one just before seven and it was just before seven thirty when he was finally able to get away. She had been waiting for him, walking out of the shadows as he made his way to his car. She was soaked to the skin, her hair matted to her scalp and her jeans, coat, and shoes were clinging to her body. She was shivering and could barely speak from the cold…or was it from the drugs? At first, he wanted to tell her to leave him alone, to stay away, but the sight of his daughter drenched from being caught in the freezing rain was too much for him. He detested her, he agonized daily over what she was doing to herself, but he knew he couldn't turn his back, no matter how much she abused him, especially on such a cruel night.

'Get in the back," he said, pointing at his car. Without hesitation she climbed into the rear seat, passenger side, slamming the door with unnecessary force. For a moment he sat looking through the windscreen. The rain blurred his vision. She leant forward holding the back of the chair trying to see his face. "I need a place to stay," she said, her voice defiant, indignant. He wiped his eyes with the back of his hand, "The rain," he said, pointing at the window, giving nothing away as to how he was feeling. He took a handkerchief from a pocket of his coat and rubbed his face, neck, and hair. Finding another in the glove compartment he passed it to her to do the same.

"We need to get you out of those clothes," he said.

"I've got no money."

He had expected the answer and was already thinking of what to do. He knew that he couldn't take her home. Carol would have a fit, but he needed to find something dry for her to wear. He noticed that her teeth were chattering, so he turned on the ignition, cranking up the heater. "There's a Primark on Vincents Walk near Houndwell Park, I know it's open until eight, we'll go there," he said.

Patricia nodded but remained silent. She let him drive off as she began to strip out of her coat and jersey. The warm air from the vents slowly raised the temperature inside the car. As they drove through the wet streets, he looked at his daughter in his rear-view mirror, occasionally catching her eye as she wiped away the hair that dangled across her face. How had it come to this, he thought? Alan Boothby, a respected doctor, yet he struggled with the physical health of his own flesh and blood! He knew that his divorce may have played some part in her current situation, but he had no way of managing her mind, her mental health. He had tried all he could. The positive, the negative, chastising, encouraging, reverse psychology, nothing seemed to get through to her. She was slowly killing herself. He detested the situation, and he was disgusted with himself for supplying her with what she had wanted. She had put him in a very difficult situation, yet he continued to stand by her, by breaking the law. He had added fuel to her fire. Why? The answer was simple because he loved her. She was his daughter, someone who would always be the apple of his eye. No matter how much he tried, he couldn't turn away from her completely. He knew that he needed to do something, he already had…he would continue to try.

"Are you feeling any better?" he asked, noting that the car was now so much warmer, and she appeared to have stopped shaking.

"A little," she answered, pained into responding to his question.

"Good."

"Can you hurry up though?"

"I'm driving as quickly as I can. With all this rain, the traffic is heavy. You can see that for……" He stopped himself, realizing that he was about to argue with her. There was no point. He knew that it wouldn't make her see anything but a red rag. She was focused on herself. He kept his eyes on the road and continued driving in silence.

He had stopped the car in the Taco Bell car park. It meant that he could run down 'Above Bar' street, the High Street of the city. He knew that it was a gamble, but with the heavy rain, he had hoped that most of the drunks, the homeless, and the drug-addled who usually frequented the place had found somewhere else to be on such a bad night. If there were any around, he prayed that they would not try to abuse or at worst mug him. The police who patrolled the area couldn't be everywhere all the time and despite the CCTV dotted around the place which recorded most of what happened there, being molested wasn't what he needed at that time of night.

He had asked her for her measurements, and her sizes, and he had rushed through the front door of the Primark store with five minutes to spare before closing time. Fortunately, despite the rain, his coat keep him dry and within twenty-five minutes he was back inside the car with three plastic bags. T-shirts, runners, jeans, underwear, a dark blue parka jacket, a jersey, and an umbrella.
She laughed when she saw his embarrassment as she stripped naked despite being parked within a few yards of the family restaurant.
"I can see better....with the lights," she said, pointing towards the Mexican franchise that was almost empty of customers. Within minutes she was dressed again. She dumped all of her old wet clothes on the front passenger seat.
"Keep them," she said, "or maybe chuck them in a charity bin. I don't need them anymore."
"Patricia!" Boothby replied, "what do you think you're doing?" he asked, turning to face her. She was sitting back in her seat admiring her new threads, pleased at what she was seeing.
"You did well, dad," she replied flippantly, ignoring his outburst, and his question.
Boothby sighed. He had tried, but he knew that he was on the losing end of any conversation with her. It was her life, and she wasn't going to listen to whatever he had to say. Before he had time to speak again, she asked him for money. He refused.
"But I need some, for food."
He shook his head knowing that she was doing what she always did, trying to manipulate him. Food was always the reason she wanted money from him, yet she always looked so thin, pale, almost anemic. He knew as a doctor what was happening to her and in time what would happen to her body if the drugs didn't kill her first. Constant illnesses, fatigue, constipation, ultimately anemia, and kidney failure.
"No!" he said firmly. "I can't keep getting you out of a hole. You need help Patricia, let me get you that help," he pleaded. "It's nutrition and support you need, not drugs."
She bit her lip and looked out of the car window at the rain still sheeting down, the wind whipping up loose fast-food papers and blowing them across the road. "Fuck you!" she spat and opened the car door fighting against the elements to get out.
"Patricia!" he shouted, but she ignored him, slamming the car door and then running to the restaurant entrance, splashing through the

water that had dammed up against the kerb. He looked at the pile of wet clothes on the seat beside him. Turning to check the back seat to see if there was anything left behind, he noticed the umbrella still wrapped in clear cellophane, the price tag mocking him. Turning to face the windscreen he made a decision. He started his car and drove off into the night.

CHAPTER 27

Brierly rarely had time to think about other things. His mind was constantly thinking of the case or cases he was working on. Ever since he had left the Royal Navy the opportunity to engage in his hobby other than keeping an eye on where Southampton FC was in the Premier League, was limited. It was even more difficult when the weather didn't play ball. During his time working on various ships, he had often found himself looking up into the night sky, wondering how the early sailors from the Greeks and Romans to the Vikings and others had used the stars to navigate their way across thousands of miles of open sea. He loved the feeling of being out on the ocean and the skies above being clear, the blackness making the night sky come alive. Depending on where his ship was heading, he would observe constellations in the Southern Hemisphere that were invisible to those in the North and vice versa, and he wondered how things must have seemed to those early civilizations. They had different beliefs then about the cosmos. Modern-day sailors knew exactly where they were and where they were going. They didn't need to pray to the Gods for safe passage, like the adventurers of the past. Raleigh, Columbus, Cook, and De Gama would have loved satellite tracking and the advanced technology of today that could have told them what was beneath the water, as well as what was in the skies above. The reliance on signs from the heavens or indeed a lack thereof must have been bewildering at times.

During Brierly's service, he had been lucky to observe many of the meteor showers that most people either knew nothing of or seldom saw. Sometimes he had been in the right place at the right time. Other times it was just pure luck. Since becoming a cop his interest in the night sky had offered a welcome release from the daily grind of policing. Over time it had become a passion and he had begun to use the resources available on the internet whenever he was able to, though at times its use was just as confusing to him as those portents of the past must have seemed to the early sailors. Learning about what he had experienced during his travels, the names that were given to the objects he had seen, and why. Where to look in the night sky, and when, all added to the rich tapestry of the heavens. He had kept a journal during his naval days detailing what he had experienced

over the years, and he looked forward to any opportunity he could to explore the vastness of the sky. He had stared dumbstruck at the Perseids, in the constellation of Perseus when he had first seen them from HMS Lancaster in 1995. Upon investigation, it surprised him to find that he had been observing particles from a comet known as Swift-Tuttle, discovered in 1862 with an orbital period around the earth of 133 years. Since then, and over the next twenty-five years he had seen the meteor showers in Orion, Taurus, Gemini, and Capricorn, some so infrequent yet so special if one was lucky to catch them. His biggest regret was the likelihood of never seeing Halley's comet. In 1986 he was way too young to even think about the stars and the sighting from earth was the least favourable on record anyway. The comet and the earth had been on opposite sides of the sun, resulting in the worst possible viewing in two thousand years. With the return of the comet only expected in 2061 he doubted that he would be lucky enough to be alive to experience the astral phenomenon. However, he took comfort in the fact that he had been able to see something else, something that few people ever had the chance to see. The Aurora Borealis, the Northern Lights, and the Aurora Australis, the Southern Lights. The latter had been easy, a trip down towards Antarctica on a naval supply vessel had meant that he had several sightings over the journey. It had taken him three attempts however to see the former. The first couple of opportunities; the timings were right and his ship was in the region but a sighting was marred by bad weather, with heavy snow clouds covering the area. The third attempt had been successful. He had taken June on a holiday a few years after they were married. At the time they had no children to worry about. They had travelled up to far north Finland during late winter/early spring and had the full experience that one could only dream of. Both had been awestruck by the beauty of the swirling sky. A mass of colours. Greens, reds, and purples had held their attention for nearly two hours as they stood transfixed, staring upward with huge smiles on their faces. Unfortunately, that was years ago and while Brierly hankered to return there, things always seemed to get in the way. If it wasn't his job, it was the kids or something else would come up causing some form of delay or requiring a change of plan.
Sitting at the dining room table he was looking through the latest edition of the Sky at Night magazine.

"You're not likely to see much over the next few weeks," June said, as she walked past him. "Tea?"
Closing the pages with a sigh and standing up, he answered her with a "Yes, please," adding, "you're probably right." He followed her into the kitchen. "It's a pity," he said, as he stood leaning against the sink, "as November is a good month to see the Taurid Meteors, perhaps with the odd fireball as well."
She smiled at him. It was unusual for him to be able to take the odd night off and think about things outside of the job. She knew that it helped him relax, though in his eyes she could see that he was torn by doing so. The two cases he had on his plate were worrying him deeply. She could tell in his voice. He would normally be much more expressive about the night sky, but tonight he was so-so. Less than enthusiastic.
"Are you okay, James?" she asked, her voice soft, caring. She passed him his mug of tea. He noted that she used his proper Christian name, James, not Jim as she normally would. It was a sign of her concern for him.
"I'm fine," he answered without conviction, taking a sip of the hot liquid.
"I'm not convinced. I know you well enough to see when something is troubling you."
He looked at her, immediately realizing that she was right. He couldn't hide anything from her. It was as if she could read his thoughts. "I'm concerned about the boys."
"The boys?"
"Yes. These cases I'm working on are worrying me."
"But surely they have nothing to do with us....do they?" she questioned, concern in her voice.
"No, of course not. But it's what I'm seeing around us that's bothering me. Anyway, I shouldn't have brought it up," he continued, sensing that he had started something he now regretted.
She looked at him, then pointed towards the kitchen door. "Let's go and sit down in the lounge. You need to tell me what's on your mind."
He followed her out of the kitchen, hoping that what he was about to share wouldn't bother her. He didn't want to burden her with his problems as she had her own. She was a people person and always tried to see the best in others, the polar opposite in some way to

himself. She used her compassion and empathetic nature in her daily life. She had a job, a calling in some ways, working voluntarily for a charity helping those with CND, predominantly infants, and young children. She also worked with adults with muscular dystrophy. It was as trying as it was rewarding. She worked hard raising money when she could and caring for those born with or gradually suffering from the genetic mutation that caused their illness. She was always advocating for more funding and support for those suffering from the disease and regularly attended council meetings to lobby for better facilities. Sometimes she and others who were passionate about the issue had success. Other times they had periods of frustration, much as Brierly himself did.

Sitting next to him, she asked him again to open up and tell her what was on his mind. He turned in his seat and looked into the face he had known for years, touching her gently on the cheek.

"You'll probably think I'm overreacting," he said.

"About what?"

He shook his head. It was as if the words on the end of his tongue needed to remain unsaid. She waited quietly, knowing that she had given him the opportunity, and he would take it when he was ready. Finally, he shared his concern. "These cases I'm working on. There is something about them that is bothering me. Something that goes beyond the murders themselves."

"How do you mean?"

"I guess it's the victims. A student and a homeless person."

"You think they are connected?

"To be honest, no I don't, other than they were both killed in a cemetery. That may be just a coincidence," he added, "No, it's more the fact that they appear to be random killings."

"And why is that any different from any other murder you have investigated over the years?"

"That's the point, it isn't…but somehow these killings have got to me. Made me realize something I hadn't considered before."

"Which is?"

He looked into her eyes, and she noticed that his own were moist, glistening in the light. It was unusual for him to be so emotionally attached to his cases.

"As I said earlier, I'm concerned for the boys. It's as if I suddenly noticed that I can no longer protect them….as I, we, used to."

"That's true, but they're not boys anymore, James, they're young men now."
"I know," he replied, "and you are right, but it's just…."
"Making you feel old?" she interjected.
"Older perhaps."
She smiled at him. She knew what he meant, but she also knew that he needed to see things in perspective. It was funny how men seemed to struggle with age. It had arisen several times over the past few years in different settings. The husbands of her friends and colleagues had suffered from it, now it was her own. It was as if a man suddenly looked in a mirror one day and became aware of their mortality, often grateful that they had children to carry on their name. Was this the start for him of a mid-life crisis or just a realization that things around him were changing?
"You know, every day I deal with people who struggle with their illness," she said, softly. "Many are not even expected to have a long-term future. But you know the one thing that I see in them? It's that they are nearly always positive. Thankful for what they have, for the support someone gives them. Fortunately, we are not in that situation. We have nothing to complain about."
"I know," he answered, "and I think that's the point."
"What is?"
"That we've been very lucky. We've brought up two kids, both of whom are properly grounded. They are good students, well balanced, a bit cheeky at times, but they don't take too many risks and have stayed away from drugs, not like some I've come across recently."
"As far as we know," she countered but agreed just the same.
"As far as we know," he repeated, though both knew that there were no signs of either Simon or Warwick giving in to the temptation of taking drugs. Brierly however wasn't naïve about his kids and he suspected that they would have encountered them somewhere at university, or at some of the parties they attended.
"Is that what is concerning you then?" she asked.
"Yes and no. It's the fact that the kids are out there," he waved a hand towards the window, "and it seems the world is suddenly out of control, and I've lost the ability to protect them."
"But it has always been that way," she countered. "It's just that we've been lucky not to have been impacted like so many others have. As I said before, the boys are healthy, we are too, and that's all you can

ask for."
"I guess so," he answered.
"Look Jim, no one can predict what tomorrow will bring. We just need to live it. To do the best we can." She pointed back to the dining room, where his magazines still lay on the table. "For all the stars in the sky, and all the astrologers out there who claim to see the future, no one can."
"I know."
"So, I understand where you are coming from, but as far as the kids are concerned you need to let them be. You can't always be there to look after them, despite your wish to keep them safe, to protect them. They need to live their own lives; they need to make their own mistakes. Though we'll always be there for them, to listen, guide them, to…."
"Give them money," he added, smiling.
"Yes, until they both leave home, we'll need to support them until they start working. But that's the point, Jim love, we both know the world is a dangerous place, but we've done our job. We've shown them that we love them. We've shown them what's right and wrong, now it's up to them."
Brierly looked at her. He knew she was right. He knew that the city, the country, had changed somehow, almost without him noticing. Death and violence were always just a day away, and always had been, but the feeling that society was now at war with itself, was all-pervasive. With social media giving a platform for hate, it was as if a sense of inevitability had crept up behind society and stood at everyone's shoulder, and the world was ready to explode. Somehow the cases he and his team were working on were getting to him like he had never experienced before. He wasn't sure why… then his mobile rang.

CHAPTER 28

The bodies of the two children lay in the shallow water. Both had been found face down. Raindrops hit the water causing tiny ripples for milliseconds before each disappeared as another hit the surface. It was as if the sky was crying. Brierly had slipped several times as he and DS White had clambered down the soft, wet bank between the road and the water's edge, the adjoining shrubs, and trees, creating a natural barrier between the two. After a drive of forty minutes, they had turned off the A32 onto Northfields Farm Lane, stopping a hundred yards along it, not far from the Chiphall Lake Trout Fishery. Blue and red flashing lights gave notice where the turning off the main road could be found. It had been difficult to see the spot through the incessant rain that had been falling ever since White had picked up Brierly at his house. The news hadn't helped Brierly's mood either. The lack of any lighting along the country road had made the journey quite treacherous given the beams of oncoming cars, which nearly blinded them at times. This was particularly the case when some careless drivers refused to dim their headlights, despite White repeatedly flashing his own as a warning for them to do so.

"Who found them?" Brierly asked Phil Sutton, who had been the one who had called him an hour earlier. The bearer of bad news who had interrupted the conversation he had been having with June.

"The farmer at the bottom of the lane. He had come down from his field on his way to the farmhouse, a little further down the road." Sutton pointed over his left shoulder, "It was just luck that he saw something drive away. Seems the vehicle only put its lights on as it turned left onto the main road and drove off towards Wickham."

"And that was strange because?"

"Because he thought he saw it turn off the main road with its lights on just a few minutes earlier. He noticed that the lights were turned off very quickly after that. A short while later he saw them come back on again."

"So, the bodies were dumped within minutes?"

"Would seem that way, which is why I called you once they were found and we got the call ourselves. The bodies have been easy to identify from the school uniforms they're wearing. They are the only

two children reported as missing from that school, so it was a no-brainer. When we spoke previously, Christ was it only yesterday?" he questioned himself, "it was the kid's mother's killing that concerned me. Now, looking at these poor bastards it's pretty clear that there is something more to this than just a random killing. In my experience kids aren't usually taken and then murdered immediately after being taken from suburban homes. Often there is a ransom request."
"So you think they were targeted?" White asked. He had been standing at Brierly's shoulder having been introduced to Sutton earlier. He had stayed silent until now, standing like a statute while rain dripped from his hair and chin; it continued to fall heavily. All three men were wearing coats, but none had any form of headgear. Their faces glistened in the bright lights that the forensic team had set up around the crime scene. Two men in light blue suits and masks, now darkened by the rain began to slowly and carefully lift the body of the young girl out of the water and place it into a body bag, leaving it open, until they had completed their initial investigation.
"Any idea how they were killed?" Brierly asked, looking towards the two men who had now started to extract the young boy from the water.
"I'll answer that," a voice from behind them stated. Just as they each turned around to see who was talking, the rain intensified. The sudden fury required them to squint as a biting wind gust made the rain appear to fall horizontally for a few seconds, straight into their faces. A small man, no more than a metre and a half in height, wearing a white Forensics suit that covered him from head to toe, supplemented with a mask, introduced himself. "Victor Wilson, Forensics lead," he said through the gauze, "and both were strangled."
"Nice to see you again, Vic," Sutton said, introducing both Brierly and White. Wilson did not offer a hand as both of his were already covered with white plastic gloves. "To protect the evidence," Wilson noted, "though I doubt we'll get much from the bodies."
"Because?" White asked.
"All this rain, and the fact that the victims were in the water for a while until we got here. Most of the evidence, if not all, including any DNA, would likely have been washed away by now. Literally."
"So how were they strangled," Brierly asked.
"By hand, unfortunately. If they had been killed with a rope or

something similar, then we may have been lucky, perhaps we may have found some fibres, but …"

Brierly glanced at Sutton, they both knew that whoever had killed the children had been very careful, meticulous. He then turned to Wilson, accepting that the Forensics team had been quite thorough already. They had been on site when Brierly and White had arrived and had already conducted their preliminary investigation before allowing the detectives to get anywhere near the crime scene. It was obvious to all that the bodies had been dumped; thrown down the bank just a few feet off the road. Sutton had already made Brierly aware that he had checked for tyre marks, but it was obvious even in the dark that with the downwards slope of the road from the A32 turnoff, the rain had washed away any possible markings from the tarmac.

Wilson pointed down towards the water as the second child was placed into a body bag. When he was satisfied that his team had all the evidence they could gather from the scene he would allow the bodies to be transferred to the morgue.

"Who could do this?" he asked aloud, not expecting an answer. He didn't receive one. Each of the policemen had seen enough killing in their lifetime yet they still found it difficult to know how to respond to such a statement. To break the immediate silence, Brierly commented by saying, "Phil, it's still your case currently. What do you want to do next?"

"I think we need to talk with the farmer down there," he said, pointing towards a large farmhouse roughly three hundred yards away. A single light shone from an upstairs room. It could be seen acting like a lighthouse, the light appearing then disappearing as the trees along the roadside swayed in the wind, blocking it, then unblocking it, from their view. The rain didn't help either. It was still falling steadily and while the temperature remained stable at six degrees celsius due to the cloud cover, they were starting to feel the cold along with the dampness.

"Do you think he'll be up at this time of night?" White asked, looking at his watch. It was just before 11 pm.

"Not sure," Sutton replied, "but let's go and find out."

They told Wilson that they were leaving the site, and he in turn advised them that a post-mortem would likely be done within the next day or two. "I'll be arranging for the bodies to go to

Southampton General. I'll give Gemma a call and she'll manage the process from there. By the time she starts her work, I'll have my initial report in her inbox." They thanked him, then with Sutton leading the way, they drove the short distance, in separate cars, to the farmhouse.

At the sound of their car doors slamming in the driveway, an outside light was turned on and a woman opened a large door, an inviting entrance to the warmth of the cottage. As they ran to get out of the rain, Brierly noted that the building seemed to be much bigger than it had originally appeared.

"Come in, come in," she said, "you must be soaked." Her accent was that of a Scot. The dialect was quite unusual. Not something one heard very often Brierly thought but remembered that Crossley had also been from north of the border, so maybe there were more Scots in the area than he had expected. Introducing herself as Maggie Anthony, she offered to get them some towels to dry themselves off while she showed them where they could hang their coats. "My husband, Colin, is just putting some clothes on. We were in bed," she advised, an embarrassed smile briefly crossing her face. She was wearing a dressing gown pulled tightly around her, with blue slippers on her feet. Brierly guessed that she was in her late fifties by the grey of her non-descript hair style. It appeared that she had already put a brush through it in an attempt to look respectable.

"Come this way," she advised. "I've already stoked the fire and Col will put some more wood on it in a minute." With a collective thank you, they followed her and walked past several rooms before they entered an artfully lit lounge. Two standing lamps and a couple of wall lamps provided the necessary light. The fireplace was beginning to give off some welcome heat and they stood as close as they could warming their hands and hoping the heat would start to dry off their lower trouser legs and their shoes.

"I'll get those towels," she said, "then I'll make you all some tea if that's okay?" With everyone's appreciation ringing in her ears, she left the room leaving the three policemen alone. For the next two minutes, it was all about them getting warm and dry. Little was said until a man in his late-sixties walked into the room. He was dressed in jeans that had been well-worn, along with a checked shirt under a dark blue jersey with leather patches sewn onto the elbows. To their surprise, he also wore heavy black boots on his feet. "I'm not

supposed to wear them in here," he said with a cheeky smile, "but my wellies are muddy from the fields out back, and my feet will get cold if I just put my slippers on…so bugger it."
Brierly smiled to himself and noted that his colleagues also saw the lighthearted side of things. Colin Anthony was a character. Standing an inch short of six feet, he seemed incredibly fit. Well-toned, slim, and with no fat on his body, even around his jowls, despite his age. It was obvious that farming was keeping the man in shape. Moving to the side of the fireplace he asked them to sit down. "Any chair you like," he said, pointing at the eclectic mix of old fabric and older leather armchairs. There were at least five of them placed in a semi-circle, all facing the fireplace. They watched as he threw four logs, each around a foot long, onto the flames. The fire was now licking at the earlier log that Maggie Anthony had used initially to get it going. "That'll work," Anthony said, sitting down in what was clearly 'his' chair. "Now gentleman," he said, "You're obviously the police, so how can I help you?" Each of them flashed their warrant cards at him proving their legitimacy before replacing them inside various pockets. Brierly let Sutton speak first. Despite both being of the same rank, Brierly still believed in respecting the jurisdiction of the crime. Until he was asked, Sutton was in charge of the case. Brierly had his own problems to solve.
"Could you tell us what you saw earlier Mr. Anthony before you found the bodies?" Sutton asked.
The old man shook his head, "Those poor kids," he answered, "never seen anything like it in my life. The way they were just dumped. Shocking it is, shocking!" Sutton and Brierly exchanged glances. It was clear that the older man would need a bit of cajoling for them to get the detail they needed from him.
"Yes, Sir, it is indeed a terrible thing, but we need to know what it is you saw….earlier," Sutton repeated.
"It was a van of sorts."
"A van?"
"Yes, you know. One of those with a sliding door…on the side."
"And you could see that from where you were at the time? I thought it was dark?" Brierly enquired. Sutton looked at him and nodded, thinking that two heads were better than none. The question was a good one. Before Anthony could answer, his wife brought the tea on a tray, placing it on a side table that rested between two of the chairs.

A typical old teapot, earthenware, was covered with a knitted tea cozy. In addition, she had also put milk into a jug along with a sugar bowl and several spoons on the tray. The policemen noticed that there were no cups, just mugs, none of which matched.
"I'll leave you to it then," she said to a chorus of thank-you's. "I'll be on my way back to bed," she continued, addressing her husband, before giving him a peck on the cheek. When she had left the room, Anthony surprised them by saying, "Yes it was almost dark, but from where I was in the field and because I was sitting in my tractor's cab, the slope of the land gave me a good view of the road."
"So, you could see that the vehicle was definitely a van?" Brierly queried.
"Yes. I used to have one meself. A Ford, diesel, two litre, I had."
"And what you saw was similar?" Sutton questioned.
"Yes."
"But you don't know if it was a Ford in this case?"
"Well, I can't be a hundred percent sure as there are similar ones about I know, but the shape of it was like my old Ford."
Sutton sipped at his tea, allowing Brierly an opportunity to ask, "I heard that you saw the van's lights go out just after it turned into the lane and then came on again a few minutes later. Is that right?"
"Yes. It made me curious. If anyone does come down the lane then if they are not coming here, to my place, they can only go on to the T-junction on Frith Lane less than half a mile up the road. This one didn't. So, when it's lights came on again I had time to take another look. By then I was much closer. I'd come down the field and was almost at the gate to turn onto the lane and head towards the house here. That's when I saw the shape as it went back towards the main road, the same way it had come."
"Did you see the driver?" Brierly asked.
"No, they were in shadow."
"Could you tell me the colour of the van? It was raining by then as well, wasn't it?"
"Yes, but it had slowed a little at the time. It wasn't too boggy otherwise I may have got stuck in the field preventing me from getting closer than I did. Anyway, it was white. Of that, I'm sure."
Brierly sat back in his chair. It wasn't much to go on, but at least there was a lead of sorts. A panel van, white, maybe a Ford. At least it was a start, something to go on.

"Oh, and something else I saw," Anthony continued, "the van had writing on its side."
"Did you see what it was?" Sutton asked.
"No, it was only a glimpse. I couldn't make out any of the words, but they were definitely on the one side, that I do know. I think one of the words began with a capital S, in red, and there was a picture of sorts below it but that's about all I notice before it turned onto the road."
The information the farmer provided was better than they could have expected, and they let him know how much they appreciated his diligence. After they finished their teas and having started to feel a little more human rather than like drowned rats, they thanked him again. They asked him to pass on their thanks to Mrs. Anthony, letting him know that one of them may need to speak with him again at some future date.
"Anytime," he replied. "Anytime at all."

White drove them back to Brierly's house. It would be one a.m. before they arrived. Sutton had left the scene separately, in his own car. Both detectives agreed to talk again in the morning after they had spoken with their individual bosses. It was necessary to agree on whose case these killings were. They each knew that no one would be happy with both of them trying to lead the same case. It was preferable that different parts of the service cooperated, rather than fought each other over a specific case. With the budget restrictions on manpower being felt across the country, there was more than enough work to go around and no force wanted more than was necessary or they could handle. It wasn't good for their stats.
When Brierly finally fell into bed he still wasn't convinced that the murders of Gretchen Millwright and her two children were linked in any way to the cemetery killings. It was something he needed to think about.

CHAPTER 29

The plan had been difficult to set up but was ultimately satisfying. It was made easier by the way they never closed the curtains in the house until they went to bed. Using binoculars while hidden in a neighbours garden on the opposite side of the road, had allowed their movements to be scrutinized and correlated. The time each child came home. The time each went to bed. The time Tom Millwright usually walked through the front door after work was also monitored. It had taken nearly eight weeks to feel confident but eventually, the decision was made. It was to be the end of one branch.

It had been simple to get an invitation into the house while she was alone, attacking her from behind as she offered coffee. The need to be careful and not leave any clues behind had been first and foremost in the aftermath. Wiping down surfaces that had been inadvertently touched while making use of her blood to contaminate the areas walked on, had taken a while longer than originally anticipated. The challenge had been to finish everything in time. Collating and bagging all the paper towels and other cleaning materials used, including sodium hypochlorite, from the relevant areas had been difficult. However, the need to be thorough had paid off. Everything had been completed before the children came home from school.
Surprising each of them as they had walked through the door had been central to the success of the plan. An injection of propofol in the neck immediately after each had been grabbed as they walked through the front door had bought the necessary time to get them away from the house. The biggest challenge, the biggest risk, had been moving them to the van. It had been a two-step process. Stage one included wrapping each inside an old carpet that had been bought for that specific purpose and carrying them separately to the car. The secondhand non-descript Vauxhall bought from a dealer on a lot in Andover for eight hundred pounds and which was subsequently squashed to a pulp at a scrap yard in Fareham, had been the best way to get them out of the house alive. They had been taken to a remote spot just north of the town of Durley, a thirty-minute drive from the house which was where the van had been parked. It had taken a minimal effort to kill them, their initial pleas and screams

for mercy silenced as they choked to death, their windpipes crushed, and precious life-giving oxygen denied them. While their deaths had been necessary, the wide-eyed faces as each was silenced still played on the mind. Their cries for help still rang in the ears.

It was quiet now. The early hours after midnight were calming. The silence stilled the mind. Only the wind occasionally rattling the windows broke the emptiness of night. Sitting alone in the dark, with nobody to break the mood made things much more comfortable. It was a time of contemplation and reflection. The boy had been easier to handle, the girl however had put up more of a fight. Whether it was because she was older or just had a stronger will to live, was unclear. The scratches on the face and the bite mark on the hand where she had drawn blood were the only signs of any resistance. After a shower using extremely hot water had been taken, each of the wounds had been treated with antiseptic cream.

The blood-contaminated clothes worn when the woman had died had been removed and replaced immediately with another set. The stained evidence was stuffed into a bag along with the rest of the cleaning materials and were the last items to be carried inside the carpet to the car. Those items including the carpet, along with the clothes worn while killing the children had been incinerated in a fire prepared in an old 200-litre oil drum bought from a scrap yard in Waterlooville. During the next twenty-four hours, the drum would be disposed of. A place in the woods, near Hambledon, had already been chosen.

With a second drink in hand, a sense of euphoria flooded throughout the body. Everything that could have been done to ensure that no clues were left for the police to find, had been. It was true that the internet provided more than just information. There was a complete 'how to' for most things. With a smile, the drink was finished. It was time for sleep. Standing up, and taking a few steps to where the tree lay, gentle fingers followed the branches that spread out from the central trunk. A knife was taken from the desk surface with the other hand and a thin spindly branch was viciously cut off.

"Another one is gone!" was all that was said.

CHAPTER 30

Alan Boothby's day had gone from bad to worse. First, it was a deluge of coughing and spluttering patients. Some were genuine and had seemingly spread their flu germs over everyone else in the waiting room, including his staff. Then, there were those who were faking their illness, expecting him to issue a sick note like dispensing toffees to a child, their hands out.

At lunchtime, just when he had hoped for a short break, his staff had put through a call that he didn't want to receive. It was another call from his father who had chastised him for not knowing where Patricia was. Phil Boothby had heard at the homeless shelter that she had been sighted in the town by some of those who had stayed there overnight. The staff had let the old man know. With vitriol in his voice, the former councillor had spared little in his choice of words.

"Did you know she's back on the streets?" Phil Boothby had asked.

Not wishing to confirm anything, or even let him know of his recent spat with his daughter, the younger man had replied in the negative and then asked if his father had been misinformed.

"Of course I'm sure. Do you think I'm a bloody idiot? I know what my granddaughter looks like, and so do many of those who use this place," he had answered angrily. "I've got lots of credit with those on the street and most are happy to keep me informed of what goes on. So don't doubt me!"

Alan Boothby sighed. Resigned to the reprimand. He had tried his best to help her. He had bought her clothes and he had offered her assistance. He wasn't sure what else he could do.

"I'll phone Anneline. I'll see if she needs any more help. Maybe I can get someone from Social Services to get involved?" he said.

"Get involved?!"

"Yes. Pat's over the age of parental control, so we can't force her to stay at home, but we can try and help her. Maybe get some outside counselling."

"But she's still a child....you're child...and my..!"

"Yes, I know....your grandchild, but unless you want to take her in yourself there aren't very many options."

"Can't you do anything?"

"Dad, I've told you before. Unless she breaks the law and the police

get involved to lock her up, there isn't too much we can do. It's up to her."
The line had gone quiet for a few seconds before Phil Boothby spoke again. He knew that Patricia would never stay with her father, not while Carol was around and it was unlikely that she would stay with him either, much as he may have wished it. The only thing that they could do was to try and find her and get her to see sense. He wanted her to go home to Anneline. To give it a try, at least until she was eighteen, and then she could make any decision she wanted to. She would be an adult in the legal sense, though not necessarily mature. It was a big ask and both men knew that it was unlikely that a solution would be found without tears.
"I don't want the police involved," Philip Boothby had said. "Think of my reputation…with the council. If this turns ugly it's possible that some of their funding for the homeless shelter and other programs may be withheld or even cut." A granddaughter of his who began causing problems around town, possibly involved in drugs and crime, wasn't the legacy that he wanted. He had worked tirelessly for the community and drugs were the scourge of society. His own flesh and blood on the streets, maybe even selling herself for money was something that was anathema to him. His disgust at the cause of her behaviour, his son's tryst with Carol, made him even angrier every time he thought of it. "I'll see if I can get some of those at the shelter to find her for me," he had said, disconsolately.
"Okay, have it your way. But I'll call Anneline anyway after I've finished work and the surgery is closed."
"Why not now?"
"Because I'm busy. I've got patients to see. Sick patients!"
"Isn't Patricia sick? Isn't it important to you, that you have a daughter who could be ill, mentally as well as physically?"
The conversation had become a full-blown argument. He didn't have time for it. Alan Boothby needed to shut the conversation down. He knew that he had raised his voice beyond what was reasonable, and it was likely that his colleagues and staff could hear him despite his office door being closed.
"Of course it's important, but I keep telling you…"
"Is she doing drugs again?" Phil Boothby had suddenly questioned, interrupting his son's response. For a few seconds, Alan was speechless, almost deflated. Did his father know what he had done,

in trying to help his daughter? Or did he think that his son was heartless and didn't care? Either way, it seemed that whatever he said had no bearing on the outcome. "I don't know," he had answered weakly. "I have no idea."
"You have no idea? Why not?"
"Because I haven't seen her since we last spoke," he had lied, not wanting to tell him about buying her new clothes and trying to get her to see sense. His desperate attempt to make her go back home and finish school. If he did mention it, he suspected his father would have another go at him for not taking Patricia back to Anneline himself rather than letting her go off on her own into the streets of the city. A stony silence had fallen between the two men. Alan Boothby listened to his father's breathing. It sounded like an angry dragon taking deep breaths and readying to breathe new fire. He waited. The tirade came as expected. "If my granddaughter ends up dead on the streets somewhere, then I'll never forgive you, Alan! You know how much that girl means to me, and for God's sake, she's your daughter. Why aren't you trying to find her?! What's the matter with you…you…coward!"
It was enough. Alan Boothby had slammed down the phone, almost breaking the handset as it hit the cradle. Office phones seemed to be less robust than mobiles and he regretted his actions the moment he felt his hand jar as the handset bounced off the table, the cord extended to its maximum, stopping it from smashing onto the floor.

CHAPTER 31

He always detested autopsies conducted on a child. Brierly was never happy to attend them even though it was part of the job. The two Millwright children's bodies had been taken to the mortuary before being brought into the pathology lab for examination. Sutton had offered to represent the police and Brierly had happily agreed. It was still Sutton's case after all. Brierly was happy to provide support to him where he could, but in the meantime, he had his own cases to run.

With the arrangements agreed upon, Brierly and his team were in the 'sit-room' reviewing what they had been able to uncover so far.

"Any update on our second victim, the unknown man?" he asked, hoping for some progress at least.

"Not yet, Sir, but DC Proctor and I have spent a bit of time on the streets," DC Hughes replied, "and we went back to the homeless shelter on Cranbury Avenue with a photo of the deceased male."

"Not a very good picture I suspect?" Brierly queried, knowing it would have been taken at the morgue.

"Exactly, Sir," Hughes continued, "but we did ask around. We left a couple of flyers with the staff there as well. Like this one here." He passed DS White an A4 page which included a photo and a request for anyone who knew the man to contact the police. It showed a hotline number that had been set up and he told Brierly that any applicable incoming calls would be automatically transferred to either himself or DC Proctor. While Brierly scanned the page, looking closely at the photo, DS White opened up a digital file in the team's case folder on the internal server within the IT network and projected the same image of the dead man onto the wall behind Brierly's left shoulder. Brierly moved his chair to one side so that he could see it more clearly. The picture wasn't particularly pleasant, and he wouldn't have been at all surprised if some at the shelter had barely glanced at it. The picture showed the man with one eye partially open, the other closed tight and the throat sewn together. The wound was still raw and the flesh buckled with the stitching. The victim looked as if he had been hit by a car. This was exacerbated by the nose and mouth which now looked like they no longer fit the man's face. Those who had seen how a body changes knew that the skin of an individual becomes pale, and ashen, losing its elasticity within a few minutes of death. The lips become dry and hard. Numerous changes to the eyes occur including corneal clouding and loss of intra-ocular tension that leads the eyelids to become droopy. With the eyes open after death, there is a deposition of dust in the exposed part of the eye. This dust, along with mucous can manifest as a yellow triangular area on the exposed white part of the eyeball which can make the eyes look grotesque. The enlarged picture on the screen confirmed this. "No wonder there have been no takers," White said, his voice sympathetic.

"What about on the streets? Anything?" Brierly queried.

"Nothing concrete, Sir," Proctor chimed in. "It seems like everyone we spoke to, had no interest in the poor man." Brierly was surprised at the sensitivity of Proctor's words. Proctor could take down anyone on a rugby field with his size and strength yet showed such compassion to the victim. Brierly liked that and guessed that it was partly because the Constable was a country boy at heart. He anticipated that Proctor would go far, as long as he didn't get too personally involved in a case and was able to maintain perspective. Disappointed at the lack of progress, Brierly asked that the dead man's details (height, weight, estimate of age) and photograph, be highlighted on the PNC as a priority, in the hope that he may have been reported as missing, somewhere. He didn't hold out much sway as he knew that there were hundreds of people across the country who died each year who were never identified, their bodies ultimately disposed of, without ever knowing who they were. However, it was worth a try.

"Will do, Sir," Proctor said, making a note in response to Brierly's instruction.

"Anything else?" Brierly questioned.

"Yes, Sir," Hughes replied, "When we spoke to the staff at the shelter about the victim, a couple of them told us, on condition of anonymity, that some of the 'guests' staying overnight are taking or dealing drugs. It's a concern because everyone who goes there for help knows that if they are found with drugs on them, they would be expelled immediately and would be banned from ever returning."

"Meaning?"

"That there is someone out there who is supplying to the most vulnerable. To homeless people who have nothing, those who are

destitute, and don't have two pennies to rub together. How else would they be able to get hold of them if they are skint?"
"Hang on," Brierly said. "You mean to tell me that someone is dealing with the destitute on credit?"
"We are not sure yet, Sir, but it needs more investigation," Hughes continued. "However, it certainly looks that way, if what we were told is true. It's bizarre in the extreme isn't it?"
"I'll say so. I think I'd better have a chat with those two individuals. Can you give me their names?"
Hughes blushed slightly and looked across the table at Proctor. Then clearing his throat, he responded to the request. "We didn't take them down, Sir."
"I beg your pardon."
"We didn't get them. The two individuals concerned refused to tell us their names. They're volunteers and they didn't want to get too involved. They said they just wanted to help us where they could. Both indicated that they love what they do and want to keep doing it, but they need to keep the trust of those they are trying to help."
"But you know who they are?"
"Yes, Sir. They seem like genuine people, but probably a little nervous about talking to us on the record," Proctor added.
Brierly reflected on this for a few seconds. It was becoming evident to him that Proctor was perhaps too understanding, and maybe he needed a mentor who could provide a bit more balance to his approach to Detective work. Brierly decided to give it some thought.
"Okay, well let's park that for a second. Maybe there is another way for me to find a way to talk to them. In the interim what about Dave Crossley? Where have we gotten to? Track?"
Evan Track looked at his notes. "Sir, from the report we received from the path lab, the knife used to kill Crossley was definitely a bread knife."
"Do we know what type?"
"It's being looked into as we speak, but from the research conducted so far, it appears to have been a normal bread knife that one can buy anywhere. At the local market, at Tesco, or any old ironmonger in most towns and cities throughout the country. Unfortunately, there was no particulate residue inside the wound, so the lab people have nothing to analyze, just the cut."
"And it's on that basis that they've concluded it was a bread knife?"

"Yes, Sir," Track replied.
Brierly sighed then pointed at the image still showing on the screen. "Okay, well let's keep digging. Surely someone, somewhere knows the man? In the meantime, Proctor, you had better come with me, we need to take a ride to that shelter."
"Sir?" Proctor queried.
"I want you to point out the two volunteers for me. I need to talk to them a bit more about what they told you and Hughes. However, I understand their reluctance, so I need to tread carefully."
"Sir?"
"I have an idea," Brierly replied, his voice almost a whisper. Touching a finger to the side of his nose, he said smiling, "nudge, nudge, wink, wink."

They were only a few minutes away from Cranbury Avenue when Brierly's mobile phone rang. Fortunately, with DC Proctor as the designated driver, Brierly was able to answer it unencumbered. He noticed that the caller was his boss, DCI Hammond.
"Yes, Dave?" Brierly said. "How are you?"
"Where are you, Jim?" A question, Brierly noticed, without any negative intonation. "Can you talk?"
"Of course. I'm on my way to see Phil Boothby at the homeless shelter with DC Proctor. What's up anyway?"
"The Millwright kids. I've just got off a call with Bill Nicholls, DC Suttons' boss."
"Yes, what about it?" Brierly answered, noncommittally, wondering where the conversation was going. He expected it was to do with resourcing. As he had deliberated the other night, two DIs on the one case wouldn't be seen as very efficient by anyone, not least those 'higher' than him.
"The case…it's yours," Hammond said.
Brierly wasn't sure if he had heard correctly, so he asked his boss to repeat what he had said. After doing so, Hammond added. "I assume you haven't seen Dr. Atkins' report yet…her observations from the post-mortems?"
"No, I haven't. After my team catch-up, DC Proctor and I got straight into the car and left the building straight away. I'm guessing that there is someone somewhere who may know who our unknown

stabbing victim is. Our starting point is the shelter which is why we are on our way out there as I said."

"Well, now you've got something else on your plate."

"What's happened, Dave?" Brierly enquired, wondering why Sutton was no longer leading the Millwright investigation. While he waited for an answer he noted that they were almost at the shelter, having just turned off Onslow Road and into Denzil Avenue. The shelter was only a couple of hundred metres away. He indicated to Proctor that he should pull over and park where he could find a spot. The Constable obliged, stopping the vehicle only twenty yards from the shelter's front door.

"Atkins has found something," Hammond continued. "It's in her report and that's why I gave our friends in Portsmouth a call." Not knowing what Gemma Atkins had uncovered was eating at him so Brierly sought the answer. He needed to understand why the killing of the two Millwright children, was now his case specifically. What had Atkins found that was so important? When they had departed the spot where the children had been dumped after their discussion with Colin Anthony and his wife, Brierly had been more than happy to provide Sutton with any support he needed. He had expected to be a backup to his colleague, to provide extra help when required. Now, based on Hammonds' comments, it would seem that it was Brierly who may need the help.

"So what did the good doctor uncover, Sir?" Brierly asked. "As I said, I haven't seen her report as yet. I'm not even sure it has hit my desk, to be honest."

"That's fair enough, Jim, so let me fill you in."

"Please do."

With the engine running and the car heater keeping them warm, Brierly listened to Hammond as he briefly summarized the findings of Gemma Atkins after she conducted the autopsies on the Millwright children.

"The clincher in all this and the reason why the case is now yours is that there is now a definite link to the murder of our homeless man."

"And so, we've now got the case because he was killed *before* the Millwright woman?" Brierly concluded.

"Yes, a case of first come, first served," Hammond said, justifying why Brierly was to take charge. The precedence of the homeless man's slaying and the similarities to the Millwright children's murders

would make it easier for the hierarchy to rationalize the investigation under one lead. The attempt at levity in Hammonds' comments wasn't lost on Brierly but he decided to ignore it, allowing his boss to continue. "Atkins has now specifically linked the killing of the mother and the kids to our mystery man."
"How?"
After a slight hesitation, Hammond said, "There are specific marks on one of the Millwright woman's hands. They are not defensive wounds. The same markings were found on the bodies of the two kids. In the same place as their mother. It was obvious that they were made deliberately, and probably by the same person."
"Which means that we have a serial killer on our hands if you'll pardon the pun," Brierly proclaimed somewhat bitterly. He noticed that Proctor took a quick look in his direction immediately after the comment. A serial killer was an unusual phenomenon in most jurisdictions on the south coast, so to be part of an investigation into one so soon into his tenure was unexpected and exciting.
"Correct, and it's the last thing we bloody need," Hammond went on. "If we are not careful there could be a major panic across the city particularly given those poor kids. I understand that there are comments and suspicions already on social media. Fingers are being pointed all over the place."
Brierly knew what Hammond was getting at. If there was widespread anger in the community and rumours started to fly about possible suspects, then things could easily get out of control. Vigilantes roaming the streets looking for a suspect could potentially derail the investigation. As it was, with so few resources available and multiple murders to investigate, Brierly and his team would need to focus all their energy on what was already a complex situation. They did not need any additional distractions. With nothing further to add Brierly advised Hammond that he would give Sutton a call immediately after he and Proctor had finished at the homeless shelter. He knew that Sutton would have preferred to be the lead on the Millwright case and to have been supported by Brierly and his team, rather than the other way around. However, despite the normal inter-force rivalry, Brierly felt that the two men had become more than colleagues over recent days. He considered the man to be a friend and consequently, he expected that Sutton would be a good ally to have, someone who he could work well with, if and when needed. Without any further

comment, Hammond terminated the call. Sighing, Brierly looked out of the car window, looking at the low grey scudding clouds blocking out the weak winter sun. Proctor turned off the car's engine. There were only a few hours of daylight left and the temperature was starting to drop as an icy wind was beginning to strengthen. Brierly shivered as he opened the car door, climbing out into the wintery gloom.

CHAPTER 32

It wasn't what he had expected. There were far more people than anticipated going in and out of the building as he walked through its front door. A heavy security gate made of steel tubing was open, fixed to a bracket on the right-hand side of the entrance. Brierly imagined that it was used at night when the shelter was closed to anyone not already inside. He noticed a photograph of their dead nameless man pinned onto a cluttered notice board on the left-hand side wall just inside the door. The picture had already been defaced with the addition of a crude moustache. It was obvious from the pieces of paper stuck onto the small corkboard that the photo was another piece of detritus to those who used the facility. Whether the same thoughts applied to the staff working there he would soon find out. The two policemen walked along a short corridor, yellowing walls on either side of them, then the passage opened up into a large hall. It was approximately fifteen metres wide by ten metres long. The room was laid out with four rows of grey plastic bench tables and white picnic chairs. Each table had six chairs on either side and there were two tables per row. With the odd loose chair at the head of a table, Brierly estimated that roughly fifty people could be seated at any one time.
"The dining room," Proctor said indicating what was in front of them, "and that's the kitchen to the right."
Brierly looked in the direction that Proctor was pointing. A large serving hatch currently locked, hid the room where the daily meals were prepared. The bolts on the hatch gleamed in the glow of the industrial lights suspended from the ceiling above. Brierly looked around observing the dozen or so people seated at the tables, some of which looked worse for wear, while others seemed vacant, almost lost or dazed. One or two were reading a newspaper, the majority however were talking quietly either to others or themselves, totally ignoring the two visitors. Noticing a neatly dressed young woman walking out of a doorway with a clipboard in her hand, Brierly asked Proctor if the door she had exited from was the admin office.
"Yes, Sir. It's also the staff room…for the volunteers."
Making their way towards the office, the sound of quiet discourse around them changed. Conversations stopped briefly as it became

obvious that two policemen were in the midst of some who despised or feared them. The woman they had noticed seemed to sense the altered tone and made her way to intercept the two newcomers. Despite Proctor's earlier visit with Hughes, he had not seen her in the shelter before. In her early thirties, slim, she had long dark, almost jet black, hair which was cut with a low fringe that seemed to be constantly in her eyes. She was dressed in jeans, brown boots, and a heavily knitted multi-coloured jumper that reached below her waist and was tied tightly around her with a black leather belt. With a large tattoo of a snake on her neck, it made her seem much older than Brierly had guessed she was. Her skin was colourless, almost translucent. It was as if she never saw the sun and reminded Brierly of the Goth movement. She had dark blue eyes and a sad smile. Her small nose was accentuated by a tiny gold ring in one nostril. She introduced herself as Janie Fenchurch. "I'm the manager here," she said.

"Nice to meet you, Miss. Fenchurch. I'm DI James Brierly and this is DC Clive Proctor." Both men showed her their warrant cards. After inspecting them she asked why they were there.

"Is there anywhere private where we could have a chat?" Brierly asked.

"About?"

Brierly looked around, noticing an intense interest from a couple of those seated at the tables. "Look," he said, "I'd appreciate it if we could just have a few minutes of your time. I'm trying to solve a murder and we are just making a few inquiries." Fenchurch considered Brierly's request and then with a simple flick of her head indicated that they should follow her. She turned around and walked back towards the admin office door. As the three of them entered the room, Brierly noticed a man sitting behind a desk and furiously typing into a computer, his fingers skimming across the keyboard. He marvelled at the man's dexterity, silently wishing that he could type as easily. His own typing speed was limited to how quickly his two index fingers could move together in unison.

"This is Wayne Anderson," Fenchurch advised, as they walked past the desk. Anderson made a brief gesture, acknowledging his name, before continuing to type. Brierly estimated the man to be in his early twenties. Fenchurch continued walking, leading the way toward a smaller room at the back of the office. On the door was a small white

plaque. A single word was engraved upon it; Refuge. A large glass window meant that anyone could see if the room was occupied and those inside the room could keep an eye on what was happening in the office itself. Once inside, Fenchurch closed the door and the three of them sat at a round wooden table, just large enough for four chairs. Despite the extra seat, with another person in the room, the space would have seemed crowded, confined, and claustrophobic. If it wasn't for the glass window occupying at least half of one wall, the room would have mirrored a prison cell.
"He's a volunteer. Twice a week, for a few hours," Fenchurch said, pointing towards the back of Anderson through the glass window as he continued to type. "He's doing some work that supports his social sciences degree requirements. We are really grateful for the help."
Brierly noticed that her voice sounded weary, despite it still being early afternoon. Her body language also indicated fatigue. He guessed it had more to do with the job than the time of day.
"So," she continued, "how can I help you?"
Without answering the question directly, Brierly asked. "How many people work here?"
She looked at him quizzically, brushing away the hair from her eyes before it fell back again. "Why?"
"I'm just trying to understand how things work. Your processes. It seems like you have a lot of 'guests' as you may call them, but not many people to help you with what I'd suggest could be a very problematic situation at times."
"How do you mean?" she asked, looking at him with suspicion.
"Well, you said that you were grateful for the help of Mr. Anderson out there. From that, I gather that it is very difficult to provide the services that you do, without people like him?"
Fenchurch nodded without comment, allowing Brierly to continue.
"So," he said, "I wondered how you manage? How you would get by without people giving up their time to help? It is obvious that you have so many needy customers."
Fenchurch stared at him, her eyes fighting with her hair. "You mentioned that you wanted to talk about a murder," she said, changing the subject. "What does that have to do with me or indeed this shelter?"
Brierly pointed at Proctor. "The Constable here, along with a colleague of his, paid a visit the other day and passed around a bunch

of flyers, one of which is on your board at the entrance to the building."
"What about it?"
"It's the murder victim that I referred to earlier."
"Go on."
"We need to know who he is. We think some of your guests may know him."
"That's possible," Fenchurch replied. "We have many individuals transit through the shelter. It's up to those who may know your victim to come forward….if they wish."
"If they wish?" Brierly queried.
"Yes…Inspector. Our guests are allowed their privacy. If they don't want to be known, then they can maintain their anonymity. Who they are is their business and we do not pry," she said, indignantly. "We provide a service to the needy, no questions asked. We are a charity, funded in part by the council, but mostly through donations. So, if …"
"So, if your guests are doing drugs, then that's their concern? Is that what you are saying?"
"What?"
"I'm asking if the taking of drugs inside this facility is okay, accepted? It's a simple question."
Fenchurch looked at both men, her eyes darting between the two of them. "We don't condone the use of any drug inside this facility," she answered. "It's our policy. Zero tolerance. Anyone found in possession of, or using drugs of any kind inside these four walls, is automatically ejected from the premises and will not be allowed to return."
"And you manage this how?"
"By observation. Every staff member and volunteer has been specifically trained to observe our guests' behaviour during the day and even overnight."
"Which is why I asked how many people work here."
"I'm still not with you."
Proctor shifted in his chair. It was time to redeem himself. "When I was here previously, we had a chat with a number of your volunteers," he said, opening a small notebook that he had taken out of his coat pocket.
"Yes. What about them?"

"They told us that they knew of active drug use on the premises."
"What?!" she replied, incredulously. "We'll lose our license to operate not to mention our jobs if that's true. Which I don't believe it is, by the way."
"Well, they were pretty insistent …"
"Who are these people?" she asked.
"I'm sorry I can't reveal names. They spoke to us on the basis that the discussion remained private. They asked for anonymity."
Brierly noted the delicious irony that befell Fenchurch. He noticed as she pushed the hair from her eyes that there was an element of anger within them. She went on the attack. "Look, if you can't tell me who advised you of this so-called drug taking, then how do I know what you've just told me is true? I can't respond to innuendo or hearsay."
Proctor turned towards Brierly, who took up the mantle. "How many people can sleep here overnight?" he asked.
A little taken aback, the accusation of mismanagement as she saw it, still ringing in her ears, she answered Brierly without hesitation. "We close the front door at eleven every night. All those inside can stay here. We have ten beds inside two dormitories." She pointed a finger over her left shoulder. "If we have more people here than beds, then we have sleeping bags and camp beds available for others to sleep on."
"And someone supervises over night?"
"Yes. We always have two people on site every night. One full-time employee, like me, and one volunteer."
Brierly did a quick calculation in his head. "So, on that basis alone, assuming there are three eight-hour shifts every day and everyone works forty hours or thereabouts, you must have a minimum of six full-time staff excluding yourself. Plus, how many volunteers?"
"Actually, we have a dozen full-timers and at least fifteen regular part-time volunteers who work on a shift rotation basis. We also have some casuals as we call them, who do a couple of hours every now and again, like Wayne out there." She pointed at the window.
"And you said those numbers exclude yourself," Brierly confirmed.
"Yes, I'm in addition to those, as is our night manager Dennis Chilton."
"That's quite a team. A lot to organize."
"You're right Inspector, but we do have plenty of need in the community as you may have already seen this afternoon?"

Brierly agreed. He had always considered those who worked with the homeless as being a certain type of person. They seemed to have a personality that was more accepting of their fellow human being's failings, and a way about them that was almost serene. Somehow able to have a connection with their fellow man that many others didn't have. They were like some of the stars in the vastness of the night sky, he thought. Shining brightly in the darkness of the everyday milieu, but seldom noticed unless someone went looking for them. He knew that she was right, there was a need, and she was helping to address it. He admired her in some ways. "Tell me about your staff and the volunteers. Have you ever had any issues recently?"
"Issues?"
"Yes, problems, arguments, specifically with the ….guests."
After considering the question for a few seconds, she responded definitively. "No, none that I can recall, and I've been here for nearly three years now."
"What about the volunteers?"
"As I said before, the guests who pass through here come and go and some never return. The same applies to the volunteers. We appreciate their help. We don't question their motives."
Brierly considered the perspective quite magnanimous, though somewhat naïve.
"Have any left recently?" he asked.
"You mean of the volunteers?"
"Yes," he replied patiently.
"We have had a couple of the part-timers leave over the past year or so. Both were university students. The casuals come and go all the time."
"Do you know why they left?"
"The part-timers?"
"Yes."
"They finished their degrees in May and left after they formally graduated. We replaced them soon afterwards."
"Are you happy with your staff?"
"Yes," she replied.
"And you have no concerns about any of them?"
"No. Everyone, other than the casuals are background checked before they are allowed to work here, and then they are trained to know what we do and what we don't do."

"So you trust your team?."
"Absolutely. Every one of them."
"What about the guests as you call them?"
"What about them?"
Brierly was starting to sense a bit of stonewalling going on but he decided to press on with his questions. "Have there been any problems between any of them?"
"I'm not with you Inspector," Fenchurch answered, frowning.
"Any arguments, disputes, even fights. Surely not every guest gets along with every other one?"
She pondered over her answer for a few seconds. "You can imagine that over the years there have been some matters, yes. But they were resolved very quickly."
"Can you give me any examples?"
Drawing on her memory she told them of a few 'minor' arguments.
"Anything more recent, more significant?" Brierly questioned. "All those you just mentioned are from several years ago."
With mock pretence at remembering anything which had escalated into violence, or was of the kind of issue that Brierly was referring to, she concluded that there were none that she could recall. Brierly knew that she was lying, her body language and facial expression gave her away. He would have to consider another way of getting to the truth. Realizing that the conversation wasn't going where he had hoped it would, he decided to wrap things up. He asked her for a list of names of the staff and the volunteers who had worked at the shelter over the past two years. Fenchurch agreed to provide it to him within the next forty-eight hours. He then pulled a copy of the same flyer that they had seen on the notice board from out of his inside jacket pocket, saying, "In the meantime, could I ask that if anyone knows this man, would you please have them call me on this number?" He requested a page from Proctor's notebook and wrote down his mobile details, passing it to her along with the flyer. She looked briefly through her fringe at the distorted face looking back at her, then quickly turned her eyes away as if the image sickened her. As she did so they noticed a man enter the office outside. He walked past Anderson who continued typing, and made his way towards the small room. Within seconds there was a knock on the door and without any hesitation, it was opened by the man.
"Oh, I'm sorry to bother you," he said, "but I need to talk with Janie

if possible?"
"Not a problem, Mr. Boothby," Brierly answered, recognizing the former councillor. "We were just about to leave."
"I'm sorry, I'm not sure if we have met before. Do I know you?" the man asked.
"We did meet some years back, Mr. Boothby, in your former life, though I doubt you would remember," Brierly replied. "Anyway, I'm DI James Brierly and this is DC Proctor." Both men held out their hands in greeting which Boothby shook firmly.
"I guess I'm getting a little old to remember so forgive me, Inspector," Boothby joked, before adding, self-consciously. "I hope I didn't interrupt anything?"
"As I said, we were just on our way," Brierly answered, looking at Fenchurch. "Though I just have one more thing to ask Ms. Fenchurch here."
"Okay," Boothby said with a smile, "Sorry to have interrupted you. I'll just take a seat outside." He left the office, closed the door behind him, and walked over to where Anderson was now standing stretching his back. Brierly watched as Boothby sat on the edge of Anderson's desk.
"He's a good man," Fenchurch said, pointing briefly in Boothby's direction. "If it wasn't for him, this shelter would have closed years ago."
"Yes, I know," Brierly answered. He had seen and heard Boothby in action several times over the years. The man had often taken centre stage at council meetings. He had spoken on the local radio, or in other public forums about the need for the shelter and the funding needed. Fenchurch smiled at Brierly's response, and he blushed slightly. It wasn't often that he received a positive reaction to comments he made while working on a case. Addressing her again, he said, "One final question then, Ms. Fenchurch."
"Janie," she replied with a smile.
"Janie," he repeated. "I know this might be unpalatable but I think that some of your guests are being less than honest with the truth."
"In what way?"
"You told me that you trust your staff…completely."
"Yes."
"So going back to what DC Proctor told you earlier. Why would several of them suggest to my officers that they were aware of drug

use in the facility?"
"I can't answer that," she stumbled. "As I told you without names, I can only assume those comments are hearsay. However, let me assure you that if I find them to be true, then there will be action taken by me....and you'll be the first to know."
Brierly did not doubt her.
"You do know that I have a board to report to?" she questioned.
"I would have thought so," he replied. "I assumed that you have a boss as well...someone who employed you. We all do."
"That's correct. It's a board made up of people from the council, the community, and a couple of benefactors. Ex-councillor Boothby is one of them."
Brierly and Proctor looked through the window noticing Boothby and Anderson sharing a laugh. Brierly wondered what the joke was. Having no further questions, the two policemen stood, shook hands with Fenchurch, and thanked her for her time. They left the room and made their way to the exit, acknowledging Anderson and Boothby again as they did so. Fenchurch remained where she was. She sat back in her chair and placed a hand over her mouth. She felt ill and closed her eyes briefly. She was perturbed. Could it be that she was missing something? Was there something going on inside the shelter underneath her nose? She would need to speak with her team. She knew the board would have some serious concerns regarding the facility if drug use or worse, drug dealing, was happening inside its very walls. She would start a subtle investigation as soon as she could. She opened her eyes just as Philip Boothby came through the door.
"I need to talk with you," he said, a concerned look on his face.

CHAPTER 33

Mary Owen sat silently between the two of them. Her father to the right and her brother-in-law to the left. They had cried, shouted, and argued until they had nothing left to say to each other. It had been a difficult day and now they were in her house, seated on her couch, in her front room. Each of them seemed lost in their thoughts. They had been required to identify the bodies. A wife, a sister, a son, and daughters. It had taken all her courage to look at Gretchen's face when the sheet had been peeled back. She had volunteered to do the same with the two children. She didn't know how she had gotten through it, but she knew that she needed to. She rationalized that she had done so on behalf of both of them, the two men now sitting on either side of her. She looked from one to the other, noticing their sunken almost lifeless eyes, staring into space like zombies. Suddenly she stood up violently, angry, arms whirling like those of a dancing dervish. Both men watched as she took a few steps away, then turned around to face them. It was obvious how raw her emotions were.

"I need to know why?!" she shouted through gritted teeth. "Why the kids?"

She received no answer, despite her imploring them, searching for a response.

Eventually, Tom Millwright lifted his face to look at her, saying, "I don't know…I just don't know."

"Dad?"

Trevor Owen had nothing to say either. All his words had dried up earlier. He refused to look at her, continuing to shake his head as if the very thoughts that he had been having were stuck inside his head, refusing to leave. As her anger intensified, she strode across the room, first one way, then the other. Her heart raced with fear and outrage. She ran her hand repeatedly through her hair as she paced up and down in front of them. Trevor Owen looked up saying, "You'll wear the bloody carpet out if you don't stop Mary. Why can't you…."

Stopping a few feet away from where they were seated, Mary looked at her father, her face red, puce, her neck blotchy, her eyes filled with hostility.

"We should call Sutton," she said, "you need to tell him everything."

"No!" Trevor Owen shouted, his objection far stronger than she had anticipated, even causing his son-in-law to rouse from his stupor.
"Why not?!" she responded, almost pleading with him. "Surely once the police know what's behind this, they will have more to work with?"
"No!" Owen shouted back. "No!"
Looking at Millwright, who seemed to be battling to focus on what was being played out in front of him, then at her father, she decided to make her position clear. "If you won't do it, then I will!" she shouted, turning her back to them both and walking away to her kitchen. For a few seconds, the two men remained seated, neither looking at the other, staying silent. From the kitchen, they heard the kettle being turned on, followed by a noise that engulfed them both. It was the sound of sobbing and wailing. Trevor Owen started to stand but Millwright put a hand on his shoulder, pulled him back down into his seat, and shook his head. Owen understood what was being suggested and he let Millwright take the initiative watching him walk towards the kitchen. Mary was standing in front of the sink staring into the blackness of early evening. The sun had set half an hour earlier and the black of night mirrored her face in the glass of the window as she looked out onto her small back-garden. With the light of the kitchen escaping outside, a small maple tree now bare of any leaves could be seen wafting in the cold breeze, occasionally scratching at the glass with its thin limbs. The branches of the tree made a sound on the window like razor blades cutting across stubbled skin, or the claws of an unseen monster. Millwright noted that the kettle had boiled already and asked her if he could help. She did not respond immediately.
"Should I make the tea?" he repeated, his voice monotone, devoid of feeling.
"Please."
Without waiting for another word, Tom Millwright began taking mugs from the inside of a cupboard. Then after putting in teabags and milk as appropriate, he added sugar.
"I keep asking myself, why the kids?" she said, continuing to stare at the reflection of herself in the window.
"Me too," Millwright answered, his voice cracking with the strain of the day.
She turned to look at him. It seemed as if he had crumpled into

himself. His back was no longer ramrod straight, his face no longer open, his entire demeanour indicating the depths of his loss. It was as if he did not know how to climb out of the pit of grief he had fallen into. She had expected him to be angry, to seek revenge, to hunt high and low to find those responsible for his pain. It wasn't what she was seeing.

With the kettle boiled he started to make the drinks. The clanking of spoons against the ceramic mugs brought Trevor Owen to the kitchen door. "I think you're right," he said.

She turned away from the window to look at her father. He made his way towards her. "I'm so sorry," he said, touching his son-in-law briefly on the arm as he passed him, a gentle moment of understanding of the younger man's grief. As he reached his daughter they embraced, while Millwright looked on. With eyes wet with tears, Mary held onto her father as if she never intended to let him leave her side again. As he watched them, Millwright saw a brief movement out of the corner of his eye. A shadow, a light, something outside. He thought it was the swaying branches of the tree, but then the inconsistency hit him. A tree with a light? Just as he realized that something was wrong, the kitchen window inwardly as a brick smashed through it, bouncing onto the countertop directly under the window before careering onto the floor. The sound of the brick punching its way into the room was deafening. Shards of sharply pointed glass shot through the air, piercing the faces, hands, and necks of father and daughter. Trevor Owen almost collapsed to the ground. Millwright leaped towards them, skating over the broken glass, the debris crunching underfoot, meshing with the howling, bitter wind now streaming through the damaged window. He noticed the blood on their cheeks and lips. In addition, there were cuts on the right side of Mary's face and the left of his father-in-law. Mary pushed him away, telling him to go outside and chase the perpetrator. For a few seconds, he hesitated. Mary screamed at him. "Go! Go!" She pointed at the back door before wiping her hand across her mouth and experiencing the metallic taste of her blood. She shouted at him again as Millwright ran towards the door, disappearing outside into the darkness. Mary held her father upright, a shard of glass had pierced his forehead just above his left eyebrow, its jagged edge protruding a few millimeters out of his soft skin. Blood streamed down his face, and into his eye. He tried to pull it out but cut his

hands and buried the offending shard deeper into the wound. He screamed in pain as the skin on his fingers he had sliced open began to sting and ooze more blood.
"Sit down, dad," Mary said, moving him towards a wooden table situated in a small nook to one side of the kitchen. It was big enough to seat two people and she pulled out one of the two lattice-work chairs for him. "I need to get something to stop the bleeding. There is a first aid kit in the bathroom, and I have an old towel we can use too." The old man raised a hand in acknowledgement then gestured to his forehead. "Keep your hands away," she complained, indicating the piece of glass he was about to touch, "I'll be back in a sec," she said.
Trailing glass fragments on her shoes into the hallway, she ran to find what she needed. When she returned, Millwright was hunched over her father looking at the damage. "Do you have any tweezers?" he asked, noticing that she had wiped the blood from her face. It didn't look as bad now, though some of the scratches were still weeping slightly. He saw that her hands had been washed as well and plasters had been placed over some of the cuts.
"What for?" she answered in response to his question.
"I think I can get the glass out."
"Okay, yes I do have some," she replied, looking at him strangely. "What did you see outside? Anything?"
Taking the first aid kit and the towel from her, he said, "Get the tweezers, and no, I didn't see a thing. Whoever had been out there has long gone, the side gate was open, and I didn't see anyone in the street either. I assume they may have had a car nearby. Anyway, while I'm busy sorting this out," he pointed at Owens' face and head, "call the police…we need to get them out here straight away…they've got to catch this bastard, and quickly!"
Mary agreed with him. Then after a quick check that her father was okay, ran off to get the tweezers from her bedroom.
"Will he need stitches?" she queried on her return, ready to pass Millwright the small tool. She noticed that her brother-in-law had managed to stop most of the bleeding on the old man's hands and face. The towel though bloodied was lying on the floor next to the old man's feet.
"I don't know but that should help," Millwright said, pointing towards the bandages from the first aid kit, that were expertly

covering both of Owens' hands. They resembled a set of children's mittens. Taking the tweezers from her, he carefully aimed at the piece of glass that lay embedded and bloodied just above the old man's eye. Mary turned, too squeamish to look, deciding to go in search of her mobile phone.
"Close your eyes," Millwright said to the old man, "and keep them closed until I say otherwise." Owen did as he was told.
With remarkable dexterity, which he later said came from working with electrical circuitry and drawings, Millwright managed to remove the relatively large glass piece embedded in Owens' forehead. Using antiseptic and additional bandages from the first aid kit, Millwright was able to staunch the bleeding in Owens' facial wounds, leaving the old man with a crown of bandages across the scalp and over one eye. A few small scars would be the only legacy. He had been lucky. The flying glass pieces could have blinded him. As he completed patching up his father-in-law's wounds, Millwright abruptly realized that Mary had been out of the kitchen for a good fifteen minutes. He could hear her talking. After receiving a thumbs up from Owen, Millwright called out to his sister-in-law. She was still on the phone when she entered the kitchen in response to his shout. The room had now become extremely cold as the wind continued to whip through the hole in the window. Millwright indicated with a shrug of his shoulders that she should move Owen to another room, while he tried to clean up the mess on the floor. As she was still talking on the phone she indicated to him where he could find a broom. She then led her father out of the kitchen.
Millwright looked at his watch, wondering why it was taking so long for the police to arrive. Annoyed at the delay he began to clean up the mess lying around him, taking care not to touch the offending brick that still lay on the floor, lodged against the bottom of the stove. He considered asking Mary for some cardboard and duct tape she may have so that he could plug the hole in the windowpane but decided to leave it alone until after the police had completed their investigation. As he contemplated the past thirty minutes, in a split second, he suddenly realized the enormity of what they had been through. His grief became absolute. The shock of what had happened to his family was now compounded by the mess around him. He felt faint and was fortunate not to keel over. He gripped the side of a countertop to brace himself as his entire body began to

shake uncontrollably. His sobs became moans then howls as his mind and heart reeled in pain and sadness. His entire world had been shattered beyond repair.
Mary could hear him from the other room. She instantly ended her call and after checking on her father, she ran to the kitchen. She saw a wreck in front of her. The man was a mess. Emotionally broken. Rushing to him and ignoring the detritus still lying around them, she held him tightly to her. As he rested his head on her shoulder, she could feel the ripples of anguish coursing through his body. Waves of emotion surfaced as moans and coughs. She tried to calm him with words of sympathy, noting that some of what she said were as much for herself as for him.
Slowly he began to calm down. She had no idea how long it took for him to settle, perhaps a few minutes she later thought, before he eventually broke their embrace leaving her shoulder feeling damp with his tears. He thanked her and then asked her for forgiveness. "I'm sorry," he said, looking into her eyes. His vision was still blurred with tears and he didn't notice that the nicks and cuts that marked one side of her face, were still weeping slightly.
"It's okay," she answered softly.
"No, it's not!" he responded aggressively. She was surprised at the potency of his outburst. His speed to anger seemed incongruous with the intimate moment they had just shared. "This has to stop. This has to stop," he repeated.
"What do you mean?" Mary asked, confused at his remark.
As he was about to reply, they heard several loud sirens. It was obvious that cars were pulling up in the road outside the house. They couldn't see any flashing lights from where they were in the kitchen. Mary turned to the door, ready to make her way to see who had arrived, the ambulance or the police. As she did so Millwright held her arm. "Tom?" she queried.
"I'm going to find the bastard who did this and I'm going to fucking kill him!" he said. The words were spat out. She stared at him for a second. She had never seen him so animated. It was as if he was someone she didn't know. Without another word, she shrugged his hand off her arm and left the room. It would be a long night.

CHAPTER 34

He had invited him over to try and make peace. Alan Boothby had eventually been able to convince Carol that they should have his father over for dinner. She had been reluctant to the idea as it was obvious to her that Philip Boothby would never accept her as his daughter-in-law, no matter what she or Alan tried. It was a fait accompli from the very beginning. Alan would continue to blame her for his son's marriage breakdown and Carol would never convince him otherwise. Anneline and Alan had produced a granddaughter, the apple of the old man's eye. Carol knew that she could never compete with that. What made things worse for her was that she was the total opposite of Anneline. Carol liked sport. Anneline didn't. She was university-educated, Anneline wasn't. She had an interest in politics, and Anneline watched soap operas and mindless TV. There could not have been a greater dichotomy between the two women.
They were sitting at the dining room table, a silence, a pause in their conversation while they ate. Carol, her auburn hair perfectly cut to suit her face, was dressed in blue jeans which hugged her slim figure and a grey turtle-neck sweater. Mid-calf leather boots covered her feet. Her face was unlined, and her make-up was subtle but elegant. Her nails were painted in a shade that matched her sweater, a silvery chrome. Being so much younger than her husband, Alan Boothby saw her as a gold digger. She had married his 'Doctor' son and that was enough for him to despise her. It did not matter to him that Carol had a good job of her own. She was a career woman. A partner in a very successful medium-sized PR and advertising agency with an office in the Westquay shopping centre. With many of their clients in the fashion industry, she felt that she always needed to play the part, to be in sync with what they wanted. Glamour, style…all the things that were anathema to Philip Boothby, who prided himself on his civic responsibility, his commitment to helping those worse off, and his dislike of all things that he deemed ostentatious or pretentious.
"So, Philip, what have you been up to recently? Anything exciting? Plans for the summer perhaps?" she asked, trying to break the dour mood that had descended over the dinner table. While awaiting a response Carol took a quick look at her husband, touching his knee

under the table with her own. A sign of concern. She waited for the answer which when it came was remarkably civil.
"The usual. A bit of this, a bit of that. Nothing too strenuous."
"Oh, that's nice."
"Yes."
The monosyllabic answer suggested that he had nothing else to add. Carol got the feeling that her attempt at conversation had been batted away like someone swots at a fly that was buzzing around their head. She decided to try again, feeling that at least she was trying to engage him. "Are you still helping down at the shelter?" she asked.
Philip Boothby knew that she was aware of his continuing involvement with the charity, but he was surprised by her comment. He always thought of her as frivolous and uncaring of others and had not expected her to show any interest at all in what he did there.
"Yes," he answered. One word, no more. He continued to eat the pork cutlet and rice that he had been served, adding extra salt to the meal which his son suggested was bad for him.
"I know…for my blood pressure, right?"
"Exactly dad."
"Well, I can always get my doctor to prescribe me some more Lipitor, can't I son?"
Alan Boothby knew that his father was being provocative, but he felt that he needed to respond. "Dad, you know that statins are designed to treat cholesterol, not blood pressure. You need an ACE inhibitor like perindopril or enalapril or something similar for that."
He pointed at the saltshaker with his knife.
"If you need anything, you can always come and see me you know," he added.
Philip Boothby had deliberately transferred his patronage as a patient from Alan's practice to another doctor as soon as Anneline and he had split. It had been an acrimonious breakup and the old man had kept away ever since. It was one of several issues between them that remained unresolved. Like any war, some battles ended in a stalemate, and some ended in retreat. This was one such war that ended with both sides staying well away from each other. A truce of sorts.
"Thanks for the offer, but I'm alright," Philip said, "Doctor Asif, always does me proud and looks after me," he continued, referring to his own medical practitioner.

"That's okay. I know he's a good man," Alan stated, knowing the GP personally, having met him on many occasions over the years.
"Yes, he is," the tone used inferring that his son wasn't a good man. Carol noticed and was going to respond but decided against it, thinking that it wasn't worth all the negative energy. She disliked how her husband was regularly humiliated in front of her. She would take it up with him later when they were alone.
"Have you heard from Patricia since we last talked?" the old man asked, as he finished the last of the meal, placing his knife and fork neatly onto his plate. Alan, with a fork halfway to his mouth, took a glance at Carol. She was looking downwards as he did so, and he was relieved that she hadn't seen his panic at the question.
"No," he replied, knowing that any interaction with his daughter would cause a row with his wife. Carol had been reasonable with him and Patricia at the beginning of their marriage but over time had become less patient as his daughter had become more demanding. Over time he had tried to hide any involvement between them from her, as he knew how she felt. Carol believed that Patricia was taking him for granted, and despite his reluctance to admit it, he knew that she was right. "The last time I heard from her, she had started her course at the hairdressing college in Eastleigh. She said it was going well," he lied.
"When was that?" Philip Boothby asked.
It seemed to Alan that his father was intent on causing friction. He noticed that Carol had stopped eating and was waiting for him to answer.
"Oh, it must have been a few months ago now. She texted me just to give me the good news that she had been accepted onto the course and that she was looking forward to starting." It was obvious to the old man that what he was hearing was a lie given the last conversation between them. He decided to hold back from asking anything else, as he could see that Carol's interest had already been piqued. He expected that she would be asking more of her husband once he had left.
"Very well," he said finally, smiling at his daughter-in-law and commenting positively about the dinner he had finished eating.
"Would you like any dessert or coffee?" she asked him, standing and beginning to stack the plates and cutlery. "I have some blueberry pie and custard if you'd like, though I'll be giving it a miss myself."

"Maybe just coffee," the older man said. "I need to watch my figure," he added, pointing at her, "not like some people."
She took his comment as a compliment though doubted its sincerity.
"How about you, darling?" she queried her husband.
"I think I'll do the same," he replied, looking at his watch. "It's probably too late to eat anything else now." With a nod, she picked up the pile of dishes and left the room. Alan called from behind her that he would pack the dishwasher and she just needed to leave the plates on the counter in the kitchen. He noticed that she did not reply but he heard her fill the kettle. With the sound of clinking cups coming from the kitchen, he took the opportunity, talking in a hushed tone, to ask the old man what game he was playing.
"What do you mean?"
"You know what I mean," Alan whispered, looking anxiously at the dining room doorway. "Bringing up Pat…in front of Carol. You know how she feels about her."
"And you know how I feel about her as well."
"Dad, she's *my* daughter, just leave it be. She's old enough to make her own decision's now."
"She's a child!" Philip Boothby replied vigorously. "A child that's got herself lost. All because of you and that…that woman," he continued, his voice loud enough that it was almost impossible for Carol not to have heard. Making a shushing sound, Alan Boothby asked his father to keep his voice down, saying for the umpteenth time that Patricia's problems had nothing to do with Carol, indeed nothing to do with Anneline and his divorce. As his father was about to respond, Carol came into the room carrying a serving platter. Carefully placed on the tray along with a cafetiere, were three cups, a milk jug, a sugar bowl, and a few chocolate biscuits, still in their wrappers. Skillfully she placed everything onto the dining room table.
"It'll take a minute or two before I can plunge it," she said, smiling sweetly at the pair of them. "So, what have you two been talking about, while I have been busy?"
"Nothing much," her husband replied, "we were just discussing my dad's pills, and some of the aches and pains he has been experiencing lately."
"Oh," she replied knowingly, "I hope that it's nothing serious, Philip?"
The old man shook his head, playing the part that he didn't want to.

He would take up the issue of Patricia's whereabouts again at a later date. He wanted Alan to do more for her, but despite his strength of feeling on the issue, he decided to hold his tongue. It would give him great pleasure to see how Carol reacted if he mentioned Patricia again, but he guessed that it was already going to be a conversation between her and his son anyway, as soon as he left to go home.
"It seems there is nothing to worry about," he said, "but Alan has suggested that I have a chat with Dr. Asif just to be on the safe side."
"That's good to hear," she answered, deciding to plunge the handle on the cafetiere, then began pouring the coffee.
The remaining fifteen minutes of dinner were spent with long silences and awkward pauses before Alan Boothby decided that it was time for him to leave. After he had put on his coat and hat, and partially opened his umbrella to brave the weather outside he asked if Carol was happy that he hadn't helped in clearing the table.
"Of course," she replied, letting him know that she never expected guests to help her. With a nod, he gave her a peck on the cheek. Then he touched his son briefly on the arm before offering a quick handshake. Leaving them standing at the door he walked to his car. Once inside, he gave them a brief wave and quickly drove off into the night.
"Well that went well..not," Alan said, as they began clearing up the rest of the items still sitting on the dining table. He now regretted the invitation, indicating to her that she had been right. That the evening had not turned out as he had hoped.
"I'm surprised you had expected anything different."
Alan smiled wanly. He explained that he had expected a better outcome and that he had hoped for something more positive to have come of the evening. It was obvious now that no matter how he tried, things would not change. She listened to his comments and then surprised him with one of her own. "Oh, by the way, Alan."
"Yes?"
"Don't ever lie to me again."
"Excuse me?" he replied.
She stared at him, turning her head slightly as if she was sizing up a piece of obscure art or an odd reflection staring back at her. Then silently, she picked up the remainder of the cups still standing on the table, placing them on the tray now packed with other items including unused spoons, glasses, and salt and pepper pots. He

waited for her to say something. He knew it was coming. Finally, she looked into his face and after a brief pause she said enigmatically, "A woman knows…" Lifting the tray carefully, she turned on her heels and left him watching her go as she made her way to the kitchen.

CHAPTER 35

Brierly had taken a good look at the mess in the kitchen. His inspection took in what he had been told had occurred, then reconciled the words with his observations. He had introduced himself on arrival. Initially, they had expected DI Sutton, but Brierly had explained to them that the murders of Gretchen Millwright and the children were now his cases to solve. He told them why. He also let them know that DI Sutton had agreed to provide any support he could, given what had already occurred. Finally, he reiterated that they could rest assured that he and his team were determined to find the killer. It was now his number one priority.

They were sitting in the lounge. The curtains had been drawn and the night kept away. He needed them to focus, despite the obvious challenges. Brierly had earlier requested that Mary Owen and Tom Millwright be seated and wait for him while he and DC Track took their time checking the area outside the kitchen window and around the side of the house. They also inspected the garden for any signs made or left by the perpetrator(s). Brierly had also allowed Trevor Owen to be taken off to the hospital to have his injuries addressed. It was likely that he would need to have stitches in his forehead according to the paramedic that attended to him, before then assessing his daughter's wounds. Mary had been lucky. The damage to her face was deemed superficial and was expected to heal relatively easily, despite some initial discomfort. However, she had been advised to see her doctor if there were any complications.

"So did any of you see or hear anything at all?" Brierly asked them a second time, his first attempt having received a confused response.

Mary had replied with an emphatic, "No," while Millwright's response had been, "Maybe."

"I thought I saw a light of sorts, but it was very brief," Millwright added.

"What kind of light, Mr. Millwright? A torch perhaps?"

"No, it was too small, it was just a sort of pinprick light. You know, one very bright but very…I don't know…sharp."

"You mean like that on a mobile phone?" Track asked.

Taking a few seconds to think about it, Millwright replied in the affirmative. "Yes, that's right. Something like mine." He picked up an iPhone that was sitting on the table next to the settee and after a few taps, the torch beam shone across the floor. He took a quick look at the beam, blinding himself for a few seconds after turning the back of the phone towards him so that it shone into his eyes. "Sorry," he continued, "that was a bit stupid of me, but yes, it was something like this." He turned off the beam, putting the phone back into his pocket.

"And this was just before the window shattered?" Brierly said.

"Yes."

"And Ms. Owen, you didn't see anything yourself?"

"No, Inspector, as I said earlier."

"Okay. We'll get our Forensics team out here in the morning to see if they can find any trace of the intruder, but from our initial observations, there isn't much out there. You have a concrete path from the back door around the side of the house to the front, so we'll be very lucky to find prints of any kind. However, you never know."

"But there must be something. What about the brick?" Millwright asked, his agitation at the questions and a perceived lack of action by the police becoming evident. It was obvious to both policemen that Millwright's anger was bubbling just under the surface of a numb exterior. They needed to be careful. Brierly got the impression that Millwright could very quickly become a vigilante and take matters into his own hands. It was the last thing anyone needed. In an attempt to settle the man down, Brierly told him that the Forensics unit would analyze the brick for any traces of DNA or any other genetic material which may be of use.

"It will likely take a few days," he added. "In the meantime, I need to ask a few questions of you both. I want to know more about the attack tonight, as well as understand the circumstances surrounding what happened to your family Mr. Millwright…about which I want to offer our sincere condolences," he pointed at himself and DC Track, who intimated his agreement. "We are sorry for your loss, Sir."

"Call me Tom, please. Mister Millwright is my dad," he replied. "And if it's answers that you need, then go ahead, ask whatever questions you like…of either of us. We've got nothing to hide."

"Fine by me," Mary echoed.

"Thank you. That's good to hear," Brierly said, taking out a small notepad from his jacket pocket. He made a show of opening and

then reviewing a couple of the pages that he flipped through before beginning to ask his questions. Track watched him quietly, realizing that Brierly was subtly teaching him an interrogation technique. "Do either of you own a van at all? A white van, a transit-type van? Possibly a Ford?"
"No," they replied in unison.
"Do you have access to one?"
"I suppose by hiring one," Mary replied, "but that's about all."
"I guess I could borrow one from some people I know," Millwright added. "Why do you ask?"
Brierly didn't answer the question but posed one of his own. "I see you're employed as a Quality Assurance manager, Ms. Owen?"
"Mary, please Inspector, and yes that's right. I work on various engineering projects."
"And you Sir, umm Tom, you have your own business?"
"That's right, I'm an electrician by trade, but I take on other work when I can."
"Such as?"
"Painting, especially in new builds or with the renovations of offices."
"Which you do yourself?"
"No, I normally sub-contract."
"So have there been any issues between yourself and any of your customers or suppliers? Anyone who you may have fallen out with?" Brierly enquired.
"What and because of that, they killed my family?" Millwright replied indignantly.
"I'm just trying to get a sense of…"
"Look Inspector, I can assure you that anyone I have ever fallen out with, as you put it, whether in my business dealings or elsewhere would never go to such extremes to get back at me. That's a ridiculous thing to say."
"Because?"
"Because….because...," Millwright stuttered.
"Because they would face your wrath?" Brierly asked, raising an eyebrow.
"No, because I would address it business-like, sensibly, practically," Millwright answered, obviously annoyed at the perceived inference.
"And what about you, Carol? Is there anyone in your circle, work or

otherwise, who you think is behind the attack this evening?"
"No," she answered. Then looking at her watch she added, "My God, it's after midnight already…is this going to take much longer, Inspector?"
"Unfortunately, it will, unless you want to come down to the station by nine in the morning where we can continue the discussion in one of our interview rooms?"
"The both of us?" she queried.
"Yes."
Mary Owen considered the offer, then realized that her father would need to be collected from the hospital at some point and be brought back to her house. She had to be available for that. In addition, the promised police Forensics team would be on-site in the next few hours. With Tom also expected to stay overnight and be around for a while she knew that things would be hectic over the next twenty-four hours or so. The thought of being cooped up in a police station room for what could be a long time did not appeal to her. She guessed that it was the same for Tom. Like him with his clients, she would have to let her boss know that she needed time off to get her dad home and settled before she could get back to work. Time, and her need for staying organized, conflicted. She already knew from Sutton that it would take a while before they could bury Gretchen and the children. He had previously advised them that the bodies could only be released, once the coroner had agreed and that could take some time. Mary felt that her life was spinning out of control.
"No, let's do it now," she said eventually, noticing Tom endorsing her comment.
Brierly looked at both of them, accepting the request.
"So, for clarity, Ms…err Mary, can you think of anyone that could be behind the attack tonight?"
"No."
Brierly made another show of checking his notebook. "DI Sutton advised me of some threatening letters your father had received recently. You are obviously aware of them?"
"Yes. We both are," Mary answered.
"And how he illegally obtained himself a gun as a consequence of those letters?"
"Yes."
"Are you aware of anything else?" Brierly queried. He sensed that

there had to be. Why would someone kill an entire family and intimidate the rest by attacking them, unless there was a link? He was hopeful that either Mary or Tom would be able to provide the answer.
"How do you mean?" Mary asked.
"Well, did you ever ask your father why he had taken such drastic action to protect himself?"
"Yes."
Brierly waited for her to continue, for her to explain what she knew if indeed anything. He let the silence between them build. He guessed that either Mary or Tom would break it. He knew that he and Track would not. Eventually, Mary spoke. "My dad received a couple of cards with dates on them."
"Cards?"
"Yes, birthday cards…and then several notes."
"Was there anything unusual about the cards?"
"Just the dates printed inside them," she replied.
"Which were?"
"My father's and my mother's dates of birth."
"And these were significant how?"
"I don't know Inspector."
"And he didn't share these cards with the police? DI Sutton or anyone else?"
"No," she replied. "He didn't take them seriously until a note arrived saying that the whole family would be dead before he turned seventy."
"Which is?"
"A few months from now."
Brierly made a note on one of the pages. "And he has no idea who sent them?"
"No."
"Does he still have them?"
"He said that he threw them away," Mary replied.
"Do you believe him?"
"Why wouldn't I?"
Taking the comment at face value, Brierly asked if there was anything else that had not been shared with the police.
"There were some bullets that were sent to him in the mail. It was the final straw. He said that made him get the gun."

"So, he still has these bullets?"
"Yes…and he kept the cards as well."
"We'll need to get hold of them asap," Brierly noted.
"They are at his house," she answered. "He showed me where he kept them. A little while ago."
"Do you have access?"
"Yes, I have a key. I can meet you there sometime tomorrow," she stated, before remembering the various happenings likely to occur once dawn broke. Putting her father's well-being first, she said, "I think it best that my dad stays with me once he's finished at the hospital, at least for a while, so after I've collected him I can leave him here while your team does what it needs to and get them for you. It will be a bit of a rush as I also need to get a glazier in to fix the window."
"I'll arrange that," Millwright said, interjecting. "Just leave it to me."
With a resigned smile and a touch of his hand, she thanked him for the offer. Brierly agreed that her suggested arrangements were reasonable. He doubted that the perpetrator would come back to the house any time soon and surmised that the attack was likely to have been a warning. With a police Forensics team crawling around the place, the next day anyone showing a special interest by staying in the immediate vicinity for too long would likely be easily identified and questioned. "I'll have DC Track here and my Sergeant, DS White meet you at your father's house tomorrow if that's okay?" he said, asking her for the applicable address, which Track took down. Brierly then asked them both if they had anything further to add. Both replied in the negative.
"I know it will be difficult for you, but please can I ask that you stay away from the kitchen and do not go into the back garden or around the side of the property until our team has completed its work tomorrow. That includes the glazier, Mr…umm, Tom. Please wait until they give you the 'all-clear'. Is that understood?"
After receiving their confirmation the two policemen stood. "Under normal circumstances, I would have a Constable come and guard the house until the morning," Brierly said, "but given the lateness of the hour I don't think it will be necessary. Are you okay with that?" he asked. "However, if you are still concerned, I'll see what I can do…"
"No, it should be fine," Millwright said on behalf of both of them. "I'm not sure we'll get much sleep anyway."

They shook hands at the front door. Brierly and Track braved the cold breeze and the spitting rain, as they ran to their car. Once inside Brierly asked for the car's heater to be turned on to the maximum. "To clear the windscreen," he said, pointing to the steamed-up glass. Track obliged, then pulled the car out from their parking spot and into the quiet street. "What do you think, Sir?" he asked. "It all seems a bit odd, doesn't it?"
"I have to agree with you, Constable, though hopefully, those birthday cards will provide us with something to work with. This case gets stranger by the day….and I still don't see how, if at all, it ties in with the murder of Dave Crossley."

CHAPTER 36

Janie Fenchurch had contacted the staff by email overnight, asking all of them to attend an urgent meeting at 11 am. Her request included the casuals and those volunteers who were able to make it. With the hall empty of guests for the hour she had set aside, she let them all know why they had been summoned.

"As most of you will know, the police have been here a couple of times over the past week or so. The first time was in connection with the death of this poor man who was murdered in Hollybrook cemetery," she raised the flyer Brierly had given her into the air. "You will have seen this on the notice board at the entrance and I'm sure many of you will have spoken with the police when they were here, trying to establish his identity." She put the flyer down and watched as several of her staff agreed, recalling their discussions with either DC Hughes or DC Proctor. "As to the second occasion, police Inspector Brierly came to see me due to the feedback he had received from his officers after their first visit. He quizzed me initially on whether anyone knew of the man in the flyer but more specifically he wanted to talk with me about some disturbing matters that the police had become aware of. He said they were informed of these by some of the staff members here. They are concerned, as am I, with the allegation or perhaps better put, the suspicion, that drugs are being bought and sold within these four walls. Either by our guests or by some of the staff. If this is the case, then it is totally unacceptable and puts the entire facility at risk, not to mention the potential of jail time for anyone caught dealing drugs." Looking around at the various faces, young and old, staring back at her, she tried to see if any of them showed any signs of embarrassment or of being uncomfortable with what she was suggesting. If there was a flicker of concern anywhere, she didn't see it. With twenty-five odd people in front of her, twenty-five staff who she needed to trust, she felt embarrassed to question their integrity and honesty. It was however something that she was compelled to do. Having discussed the matter with her board the previous evening she had been encouraged to act decisively, so she decided to come right out and ask those assembled.

"Does anyone know of or has anyone seen any evidence of drugs

being dealt or used here?" she stated forcefully.
Despite her blunt question, she was met with a stony silence. Many of the staff sitting in the makeshift rows of chairs, normally used in the guest dining room, looked down at their hands or the floor. Some seemed to be thinking but others stared blankly. The atmosphere was tense. She sensed that someone knew something but was afraid to mention it publicly. She offered a lifeline.
"I appreciate that it may be difficult to talk openly in this forum and I will understand if anyone would prefer to talk with me privately if you do have any information. Please can I ask you to think about what I have said very carefully? We provide a service to the community. We are trying to keep people off the streets. To keep them safe from harm. Dealing and using drugs is contrary to our ethos and while I'm sure most of us understand why drugs are used; we cannot allow this facility to be a place where guests or staff actively ignore and abuse what we stand for." Deciding that she had made her point she asked her audience if anyone had any questions. Once again, she was met with silence though a few coughed quietly or shifted in their seats. She noted who they were and stored the information in the back of her mind. If she was right, she expected several of them to seek her out. While she was disappointed at the prospect, she was pleased that some would have the fortitude to act.
"Okay then," she said in conclusion, "let's prepare for the day. Those who are on shift please get ready to welcome our guests. Those that have come in, especially for this meeting, thank you so much for your attendance. I'll see you again soon." With a smile and a flick of her hand, the meeting began to break up. Some of those in the room made a beeline for the exit, some headed to the kitchen and others began rearranging the room so that guests could sit at the tables and eat the small lunch that was to be provided to each of them.
Fenchurch made her way to her office. She half expected to have one or two of those she had just addressed in her office by the end of the day. She hadn't anticipated there would be any immediate reaction. It would be unwise for an individual who wished to remain anonymous to their fellow staff members, but who had information about what was going on, to rush off to Fenchurch's office as soon as the meeting was over. Not only would they be in potential danger from those they 'fingered,' but they would likely need to provide evidence of sorts before she would take them seriously. Allegations were one

thing, but the provision of proof was something else. Being a whistleblower came with its own issues and often the innocent party came out worse for wear. She opened the door to her office and stopped briefly as she noticed a man sitting crossed-legged on the opposite side of her desk. He was reading what appeared to be a report. "Aah, good morning, Janie how are you?" Philip Boothby said, beginning to stand as he placed the document back down on her desk.
"Oh, what a surprise," she replied, with genuine sincerity, "what brings you here Mr. Boothby?" The old man asked her if they could have some privacy and despite there being no one outside in the short passageway between the dining area and her office, he reached over from his chair and closed the office door.
"It's about my granddaughter, Patricia…Pat," he said, "I'm very concerned about her."
Fenchurch was a little confused. Boothby had never mentioned her before in any way with or in the context of the homeless shelter. She asked him to elaborate on his concerns. For the first time in her dealings with him over several years, he seemed genuinely embarrassed. His demeanour indicated his obvious worry. "I'm afraid to ask this, which I why I wanted to talk with you in private, but I need a favour."
"Go ahead, Mr. Boothby. I'm happy to do whatever I can to help."
In a quiet voice, he said "I think Pat has been living on the street recently and I have reason to think that she may have had some dealings with some of our guests."
"Dealings?" she queried.
"Yes, as in…buying illicit drugs."
"I thought your granddaughter was living with her mother. Where was it..err, Romsey?"
"Eastleigh."
"Yes, Eastleigh, sorry. I remember you telling me at one of our board meetings a couple of months back. She had started a course or something?"
"Hairdressing," he reminded her.
"Has something happened?" she queried, beginning to understand his concern. "To drive her to the streets I mean. And how do you know that she has been around here? Has anyone seen her?"
Boothby sighed. "I've spoken with her mother the other day. It was

she who called me. She told me that she had no idea where Pat is. It seems she just walked out one morning to go to college and never came home."

"Did she report it to the police?"

"No. Patricia has done this before. So Anneline, her mother, thinks that because she reported it previously and she came home eventually, the police would think that she was being paranoid."

"That's a bit rich and unacceptable, isn't it? Though with police numbers being stretched nowadays, it is hardly surprising that she feels that way. It seems they pick and chose who they look for and who they don't."

"And that's my concern," Boothby replied. "I don't think anyone is looking for her."

"What about her father?"

"I'm sorry, but I'm not going there. I've had more than enough conversations in recent times with him on the matter."

Fenchurch understood what was being implied and asked the question that she had been wanting to since he first brought up the subject.

"So what makes you think she has been in the area or even had dealings with anyone who has spent time with us here?"

"It's just a guess. A feeling I suppose. Patricia has her problems, there is no denying that," he admitted, "and her default has always been to get access to money. It's her innate survival mode kicking in."

"Okay, but I'm still unsure where we come in."

With a look of desperation on his face, Boothby said, "I spoke with my son at dinner last night. He tried to tell me that he knew Pat was in Eastleigh, however, I knew differently. As I told you, Anneline, Pat's mother had already told me that she was missing."

Fenchurch indicated her understanding, signaling for him to continue. "So please forgive me for my next comment, but from what I knew already, it told me that my son was a liar."

"I see, but…" she queried. However, he didn't hear her reply but continued with his explanation.

"It's just a guess, but I think Pat's first port of call would have been to try and get money from my son. If she was unsuccessful, and I guess that she was, then she would have reverted to something else."

"You mean stealing? Prostituting herself? Why she would not come to you, Mr. Boothby…or seek help in a shelter like this one?"

Boothby looked into her face, a sad look in his eyes. "Pat knows how I feel about her behaviour and my stance on the use of drugs…as you know from our board conversations it was me who set up the no-drugs policy that everyone is required to abide by."
"Yes, I do," she answered.
"It was one of the conditions that the Council insisted upon as being part of our charter before they agreed to provide funding to set up this place," he added. "I fully supported the position then and I still do."
"As does everyone who works here," she confirmed.
"So that's why I am concerned. As I already mentioned, Pat has done this type of thing before, particularly the running away, but the last time she did so, she ended up smoking marijuana and getting into other drugs," he continued sadly. "The problem is despite my strong aversion to drugs, she also knows that I love her. She is my grandchild after all. So, while she wouldn't come to me for help as she is so bloody-minded, she is not dumb. In fact, I would say that she is too street-smart for her own good. Even at seventeen-years-old."
"Which means?"
"It means that she will find the easiest way to get what she needs, food, alcohol, clothes, anything at all, and having said that, even a place to stay. So because she knows of the shelter here due to my involvement over many years, I suspect that she may make her way here at some point. She may even try to use my name to inveigle her way in. With the weather at the moment, she can't stay on the streets forever, and with two people killed recently where a lot of homeless people normally go at night, I'm not sure she would want to take the chance of being on the streets."
"You mean sleeping in the cemeteries?"
"Yes. To be honest it's why I'm so concerned for her. It's why I need your help."
"What are you suggesting?"
"I would like you and the team to keep a look out for her, and if she does come here, to let me know."
"I'm sure we can do that for you, Mr. Boothby."
"Thank you, but I need something else."
"What is it?"
"I need to know if she's back into drugs."

"I'm not sure how we can help with that," she answered, "why do you think we can?"
"The same reason you spoke with your team just now, the follow-up from the police inquiry that we discussed at the board meeting last night. If someone is dealing drugs here, it is likely that at some point they may come into contact with Patricia. It's a small community and I think it will only be a matter of time before whoever is involved will find her or she in turn will find them."
"Isn't that a long bow to draw?" she asked.
"No, I don't think so. I'm just putting two and two together."
"I suppose so, but…"
"And perhaps there is a bit of selfishness involved as well," he interrupted. "The reason why I wanted to talk with you privately."
"Go on," she said, unsure of where he was going with his inference.
"Well, if we can find her before the police do, then I'm hoping that I can get her to drop her involvement with drug taking and take her back home before she is charged with anything. I'm afraid if she gets a police record then it can affect her future."
"That's very true. I agree with you. She would be very silly to end up in court or worse, in prison."
"Exactly. Which is why I hope you and your team will be discreet. If you can put the word out quietly to let me know if Pat comes here or if anyone sees her on the street trying to buy or sell drugs, that would be appreciated. I'd like to limit any police involvement as I'm hoping to protect my own reputation as well. To have my grandchild stealing to do drugs or something worse is not something I'd like publicized," he added.
"But surely no one would blame you for how your granddaughter acts, Mr. Boothby? All adults ultimately have to take responsibility for themselves and their actions do they not?"
"That's true, but Patricia is still a child. Over many years I spent a huge amount of my time while on the council advocating for the protection of children within the community. I petitioned for drug treatment programs and the establishment of shelters like this one," he said. "During that time, I made a lot of noise, and with it, lots of enemies. I even excoriated the police when they seemed to turn a blind eye to some of the things that were going on with the younger people, especially youth prostitution and drug taking in nightclubs and on street corners. You can imagine how it will go down if it turns

out that my own flesh and blood is involved in something I spoke out against!"
Fenchurch considered his comments and then conceded to herself that while his request was flawed in that there was more than a small element of self-preservation involved, she believed that he had the best interest of his granddaughter and the shelter at heart.
"I'll see what I can do," she said, finally.

CHAPTER 37

He had been trying to think while at the same time looking through the new edition of the 'Sky at Night' magazine. It was unusual for any of the boys to be at home so early, but Warwick wanted to watch the Champions League game between Arsenal and Bayern Munich. The kickoff was at eight o'clock and the game was already underway. Fifteen minutes into the match and the German side was already one nil up.

"I hope they lose," Warwick said, who was a Chelsea supporter. "It will serve them right for being so bolshie last season." The Gunners had finished runners-up in the Premier League only five months earlier, just two points behind Liverpool who had stolen the title from them in the very last game. Chelsea had finished fourth behind Tottenham, but their game in round two of the Champions League was only in a week's time. They had won their first-round match in their Group, (Group E), three-one, against Montpellier at Stamford Bridge, much to Warwick's delight and that of thousands of other Chelsea fans. Brierly hardly noticed the comment, he was concentrating on a number of questions that were bouncing around in his head. Questions related to different crimes to which he had no obvious answers. The white panel van with the letter S on the side? The different murder weapons used to kill Crossley and the homeless man? What had happened to them? Had they been disposed of and if so, where? By whom? The birthday cards and associated letters. The strange markings on the hands of the victims, the children in particular. What did they mean?

His thoughts were interrupted as Warwick let out a groan.

"Damn!" Warwick said, pointing at the TV, "Surely that was offside?"

Brierly realized that his son was agitated and that Arsenal had equalized. His son's reaction to a soft goal scored by the Gunners was one of huge disappointment and Brierly noted the change in his attitude to the game as Warwick jumped off the couch and raced to the kitchen.

"Do you want some tea, Dad?" his son asked, just as June came into the lounge. She had been in the bedroom reading, preferring the peace and quiet of sitting on the bed rather than trying to compete

with the noise of a football match. On hearing the agonized cry of her son, she decided to check out what he was up to. She had an idea that his reaction to how the game was going was behind his comic anguish. "I'll have some too," she called out, letting her son know that she had heard his generous offer.
"No problem," Warwick replied, beginning to clink mugs, spoons, and milk bottles together.
"How are you doing, darling?' she asked, noting Brierly's frown, as he flipped through the pages of his magazine without spending too much time looking at any in particular.
"Not too well," he answered, putting the magazine to one side and giving her a sad smile. "I'm sorry I was a little distant over dinner earlier, but I've been trying to work out why anyone would want to murder an entire family and I'm struggling for a motive. I can't even see any rationale at all."
June touched his hand, recalling how only an hour earlier they had finished eating and she had cleared away the table. During the meal, they had hardly spoken to each other. It was a sign that Brierly was feeling stressed, that there were too many things on his mind, and he was unsettled. She had wanted to share her day with him but had concluded that discretion was the better part of valour and had retired to their bedroom to give him the necessary time and space to think. Given his comment, she wasn't sure now if it had been a good idea. She changed the subject, hoping to lighten his mood. "Anything of interest?" she said, pointing at the magazine.
"Not a lot to be honest," he replied, still sounding downcast. "Though irrespective of what's being alluded to, it's a moot point. The weather has been so bad, it's impossible to see anything through the cloud cover and the rain that's been hanging around for the past fortnight or so."
"And this prevents what?" he continued.
"The ability to look at anything…anything that makes sense or is worthwhile."
"You mean with any clarity?"
"Yes, essentially."
She looked at him quizzically. "Does that apply to the cases you are working on?"
"I guess so," he answered, beginning to understand what she was suggesting. "Yes, there is something. Something that I can't see past

yet."

"The cloud equivalent?" she queried. "The same type of thing that prevents you from seeing into the night sky?"

"Yes," he answered. He knew that what she was inferring was correct. In a situation when an astronomer, be they amateur, professional, or casual, wanted to search the heavens, they would use tools and instruments to get above a dirty sky. Binoculars, telescopes, ground-based or on the high mountains of the world, satellites, and other means were all at their disposal. A cloudy day or a desperate sky was not the end to looking upwards, it was just a challenge. Brierly realized that June was throwing out a challenge to him. A challenge that he needed to work through. One that required him to peer through the clouds that hid the truth behind the murders of Crossley and the other victims.

"I'm surprised that you even bother to read that magazine, dad," Warwick interrupted, putting down a mug of tea on the table. "I'm sure you'll get a better outcome and a better view of the stars by using an app. Surely there are plenty of them around?" he added before settling down again to watch the game.

Brierly gave Warwick's comment some consideration and acknowledged that he was probably right. There were other tools, other brains, available to be leveraged and that could be used in his star-gazing pursuits. Tools more sophisticated than the articles and diagrams published in a magazine, no matter how revered the publication was. There were people far more qualified than he who had worked on such problems and had found solutions. The Apollo program, the international space station along with the Hubble and James Webb telescopes were evidence of that. Brierly knew that what June had indicated, required him to think beyond the obvious, to think outside of the box. Somewhere beyond the clouds whirling throughout his mind was the answer to the case, but where? He needed to find a way through. In the interim, however, he decided to bite the bullet and take up Warwick's suggestion. "Can you help me with my phone," he called haltingly, hoping he could be heard above the sound blaring from the TV. "I'm not sure what to do."

Warwick was engrossed in the football. June had joined him on the couch where she had begun working on a spreadsheet on her laptop computer. She gave him a gentle push with her elbow.

"Your dad is calling you."

"Okay, okay," Warwick replied, standing up. With one eye on the TV, he began to walk towards the lounge doorway before letting out a loud 'woah' sound as a Bayern Munich striker headed the ball against Arsenal's crossbar.

"Sorry, dad, I just want the Germans to stick it to them," he said. "How can I help?"

Brierly passed his son the mobile. "That app store you talk about, can you get this for me?" He pointed at his magazine now lying face down on the table. On the back cover was an advertisement for something called Star Walk 2 which was described as a 'Stargazing App to view the night sky through the screen of your device.'

"It's free as well," Brierly continued, watching as Warwick caressed the phone, his fingers rapidly tapping away. Without breaking concentration, Warwick completed the download and passed the device back to Brierly. "All done," he said, "and I've opened it up for you."

With a smile and a thank you, Brierly watched his son walk the few steps back into the lounge. He didn't know how to operate the new application, but he was excited by the thought. He looked down at the screen which showed a night sky and a horizon along with several boxes, a compass, and a menu. He was pleased that he now had something modern to use, a tool that would hopefully enhance his understanding of the night sky even more. He began to press on various names of stars and planets as he scrolled around the screen, watching various details appear about each. Some were extensive, others limited. He lost track of time as he continued exploring. It was only when Simon, his eldest son, walked past him on his way to his bedroom that he realized how much he had become engrossed in what he was reading.

"Good night, dad," Simon said, smiling at the way his father concentrated on the screen.

"Oh, night, son," Brierly answered, suddenly aware that he hadn't spoken to his eldest at all, throughout the entire evening. Indeed he hadn't even noticed when Simon had arrived home. After his son had climbed the stairs and Brierly heard the bedroom door close, a thought suddenly struck him. He wasn't sure if it was relevant to the Crossley case or related to the Millwright family, but something began to niggle him. He couldn't see the connection, but he was convinced that it was relevant. He would share his thoughts with his

team in the morning and see if what he was thinking made sense. He looked at his watch, noticing that it was nearly eleven o'clock. Warwick was still sitting in front of the TV watching the soccer pundits review the Arsenal game. It seemed from what Brierly could hear that the Germans had been beaten and that one of the pundits, an ex-Arsenal player, was currently praising the home side for their application and tenacity. Brierly stood and stretched, yawning as he did so. He felt a gentle crack in his spine. Calling out a goodnight greeting to Warwick he made his way to bed. June was already snuggled up, reading. She gave him a glance over the top of her book as he placed his phone and wristwatch on the bedside table.
"What are you reading?" he asked.
"It's a memoir, by Pauline Collins, the actress."
"Oh," he replied, only half listening. "Any good?"
"I've just started it. I'll let you know," she replied with a smile. He smiled back in silent acknowledgement as he headed toward the bathroom. He was just about to start brushing his teeth when he heard his mobile phone start to vibrate. June called to him, checking whether he had noticed, and reached across the bed to answer it. After a quick rinse of his toothbrush and a sip of water to clear his mouth he took the phone from her.
"Hello Barry, what's so urgent that it can't wait until the morning?" he asked, knowing full well that DS White would never call him unless the matter was important.
"We've found a van, Sir. A panel van…a Ford. We think it could be the one used to transport the Millwright kids."
"Are you sure?" Brierly asked, looking at June and mouthing a silent apology. She waved his concern away, a call late at night was par for the course and she knew what it meant.
"Yes," White continued, "well, at least we think it is."
"Think?"
"Yes, Jim. The Forensics boys are already on the scene. They are trying to verify if my hunch is correct."
Brierly was surprised that White had concluded that the vehicle in question was the one used by the Millwright children's killer. It seemed premature for him to have done so. Particularly without any definitive evidence.
"Where was it found?" he asked.
"It was dumped about four miles from where the kids' bodies were

found. It's a country road called Ashley Down Lane, and it's surrounded by woods, not far from a place called Boarhunt."
"Bloody hell, never heard of it."
"Me neither, Sir," White responded, reverting back to formality, "but the vehicle does seem to fit the description we were given by Colin Anthony."
"What makes you so sure it's the right van though?" Brierly asked a little sceptically, still not convinced that White's hunch was correct.
"A couple of things. Firstly, it's a Ford and secondly, there is some writing on the side of the sliding door along with a graphic of some sort. It looks like a couple of the words may start with large red capital letters."
"May? Aren't they obvious?"
"No Sir, that's why the call, the urgency. The van was torched. Some of the paintwork has blistered and has peeled away. It needs experts to decipher them."
"So that's the reason for Forensics being on-site already? To try and confirm your thinking?"
"No Sir. It's because when one of the local lads got out here to investigate, they found a corpse inside the van. The body has been burnt beyond recognition!"

CHAPTER 38

The flashing red and blue lights of the ambulance lit up the perimeter, while the bright white light set up by the Forensics team was focused on the twisted still smoldering shell of the van. The road had been blocked off in both directions using a couple of squad cars, each stationed a quarter of a mile away from the suspected crime scene. Blue and white tape tied to trees on either side of the road created an exclusion zone for anyone not required to be there. The tape flapped in a bitter wind that threatened to tear it apart, and the smell of charred flesh permeated the immediate area. Despite its strength, the breeze was not strong enough to expunge the pungent odour of death into the night sky.

It had taken Brierly less than an hour after he had finished his call with White, to get to the scene. Along the way, he had called Sutton, who had been asleep. Brierly had advised him of what had happened, then asked Sutton for a favour. Sutton had agreed without hesitation, accepting to stand in for White the next morning, and meeting DC Track at Trevor Owen's house to collect the bullets and cards that Mary Owen said her father had kept there.

As he clambered under the tape, showing a stern-faced Constable his warrant card, he noticed the young policeman stamping his feet and rubbing his hands together from the cold. Clouds of condensing vapour disappeared on the breeze as he blew onto his exposed fingers. Brierly noticed White was standing a few yards behind a couple of white-suited forensic team members, talking studiously. He called out to him, realizing that he couldn't tell if the forensics folk were male or female as both were partially bent over. They were looking into a twisted, blackened metal, hulk. Their torches scanned the inside of the van through a half-opened sliding door. It was so badly twisted that it would never close again. As he walked towards White from the rear of the van, carefully standing on a series of white steel plates already dotted along the ground, he noticed that there were no number plates attached to the vehicle itself. Moving to see what remained of the front of the vehicle, he saw where the flames and intense heat had blackened and scorched the seats, blowing out the windscreen and side windows. It was there that he saw the remains of what used to be a human being. The body was in the driver's seat, inexplicably with the car seat belt still strapped across what was left of the victim. The smell of burnt rubber and flesh assailed Brierly's nose and mouth and he gagged slightly, before taking a handkerchief from a pocket and partially covering his face. He felt slightly envious of the Forensics team as they were wearing masks. White, he noticed, had neither.

"Who found him?" Brierly asked, taking a few steps away from the hulk and walking around to the front of the van, staying far enough away not to disturb anything on the ground. White joined him pointing through the glassless window at the blackened figure, which despite a lack of a face, still seemed to watch them as they moved.

"A motorist on his way home. Seems like he uses this road as a shortcut whenever he's late. His name's Daniel Shepparton and he lives in Southwick. He's a rep of sorts."

"So where is he now?" Brierly asked looking around, noticing one of the two white suits had started to walk towards them from the other side of the van.

"He's at home. He called 999 when he could. The signal here is pretty patchy and his mobile was low on battery apparently. It seems he couldn't find a phone box locally so he called it in from home." Brierly instinctively looked at his own phone noticing that he only had one bar.

"I've sent DC Hughes to take a statement from him, and if we need to, I'll get the poor man into the station for a chat," White continued.

"Okay," Brierly replied, just as he recognized the person occupying the white suit that was now standing right in front of him. He was surprised that White hadn't mentioned anything.

"Hello, James," Robert Tankowski said, his accent seemingly heavier with the oppressive nature of the darkness surrounding them. "Fancy you being involved with this lot!" he added, removing his mask before pointing at the shadow behind the melted steering column. There was no steering wheel left other than a piece of twisted plastic distorted into an obscene figure eight which appeared to snake back into itself.

"Any ideas, Bob?" Brierly asked.

"Meaning?"

"Identity of the victim perhaps?"

"Not at this stage. We don't even know the sex. Looking at what is left of the body, it's possible that it could be either."

"Was he…or she," Brierly corrected himself, "dead or alive when this all went up in flames?"
"Still too early to say," Tankowski replied. "It looks like they were tied to the steering wheel with what I think was a bicycle lock. I'll check that later, but you can see the remnants of the metal innards still wrapped around the hands." Tankowski pointed towards the shattered windscreen. "When we get the body to the lab, we can check how seared the lungs and trachea are to see how deeply they were breathing in all the fumes and heat. If he, or she, was alive, I hope they hadn't been conscious, it's a hell of a way to die."
"I agree."
"Being unconscious, if he or she was, would have been a godsend I suppose?" White added.
Tankowski did not reply. Death in whatever form was his bread and butter, but despite all his years as a Forensics practitioner he still struggled with what he saw at times. "We had decided not to move him/her until the senior officer on the case had been to see the scene for themselves. I assume that's you James?" he asked.
"Yes, it is."
"Good. Well, you know our drill," Tankowski continued, "so, I'll be led by you as to when you are happy for us to move the victim and clear the site. In the meantime, is there anything you would like to see?" Tankowski looked up into the night sky noticing the swirling wind brushing the tops of the trees and sending the branches in multiple directions. He hoped that the cloud cover would remain without disgorging rain. If it did, it would make their job gathering any evidence around the vehicle so much more difficult.
Brierly raised a hand indicating the charred structure. "DS White here told to me that there was something written on one of the panels. It could be a vehicle that we are looking for. Where is that? On the other side?" Tankowski pointed, then advised that it was okay for them to walk to the darkened side of the van as long as Brierly and White were careful with their feet, keeping to the footplates. Using a torch previously provided by Forensics, White scanned the blackened paintwork of the van and pointed out where the lettering along the side of the vehicle used to be.
"You can see here, Sir," he said, shining the light along the distorted panelling behind the passenger window, now empty of glass except for a few pieces of twisted clear shards. "Parts of words here and

there." Brierly stared at the blistered paintwork. It still seemed hot to the touch and some of the decals seemed to bubble slightly. The only letter he could make out was the large S which had been painted on at some stage in bright red, now darkened by the heat. Somehow the flames and the heat had spared the driver's side of the van from twisting completely. Brierly's first thought was that the word should read 'Southampton' as the colour reminded him of his favoured football team. However, the remaining letters did not conform to his expectation.

"It looks like S, something, o, something, lf, capital *D*," Brierly said, trying to read the words, squinting to where White was pointing the torch beam. He was unable to read the rest. "What do you make of it, Sergeant?"

"I'm not sure, Sir, but take a look at this." White shone his light toward the back of the van. The rear doors were still closed, fused together by the scorching heat but bulging outwards in some places. "Here," he said, "this graphic, it looks in part like that of an arm and a column of some type. Can you see it? Also, there appear to be a few numbers below it, I think it's a phone number, but most of them have been burnt off. I can make out two of them, but that's it."

Brierly peered a little closer. In the dark and with the bright light focused on a small area, Brierly's eyes were becoming accustomed to the gloom. "I can certainly make out something," he agreed. "Just give me the torch for a second." Once in his hand, he shone the light in a small circle trying to see a little clearer what White was suggesting. He took his time, bending down occasionally, being careful where he planted his feet, and inspecting where the paintwork was less damaged. The smell of the burnt tyres from his left side attacked his senses but he tried to ignore the stench while he concentrated. Around him and on the other side of the van, the Forensics team continued working while the paramedics waited. White watched as his boss took a few more seconds staring at the burnt image before handing back the torch. "I've seen this before," he said finally, "the logo, the graphic, I'm sure I've seen it around the city, but I'll need to check once we are back at the station. Can you take a photo on your phone?" White took a few. Finding out where the van came from would be a good start to their investigation, but who the victim was and how they got there was a different story.

"Are you finished, Inspector?" Tankowski's voice boomed,

interrupting the relative silence Brierly and White had shared for a few seconds. "Do I have your permission to move the body now as I'd like it to be taken to the morgue, while we continue with our other work?"

The two policemen took a few steps back towards the front of the vehicle, walking from the shadows and into the white lights that burned brightly on the opposite side of the van. For a few seconds, both were partially blinded by their intensity. As he accustomed himself to the light again, Brierly realized that he was facing the blackened body still slumped in the driver's seat of the van. He stared at it for a few seconds, thinking. White waited, the grisly sight sending a shiver up his spine.

"Okay, go ahead, Robert. I think we're done here," Brierly answered eventually, after which Tankowski indicated to the paramedics that they could start the process of extracting the victim. As they did so, Brierly and White made their way to their cars, climbing under the blue and white tape that still fluttered madly. Turning to his Sergeant, Brierly said, "Get the team together, other than DC Track. I want everybody there by eight in the morning. We've got a lot of work to do, and we need to find some answers quickly. If we aren't careful, this could escalate badly and we could all be heading for hell in a handbasket." The emphasis was not lost on White who knew that Brierly was extremely worried. The latest victim was going to add considerable pressure on the investigation and with no idea who the victim was, they were not too far from finding themselves in the middle of a minefield. If that happened then every step they took could end with it blowing up in their faces.

"Okay, Jim, understood," White replied. The use of Brierly's Christian name confirmed that he understood how personally his boss was taking responsibility to find the killer or killers of the badly burnt victim. White knew that their friendship transcended rank at times. This was one of those times and by addressing his boss the way he did, he was letting him know of his support and that he would be watching Brierly's back.

"And another thing." Brierly continued, "we need to keep it out of the press until I've had a chance to inform DCI Hammond. He'll likely need to speak with the Chief Constable as well. She'll probably want to talk with the press first before they find out and start asking difficult questions." White smiled. Knowing the politics of the Force, he was glad that he didn't have to face the 'higher-ups' at times like this. He knew how things worked. They took the praise when they could and disappeared when the going got tough, leaving the press hounds to dog the poor DI or DCI about their actions taken and the results achieved. "I'll inform the team to keep schtum," he replied, in response.

"Thanks, until we have any answers there will only be speculation and you know how the press can sensationalize things."

"Agreed, but you have to admit boss that this killing is bizarre."

"I'd go so far as to say it's sick, Sergeant. Whoever did this, has somehow lost the plot. What we need to work out is why. Before they kill again."

White could tell that Brierly was feeling edgier than ever. He decided that he had said enough. The two men walked the remainder of the way to their cars in silence. They found that they had parked each just thirty yards apart from one another. White sat for a second and watched as Brierly started his car, a three-year-old Honda Civic, which he rarely drove himself. Normally Brierly was a passenger in an unmarked police car, driven by White or one of the DCs. The Honda remained where it was, the headlights facing down the road, tail lights glowing and creating an eerie red blush on the surrounding trees. White could see that Brierly was writing something. Starting his own vehicle, he turned up the heater to 'high' to take the chill from his bones, he then waved a quick goodbye to his boss and headed for home. He knew that in just a few short hours things were about to get hectic.

CHAPTER 39

She watched him as he entered the building. Despite wearing several layers, and the coat he had bought her, she was still feeling the cold. The small blisters on her hands were less painful now but were a remnant, a reminder, of her getting too close to the fire. The things he had bought her had been sufficient to keep her warm, but she had flogged some of the items, giving her just enough money for food. Now, she was broke once again and it had been a difficult night. Having sold herself twice she had intended to use her earnings to buy drugs. It was a transaction that she had regretted. Handing over the money, then receiving a fist to the head, the bastard had stolen her cash and run off. After walking the streets for a while looking for him she had finally given up. All she had to her name was an empty backpack. Fortunately, she had been able to find a bed for the night in the City Life church where she had been welcomed without question, despite the lateness of the hour. It had been a decision that did not sit well with her. Her independence was everything, but she had needed to sleep, and the streets seemed particularly dangerous now. The usual haunts like shopfronts, park benches, and under the cemetery trees, had been fortified in some places. Metal grills limiting access to certain areas and increased security personnel in shopping areas made finding a warm and dry space more difficult. Those lost to society were beginning to take notice that sleeping in doorways and under bridges was no longer as safe as it once was. Violence was becoming endemic. Finding ways to protect themselves, knives, whistles, and even small swords were hidden under the cardboard and dirty blankets they often used as beds. Those who resisted going to shelters were starting to pair up for the night, feeling safer with a buddy next to them. Two pairs of blurry eyes were better than one. Word on the street was that something was going on. The homeless were at greater risk now. If the weather and the drugs didn't kill them, then…..

Patricia had left the City Life church well before the majority of those sleeping there had woken to face the day. She had only stayed a few hours. Enough for a short nap and a shower. When she had walked out of the door, despite a genuine plea from a staffer for her to have something to eat before leaving, she was determined to have him pay more. It was her right, his obligation, she thought. Waiting for five minutes to ensure he had settled in his office, she walked across the road leaving her hiding place behind a row of cars parked opposite the surgery building.

After pressing the button on the outside of the glass door to gain access she made her way into the waiting room, where six patients were already seated. Some were coughing and spluttering while others stared quietly at the silent TV affixed high on one of the walls. The vision advertised certain medicines and drugs and indicated the treatments available at the surgery to combat the types of illnesses impacting the community. Flu jabs, regular check-ups, sick notes, and mental and sexual health support, amongst others.

She walked up to the reception counter which was manned by a bespectacled middle-aged woman who was busy arranging a series of small brown envelopes into some form of sequence. Patricia guessed that it was the personal files of the patients seated behind her. While she waited for the woman to acknowledge that she was standing before her and wasn't a glass ornament to be ignored, a figure loomed up from behind, touching Patricia on the shoulder. Feeling aggrieved at being ignored by the receptionist, she turned around to face the figure.

"Will you leave the fuck alone!" she shouted. An audible gasp from the patients quietly sitting in their chairs could be heard as she stared into her father's face. She ducked her head slightly as he took her firmly by the arm, telling the receptionist that he would handle 'the girl' and simultaneously advising her that he would start seeing patients 'shortly'. He led Patricia down the short passage to his consulting room and once he had manhandled her inside, closed the door firmly, locked it, and pushed her down into a chair next to his desk.

"What do you want?" he asked.

"It's good to see you too," she replied sarcastically.

"What do you want?" he repeated, "And why here?" his angry tone indicative of his irritation.

"Money," she answered, rubbing her upper arm where he had held it. "And anyway, because I've got nowhere else to go."

"What about going home?"

"To live with that fuckwit?" she answered.

"Hey! Hey!" Alan Boothby replied, "that's no way to talk about your mother."

Patricia smiled, "You don't know do you?" she sneered.

"About what?"

"Mum, she's got a partner. A lover," she said, emphasizing the point.

Boothby smiled to himself. He didn't care what Anneline did with her life, and he had no issue knowing. If Patricia thought such news would impact him in any way, then she was wrong. Jealous was something he wasn't.

"Is that why you aren't at college?"

"Because of him?"

"Yes."

"No."

"Then why?" he asked.

She stared at him with narrowed eyes, trying to work out what angle to use to get what she wanted. Eventually, she broke her gaze, changing the subject. "I just need money."

He turned his back on her and looked out of a curtained window, watching a young couple hurriedly pushing a pram in the direction of the surgery door. He recognized them as one of his patients. He guessed they were coming to see him.

"I thought we've been through all this before. I'm not going to give you any more money, or drugs, or anything else," he said firmly. "It's time for you to grow up and go home."

She looked at him, her expression calm but inside she was seething. He had said the same thing many times before, but she sensed that now he was serious about not helping her. She decided to play the only card she had left. "Then, in that case, I'm going to the papers."

"To tell them what?" he goaded, "that you are an addict?"

She bristled at his response, finding herself at a loss for words. She had expected that he would just cave in and offer her something at least to get her out of the surgery. Now she wasn't so sure.

"You know that you are not the first daughter of a doctor to go off the rails," he said, "and frankly other than me, your mum, and your grandfather, no one cares. No one wants to hear your story. People have their own lives to lead…." As he spoke, she noted the words he had used. That he, along with the others, still cared for her. His earlier comments she took as a bluff, so she decided to stake her claim, to make her pitch, to get what she wanted. "I've got photos," she said.

"What?"
"I've got photos. Actually, it's a video."
"About what?" he queried.
"You…a while ago…giving me the drugs. I've got a video." She took a mobile phone from the back pocket of her faded jeans. "On this."
"You filmed me?" he asked.
"For insurance purposes," she smiled, waving the phone in her hand. He lunged towards her, attempting to grab the device but she was too quick for him, slapping him across the face as she jinked away from his grasp. The shock of the heat on his cheek made him stop. He held a hand to his jaw feeling more embarrassed than pained. He sat down at his table. She watched him cautiously before turning towards the door and unlocking it. "Do I get what I want, or do I use this?" she asked. He looked into her eyes, noting a small glint of victory. She waited for a few seconds sensing that he needed to process that he had lost the battle. "Well?" she asked, impatiently.
"No!" he replied, deciding that he would face the consequences of his previous misdemeanours if that's what it took to get her to see sense. He desperately wanted her to get straight, to get off the drugs, to go back to her original career pathway, to go home. The words of her grandfather were ringing in his ears and they haunted him.
He did care about her, she was his flesh and blood, but he knew that he needed to be cruel to be kind. He should have pushed back ages ago but from now on, he would.
"Do what you want," he said, challenging her, "but you are getting nothing from me." She looked at him feeling confused. The lack of sleep and her need to get high as soon as she could was making her feel uneasy and desperate. She glanced around the room, looking for something to use, to get him to see sense and give her what she wanted. She had expected it to be easy, but now a sense of panic rose within her. She noticed a few small instruments in a metal tray on top of a cabinet. Items for excising skin lesions and suturing wounds. He had started to turn his back on her, readying the computer on his desk for the day. His dismissive nature angered her, and she grabbed what appeared to be a scalpel of sorts from the top of the cabinet, sending the rest of the instruments crashing to the floor. She pushed the blade against his throat.
"I could kill you right now," she said, through gritted teeth, "and don't think I won't!"

Boothby felt the cold steel pressing against his tightening skin as she held his head to one side with her other hand. "Now give me what I want!" she shouted.

"No," he replied, hearing voices outside his office door coming closer. He guessed it was one of his surgery partners or possibly a concerned patient.

She moved the scalpel across his windpipe, a motion that suggested that she was about to cut him. He tried to speak but she pulled his hair, dragging his head onto his left shoulder. He waited to feel the slice and his throat open up with a flood of crimson, but it didn't come. Her hand began to shake and then as quickly as she attacked him, she dropped the scalpel onto the floor, opened his door, and ran. As he felt the skin around his throat where the scalpel had punched the flesh, he heard her shouting obscenities at him and the patients in the now crowded waiting room that she had to barge through to reach the exit.

"Are you alright, Doctor?" the receptionist asked, as she reached his open office door, a look of concern on her face.

"Yes, I'm fine, thank you, Sue," he replied, "sorry about all that."

"Can I get you anything?"

"No, it's alright. I'm just about to call the police," he replied, reaching for his phone.

CHAPTER 40

He had barely slept, finally getting into bed just before three-thirty in the morning. His mind was racing and before he fell into a restless sleep, he remembered where he had seen the logo. When he awoke less than three hours later, he knew that he would have to rearrange a few things. He quickly showered, much to June's surprise as she was the one who was usually first into the bathroom. Then after hurriedly dressing he followed up on a voice message he had left overnight for DCI Hammond, which he had made on his drive back home. Hammond had not yet heard the message so was grateful to be able to talk firsthand about it. Brierly shared the details about the burnt-out van and the assumption that it was the vehicle used to transport and dump the Millwright children. Hammond agreed with him that while it was still to be confirmed, the evidence seemed to suggest that Brierly was right. The issue of the body inside the van concerned Hammond particularly.

"So, you're convinced that the victim was murdered, that it wasn't a suicide?" he had asked.

"Yes, I'm pretty certain," Brierley had replied. "I'm sure Forensics will confirm it, but just looking at the evidence, the location, and the fact that the victim had been tied to the steering wheel, I'm almost a hundred percent. If the victim was going to commit suicide, there would be evidence of some kind relating to an ignition source. There was nothing to suggest that in the immediate vicinity."

"What about further along the road? Maybe the individual disposed of it elsewhere?" Hammond challenged.

"Well, I suppose that's possible but highly unlikely don't you think? And anyway, why lash yourself to the vehicle? Surely you would try and keep the option open to change your mind. Attaching oneself to the van rules that out. No, Sir, this was definitely a murder."

Hammond had concurred knowing however that if the Forensics team concluded differently then they would have an entirely different problem on their hands. They both agreed that finding out who the victim was, was of paramount importance and that time was of the essence. Also, the need to keep the Chief Superintendent abreast of developments was key to giving Brierly and his team air cover from any potential fallout. Brierly and his team needed to focus all their

energy solely on solving the crime, they didn't need distractions from outside or even internal influences.
"If you need more resources, I'll see what I can do," Hammond had offered, to Brierly's surprise. "But we need to sort this out quickly otherwise both our arses may be on the line."
After thanking Hammond for his support, Brierly had then called DS White who was already in the office and suggested a change of plan for the day. He asked him to ensure that when DC Track arrived back from collecting the cards from Trevor Owens' house that the entire team was to be ready for a briefing. "Around midday," he had said, acknowledging that the start time was later than their normally scheduled meeting. In the meantime, he requested that DC Proctor collect him from his house as soon as possible.
"Where are you off to, Sir?" White questioned.
"I remembered where I had seen that logo," Brierly had replied, "and I have worked out what those words are. Maybe you can check the address for me in the yellow pages." White knew that Brierly preferred looking at a paper trail than going online to verify detail, notwithstanding the speed at which information and data could be gotten via the web. "That's what we have IT experts for," he had said many times previously.
"Go ahead, Sir. I'm at my desk. I can do a quick Google check for you," White had said.
"I think it's something like Stotts Self Drive. At least that's what I believe they are called."
Brierly had waited patiently as he heard White type on his keyboard. While he did so, June had come into the kitchen where he had been standing with his phone firmly stuck to his ear. She had given him a peck on the cheek and offered him a pair of earphones to plug into his phone, but he had shaken his head while White had confirmed the name of the van hire business and had told him the address.
"Give the details to Proctor and tell him to get here straight away," Brierly had requested, outlining what he wanted the rest of the team to focus on, while he and Proctor were absent. As he waited for Proctor to arrive, June had told him that she was likely to be at work for the whole day. She had also mentioned that Warwick was asleep and was "staying at home to work on a uni assignment," which was why he had stayed up to watch the football the previous evening. In addition, she let him know that Simon was soon to leave for his

lectures. Brierly realized that having gone out into the night as he had, Warwick had still been watching TV when he left, and Simon had already gone to his room, leaving him unaware of what their schedule for the day was. By getting up earlier than normal, and already busy with his calls, the routine of seeing his sons around breakfast time and knowing what each was up to had been disrupted and he felt guilty about it. He kept the feeling to himself, not wanting to bother June, but while he waited for Proctor to arrive, he felt the pang again of getting that little bit older and of his family growing ever more apart. It was an uncomfortable feeling, but he knew it was part of life. He hadn't wanted to think about it too much as it was an unnecessary distraction, and he was glad when Proctor finally arrived. Before his DC had turned off the car's engine, Brierly was out of the front door, calling out his goodbyes, braving the dirty grey sky outside. The heavy rain-sodden clouds were threatening to turn the still-dry morning into another miserable wet afternoon. Brierly kept his coat on as he clambered into the passenger seat. With a quick, "good morning," he asked Proctor if he knew the way. "It's in the Sat nav, Sir," Proctor had answered, pointing to the dashboard.
"Good man," Brierly had replied, pleased to be on their way. "Good man."

"So can you tell us who borrowed it?" he asked.
They were sitting inside a small office, the sound of a radio mixing with the soft patter of rain tapping gently on the roof of the portacabin. It had taken them just over twenty minutes to get to the premises on Hawkeswood Road after crossing the river Itchen. Having introduced themselves, Brierly and Proctor were taken behind the small customer counter by a young woman in her mid-twenties. She was tall, about Brierly's height but it was obvious that she was enamoured with Proctor. Being six inches taller than them both, his good looks and Gloucestershire accent seemed to make her weak at the knees and she was constantly sidetracked when answering their questions. Brierly tried to be patient. Her name was Fiona Black, and she was the booking manager. Her straight dark hair was a testament to her surname. Brierly noticed that it was so straight and so dark as it tumbled halfway down her back. He surmised that it must have been recently dyed. He watched as she typed on her

keyboard, her nail extensions clacking on the keys. As he waited for her to find the information they sought, Brierly wondered why the young women of today seemed to want to adorn themselves with unnecessary additions to their bodies. Piercings, hair extensions, eyelash adornments, nails five centimetres long. Was there nothing that couldn't be added to? Then he noticed a few inches below her right ear, peeking out above the grey polo neck jumper she wore, was the top of a tattoo. It seemed to be the tip of a wing. Angel? Bird? It didn't matter, it just made him feel a little older. Strange in a way, he thought, given he very nearly had one done himself while he was in the navy, but he had resisted. Maybe he shouldn't have.

"Are you sure it was one of ours?" she asked, interrupting his thoughts, turning from the screen to look at him before smiling at Proctor.

"Yes, I'm confident," Brierly replied, referring back to his initial query where he had advised her that they did not have a registration number for the van. They were still hoping to get chassis and engine numbers at a later stage to check with the DVLA, but in the meantime needed her assistance to verify that the van was indeed one of their vehicles. "Look is there anyone else here who could help us?" he queried, hoping to find someone more interested in assisting him rather than flirting with his DC. Sensing his annoyance Fiona Black said, "Okay, okay, let me check again."

"Maybe Fiona, the van is not overdue yet," Proctor said, gently, belying his bulk, and sensing that a softer approach may be able to help smooth over his boss's impatience. "Perhaps you can look at all the vans that are out?" he added.

Turning to Brierly, Proctor said that perhaps the van had been hired out for an extended period so that it wasn't expected to be returned in the short term. Accordingly therefore Stott's wouldn't be looking for it and it may not appear in the returns listing for the current week. Brierly agreed that it was a good idea to widen the search. "How many vans like the one we are looking for do you have?" he asked her.

She tapped on her keyboard and then said, "We have thirty-six Fords of all different sizes. Twenty-five Peugeots and twenty Vauxhalls plus a few other makes and models."

"That's quite a lot," Brierly queried, "where do you keep them all? There's not enough space around here," he added, noting how small

the yard and the parking area next to the offices were.
"We have a facility at the airport where we keep most of the vans. It's where most of them are collected from and dropped off by our customers. This is more of an admin office. Where we do the billing and payment collections from."
"Customers don't pick them up from here then?" Proctor queried.
"On occasion they do, but generally not."
"Any luck?" Brierly asked, pointing at the computer terminal, the screen facing away from him. He was still trying to get her to concentrate.
"From what I can see, there are eleven Fords out at present. Four are those of the type you said you were looking for."
"Do you know who hired them?"
"Of course. Every borrower needs to provide credit card information before they can take out one of our vehicles, and on collection or delivery they need to…"
"Excuse me," Brierly interrupted, "delivery?"
"Yes. We also understand that not every borrower has the time to collect one of our vehicles, so we offer a service whereby we deliver to wherever the customer requires us to drop it off." Brierly noted the sales pitch and another smile in Proctor's direction. "We charge for that of course," she added. "Time and mileage."
"So, were any of the four of the type we are looking for, dropped off anywhere?"
Fiona Black checked her screen. "No," she answered, "they were all collected."
"Okay, so what about the driver or the person who hired the vans? Do you have that information for me?" She looked at the data in front of her, before typing a few more strokes and clicking on the wireless mouse sitting alongside the keyboard. "That's strange," she said eventually, a frown creasing her forehead, almost making her extended eyebrows touch in the middle.
"What's strange?" Brierly asked.
"There are two vans of the same model, hired one day apart, but both of them are only due back in exactly two weeks."
"So why is that unusual?"
"Because both were hired online by the same person, using our web portal and both were paid for using a pre-paid debit card, not a credit card."

"I thought you said the customer needs to pay with a …"
"I did, that's normally the case," she interrupted, "but it seems the customer also took out full insurance cover on both the vans, and on collection paid a thousand pounds cash for each to cover any excess should there be any damage. It looks like the bosses were happy with the arrangement."
"What about the license check? Was that undertaken?"
"It says here that a check was done, yes."
"On the day of collection?"
"I assume so, though I'm not sure how well it's done."
Brierly nodded. He guessed that as long as insurance was taken out in full and the excess was covered, the company didn't care if the driver damaged, stole, or even wrote off the van completely.
"What about CCTV, do you have any in your collections area?"
"No. We only have it in the shop here and where we keep our vans overnight."
"Okay," Brierly said, "In this case, do you have a name for us in relation to the two vehicles?"
"According to the data, it's Mr. Wayne Anderson."
She provided them with an address.

CHAPTER 41

Mary Owen was on her way to the hospital. She had managed to find what she had been looking for and had revealed to Sutton where her father had stored the cards and the offending bullets. He in turn, once satisfied that he was not going to contaminate them in any way, had placed each with gloved hands into individual plastic evidence bags and had sealed each. Then he recorded the details of where the evidence had been found in a case log, noting the date, time, and address. He had then requested that she sign the necessary paperwork, confirming the information noted on the outside of each bag, before handing over each to DS Track. After Track had left them to make his way back to Southampton Central, Sutton had told her that he planned to call DI Brierly later in the day to check if he wanted any additional assistance with the case. He had indicated to her that given his initial involvement in the matter he would happily oblige when he could, notwithstanding his own caseload was growing. Now as she drove, her mind turned to what had occurred the previous evening. She was mad at herself for not informing the police about the threats her father had told her of much earlier than she had. She was also angry because she hadn't told them everything. She agonized over whether her sister would still be alive if she had spoken up, or indeed whether her niece and nephew, those beautiful children, would not have suffered if she had. She was also annoyed at her brother-in-law. He was meant to protect his family and in her eyes, he hadn't. She knew that Tom was capable of carrying out his threat of revenge on whoever the offender was, but who was it and why would he even think it? And what did he mean by his comment, "this has to stop"? Did he know something that he wasn't telling her? She tried to rationalize his outbursts but failed. Maybe the answer was in the cards or the bullets? Or maybe there were other reasons behind her sister's killing? As the thoughts filled her head, she realized that she wasn't concentrating on the road. Suddenly the rear tail lights of the Sainsburys delivery truck directly ahead flashed several times and penetrated her glazed eyes. She instinctively slammed her foot down on the brake pedal, completely forgetting to change down her car's gears. At the last moment, she stamped on the clutch bringing her car to a screeching halt, inches from the back bumper of the bright orange vehicle which towered above her car. With a jolt she flew forward and then backward in her seat, the belt across her chest doing its job and preventing her from smashing into the windscreen. As her momentum ceased, her heart was racing, and she immediately burst into tears. She sat for countless seconds, her eyes stinging as the warm liquid ran down her cheeks. It was only the loud hooting of cars stuck behind her that brought to her attention that the truck ahead had moved on and was now a further hundred metres down the road. With a silent apology and a wave of her hand to acknowledge her error to the driver immediately behind her, she wiped her eyes, placed the car into gear, put on her indicator, and turned left at the very next road. When she was able to, she pulled into the car park of a small shopping centre. After turning off the engine she sat quietly for a few minutes, taking deep breaths and trying to stop her trembling hands. She had never smoked in her life, but she felt that if she did, she would gladly have had a cigarette there and then.

He had bandages around his head and on both hands. Some of the stitches hid behind gauze but on both sides of his face, there were others circled by yellow iodine and red mercurochrome. He looked worse than he probably felt but to see her father like this was almost too much to bear. After she had settled herself down, Mary had driven the rest of the way to the hospital intending to stay calm. The investigation of what had happened and who was behind it was now in the hands of the police. All the evidence she had access to was now where it needed to be. Her attention now was focused on getting her father home. He would stay with her until the case was resolved. Tom would move into her father's house in a couple of days so that it wasn't left empty and would remain there until he was able to return to his own place. She knew that whatever was ahead of them would not be pleasant or easy, and she had knots in her stomach just thinking about it. With the intention of not showing him how she was feeling, she had walked into the four-bed ward, noticing that he was the only patient there.

"They said I can go home now," Trevor Owen said impatiently. He was sitting on the side of the bed where he had been waiting. He was

fully dressed which surprised her given the bandages on his hands.
"The nurses helped me," he said, beginning to stand. As he slid off the bed, she noticed him wobble slightly and moved quickly to stop him from falling.
"I'm alright," he said angrily, "leave me alone. I can stand on my own two feet. I don't need any help." He pushed her away with his elbows. Taking a step back she noticed that the bandage across the front of his head was just above one eye. It seemed to her that it may be affecting his vision.
"Can you see out of that eye?" she asked, realizing that the bandage and lint were protecting the cuts and the stitches.
"Yes, of course, I can," he answered, "and I 'see' it's time to go."
She told him to wait where he was while she confirmed that he had already been discharged or whether there was additional paperwork to be completed.
"We are just waiting for some medicines to come up from the pharmacy," one of the on-duty nurses said to her. "Once we have received them, I'll bring them through to you and he can go after that."
Mary thanked her and made her way back to the ward.
He was standing at the window near his bed, looking down at the mass of cars that filled the hospital car park. Numerous others were being driven around trying to find a place to stop and offload patients and visitors. The constant movement looked like giant coloured Lego blocks moving into and out of oblongs of grey tarmac. Owen was glad that he wasn't experiencing the frustration of the drivers below him, before suddenly recalling how he had hit the child in the Asda store car park with his own vehicle. He hadn't heard how the little girl was doing and the police had not been in contact with him to ask him any further questions. It seemed that no news was good news, and he was hoping for the best for her recovery. How ironic, he thought, given he had just lost a daughter himself.
"We should be able to go soon," Mary said, interrupting the silence. Owen turned and gave her a half smile. It was the most she could expect from him and while it was better than his earlier protestations, she was extremely unhappy with him. He wasn't aware yet that she had been to his house and had given the police access, allowing them to take the birthday cards and the bullets that he had been hiding and ignoring for so long. She hoped that he would understand the

reasoning for her decision, and the urgency needed. She would tell him what she had done when they got back to her house.
"How long?" he asked, the irritation within him bubbling to the surface again.
"Look, dad, I don't know. It will take as long as it takes."
He mumbled a response under his breath, but she ignored it and sat down on the single chair next to his bed. He turned his back on her and stared out of the window again, thinking that he had made a good decision to move the gun from the place where he had hidden it originally.

"Cancer?"
"Yes," she replied, "and it looks like it's spread to your lymph nodes."
"But I've had no symptoms."
"Which is why we ask everyone to have a colonoscopy every few years or at least have the old FOBt test."
"My doctor never insisted."
"Any such test is always voluntary, but that's by the by now. What we need to do is get you into surgery asap."
"What does that mean exactly?"
She took out the results of the PET scan and the report that accompanied it.
"Well, you are at stage 3. With luck, if the tumours can be removed, we can limit the chemo. I'm not sure radiation is an option just yet, but we'll see how we go."
"And what happens if I don't have treatment?"
It was a question that nearly every patient asked, and as a doctor, it was the one that they never really wanted to answer. Unfortunately, it was often the most difficult question, and the prognosis was never as clear as people would like. "That depends, but generally between one and two years."
She let the answer sink in. Once she was sure that the patient had processed her comment, she said, "The good news however, is that with treatment, surgery, and chemotherapy the results are so much better nowadays. Survival rates of five years and longer are as high as seventy percent. Perhaps that puts your mind at rest somewhat?"

"Will I have to wear a bag?"
"An ileostomy bag?" the doctor queried.
"Whatever it's called, yes."
"It's possible, but let's not get too far ahead of ourselves. There is way too much water to go under the bridge before then. At stage 3 as I mentioned, the surgery and the chemo will hopefully be enough. If that's the case, even in a worst-case scenario, a bag will likely be temporary."
"That's good to hear," the patient replied a sense of relief in their voice. "It's just that I have a couple of things to resolve, and I need as much time as possible to finish them."

CHAPTER 42

"What do we know about him?" Brierly asked.
The team had come together, their sandwich and other fast-food papers along with plastic cutlery had been thrown away into the rubbish bins outside of the room. Brierly's distaste of food on working surfaces, where papers and files were being worked with was well known. The only exception he allowed was coffee and tea, water, or individual cans of soft drink. Beers for celebrations, after a case had been cracked, could be drunk at their local. His need to keep things tidy in the office was legendary. Brierly was seeking an update on Wayne Anderson before they moved on to the cemetery murders. With DS Track on his way back from Trevor Owens' house, they needed to address the immediate problem, the torching of the Stotts' van and the apparent murder of the van's sole occupant. The story of the torching had already made its way into the local paper, however with the agreement of the editor and the Chief Constable no mention had been made about the body found inside it. Brierly had called White as soon as he and Proctor had finished talking with Fiona Black, asking him to get Hughes to find out as much detail as he could on Anderson. That was three and a half hours earlier. Not much time to do any significant digging.
If she hadn't taken as long as she did before giving them a name, Brierly may have been able to give his team more time to do their work. As it was, Black was still enamoured with Proctor when the two of them left her, Brierly rolling his eyes as she tried to slip his DC her phone number. Brierly sensed that time was against them, the press would not be as accommodating for long. So far they had played the game, however, the friendship could be stretched only so far before it broke. They had to find something with which to arm the Chief Constable and Brierly needed the answers quickly.
"Not much, Sir," DC Hughes replied in response to the question. "It appears from the call I had with the University, that Anderson is a genuine student, and he lives on campus in residence. He is originally from Kesgrave on the eastern edge of Ipswich and as far as I can establish, he's never been in trouble with the police. He's not on any d-base at all."
"Does he have a family?"

"His parents are still alive, yes, Sir. They live in Bury St Edmunds where his father works at the Greene King brewery. He has a sister who is a bit older than him. She's married and lives with her husband in Glasgow."
"What about friends, girlfriends, acquaintances?"
Hughes looked at his notes, indicating that he had only been given a limited amount of time to make his inquiries and to search the various in-house tools and programs at his disposal. What he had found wasn't particularly helpful. "Not got that far, Sir. The only thing I have been able to establish is that he plays football for one of the university teams at Eastleigh."
"Okay, well see if you can find out anything else about him. We need to know his movements last night. Who he was with, where he went…everything! DS White?"
"Sir."
"While DC Hughes is looking deeper into Anderson's background, I think we should bring him in for a chat anyway. Let's see what he has to say for himself," Brierly declared. "DS Proctor, once we are finished here, I want you to go with Sergeant White and bring Anderson in for questioning." White turned to look at Brierly, giving him a thumbs up. They might have received the break they needed, but everyone knew that they would need to proceed with caution. The step being followed in line with standard procedure was to ask Anderson "to have a chat." The man was not being arrested, as while he was under suspicion, they still needed more evidence before he could be charged with anything. At least things were moving in the right direction, however, the challenge they faced was how to manage the various pieces of evidence they needed to collect. The team was being stretched and as things gathered momentum, there was potential for mistakes to be made. Not good for anyone, especially if such errors became public. It would be a very career-limiting situation if the Chief Constable was embarrassed in any way. Relationships with the press were always fragile and relied a lot on goodwill, with the occasional threat if needed. So far that wasn't necessary. Brierly decided to move the conversation on.
"DC Hughes, I know I sprang the Anderson research on you, but do you have any update on Crossley or the other unknown victim? Anything at all?"
"Nothing as yet Sir, but about the latter I have been in touch with

our missing persons unit to trawl through their database. The pathology report gave us some more detail about the man's approximate age, and his overall health before his death. We are using that to….."
"Health?" Brierly queried, interrupting Hughes' flow.
"Yes. It seems he had emphysema, heart disease, and his liver was well on its way to packing up."
"A smoker and a drinker?"
"The report from Doctor Atkins makes that conclusion, yes, Sir."
"Anything else?" Brierly queried.
"Doctor Atkins arranged for some DNA samples to be taken. Unfortunately, it appears as though the only ones available so far were those of the dead man. They've been sent for analysis to our lab boys to check if they can find a match on their dbase anywhere. It's still a long shot as we've got little else to go on at this stage, the flyers and the appeal we put out have produced nothing at all, even those living on the streets couldn't help us."
"Couldn't or wouldn't?"
"Take your pick, Sir."
White smiled at Hughes' response. Everyone on the team knew the answer to the question. The police were *persona non grata* as far as those who used the city shelters were concerned. They always were, and always would be.
"And Crossley, what about him?" Brierly asked.
"Still nothing, Sir. His mother has gone back up north. Until the body is released, they can't hold a funeral and as she had to get back to work there is nothing for her to do but wait."
"The poor woman," White said under his breath, with which Brierly concurred.
"One other thing, Sir," Hughes began.
"Yes?"
"I've asked the local NCA member to see if they have any information about Crossley. Whether he was on their radar in any way."
"I would doubt that DC Hughes," Brierly replied, "he was hardly Mr. Big around here."
"I know Sir," Hughes said, looking a little unhappy at Brierly's putdown. "I thought they may be able to shed some light on who he may have been dealing with. His supplier and his clients."

Noticing his DC's tone, Brierly apologized for his comment and thanked Hughes for using some initiative. The apology was accepted with a smile. As Brierly was about to ask another question, DC Track entered the room, slightly out of breath. It appeared as though he had been running. "Sorry I'm late, Sir," he said, "but the traffic in the city was ridiculously busy. I couldn't find a spot to park in all the usual places, so I had to carry the stuff from the Owens' all the way from the Dunhelm parking lot. Even our lot outside the building is full. What's worse is that I've only got two hours," he complained.
"It's the league cup game tonight, Man U. That's why it's so busy around town," White said, "Kick off at seven. No wonder!"
Brierly had forgotten that his beloved Saints were hosting the current Premier League leaders. Normally he would have hoped to use his season ticket to attend the game but with everything on his plate, it was out of the question. He was surprised that neither of his sons had asked to use it. Obviously, they had other things to do. It was then that he noticed the damp patches on Track's jacket shoulders. "Is it raining again?" he asked. The room they were sitting in was windowless. It was used frequently by investigating teams when cases required attention, twenty-four by seven. With no awareness of the changing light outside, the teams and individuals were able to work for longer hours without the mind suggesting that it was time to sleep. It was akin to preventing jetlag by fooling the brain as to what time of the day it was. Brierly had anticipated that with things starting to move, his team would be spending most of their time there.
"Yes, Sir," Track answered. "It's actually coming down pretty hard. Not to mention that it's bloody cold as well."
Brierly shivered involuntarily despite the warmth of the room. He sat hunched up in his chair as if he was cold. His body was bent into the gnomelike position that had earned him his nickname.
"I dropped off the evidence bags with the items that DI Sutton and I collected, downstairs, Sir," Track continued. "I'm assuming you'll want to have a look at them as soon as possible?"
"Yes, I will. Probably once we've finished here. Thank you, DS Track."
"No problem, Sir."
"Good. Well now that you are back, once you've been able to sort out your parking arrangements, I'd like you to help DC Hughes. Could you get hold of Doctor Atkins and ask her when she expects

to give us something, anything, about last night's murder victim? Sex, age, anything she can. There has to be some link between the poor soul and the Millwright murders."
"Maybe the items that DC Track has brought back will shed some light on what's going on?" White replied.
"Perhaps. I'll have a look at them while you and DC Proctor bring in Anderson. I'm looking forward to having a chat with him," Brierly answered. "Meanwhile there are a couple of other things I need to check. I have a feeling that I'm missing something though I'm buggered if I know what it is."

CHAPTER 43

She was sitting at her desk having left him at her house once he was settled and she had been able to leave him alone. The kitchen window had been replaced by the time she had arrived home from her visit to his house and brought him from the hospital. Tom had waited for them, which was a relief before he had to depart himself for Rownham. He had told her that he was feeling anxious about what had happened the previous evening and he hadn't wanted to leave them. However, he had explained that his subcontractors were seeking payment for the work they had done for him to date, and because he had been away from the site for a few days they had been getting nervous about it. He also mentioned that the Forensics team had completed their work and that they could use the kitchen once again. The garden and the path alongside the house had been searched for evidence and he had been told that everything the police had been able to find, which was very little it appeared, had been taken, and was no longer off-limits. When she walked with him into the kitchen to inspect the new window, she noticed that the offending projectile thrown through the old one had been removed from the kitchen floor, but she noticed the scars and scratches that it had left behind on the countertop as well as on the tiled floor.

Now, as she sat staring at her computer screen, she didn't want to think about it anymore, however, she found that she couldn't concentrate on what she was supposed to be doing. Arriving at the office just before lunchtime had thrown her schedule out, making her feel uneasy. Although her boss had been understanding, she had missed several early morning meetings and with the added pressure of being absent for a couple of days, she found that she was becoming overwhelmed. The stress, the fear, and her concern about what could still happen made her more agitated. The fact that she still couldn't bury her sister or Gretchen's children and had not yet told the police everything she knew made matters worse. It was a dilemma that she would have been able to handle under normal circumstances, but the promise she had made to her father weighed heavily on her.

Earlier, as she had arrived at her office, she had sat down and was starting up her computer when she received a call from one of the design team on the project she was managing. He had wanted to make a change to the project timeline. After listening to his excuse and realizing the implications of what he had told her, she shouted at him with unrestrained anger. Cost blowouts, time delays, and contractual penalties were the likely outcomes of his suggested amendments. These were likely to cause her to miss her own KPIs and affect her standing, and deemed efficiency within the business, not to mention any financial bonus that may come her way. Normally she would have been more philosophical and would have looked to arrange a variation of the project with the client to compensate for the changes. That was the normal approach. However, with everything that she had endured recently, she blew the matter out of all proportion. It was all a bit too much for the caller who had slammed the phone down in her ear causing her to break into tears. Her normally strong exterior was shattered into a million pieces, and she had wept openly for several minutes before finally composing herself as her phone rang again. With the office door being closed, and no one to hear her crying, she was able to hide her emotions as she spoke calmly to the caller.

Recognizing the voice on the other end of the line she said, "Oh, hello Inspector, how can I help you?"

"I was wondering, Ms. Owen if you could spare me a bit of your time?" Brierly asked. "I've just been reviewing the details on those cards that DC Track and DI Sutton collected from you this morning and I have a few questions. Are you able to come into the station tomorrow?"

Mary asked him if it was possible to have the meeting the day after, as she had so much to do, her diary was full, and she also needed to ensure that her father was not left on his own for too long. "I would have come after work tomorrow," she said, "but that might mean that I only get home very late, and I'm concerned that dad will be on his own, way after dark. I'm still worried that someone may come back to the house, and if he's on his own…"

"Yes, I can understand that. What about Mr. Millwright? Won't he be home?"

"Tom? No, he's working on his own business projects. A bit like me, he's trying to catch up after all that has happened. He'll be home much later than I will."

"I see," Brierly said, wondering how quickly things change. Perhaps Millwright was able to move on more speedily than Brierly himself

would have been able to if his family had been murdered as recently as Millwright's had. Maybe keeping busy was a personal defence mechanism, he thought. Maybe it was how some people managed at a time like this. Maybe….?
"Very well, but just so you know," he continued, "my concern is that we have to find whoever murdered Mr. Millwright's family and who attacked you before they strike again. Time is against all of us, and I urgently need your help to resolve this matter."
"You have that Inspector, in spades!"
"Good. I look forward to seeing you down here at the station, the day after tomorrow. Can we make it at nine am?"
"Yes, that will be fine," she answered.
After she had put down the phone she wiped her face with a tissue. A box, nearly empty, sat on one side of the desk. Grabbing another, she blew her nose and then threw it into the plastic paper basket already half full under her desk. Sitting back in her chair she took a deep breath trying to calm herself. What she had told Brierly was true. She was concerned for her father, but she was also concerned for herself. Tom staying at the house with them for a while was a comfort. She knew that it couldn't last however and that he would eventually move back home once he was allowed to. She wasn't sure what Brierly wanted to talk to her about specifically, but whatever it was she hoped that he was getting closer to an answer.

She tried to recall what had happened, but she still wasn't sure if she had seen it or whether it was a dream. She was trying to stay calm but she felt that everything around her was turning upside down and inside out. It was like a trip, but she knew that this time it was for real. It had happened before she had been able to take them. Was it really last night she thought? The darkness she had wandered through for hours had slowly turned to a grey damp day. She was only partially awake now and it was well after midday. The thick, muddy clouds had been traversing the sky when she opened her eyes for the first time. The breeze was slow but cruel and the trees above her bent and swayed. The thin canopy had given her some protection from the occasional raindrops that the sky ejected after she had fallen asleep. She had been grateful to find the spot. She used it as often as she could. It was a spot known by a few who preferred to stay away from

the shelters, and she used it whenever she could. Sometimes others who shared the streets with her or were trying to hide could be found there. She had been lucky to find it unoccupied this time.
After she had escaped the surgery, she had decided to try and keep away from the spots where she would normally hang out. She had disappeared into the bowels of the city, finally finding a charity bin to raid. With a discarded jacket and wearing a second pair of tracksuit bottoms she had found there, she had managed to stay warm during the day, eventually eating a cold tin of beans and some luncheon meat that she had shoplifted from a Seven-Eleven. She had expected her father to contact the police, but it seemed he hadn't. From those she knew from the street, there was no word that anyone was looking for her. Relieved, she had hidden in a squat until the 'itch' had come back and she needed to fulfill it. Without money, she had used her knowledge of the city, and eventually, she had been able to score, having found herself a new dealer. He had been generous, giving her two packets, but only after she had fucked him. It was a small price to pay she thought, given that she needed the hit. It was while she was heading back to the park that abutted the cemetery to 'feel the kick' and then rest that she had seen the incident. The van had been parked in an unusual spot, just off the road and hidden by the trees that surrounded the graveyard. At first, she guessed that it was there being used by lovers and despite the cold she had decided to watch and wait, her curiosity getting the better of her. Standing behind the trunk of a tree approximately twenty yards away and at an angle she had a clear view of the passenger door. However, from her vantage point, she had only been able to view a silhouette of the person in the driver's seat. As a result, she had been unable, initially, to see if the driver was male or female. Within minutes of her stopping to observe what was going on a figure had approached from the front of the van and had tapped on the driver's-side window. After a brief conversation, the individual had run around the front again and climbed into the passenger's seat. Another drug deal she had thought, not the tryst that she had originally imagined. She waited for a minute or so expecting the passenger to exit once the deal had been done, but there was no movement. Nothing. Feeling the cold and the need to ingest what she had earned with her body, she decided to move on when she saw the passenger door suddenly open. The passenger was just about to get out of their seat, their back to the driver when

suddenly she saw the glint of what she thought was a knife but then realized that it was a hammer. A blow struck the passenger from behind, the thud could be heard from where she stood. The crack against the skull and the cry that followed made her skin crawl. In horror she saw the passenger crumple face down to the ground, then try and stand, reaching for the side of the van and the door to regain their balance. As she watched, unsure what to do, she noticed the driver climb from their seat, and walk around the side towards the back of the van, where she lost sight of them for a few seconds. The driver then appeared from the shadows and approached the still-dazed passenger from behind, smashing a second and third blow with the hammer into the skull. Throwing the hammer into the footwell of the passenger seat, the driver then lifted the now unconscious body into the van, then gently closed the door. Patricia Boothby gaped at the scene, staring as the driver took out what she concluded was a mobile phone from a pocket and turned on the torch function. The driver scanned the ground quickly looking for anything that could have fallen onto the dirt floor. She watched as a shoe scuffed the area removing imprints made in the soil. It was an obvious attempt the make the immediate area appear normal. In the few seconds that the light shone, her jaw dropped and a hand flew to her mouth suppressing a scream. The silhouette she had observed earlier had morphed into a face. The beam of the dying torch briefly lit the driver's features. It was a face that she had seen many times.
Now in the cold of the early afternoon, her nerves were jangling as she looked upwards from where she lay. The cold had woken her, but the dream was a nightmare and the face within it haunted her. Had her mind been playing tricks? She sat up stiffly. She was unsure what to do. Then she smiled. It was an opportunity too good to miss. She would use what she had seen, to her advantage.

There were still two branches of the tree that needed trimming. One had been partially removed but was still alive. The other had somehow continued way beyond its years. Having received the unwelcome news, both would now need addressing before the task became too difficult. Time had never been a factor before, but now things had changed.

CHAPTER 44

"So, what can you tell me about this?" he asked, pointing at an A4 page that showed the order details.
"I don't know what you are talking about."
The four of them were sitting in an interview room. It was now just after seven thirty in the evening and they had only just started the conversation. It had taken a while to find an available Duty Solicitor, but eventually, Craig Julies agreed to support Wayne Anderson in the discussion with Brierly and DS White.
After Anderson had been tracked down at his university residence, he had agreed to accompany White and Proctor to the police station. Having been advised that he wasn't under arrest but was under suspicion, it was suggested to him that it was in his best interest to cooperate with the police as they conducted their inquiries. He had gladly agreed. Now he wasn't so sure. The sight of the machine recording their conversation, an old-fashioned cassette tape whirring around on a pair of spindles unnerved him.
Brierly pointed at the single page that lay on the table separating them, Anderson and Julies on one side, the two detectives on the other. He noticed the beads of sweat that were forming on Anderson's brow.
"So, you had nothing to do with this?" Brierly asked.
"I don't even know what it is," Anderson replied.
Brierly smiled. "Okay, Mr. Anderson," he answered, "let me explain it to you. This," he pointed towards the page, "is an order confirmation, and it is from a company that hires out transit vans."
"So?"
"Well, it's in your name. Could you tell me why?"
"I don't know," Anderson responded.
"You don't know?"
"Look Inspector," Julies chimed in. "If my client indicates that he doesn't know the reason why his name is on this order, then perhaps you need to consider that what he is saying is indeed the truth."
Brierly stared at the DS. He was a man in his late forties, with deep green eyes and a round face, almost moon shaped. With a large nose that resembled a beak, he also wore a bushy moustache reminiscent of the 1970s. He was bald except for hair around the back of his head

that had been shaved down to its roots. A portly man of medium height but one who was very well-dressed. Neat dark blue suit, a blue tie, and a crisp white shirt that seemed to Brierly had only been put on a few minutes before. He wore highly polished black leather shoes that reflected the overhead light whenever he crossed his legs and he spoke with an accent that suggested the Midlands.

"Very well, Mr. Julies, I'll park that for the moment."

"And by the way, Inspector," Julies interrupted for the second time, "I have already advised Mr. Anderson that if he feels he does not wish to answer any questions, then he is not under any obligation to do so, given he has not been charged with anything at this point."

"Noted," Brierly answered, condescendingly, much to Julies' annoyance.

Wayne Anderson was uncomfortable with the exchange and decided that he wanted to get the interview over with as soon as possible, saying, "I have nothing to hide Inspector, so ask me whatever you want, and I'll try and answer whatever I can. However, let me assure you that I never ordered the vehicle you are referring to. I had no need to."

"Let's take a step back then, shall we, Mr. Anderson?" Brierly continued, tapping White with his leg underneath the table, a pre-planned strategic move they often used to bring him into the discussion. It was the good cop, bad cop tactic, whereby each played their respective roles. Today White was the good guy. He listened while Brierly continued his questioning, ready to jump in when necessary.

"We have in front of us, Mr. Anderson, and for the benefit of the tape recording, it is a single-page online order form. It has been completed with your name, address, and driver's license number for the hire of a Ford Transit van from Stotts Self Drive in Hawkeswood Road, Southampton. How can that be Sir?"

"As I told you before, Inspector, I have no idea. And I repeat, I can assure you that it wasn't me who hired that van."

"I find that hard to believe, Mr. Anderson," Brierly continued. "You'll need to do better than that."

"But I.."

"Why did you kill them? Why?!"

"Sorry?"

"I'm sure you know that it's 30 plus for murder!" Brierly continued,

his voice rising much to Julies' annoyance.
"What?" Anderson queried, his body beginning to shake, "What the fu..?"
"Who was it!?" Brierly shouted, cutting Anderson off mid-sentence.
"Inspector!" Julies said angrily. "Please! Can't you see my client is distressed? Can't you accept that he does not know anything about the matter? Isn't it obvious?"
"No, Mr. Julies, nothing is obvious," Brierly answered. "I'm dealing with the facts as presented to me and unless your client can convince me otherwise about this document, I'll be charging him with murder." Brierly knew that his comment was a gamble. While they had the details from the van hire company, what was still missing as far as Brierly was concerned about Anderson, was a motive. So far, they had been unable to find a link between the student and the Millwright family and it bothered him, despite the information they had garnered so far. Brierly was hoping therefore that something would come from the interview. While his team still searched for clues and tried to establish Andersons' movements the preceding few days, the opportunity to question the man directly was too good to miss. The direct approach had the potential to provide them with all the answers they needed. The issue they faced was whether the man would crack or not.
Julies considered Brierly's last statement and responded by saying, "I'd like to ask for a few minutes break while I talk with my client, Inspector. Please give us that courtesy."
Brierly agreed, beginning to get a little concerned about his own behaviour during the questioning. He had conducted many such interviews in the past and always prided himself on keeping calm and reading the body language of those he was interviewing. When he did that, he was usually able to spot the lie, the untruth, the game being played. He knew that his outburst related to the need to make progress on the cases they were working on. He sensed that not getting traction was affecting his judgement. Stress was always there, with him and with his team. Somedays were worse than others, but right now he needed answers and he needed them quickly. Many people were depending on him, and he was feeling the pressure. It was at times like these that he needed his hobby, his interest in the cosmos and the stars. How ironic he thought that he needed such a circuit breaker to ease his mind, to free it up for a while, and to keep

him grounded. Unfortunately, because he was still at the police station much later in the evening than he would have liked, he knew that tonight he would have no time to indulge. Even less time to work on understanding the app that now occasionally caused his phone to buzz! It frustrated him. Ever since Warwick had loaded it onto his phone, he had wanted to use it, learn more about it, and do practical things with it. His hobby helped him relax, helped him think. Unfortunately, the weather wasn't helping his mood either and until there was a break in the cloud cover sitting over the south of the country, he wouldn't be able to see anything of significance anyway. It was annoying and frustrating on so many levels.

They had left Julies with Anderson and he waited with White outside the interview room, having given the pair fifteen minutes to talk. With a cup of tea that he had been able to source from the kitchen just up the passageway, Brierly apologized to his Sergeant for his behaviour through sips of the scalding liquid. "I understand, Jim," White said in response. Being colleagues and friends, White was able to use the diminutive of Brierly's Christian name, as he sensed it was the right time to do so. He wanted his boss to know that he concurred with him on the need to take advantage of the breakthrough they had made in at least one of the cases they were running.

"Thanks, Barry," Brierly replied, "Let's hope that we're not barking up the wrong tree here. Anderson seems quite convincing. What do you think?"

Considering his answer for a few seconds, White said, "It's possible that he's telling the truth, but we have a couple of things up our sleeve, so let's see how he handles them. We'll know pretty quickly if he's on the level or not."

Brierly agreed, telling White to take the lead when they re-entered the room. Then at the right time, with a tap on the knee from DS White, Brierly would take over again.

"Thank you for the break, Inspector," Julies said, once they had retaken their seats. "My client and I have had a look at this document while you were out," the DS picked up the A4 page that was still lying on the table, "and we think we have the answer."

"That's good to hear," White said, beginning to play his role, "why don't you enlighten us?" he continued, sarcastically.
Julies allowed Anderson to explain. The student cleared his throat, then looking Brierly straight in the eye said, "I admit that the details on the form are mine, but I can assure you, as I told you earlier. I did not order any van."
"And you had nothing to do with the torching of it?" White said cynically, but calmly.
"Torching?"
"Or of killing those children?"
"Children?" Anderson questioned, clearly taken aback by the statement. It was the first time anything along the lines of murder had been raised.
"Yes," White continued. "Those innocent kids."
With a plea of desperation in his eyes, Anderson raised his hands to both sides of his head, holding the palms over his ears as if refusing to listen to anything further they had to say. Brierly stepped in, tapping White under the table but wanting to hear how Anderson was going to respond to White's proposition. He had watched how the questions, like his own, had affected their prime suspect but was now ninety-nine percent convinced that they had the wrong man. He still wanted to test him a little further however before coming to a final conclusion. He knew that suspects could often be good actors as well as good killers.
"Mr. Anderson, Mr. Anderson," he said quietly, "you indicated that you had an answer for us. If you believe that what we have questioned you on is incorrect, then now is your chance to put the record straight. Tell us what you think has occurred here."
The young student rubbed his eyes, and tears of frustration fell onto his cheeks before disappearing into the folds of a handkerchief that he had taken from his jeans pocket.
"I think somebody stole my identity," he said.
"So, it's as simple as that is it?" Brierly questioned.
"Yes."
"And how and when did this happen?"
"I have no idea."
"And you expect us to believe it?"
"Yes, because it's the only explanation."
Brierly looked up at the clock above the only door to the room. It

was perched directly behind Anderson and Julies. An old-fashioned analogue clock with a white face and black numbers. The second hand slowly moved from one digit to the next with an inaudible click. It was now 8:45 pm. "You see that clock behind you, Mr. Anderson?" Both men opposite him turned to see where Brierly was pointing. "You could be out of here by 9 pm if you can convince me why I should believe you. Alternatively, we could be here until tomorrow morning. I'll let you decide what you want to do."
"Inspector, I must ...," Julies began.
Cutting him off, Brierly said, "With respect Mr. Julies, can I add something else before your client responds?"
With a sigh, the DS indicated that Brierly could continue.
"Before you reply Mr. Anderson, I'd like you to think long and hard about what I am about to say," Brierly stated ominously, leaving a few seconds of silence before continuing. "While my Sergeant and DC Proctor were on their way to collect you, our IT team has been out to Stott's and were able to trace the IP address from where the van was ordered. The actual computer that was used to make the transaction." Though Brierly had no idea what IP addresses meant technically, nor indeed how to trace them, the internal 'IT geeks' had briefed him on their findings. It was a vital piece of information and something to potentially break open the case.
"I'm not with you."
"It was your computer. The one I saw you using at the shelter a few days ago."
Anderson was incredulous and looked at Julies who had stopped writing his notes. He then turned to face Brierly and White, looking from one to the other, noting that both were waiting for his reply. Eventually, he said, "That just proves my point, Inspector."
"What does?"
"That someone stole my identity."
"And how have you come to that conclusion?" White asked.
"Because I'm not the only one that uses that machine. It's a shared facility for all staff. I only work there a couple of days a week as you know."
Brierly had already anticipated what Anderson was now suggesting. He had checked with the IT team for the specific date that the order for the van was placed. In addition, while Anderson was being brought in, he had spoken with Janie Fenchurch to check whether

the student had been working on that day and at the time the transaction was concluded. Fenchurch had confirmed as much without questioning why Brierly needed the information. He relayed the same details to the student, who leaned over to Julies and whispered into his council's ear. Julies nodded and with a smile said, "Inspector, my client is suggesting that he wants to leave. You mentioned to him earlier that he was not under arrest, but solely here for questioning. Am I correct?"

"Yes."

"My client has advised me that what you have set out so far is nothing but a diatribe of circumstantial evidence and as he has already told you, he had nothing to do with this van you are suggesting he rented. So can we go now, please? My client has nothing further to add."

Brierly bristled at Julies' comment but felt it best to remain calm at this stage of proceedings. "Before I let that happen, I think it's best if your client gives me a better reason as to why I should believe him before he goes," he answered. "From what I have heard so far, I think I have enough evidence to charge him, and I may well do it unless he can give me something else. There are too many elements linking him to the van for us not to conclude his involvement." He looked directly into Anderson's eyes as he spoke, the stare making the student very uncomfortable. In response and slightly wide-eyed, the student said, "Inspector Brierly, do you know how many people use that computer at the shelter?"

"No, tell me."

"Upwards of ten people."

"And your point is?"

"I think one of those people placed the order."

"With your details? Using your driving license? Come off it!"

"It's the only explanation," Anderson replied, tears beginning to well up in his eyes again. Brierly began to get a sinking feeling in his stomach. Perhaps Anderson wasn't a good actor? Perhaps his appeal for understanding his position was genuine.

"Can you tell me what you think happened then?"

Anderson reached into his jacket and pulled out a thin wallet. He then removed his driver's license and dropped it onto the table, the plastic coming to rest on top of the A4 sheet. "My wallet is always in my jacket pocket. When I go to the toilet, have lunch, or need to talk

to someone at the shelter, I don't always log out of the system, especially if there is no one else around who wanted to use the machine. As you may have seen, there are a couple of computers in the shelter."
"Go on."
"I think someone found my wallet, got onto the machine, and used my license details to make it look like it was me who placed that order."
"Conveniently?" Brierly said.
"It's the only explanation. The admin office in the shelter often has just one or two people there at times, especially if Janie or Dennis are busy with the 'guests'."
"And you're telling me that at some point while you were away from the desk, someone working there has tried to frame you?"
"A worker, a volunteer, or even a guest, yes! If they knew what they were doing, it's possible they could have done it in just a few minutes. While I was away from the desk."
Brierly sighed. He was getting more concerned. What appeared to be cut and dried originally now looked like it was unravelling at a rate of knots. He had hoped for a quick confession or at least something more concrete, a mistake perhaps, that would have allowed him to hold Anderson in custody. That would have given them more time to find enough evidence to have him charged; DNA at the Millwright home or on the brick that could be matched back to the student. Now he wasn't so sure. The lack of a motive was also still a concern, though he knew that not every murderer had one. Sometimes, people had other issues. Mental problems, previous abuse, or the use of drugs, all of which could affect their behaviour. In some cases however a killer was just evil and liked the thrill of the chase. As Brierly considered the next steps, he noticed that those across the table, along with White, were waiting for him to respond to Anderson's utterances.
Looking at the DS he reluctantly said, "Your client is free to go, Mr. Julies." Then addressing the young student who had expelled an audible cry of relief at hearing Brierly's words, he added, "Thank you for your cooperation, Mr. Anderson. I apologize for any inconvenience we may have caused you, though I must warn you that we may need to speak with you again should further information become available to us."

Anderson and Julies rose from their chairs in unison. White turned off the recording device and walked out of the interview room with them, leaving the door ajar. Brierly stayed behind, remaining seated, thinking while staring at the order form still lying on the table. A few minutes later, White reappeared at the door, stopping at the threshold and leant against the door frame.
"Time to go home, Jim?"
Brierly looked up, "At least it wasn't a total failure," he reflected.
"How do you mean?"
"If it wasn't Anderson who ordered that van, then whoever killed those kids, and left us with our burnt victim, must be someone at the shelter. Our job now is to find out why and more particularly, who!"

CHAPTER 45

Carol was extremely upset with him. She couldn't understand how he could let things lie, why he hadn't had her arrested.
"Because she's my daughter," he said, "and despite what you may think, it's better for her to get help, rather than a custodial sentence."
"But she tried to kill you, stabbed you in the bloody neck, for God's sake!"
"Don't I know that?" Alan Boothby replied, feeling the unhealed scar on his throat and remembering the embarrassment he had suffered when the staff realized who his assailant was. It was compounded by the inquiries from his colleagues. Even as the stitches were being inserted by his nurse they wanted to know more than he was prepared to answer. The question of the staff and his colleague's security was the first subject for discussion at the practice meeting earlier in the day. Boothby knew though that if Patricia had really intended to do him harm, she could have pierced a jugular vein or even worse stuck the scalpel straight into his esophageal veins potentially killing him. On that basis alone he wanted to defend her despite Carol's obvious objections. They were sitting at the dining room table having dinner where only a few days before she had been humiliated by her father-in-law and where her husband had lied to her. She had not forgiven him for that and was less than impressed with his reaction to Patricia's attack.
"So, what are you going to do about it? Have you told Anneline?"
"Nothing and no," he answered.
"Why not?"
"Because!" was his simple answer.
"Because what? Because you're afraid you failed her? Because you left her mother for me, and you feel guilty about it? Because your father still holds you accountable for her…."
"Enough!" he shouted. "Would you please just stop?" He closed his eyes tightly, clenching his jaw and turning his hands into fists. He took deep breaths trying to tame his reactions. Carol waited for him, the silence between them uncomfortable. Eventually, he answered her questions. "She's ill. She needs help and more importantly, she's *my* daughter."
"But you told me that she doesn't want any help," she retorted.

"Yes, I did."
"So how can you help her if she refuses to accept it? If she doesn't want to be rehabilitated?"
"You keep trying," he answered, "it's what parents do."
Carol looked at him, feeling the jibe. With no children of her own, her view on parenting was quite simple. Direct and almost cold. It was a trait that he had only become aware of later on in their relationship. Their affair had been passionate, full of promise, regular liaisons which compensated for the lack of intimacy with Anneline. When he finally left his wife to move in with Carol, he justified the breakdown on the basis that Anneline had rejected him. That they were a couple in name only and he felt that he was nothing more than an income provider. Anneline left the workforce when Patricia was born and never went back unless she absolutely needed to. He on the other hand found himself working longer and longer hours, staying away from home as much as he could. He wasn't sure how much of a father he was, but while he was in the home, he did all he could for his daughter, though Anneline made it clear to him that it wasn't ever going to be enough. When he met Carol on a golfing trip, a game he now no longer played, but she still did, he realized very quickly what she offered him. Laughter, light, fun, desire, everything that was missing in his marriage. Because he had hidden behind the façade of a happy life for so long, when he walked out of the home for the last time, he surprised everyone. His family, friends, and work colleagues were stunned, and many were disappointed, especially his parents. They made him feel guilty and despite trying to shake off the shackles, he had never been able to lose them completely. He was racked with guilt at times, especially when alone, and it was this feeling that continued to gnaw at his soul.
"I'm sorry," he said, noticing how Carol had reacted to his less-than-subtle dig at her. Strangely, however, he felt that he shouldn't have apologized at all. He did not need to and didn't think one was warranted. He realized that he needed to be honest with himself, to be true to his feelings. Perhaps their relationship wasn't as strong as he thought it was. She accepted his apology somewhat reluctantly and began to collect the empty plates, cutlery, and cups from the table. He watched her as she walked away. He remained seated. Her back to him he noticed a knife and fork that she had missed, still on the table. It was a carving knife, roughly eight inches long that he had used to

slice the pork she had cooked for dinner. He picked it up and as he was about to call her, he stifled the words, swallowing them. With the knife in his hand, he aimed to throw it at her back, to send it right between the shoulders, but he hesitated. Before he went any further, the front doorbell rang, and he lowered his arms. She turned to speak to him, her hands full and she asked him to see who had rung the bell. After putting the knife back on the table, he strode to the door, opening it slowly. Standing on the threshold was the last person he expected to see.

CHAPTER 46

Brierly still couldn't understand how the app worked. He had decided to read through the manual but before he could, he had to seek help from Simon to print the document out for him. Fortunately, his eldest son had been at home and had enough paper in the printer in his bedroom to be able to oblige. The document was a little heavy going, but Brierly persisted with it, giving June the chance to work on a new fund-raising exercise for her local CND branch.

It was quiet throughout the house; particularly given Warwick was out for the evening. Being the loudest of them all, his youngest always seemed to be active. Even watching the TV, especially sports, he was the most vocal. As Brierly read, he occasionally found that his mind wandered back to the ongoing investigations. From what they had gleaned so far, the common denominator in the murders appeared to be the shelter on Cranbury Avenue. The link seemed clear, but the who and the why were still out of reach. They knew that Dave Crossley was dealing. With whom was still unknown, but it wasn't too far-fetched to suggest that he had some clients who used the shelter. The obvious question was whether Crossley was murdered by one of them.

Did someone witness his murder? Was that why the Millwright family had been decimated? Where did Trevor Owen and his daughter fit into the equation? Did they know something that they still hadn't told him? He contemplated the various computations, struggling to see where the two unknown male victims fitted in. One dead in a cemetery, and another burnt to a crisp in a van.

June's voice offering him tea suddenly interrupted his thoughts. He found himself looking at the Star Walk app. He was frustrated that he knew the names of the planets, the more significant constellations and that the current northern pole star was called Polaris, the brightest star in Ursa Minor more than 400 light years away from earth, yet he didn't know how to use the tool itself properly. As his fingers moved around the screen, names like Cepheus; The King, Cassiopeia: The Queen, Perseus, Andromeda, Cygnus, and many more appeared. Brierly knew many of the names were mostly of Greek or Roman origin, sometimes however there were equivalents for the same star. He also knew that many of the constellations that

popped up as he moved the screen around, had first been mentioned as long ago as the second century BC by the astronomer Ptolemy. He decided that when he had the chance he would look into the background of how the stars and planets became to be named as they were, and how they used to fit in with that specific societies thinking at that time. While he marvelled at today's technology, and the amount of knowledge found on the small screen of his phone, he also wondered about the creative minds that had looked up into the night sky and imagined what they did. How they could draw pictures in their heads and then with the help of the stars were able to navigate their ships across the oceans. He remembered when he had first looked at the very same celestial objects himself. Years ago, when he was in the navy. Despite the passage of time, his interest in the enormity of everything beyond the planet had never waned. He wasn't a religious man by any means, and he had no strong feelings either way about a supreme being having created what was in the sky above, but he did occasionally think that there were forces, out there, that seemed to take him on a journey, gave him cause to think.
"I said, do you want some tea?" June repeated, raising her voice slightly to focus his mind on her rather than on the phone.
"Oh, I'm sorry, yes that would be great," he replied.
With a smile, she left him alone and went into the kitchen. The ritual of tea before bed had begun. In the interim, Brierly stared at his phone's screen again, idly moving around the night sky. As he did so, various names of stars and constellations he had never heard of jumped out at him. Names such as Cetus; the amazing one, Lacerta; the Lizard; and Rastaban a star in the Draco constellation whose name comes from an Arabic phrase meaning 'head of the serpent'. As he read the details written on the screen, he noticed the stars' name was also known as Alwaid, meaning 'who is to be destroyed'. He wondered why before continuing to scan the virtual night sky again. June brought him his drink and suggested that he stop for the night. He agreed. For the rest of the evening, he tried to concentrate on June and what she was telling him about the new project she was working on for her charity. She had started planning workshops and arranging talks by local personalities including chefs, comedians, and magicians. She hoped to sell tickets to each event which would raise even more money for her cause. Ten thousand pounds 'net', was the target.

"That's a large amount," Brierly said.

"I agree, but if we don't try and aim big, we'll never be able to get the new equipment we need."

Brierly nodded. He knew that all charities struggled most of the time. There was only so much money to go around, and it never stretched as far as was needed. To some degree, the situation she described was like the police force. There were never enough resources to meet the challenges of the day and they also had to do what they could. This, despite the public expectation that every crime be solved and every recalcitrant, caught. Unfortunately, this was no longer possible or realistic. Now it was all about priorities, optics, and politics. Society was the worse for it.

"Is there anything I can do to help?" he asked.

"Such as what?"

"I don't know," he shrugged, "but if you have a raffle at some point, I can try and have some of those at the station buy a few tickets."

She smiled at his offer knowing that he was genuine, but raffle tickets were no longer the main tool used in raising funds for her charity. The modern way was to create a donations page on the web with a target or goal set within it. Sometimes a crowdfunding page would be used. There were several other alternatives that she had thought of, but they would be looked at later if needed.

"Look, love, thanks for the offer, but I have a few ideas so don't worry." She was not trying to sound condescending, and she hoped the humour in her voice indicated that.

"Like what?"

"Well, the easiest way is just to ask for money. A lot of people do it nowadays and it's amazing how the public supports a good cause."

"Ummm," Brierly replied, wishing that the very same public would support the police better than they seemed to do. Where were the days when respect for authority meant that the world was a safer place for everyone? It was perhaps a rhetorical question when he considered it properly. The police and their masters, the politicians, had not done themselves any favours with the public. Corruption, nepotism, dishonesty, fraud, and manipulation were like millstones around the neck of those in the force today. There was always someone working in their own interest, trying to get what they could out of it. Brierly wondered if the same thing had occurred when the old stargazers looked up at the heavens thousands of years before.

What had the stars seen in the past that were being replayed today? With a sigh, he realized that nothing had changed over time. Man's inhumanity or indifference to one's fellow man, was the same today as it was thousands of years before.

June looked at him, noticing his frown and his 'thinking' face. She knew that he wasn't concentrating on what she was saying but was rather wrapped up in his own thoughts. It was always this way. A case would land on his desk, and it would take over his life at times. She had seen it before, many times, and she understood why it was. Most of those involved would become obsessed with trying to solve a case. Some got in so deep that they lost perspective. Families were often destroyed, officers became drunks, and divorce became the norm. Unfortunately for those affected there was very little support. Sympathy yes but putting back the pieces of broken lives was almost impossible. June realized how lucky she was. Brierly hadn't lost sight of what was important to him and for that, she was grateful. Knowing he needed space, she decided to go off to bed, leaving him with his thoughts.

"I'll be up in a little while," he said, as she removed his empty cup and took it into the kitchen, placing it into the dishwasher along with her own.

Once he was alone, he picked up his phone again, opened up the app, and spent the next few minutes trying to improve his understanding of how it worked. With limited success and realizing that until the rains stopped and he had a clear sight of what the app was suggesting he could see in the sky, he closed it down, placing the phone back on the table. He suppressed a yawn and stretched, before turning off the light and making his way to the bedroom. June was in the bathroom and had switched on the table lamps that sat on chest of drawers on either side of the headboard. As he sat on the edge of the bed tucked up in his gnomelike way, the phone that he had placed next to his lamp began to ring. He groaned, looked at the screen, and knew that he had to answer it.

"Good evening, Gemma," he said, acknowledging the lateness of the hour. "What's so important for you to be calling me at this time of night?" It was almost 11:30 and late calls were generally bad news. Phone calls from the Head of Pathology at the University were both unusual and rare, and Brierly's tone foreshadowed his expectation.

"And a good night to you too," Atkins replied, sarcastically. Her

attempt at humour wasn't lost on him, however. Having worked together for years now, they had a relationship that to outsiders looked the same as that of a long-married couple. With a gentle laugh, Brierly encouraged her to continue.
"Some interesting information came through about an hour ago while I was busy with another autopsy. I thought it couldn't wait until the morning, given the circumstances."
"The circumstances?" He had so many things on his plate, he wasn't sure which one she was referring to. "Is it in connection with the corpse in the van?" he asked, hoping that there had been a breakthrough. "Have you been able to identify him or her?"
"No, I think that may take a little longer than I first thought. No, it's the others. The student, Crossley, and the man found with his throat slit in Hollybrook cemetery."
"What about them?" he asked, recalling that the initial conclusion reached of how each was killed was with different types of knives.
"No, that conclusion is still correct," she replied. "No, this is something far more interesting."
"Go on."
"The results of the DNA tests we ran on both Crossley and the other man have just been released as I said."
"And?"
"Well, you won't believe this, but they were related."
"What?"
"The DNA tests we did, indicate that they were family."
Brierly sat stunned for a few seconds, silent, immobile, just as June walked into the room.
"Are you okay?" she asked, a worried look on her face. Seeing him sitting down, a phone to his ear but with staring, unfocused, eyes. The sight disturbed her. It looked like he was having a stroke.
"Yes, yes, I'm fine," he said, indicating that he was talking on the phone. June smiled, relieved at his response as he continued questioning Atkins' findings. "By family, you mean…?"
"I mean, the results of the PCR tests suggest with 99.999% certainty that Crossley was the son of the murdered man in the cemetery."
"But..?"
"I thought you might find it interesting," Atkins said with a smile in her voice. Brierly was still trying to work through the implications of what he had been told and for a second she thought he had

terminated the call.
"Yes," he said eventually, "that is interesting. Thank you, Gemma, you were right to call me. It's given me a lot to think about."
"I'm glad I could help Jim," she replied, "and with that, I'll get back to work."
"Before you go, just going back to the body in the van, is there anything you can give me on the victim?"
"You mean anything of note?"
"Anything at all would be good," he stated, still unsure whether Atkins and her team had started their examination yet.
"We still have a few things to do before we get there. Once I've done what I need to, I'll send over my report," she replied.
"Will you call me if you find anything unusual," he queried, "as with the Crossley situation?"
"Yes, of course,"
"Thanks again, Gemma…for the update."
"No problem," she answered, "goodnight, and give June my best."
"I will do," he answered, closing the call, his mind racing.
"Are you okay?" June asked. She was sitting up in bed, the Pauline Collins book lay open in front of her. He hadn't noticed that she had undressed and climbed in.
"Yes, I'm okay. That was Gemma Atkins"
"I gathered that," she answered. "I assume it was something important?"
Brierly nodded, telling her that he would need to make a quick call before he could join her in the bed. With a grin, she patted the duvet saying that she would try and keep his side warm, then began to read as he walked from the room. It took ten minutes for him to finish what he needed to do. He would follow up with those he had spoken with and sent texts to, the next day.
Suddenly realizing that it was already past midnight he climbed into bed. June put her book down, and they both turned out their lights. As they lay in the dark, they heard Warwick arrive home, barging his way into the kitchen. A few minutes later they felt him closing his bedroom door with a bang. Simon had been in his room for most of the night and his light had been off when Brierly had finally come to bed.
Neither of them were able to sleep and June could tell that he was thinking. Occasionally he would sigh and rub a hand across his brow.

She was used to it, but tonight he seemed particularly anxious, and she asked him why. Brierly told her what was concerning him, and she let him talk, allowing him the opportunity of expressing his thoughts into the darkness, knowing that whatever he shared with her was their secret. After a few minutes, he finished speaking, putting a full stop to his observations. He had said enough. He was lying on his back, his arm around her as she snuggled into his chest. He kissed the top of her head slowly running his hand through her hair. She held him tighter, her arm now around his waist. "How tired are you?" she asked.
"I'm awake, unfortunately," he replied.
"Good," she replied, "I have an idea."
He smiled. He knew what she meant. Twenty minutes later they were both spent.

CHAPTER 47

Mary Owen waited patiently in the reception area. She had arrived early and she hoped to be heading back home before midday. She was very concerned about leaving her father alone, but she had no choice. Tom was working and she would do anything she could to help catch whoever was threatening to kill her and the rest of the family. She felt like she had a target on her back and every time someone walked behind her, she felt her skin tighten, almost readying herself for a knife to be planted between her shoulders. With Brierly asking her to come and see him specifically, she was hopeful that progress was being made and that she could walk out of the police station feeling confident of an arrest. Would she be disappointed, she thought? Was it too much to expect?
She was still struggling with the murder of her sister but found the inability to bury her and the children even more distressing than the threats to her own safety. Despite her fear and concerns for Tom and her father, she wanted closure on Gretchen and the children more than anything else in the world.
"Would you come this way?" the voice said.
She looked up into the face of DS White. She had been miles away and had not heard him approach. Standing up, she followed him through to an interview room on the ground floor. He asked her to take a seat, offering her tea, which she accepted. He left her alone while he went to make the arrangements. As she waited for Brierly to arrive a young Constable brought the drink for her in a plastic cup. She thanked him as he left her alone again. Looking around the room with its grey-painted walls, and a single desk with four chairs, she sipped her drink, occasionally blowing on the scalding liquid. The room reminded her of those she had seen on TV and in films. A place that seemed innocuous enough, but if the walls could speak…..?
A gentle knock on the door was followed by the entrance of Brierly and DS White. She stood up, shaking Brierly's hand who then thanked her for coming into the police station. He asked her to take her seat again and to get comfortable. Apologizing for the urgency and the early meeting, he explained to her why he wanted them to meet.

"I've been looking at these birthday cards again," he said, taking them from a file he had been carrying. The cards were opened flat inside sealed plastic evidence bags, the front, back, and insides easily readable. "I'm still at a loss as to what they mean," he said. "Apart from the obvious, the dates, there is nothing unusual about them is there?"
"No," she replied.
"Yet they frightened your father so much, that he went and bought himself a gun, without a license…and illegally."
"Yes. Though as I told you previously, it was the note he received about all of us, his family, being killed that made him do that."
"Aah yes, the famous note," Brierly said. "A note which we've been told was thrown away, but…"
"It was thrown away, Inspector!" she interrupted, "I believe my father when he says that it was," she pleaded.
"Okay, let's accept that to be the case for now," Brierly answered. "But what I'm trying to understand is a motive behind all of this. How it relates to your sister's murder and that of her family? Something appears to be missing. The dates on the cards, as we know, are those of your parents' birthdays but there are no cards with your birthday or that of your late sister. Nor of her husband or her children. Why is that?"
"I don't know."
"So, I'm expected to believe that someone is out there intending to kill your father and the rest of his family for no apparent reason?"
"Yes," she replied.
"I'm sorry, Ms. Owen, I'm afraid you need to do better than that. There is something behind all this and I think you know more than you are telling us." Brierly looked at White who remained passive, staring across the table at her. It seemed like he was looking into her soul. His gaze made her uncomfortable. He was playing the game exactly how Brierly had asked him to.
Mary Owen shifted in her seat. Brierly knew that he was close to a breakthrough. He decided to play another card. "What do you know of the injuries your sister and her children suffered when they were murdered?"
"I'm sorry?" she questioned, not wanting to think about Gretchen's pain.
"The injuries, how their bodies were defiled," Brierly said,

emphasizing the last word for effect.
"What?"
"I said, are you aware of how your sister and her family were scarred?"
"I'm not sure what you are talking about, I heard from Tom that the kids were strangled to death, and Gretchen was…." Her voice drifted away, and tears started to form making her eyes glisten from the lighting above.
Brierly had had enough. "Look, Ms. Owen, I may have misjudged you, maybe not, and perhaps you are not fully aware of what I'm referring to," he said, convinced of his assessment of her but careful not to be too dogmatic in his comments, "so I'll give you the benefit of the doubt for now. However, let me ask you this. We have found cut marks on the bodies of the Millwright family, cuts that were deliberate and were intended, I think, to send a message. Do you know anything about this?"
"Cuts?" she queried. "What type of cuts? Where?"
White turned his head slightly to look at Brierly, wondering how his boss would reply to the question. He watched as Brierly contemplated his response. They knew that the same cuts were found on the body they now believed to be Dave Crossley's father, and while the link with the Millwright family was tenuous Brierly guessed it was relevant somehow. Trying to find out to what extent, however, was their challenge. Finally, Brierly said, "On the fingers. One specific finger in fact…on the left hand. Now, why would that be?"
He had just finished the question when Mary Owen's chest rose in panic as she took a deep breath and then exhaled violently. It was as if she had something stuck in her throat. The two policemen wondered if she was having a panic attack and offered her some water, telling her to breathe slowly, to take her time, and to settle herself down. While they waited for her to recover her composure, Brierly sensed that he was almost there. He remained patient. It took a few minutes before she was in a position to continue and after an apology, she decided that it was time to let him know what her father had tried to protect.
"I can only tell you what my dad has told me, but the cuts as you call them are a message, yes. Just like the cards."
"What kind of message?" Brierly asked.
"That what was done would be avenged."

The two policemen looked at each other, uncertain as to where she was going with her comments.
"You mean someone is seeking revenge?" Brierly questioned. "For what?"
"A murder."
Her response took them both by surprise. It was the last thing they had expected, initially unable to comprehend what she was referring to. The tables had turned somewhat, yet Brierly knew that he was getting closer to the truth. Before the meeting they had planned how they wanted to run the meeting, the questions they expected to ask, and their specific line of inquiry. Brierly had a hunch about what was going on, but he hadn't anticipated what she was now telling them. Was all their planning about to dissipate like the mist over a river when disturbed by a strong breeze? He encouraged her to explain herself.
"It's a long story," she continued, "but it all makes sense now."
"Does it?"
"Yes, to me anyway....and to my dad," she answered sadly. Then as she considered what to say next, it was as if a light switch had been pressed. Her voice changed, becoming guttural, her anger obvious. "He should have told us earlier!" she exclaimed, a fist slamming into the table. "Maybe Gretchen and the kids would still be alive!"
Brierly put out a hand and touched her gently on the arm. He felt her trembling and with words of understanding, tried to calm her for the second time. He realized that the conversation was going to take far longer than expected. He asked her if she wanted a break, but she declined, telling him that she didn't want to make the same mistake as her father had and keep the secret hidden any longer. As he was about to ask her to continue, he felt his phone that he had left in his jacket pocket vibrate. He ignored it. The call ended but was followed shortly after by a voicemail message. He would listen to it when he had the chance.
"Tell me about the murder you mentioned," he asked. "Why is it relevant to your sister's killing?"
"I think...I don't know who, but...," she stuttered, "I only know why."
"As revenge for someone else's murder?" White queried, speaking for the first time.
"Yes."

"Whose murder?" he questioned again, "and when was this?"
"The sister of my great grandfather….in 1927."
"What?" White asked, his voice indicating the incredulity he felt with her response. "1927? That's just shy of a century ago. I can't…"
"What makes you so sure of this?" Brierly asked, interrupting White's almost apoplectic reaction to her statement, hoping to get her to focus again on her story.
"My dad told me that in one of the notes he received some time ago….."
"That he threw away?"
"Yes," she answered, acknowledging his interruption.
Brierly smiled, gesturing for her to continue.
"Well, my dad said that the note contained a riddle of sorts saying something about the dead having woken up and the remaining line would soon be broken."
"And that makes sense to you?"
"It didn't initially, but it does now."
"Because?"
"Because it fits with what's happened. The cuts on the fingers that you mentioned. They confirm it."
"I'm still not sure I understand," Brierly said. "Explain it to me."
"Were the marks on the ring finger?"
Not wanting to give too much information away, as he was still trying to test what she had said versus his own developing theory, he took a few seconds respite before responding with a small gesture of confirmation.
"Then I'm right. It is all about ending the line," she said.
Once again, the two policemen found themselves looking at her dubiously. Mary Owen was making statements that made no sense at all.
"Tell me about this murder. From 1927," Brierly requested, trying to find some logic to her ramblings.
"Okay, okay, I'll try and keep it simple, but you need to understand that I can only tell you what I know, what my dad told me. The rest is conjecture on my part."
"We're all ears, Ms. Owen," Brierley replied in an attempt to remove any doubts she may think they had. Following up and separating fact from fiction would come later.
"In 1927 my Great Grandfather, called Fred Amberley killed his only

sister. Apparently, and according to my dad, it had to do with an expectation. Something Fred hoped to inherit from his mother, but when she died, the inheritance went to his sister, Susan Amberley, instead. A few weeks after their mother's funeral, Fred, and Susan, who was married to a man called David Warrington, had a huge row while she was visiting him. Fred struck Susan with a metal rod he used to stoke the fire. He hit her several times, bludgeoning her to death. He tried to hide the body but was seen by neighbours and was eventually charged."

"What happened to him? To Fred?" Brierly asked, knowing that once he had a chance, he would have his team do some digging to verify the facts from any fiction in her statement.

"He was hanged. In 1930."

The answer seemed quite definitive, but the story she was telling didn't seem to stop in the 1930s so Brierly encouraged her to continue.

"Before the killing, Fred had a daughter. In 1924. Her name was Sarah, my grandmother. Being three when the murder took place and only six when her father was hung, she had no understanding as to what happened to her dad. His fate was kept from her, for a long time. In those days people didn't talk about things like that. It was only later that she found out the full story."

"From whom?"

"Someone she worked with apparently, who had read about it. In the years after the war, through the 1920s and the depression that followed, including World War two, and up until the 1960s, most people lived, worked, and died in the same area, never moving far away from where they were born. So, I guess it wasn't unexpected that paths would cross and that the story would circle back to her."

"Yes, that's true," White agreed, "a sense of community was very real back then."

"And you hadn't heard this story before?" Brierly asked.

"No, my father only told me a few days ago. He said it was one of those things that the family tried to bury. It seems my grandmother never even told her husband. She only told my father when she was on her deathbed."

Both policemen nodded, both aware of how family secrets were often revealed within the context of a forthcoming death. They had seen many such cases where the past was kept hidden, only to reveal

itself in ways that were never intended, and the outcome was often disturbing.
"What was the inheritance that caused Fred Amberley to murder his sister?"
Mary Owen looked directly into Brierly's eyes. She seemed embarrassed. "It was predominantly jewellery. But there was one piece, a ring, a wedding ring that had been his father's, that he specifically wanted. He thought it would be valuable, a kind of treasure."
"Because?" Brierly enquired, raising an eyebrow.
"Because his father, Wilfred, died, on the Titanic. He was an officer on the ship. Apparently, he gave the ring to a young man who he helped get into a lifeboat and asked him to get it back to his wife, Joyce Amberley, my great, great, great, grandmother. The young man concerned, as were most of the crew on that crossing, was from the Southampton area. He was able to find Joyce and eventually return the ring as well as a locket. As I said earlier, there was a sense of community back then."
"Who was this young man, this survivor?" Brierly asked.
"His name was Samuel Warrington. He was killed during the war, in 1917."
Brierly frowned. She could tell that he was thinking. "You said the name, Samuel Warrington, just now, but didn't you say earlier that Susan Amberley was married at the time she was murdered?"
"Yes, I did."
"To a David Warrington as I recall."
"That's right. They were married in 1919 but they had met when Samuel Warrington found Joyce in 1912 after he survived the sinking. The families became very close after that."
"What happened to David, after his wife was murdered?"
"I don't know Inspector."
"Can I ask you a question, Ms. Owen?" White jumped in, trying to piece a few loose ends together. Pieces that he couldn't get his mind around.
"Sure, go ahead," she answered, relieved that she had been able to get some of the burden of secrecy off her chest.
"Sarah, your grandmother. If she was only six when her father was hanged, who brought her up, who looked after her?"
"That's another family secret as well," Mary replied. "Sarah was

looked after until she was three by a couple of lady friends that Fred had managed to snare. It seems he had fathered her out of wedlock, which was a big no-no in those days. He was also wounded during the war and suffered what we would call PTSD today. They called it nerves back then."
"And?" White queried, still seeking an answer to his question.
"Around her third birthday, Sarah was put into an orphanage until she turned 16 in 1940. She left school and went to work in a Royal ordinance factory up in Staffordshire. I think it was a place called Swynnerton. After the war, she married my grandfather, Neville Owen in 1946. My dad was born in 1953."
"One of the dates in the cards," Brierly said, recalling the date from his memory. Having studied the cards she had retrieved for them, he now began to understand how things fitted together.
"Yes," she replied.
Brierly made a note, adding it to a number he had taken down as Mary Owen had told them what she knew. "Which brings us to you and your sister, and her children," he said, "the end of the line. Isn't that what you called it?"
"That's right, Inspector. That's apparently what my dad remembers the note saying."
"But he has no idea who sent it?"
"No."
Brierly shifted in his chair. He was beginning to feel a little stiff. Sitting as he had been in his usual position, bent over as his nickname suggested. His back was also starting to ache. With a finger stroking his cheek, while he considered his next question, he looked like the gnome he had become to be known as. He decided to stand, offering the same option to Mary and DS White, but both declined. Taking his time, he slowly uncurled himself before walking a few steps away from his chair and then turned back to face her.
"Earlier you said this was all about revenge, and you've suggested a reason, however implausible as to why…"
"Implausible?" she asked a tinge of anger in her voice.
"Yes, at least at face value. However, I'm not discounting it immediately. What I'm trying to …"
"You don't believe me, do you?" she interrupted.
"I just.."
"You think I'm delusional, that it's all made up, don't you

Inspector?"
Brierly sat down again, his sigh audible. "Look, Ms. Owen, as I said, I'm not suggesting anything. I'm just trying to work out who would kill your sister and her children, and then threaten to do the same to your father, yourself, and Mr. Millwright, all because of something that happened over a century ago. I can't see a reason, a motive, despite what you have told me."
His comment hurt her. He could see that she was wounded, a sense of despair seemed to bubble up inside her. She kept her head lowered. He knew he needed to provide her with something to cling to. With the silence between them palpable, he said, "If it's any consolation, one thing I can tell you, Ms. Owen, is that I won't rest until I find out who killed those children and their mother. That I promise you."
She looked up at him. With tears in her eyes, she said, "That's all I can ask Inspector. That's all I can ask."

White had taken her back to the reception area while Brierly waited for him to return. It had taken a couple of minutes, during which Brierly had scanned the notes that he had taken. When White entered the room, Brierly asked him to take a seat and they reviewed what they had discussed with her. After fifteen minutes, they had decided what the next steps would be and both men left the room. They would reconvene after lunch, with the rest of the team. White made his way back to his desk, while Brierly went to brief DCI Hammond on the approach he had decided to take. As he climbed the stairs to Hammond's office, he remembered that his phone had buzzed during the meeting with Mary. Taking it from his pocket he noticed there was a phone message, the number, was unknown to him. He decided to take a quick listen and was surprised to hear a voice that he recognized but couldn't place it until the caller mentioned the name; Jill Tucker. She sounded slightly out of breath as if she was calling while walking, but her voice had an edge to it. "Inspector Brierly, could you call me at your earliest convenience, please? It is very important that you do. Thank you...," and with a sense of urgency, she repeated her contact number for him. Brierly was intrigued by the call as he hadn't thought about their conversation since he had met with Christine Grovedale in the Bellemoor Tavern just before the Millwright killings. Having put things on the back burner, he realized that he had let the Crossley murder slip a little. With the update from Atkins that Crossley and the homeless man were related his caseload was becoming more complicated. With Tucker now wanting his attention as well, he was facing the daunting prospect of managing his time and his team across multiple lines of inquiry. As he entered Hammonds' office the thought of needing more resources was top of mind. He found his boss unsympathetic. The message was that they would need to do more with what they had.

CHAPTER 48

The pain had started slowly and while it was obvious something was wrong, the tests and appointments had been put off for months, with the resulting outcome. With the drugs already on hand, and those from the clinic it had become manageable, but for how long? With the diagnosis and the need for surgery within the next few weeks, the need to finish the job and cut off the last few branches had become paramount, and it meant that action needed to be taken before the tree had an opportunity to flourish again. Any hospitalization before the job was complete would mean that all the earlier work would have been for nothing. The biggest concern was whether the pain from the cancer, which was getting worse by the day, would become so debilitating before time ran out and the surgery had to be done. Or, would another chance avail itself beforehand?

Looking at the tree and how the upper branches mingled together intensified the irritation and exacerbated the pain that shot from the middle of the abdomen and through the spine and up into the chest. Doubled over, knife in hand, a slash at the three remaining limbs tore the paper on which they lay with a jagged line, a Z shape ripping through the tines that bound them. The blade dropped to the floor as the paper floated in pieces around it, landing gently on the floor. A scream of anguish echoed in the night.

CHAPTER 49

The morning had flown by and Brierly was able to make the one phone call that had been requested of him. After meeting with Hammond and providing him with an update on his cases, he spent the rest of the time in his office. He had asked to be left undisturbed, except for being brought his tea. The balance of his time alone was spent trying to fit the various strands together. He found himself winning at times, then losing at others. Occasionally his phone would buzz, and he would see a message of sorts pop up from his Star Walk app. These were small news feeds such as the planets nearest to the moon in the next month. How to see satellites, and what did the Greeks call Saturn?
He had become irritated with it as he could not work out how to stop being interrupted by the irregular 'pings'. It was made worse by the fact that even if he was able to apply what was being messaged, the sky was filled with dirty dishwater-coloured clouds, which prevented him from seeing anything at night anyway, and given the weather forecast would likely be the same for the forthcoming week. He knew he would need to speak with Warwick or Simon when he got home and get them to help him sort it out. He looked at his watch realizing why he felt hungry. It was already after 1 pm and he had just over forty-five minutes available to him before his meeting in the situation room. He decided to take a quick walk, alone, to Mi Rice on Commercial Road, where he looked forward to a hot chicken rice lunch and a cup of tea. He needed it, the cold outside chilled his bones. With the wind whipping at his coat, he walked with his head down, thinking of the meeting with Mary Owen…. "Motive!" he said to himself, as he dodged through the crowds, "motive!"

"I want them brought in, first thing tomorrow," he said to DS White, referring to Damson and Klein and the need to question them again. "And another thing, I want you to find out whether Crossley's mother had any idea as to why her ex-husband would be in the area and whether he really was homeless."
"No problem, Sir," White replied, the informality they had shared

earlier now a thing of the past.
"One other thing, we know that Crossley was dealing, and we think he had customers who used the shelter on Cranbury Avenue. So with the shelter being the place where the van with our other dead body was ordered from, the link is obvious. But who is behind it all, that's the big question."
"And the why, Sir," DC Hughes noted.
Brierly looked around the room at his team, their faces showing that they expected him to respond to the point that Hughes had made. He smiled, saying, "I think I know the why, now. I just need to work out the who."
The remainder of the day was filled with discussion and instructions regarding the story Mary Owen had shared with Brierly and White. Follow-up and validation were critical. They had to leave no stone unturned, despite some cynicism that arose from a few of them who considered her tale to be fanciful.
By the time Brierly left the office, it was already dark. As he walked onto the street taking a short stroll to his car, he looked up briefly. The clouds had parted for a few seconds, and he had sight of a few stars for the briefest moment. He knew that it would be a full moon in a few days, but that would be at 11 am, hardly the time of day to see it, and even less likely to anyway, given the expected weather. He could hardly wait for the Spring and Summer when the clearer nights, despite being shorter, would give him chance to view the sky more clearly. By then he hoped that he would have mastered his Star Walk app. Either that or he would have ditched it. With eyes now looking downwards, he continued his walk. As he climbed into his car, the rain started to fall. Not for the first time, he thought, "Bloody typical!" he said to himself.

She was shivering again, and a cough had started. She spat phlegm onto the pavement. She didn't care about the sideways glances she received from passers-by. When they did make eye contact with her, she told them to "fuck-off" even if there were children around.
He hadn't wanted to help her when she had turned up. He wouldn't even let her cross the threshold, quickly closing the door behind him so that the bitch, Carol, didn't see her. They had stood outside, him

speaking quietly and she tried to tell him what she had observed. She wanted money and he refused her again. She had begun to make a scene, raising her voice and making a threat to expose him, before getting the reaction that she wanted. He had finally relented, meeting her a half hour later just around the corner from his house, having made an excuse that he received a call from a patient that required an urgent prescription. The excuse to get out of the house had worked but he had told her that he was on "borrowed" time. He had given her thirty pounds and some Naltrexone to ease the cravings. She had subsequently thrown away the pills, having no intention of taking them. She wanted a hit first. Tomorrow she would make her way to her grandfather's house, but not before making the phone call.

If only she could stop the shaking.

CHAPTER 50

He had anticipated a busy morning and Brierly had realized that he would have to split himself into three if he expected to be involved in all the conversations. Knowing this was impracticable he gave White and Hughes the task of questioning Damson and Klein, then requested DC Track to work with the backroom support teams to look into Mary Owens' story. She had provided them with plenty of information, the question was whether it would stack up. Meanwhile, he and DC Proctor would be off to meet with Jill Tucker. During the call he had made to her she had sounded extremely concerned about something but would not say what without meeting with him face-to-face. Once they had finished with that meeting, he and Proctor intended to go on to see Janie Fenchurch at the homeless shelter on Cranbury Avenue. They needed to follow up on what Anderson had told them. With any luck, Brierly expected to be back at the station in time for the next situation meeting which was scheduled for four that afternoon. He always enjoyed times like these. As the strands of a case slowly became clearer and the various pieces of the jigsaw started to fit, despite them not making the complete picture, his mind would begin to form an outline. The threads that once had little connection would begin to intertwine, knitting themselves together like a patterned cloth to ultimately reveal the full picture. He knew that they were still some ways away from making any arrests, but somehow, he felt they were closing in steadily. It was now a matter of time. Unfortunately, that wasn't always on their side. Hammond was already making noises about closing cases, putting them into the unsolved file, the too-hard basket which would later become the responsibility of the cold case team. Brierly disagreed with his boss and requested a stay. Reluctantly Hammond had agreed but told Brierly that he and his team were now on borrowed time, emphasizing the point strongly, in words that required no interpretation.

"I understand, Sir," Brierly had said.

"Dave," Hammond relayed, "when it's just us two, Jim, it's Dave. Remember?"

"Yes, S…Dave," Brierly had responded. "Thanks for the support. I know it's a touchy subject, resourcing, and cost, but I'm confident

we'll get whoever is behind all this…we just need a little bit more."
"I know, but as I keep on saying, it's not a luxury that we have plenty of," Hammond had repeated.
Brierly had stood, ready to leave his boss's office, when Hammond had indicated how much pressure he was under regarding his own position, and his own case load. Brierly had responded empathetically. Each knew what the other faced in terms of challenges sent down from the hierarchy. There was a rapport between the two men, both knew the game being played above them. Brierly let his boss know how he appreciated the air cover Hammond provided.
"I hope you do, Jim," Hammond had replied, "I really do….for both our sakes."
With such an endorsement, Brierly had left the room. He knew it was about as good a conversation as he could have expected. Now it was up to him.

The lines around her mouth and eyes seemed to have developed rapidly. Jill Tucker was still incredibly attractive despite the concern now etched on her face. DC Proctor had been introduced to her when she had answered her door to Brierly and the young constable. Upon them entering at her invitation, she had observed the man from Cheltenham with interest. His six-foot-four frame towered above her and his good looks added an extra special dimension to the room. The previous visit was in sharp contrast to what Brierly was now observing. Between himself and White and both of them being middle-aged, their looks were of lesser interest to her compared to how she undressed Proctor with her eyes. The young constable was uncomfortable at the attention, his ears glowing red as she held his gaze a little too long.
Brierly thought the situation was odd, given her proclivities elsewhere. He decided not to push the issue as he could be wrong. He would talk with Proctor after they left, though he expected the constable would pick up the drift of the conversation with her sooner rather than later.
"Can I offer you some tea or coffee before we start?" she asked, looking to Brierly before smiling at Proctor.

"No, I don't think so Ms. Tucker," Brierley answered, "we need to be moving along as soon as we can as we have another appointment later. Thank you anyway."
"That's no problem at all. I just thought I would ask."
"It's appreciated, but let's get back to the reason why we are here," Brierly said steering the conversation to where it needed to go. "You mentioned when we spoke yesterday that you had something you wanted to share that couldn't be discussed on the phone. Would you like to elaborate?"
"It's about Christine," she said, her mood suddenly changing, becoming more serious, no longer flighty or frivolous.
Brierly needed a second to connect the dots before saying, "Oh, Ms. Grovedale?"
"Yes."
"What about her?"
Tucker lowered her eyes, and worry lines again appeared across her forehead and around her mouth, blemishing her smooth skin. Brierly noticed her hands appeared to be shaking slightly and her lip trembled. Speaking softly, she said, "I am concerned for her safety. Very concerned."
"Because..?"
"Because she has been beaten. Savagely beaten, several times in the past few days."
"Do you know by who?"
"Yes," she answered coyly.
"Would you like to elaborate?"
When she looked up at him, he could see tears in her eyes. He wasn't sure why she was hesitating with her response, but he waited patiently while she gathered herself together. He found it odd that she looked so vulnerable now given their previous meeting and the confidence she had exuded then.
"It was Terence."
"Terence Silver, her partner?"
"Yes."
"Do you know why?"
"No, but Chris, sorry Christine, told me that he had hit her several times. Her bruises were so noticeable that she had to take time off from work, from school."
"She spoke with you?"

"No, she texted me, from her bedroom. She was so frightened that she locked the door while he rampaged through their house. He didn't go to school either. Apparently, he didn't even take the dog for a walk as he usually does each day."

Brierly recalled the meeting that he had with Silver when Dave Crossley's body had been found. There had been something about the relationship between Silver and Grovedale that had unsettled him at the time, but he hadn't been able to put his finger on it. Was domestic violence the answer?

"Did you ask why she hadn't contacted the police?" he asked.

"Yes, I did and that's why I wanted to see you in person."

"Go on."

"Well, Christine said that he had threatened her."

"All the more reason for her to call the police, don't you think?"

She grimaced in response, saying, "I agree Inspector. I would have thought so, but it appears that he threatened to kill her if she tried."

Brierly sat up a little straighter in his seat. His experience told him that couples often argued, and things were said, but threats to kill were usually infrequent. He asked her to elaborate further if she could.

"It seems he held a knife to her throat, a bread knife, he drew blood."

As she spoke, something triggered in Brierly's mind. He barely noticed her next comment. "Christine said that the knife he threatened her with was new, she hadn't seen it before, and he told her that he would kill me as well if she told anyone about what he had done to her."

"Because of your relationship?"

"Yes."

"Do you know where Ms. Grovedale is now?"

"I think she's still inside the house. She's too scared to go anywhere yet. Terence is effectively keeping her prisoner." She began to sob, and Brierly asked her if she would like him to arrange for a female officer to stay with her while he followed up on her complaint. She declined the offer, letting him know that she had work to do and it would keep her mind off things, but she appreciated the gesture. Her preference, she said, was for the police to follow through on what she had told him. Brierly agreed, appreciative of her response. He half expected that due to his discussion with Hammond, he would have been unable to fulfill the offer anyway. As their conversation came to its logical conclusion, he told her to be vigilant and to contact him immediately should she have any further concerns. He thanked her again as he and Proctor shook her still shaking hand, promising to be in touch once they had concluded their investigations. Brierly knew that they needed to be careful as allegations were one thing, proof was something else. If Christine Grovedale refused to press charges against Silver, then things could take a very different turn. Brierly had an idea. He made a call to DS White.

The shelter on Cranbury Avenue was busy. By the time Brierly and Proctor had been able to find a parking spot after the drive from Jill Tucker's house and walk into the place, those who had arrived for a free feed at lunchtime were either still seated at tables or were wandering around, being offered support from the various staff members. Having made their way into the office, Brierly noticed that there was no sign of Wayne Anderson at the desk he normally used. However, there was someone else sitting at the computer. A young woman, who introduced herself as Tas de Konig, a student from Holland. "I only started two days ago, so I don't know very many people yet. I'm just a volunteer," she stated after Brierly and Proctor had introduced themselves, showing her their warrant cards and unsettling her slightly. "Don't worry," Brierly replied, "we're here to see Ms. Fenchurch. Do you know where she is?"
The young student, whose face had flushed, making her freckled skin shine, pointed towards the meeting room with the glass window. "At least I know Janie," she smiled.
Brierly looked towards the back of the office noticing the door to the meeting room open. Janie Fenchurch and Philip Boothby walked out of the office speaking quietly. Noticing the two policemen, Fenchurch greeted them, and Boothby did likewise.
"We saw you through the window," Fenchurch added. Mr. Boothby and I were finishing our meeting, just as you arrived. Perfect timing."
Looking at Brierly, his back ramrod straight, Boothby bemoaned the recent events affecting the facility. "I don't know what's happening in the city, but as Janie and I were just discussing, the drug problem seems to be getting so much worse. We are being inundated with

more and more people looking for our assistance. It's becoming much harder to accommodate everyone in need. Are you seeing that Inspector…in your everyday work?" Brierly tried to be diplomatic, conscious of the young student sitting a yard or two behind them. He didn't wish to alarm the poor girl, but he did need to answer the question. "I would suggest that there is a problem, yes, but I'm not sure it's any worse than in any other city across the country." He noticed Fenchurch nod in agreement, but his comment didn't seem to satisfy Boothby.

"I'm not sure I'd agree Inspector. I've been involved in public service nearly all my life, as I suspect you have, and I can tell you from experience that homelessness and violence on our streets seem to be reaching epidemic proportions. Just look around outside," he gestured towards the office entrance, "just look at the number of people wanting a bed or a meal. There are so many, a large number of whom are drug affected as well."

"That's why we are here, Mr. Boothby," Brierly replied. "We are likewise very concerned about the drug problem that you just mentioned. We need to have another chat with Ms. Fenchurch here, as we continue our investigation into the matter."

Brierly's comments appeared to placate Boothby slightly. "And I suppose that means you are looking into the recent violence across the city, as well as the drug issue?"

"Yes," Brierley replied, "but as you would expect I can't go into the specifics of our investigations."

"I understand. I think the entire city is concerned about what we have read in the papers recently. Those poor children and their mother, not to mention the individual killed in the van fire."

"Yes. It was a shocking crime, wasn't …?"

"And what about the poor man whose identity you were looking for?" Boothby interrupted. His natural inclination to take over the conversation as he would have done at previous council meetings. "The man whose face was plastered all over our walls. Has he been identified yet?" he asked.

"As I said, Mr. Boothby, I can't comment specifically but if it is any comfort to you and Ms. Fenchurch, I can say that we have made a breakthrough of sorts and we are following up that lead as we speak."

With a grunt of acknowledgement, the ex-councillor accepted Brierly's words as an indication of progress. He then turned to

Fenchurch and thanked her for her time. "Well, I'll leave you to it then," he said in finality, offering a hand to Brierly and then to Proctor, who seemed slightly intimidated by the old man despite being so much taller than him and with a physical presence that would make any front rower shake in their rugby boots. They watched Boothby leave the office, hearing him calling someone outside before Fenchurch indicated that they should make their way back to the meeting room that she and Boothby had just vacated. Once they were seated, Brierly explained to Fenchurch what they now knew about the man whose death had sparked their investigation and the link to the shelter.
"We don't think he had anything to do with drugs," he said.
"That's a relief," Fenchurch said, her comments indicating the weight that had been lifted from her shoulders.
"Having said that," Brierly continued, "we believe that drugs were and are still being sold to some of the people using the shelter, we just don't know who that source is yet. Our investigations are continuing."
"Do you think it is one of the staff?" she asked, her concern returning, etched again onto her face, "Or is it someone using the facility?"
"At this stage, I can't tell you. But I do want to ask you to remain vigilant and should you see anything suspicious to call us immediately."
"Of course, Inspector," she replied. "The sooner this issue is resolved, the better. Mr. Boothby and I, as well as the rest of the Board, are particularly concerned about what would happen to us if our funding was suddenly cut or our license to operate was revoked. Not only would we be unable to serve those who are the neediest in our community, but also some of us would lose our livelihoods as well, not to mention our reputations." Brierly understood what she meant. He was acutely aware of having to fight to keep doing what he loved. What his team loved. He didn't show it but inwardly he felt as she must have done. Walking the tightrope of expectations from the public, she, like him, was expected to meet demand. This was despite limited resources and the ability to service that demand properly. He found himself feeling despondent, sombre. As he silently contemplated his thoughts, a piece of the puzzle suddenly fell into place. He stood up abruptly, catching Proctor and Fenchurch by

surprise. Thanking her for her time, he marched from the room, offering a quick goodbye and a smile to Tas de Konig as she tapped away at her computer.
He needed to get back to the office and told Proctor to drive as quickly as he possibly could.

CHAPTER 51

She helped him through the door. It had been a difficult journey and seemed interminable. He had stayed quiet for most of it particularly after she had told him that she had taken DI Sutton and DC Track into the house and had allowed them to take away the cards and bullets that he had kept in his drawer.

"You knew it was necessary didn't you, Dad?" she had asked. His response had been a shrug and a heavy sigh. As they drove she had fought against the feelings of anger and frustration at his thoughtlessness. He had lost some of his immediate family, yet he appeared unwilling to act in any way at all that was rational.

"You told them everything then?" he had queried.

"Yes, at least everything you told me."

He had grunted in reply, then touched his head, still bandaged, the stitches hidden beneath the cotton and gauze.

They sat down now, opposite one another. He was unwilling to look at her, but she was desperate to ensure that he was okay, both physically and mentally. He had been allowed to come back home. Tom had likewise been given the okay to return to his place.

He looked around at the familiar surroundings, the lounge, his lounge. For some reason, it appeared foreign to him. What he had known before was no longer. What Mary had said in the car was true. Life had changed. It felt wrong, however, almost an untruth. He hadn't had the chance yet to lay his daughter, or his grandchildren to rest, so was it really true that they were gone? He knew consciously that it was the case and he bore the scars of why, literally and figuratively, but he wasn't yet ready to accept it. Not before he had done what he knew he needed to do.

"Will you be okay?" she asked, breaking into his thoughts.

"Of course, I will," he responded, his tone curt.

She bit her tongue not wanting to start an argument. "I'll call you later, after dinner, to see how you are going," she added. "Is that alright with you?"

"Suit yourself."

"Look, Dad," she began, her ire starting to rise, "if you don't want me to, then I…"

"I don't," he answered. "I can look after myself."

"Really?" she replied, incredulous at his arrogance.

"Yes. Really!"

She decided not to rise to the bait any further than she already had. It was of no use, not anymore, not now. It wouldn't change anything that had happened. It was out of their hands. Mary knew that she could no more. It was over to the police.

"I'll go then, should I?" she queried, looking at her watch. It was almost four thirty and the sky had dimmed under a damp ceiling of grey. She noted that the brief interlude of breaks in the cloud seen occasionally were over now. The sun had hardly shown its face throughout the day, with the odd exception of a few minutes here and there.

"Yes. See yourself out," he ordered, unwilling to get up from his seat.

"I need to be back at work tomorrow," she advised getting up from her chair. "I doubt I'll have much time to call as I need to catch up on a few things, but as I said, I'll call you later tonight. Perhaps before I go to bed."

"As I said," he responded, "it's up to you."

Mary looked at her father closely. She looked into his eyes. He diverted his gaze away from her and she noticed how old he suddenly seemed. Walking towards him she made her way to kiss his cheek but as she bent forward, he moved his head sidewards. She hesitated. His actions were as unusual as they were unexpected. Picking up her car keys and coat she strode silently to the front door. He watched her walk away, his eyes boring into her back. She decided not to turn around and say her goodbyes. Opening the door and walking out into the rapidly darkening night, she resolved to leave him a message by slamming it as hard as she could. Trevor Owen barely flinched. He turned slightly in his seat, following her through the still-open curtains as she strode along the pathway and climb into her car. She reversed it back onto the road, and he watched her disappear as she drove away to his left. Standing up slowly, he leaned on the arm of his chair and leveraged the support it provided. He felt his knees crack slightly and cursed them. He ambled to his kitchen dragging a dining room chair with him that he collected on the way. Once he had steadied it and had covered the seat with a small dishcloth, he clambered on top and reached for a biscuit tin that he had hidden at the very back of the highest shelf in the furthest cupboard from the kitchen door. Stretching he was just about able to reach it. A Quality

Street tin, the colours now faded, old, and given to him years before. A Christmas present from his late wife, the contents long gone. After carefully stepping down from the chair he placed the tin onto the dining room table, before putting the chair back from where it came. Order had been restored.

Slowly he removed the lid of the tin. Inside, covered in tissue paper, was a gun that he had surreptitiously hidden away. He picked it up feeling the cold metal against the palm of his hand, his index finger automatically finding itself on the trigger. He knew the gun was loaded. He had made sure that it was. If he needed access to it in a hurry, he knew where it was and that it was ready to be used. Instantly.

He smiled at how balanced it felt. It was unlikely that the police would have searched for it. They had no reason to, though he wasn't sure if Mary had. He suspected that she may have tried, particularly as she knew where he had stored the cards and the bullets that were now in the possession of the police. He guessed that she might have suspected him of obtaining a second gun. It would be typical of her, he thought. Placing the barrel of the gun to his temple he felt the end, the muzzle, against his skin. A shiver ran down his spine, a premonition. He moved the barrel along his cheek, stopping at his mouth. Parting his lips, he felt the metal against his teeth. He wondered what it would feel like to press the trigger. For a few seconds, he closed his eyes, feeling the weight of the gun in his hand, the barrel inside his mouth. The skin above his eye throbbed under the bandage. He knew what he needed to do. He would make his peace with her, he thought He would do that tomorrow. He felt she needed time to digest what had happened to her sister and her children. To him! As he stood in silence, he lowered his arm, the gun pointing toward the floor. He opened his eyes just as his doorbell chimed. He quickly placed the weapon back into the tin, covering it with the tissues and closing the lid. The doorbell rang again. With no time to return the tin to its hiding place, he went to answer the door.

CHAPTER 52

He wasn't at home, and she was furious. "Fuck, fuck, fuck!" she screamed, kicking at the wooden door, anger coursing through her like the drugs she ingested would course through her veins. "Where are you?" she shouted into the night, her voice pleading but lost to the neighbours who were all safe behind closed and curtained windows. TVs blaring at tired eyes, rooms heated to keep the cold away, and minds ignoring the outside world.

She was shivering again. She hadn't been able to find anyone to give her what she needed and her normal supplier was unavailable, not responding to her texts. She had limited cash now. The thirty pounds she had managed to scrounge was almost gone. A meal from McDonalds, another coat from a Charity shop, a 5-pound recharge of her phone and some cigarettes to be used as barter meant that she had little left over. She had promised that she would use the money to go back home but she had lied and now the cold and damp were beginning to get to her. She had been on the streets now far longer than she had expected, but she would be damned if she ever went to a shelter for professional help. A bed in a church was the extent of her willingness to seek aid or handouts.

She knew that he would come home at some point, but she didn't want to stick around for too long. The darkness could be cruel, and unsettling with dogs barking at strange sounds, some in their gardens, and occasionally one in the street with its owner being dragged along the damp pavement. She had walked around the area for a while before making her way to the house and upon arrival, had noticed a light on in the front room. It was obvious however that it was just for show. A pretence, an illusion designed to keep people guessing whether anyone was at home or not. Standing in the shadows her feet slowly going numb with cold, she decided that she could wait no longer. Not wanting to call him, or text him, she would come back later. In the meantime, she would leave the police a message, albeit anonymously. She believed that it would give her leverage and she could always send them on a wild goose chase if it suited her. She knew the name of the detective that was in charge of the case, his name having been mentioned in the newspaper. She had read the story in the library where she had spent a portion of the previous day trying to stay out of sight and also keep warm. With no alternative, she slipped out of the garden walking through the gate as if she owned the place. The street was deserted. A strong breeze brought by a cold front had sprung up. She had been protected from its effect while she had remained hidden in the bush, but now she felt the full force. The wind chill factor took the temperature down to low single digits and her face and hands were exposed to its brutality, turning blue as she walked away, head down, from the house. A soft rain that had started to fall minutes earlier made the pavement even more slippery underfoot. After walking for a few minutes she found herself at an empty bus stop and leant up against the glass, trying to keep out of the breeze. The rain began to increase in intensity, the squalls lit up by the orange glow of the streetlamp that stood forlornly a few yards from where she had curled into herself, trying to keep away from the fingers of the icy wind. Puddles of water settled around her feet, and she stamped her trainers on the bus stop's cement base as hard as she could trying to get some feeling back into her toes. Taking out her phone and trying to disguise her voice she dialled nine-nine-nine. Once the call was answered she spelt out what she knew, asking for the message to be passed on. Before she could be asked any questions, she terminated the call and immediately switched off the phone. As she did so, she noticed the car she was hoping to see drive past the bus shelter and continue in the direction she had come. It was obvious that she hadn't been seen. That would work in her favour. She decided to head back to the house. It was time.

"This thing is going to drive me bonkers," he said aloud. He was staring at the screen of his phone, sitting alone at the dining room table. June was in the lounge and the boys were still not back from their lectures at the university. A number of magazines and books about the cosmos were scattered across the tabletop. He had been trying to reconcile a reminder he had received on his phone about the planet Saturn. The Star Walk app had sent a message saying that the planet was visible at good resolution all night and had shown a timeline advising where it would be during the next 24-hour period, including the position above the horizon and at what angle of degree.

With the poor weather conditions outside, Brierly had decided it was unlikely he would see anything at all, not even the moon, let alone Saturn, Mars, or Jupiter, despite what the app indicated.
He knew that the recent weather was the major cause of his frustration, but he found himself taking it out on the very tool he had acquired to help him uncover the mysteries of the night sky. Placing his phone to one side in a fit of pique, he began scanning through an old edition of the Sky at Night magazine. He located what he was looking for and wanted to check whether the app was accurate or not. As he read, he found his mind wandering as he tried to follow the article. Saturn was the name used for the planet. Saturn, a God of Time in Roman mythology. Yet in Greek mythology, the name used for the same God was Cronus or Kronos. Brierly was surprised to find that there was no planet or star with the name Cronos, but a star some 320 light years from Earth, number HD 240430 according to the article, had been given the nickname. He wondered why. As he read further there was a reference to the genealogy of Cronus. According to Greek Mythology, he and his sister Rhea, whose father was Uranus, produced a number of deities including Hera, Poseidon, Hades, and others, but most importantly Zeus, whose Roman equivalent was Jupiter. In the article, he also saw a graphic indicating the names of the various generations that followed Cronus. Some he knew like Apollo and Athena, but it was Aphrodite who stood out. According to myth she was formed from the white foam created from the flowing blood after Uranus's testicles had been thrown into the sea by Cronus who castrated his own father. Cronus/Saturn had devoured his offspring as soon as they were born. Before Zeus killed Cronus, he used a special drug to make Cronus disgorge his previously devoured siblings.
Charming! Brierly thought. As he read further, the article revealed that HD 240430 is a devourer of other planets so the nickname suited it appropriately. Brierly had previously found it strange that most of the planets had Roman God names, but now he understood why. The Greeks had never conquered Europe so most monikers used for planets and stars were taken from the Romans whose ancient astronomers had mapped the skies during the time of occupation. Some planets however had only been discovered many centuries after the Roman Empire had disappeared which resulted in most being labelled with a number rather than a name.

As he finished reading the article it reminded him that families had fought, argued, and occasionally killed each other over many generations. Nothing was new. Jealousy, and hate, were always present, but was it more prevalent today he wondered? Or were we more aware of it due to social media, the likes of Facebook, Twitter, and other platforms? From the observations made in the article, family disputes, even in mythology had been around forever. Brierly didn't need any convincing of that, given his experiences in the police. As he contemplated again what he had read, linkages began to form. The past, the present…Suddenly his thoughts were interrupted as his home phone began to ring.
"I'll get it," June called. "I hope it's not the boys stuck somewhere," she added. Brierly smiled to himself, it was not even nine pm. Despite her relatively easy-going demeanour, June worried about the boys more than she would ever care to admit. He knew that both his kids, now young men, were sensible, and had their heads screwed on properly, but even so, anything could happen to anyone at any time. He felt a shiver run down his spine. Trying to ignore the sensation, he flipped over the page of his magazine, his phone still lying untouched where he had placed it forty-five minutes earlier. The App was still open but the screen was dark.
"It's for you," June said, standing over him, her hand outstretched offering the handset that she had carried from the hallway. He hadn't even noticed that she had come back into the room.
"Oh, sorry love," he replied apologetically as he took it from her. She turned to walk away. He sensed that she felt relieved that the call had nothing to do with the boys.
"Yes?" he enquired.
At the other end of the line was a familiar voice; DS White.
"Sorry to bother you at home, Sir, but we've received an anonymous call that I thought you should know about."
"In connection with?"
"An abduction, possibly a murder. The caller seemed a bit vague but there was something said that could have a link to the killing of the Millwright family."
"What was that?"
"The person said that they saw someone attacked and bundled into a van. She indicated there were drugs involved."
"She?"

"Yes, Sir. The voice appears to be that of a young girl. She tried to disguise her voice, but she used phrases that teenagers of today use."
Brierly was intrigued. "Did the caller say where this all happened?"
"Yes, in the Hollybrook cemetery. In addition, she said when. The timing seems to fit with when the burnt-out van was found on Ashley Down Lane. It's too much of a coincidence for it not to have merit….unless there is another killer out there."
Brierly considered White's remarks before saying, "I think you are right Barry, but there is still something that doesn't make sense."
White waited for Brierly to elaborate. "Why now?" he asked.
"Sir?"
"Why make the call now?"
"Guilt? Fear? Revenge?"
There it was, that word again; Revenge. Brierly got up from his chair, his mind racing ahead of itself. "Do we know where the call was made from?" he asked.
"Not as yet, Sir. The technical boys are doing their best, but they think it was from a phone with an unregistered sim card."
"Bugger."
"There is one good thing though, Sir," White continued, understanding Brierly's frustration.
"What's that?"
"The message. The caller specifically asked for it to be given to you personally."

Jill Tucker pressed the button on her phone. Her call had gone unanswered again. She had tried all evening to get through but there had been no response and no reply to her SMS or Whats App messages. She could see that there had been no activity on either for the past 18 hours. She was extremely worried. Had she done the right thing? She would try again in the morning. If there was no reply, then she would take a drive to the house.

CHAPTER 53

He had arrived at six in the morning. With so much to get through Brierly had called for the situation meeting to start an hour earlier than usual. After he had finished his call with White, he had contacted Hammond who had been out at a function until ten but had taken a call soon after. They had spoken for nearly an hour. Hammond had listened intently and agreed to Brierly's request to have extra resources made available to him. Brierly had been so involved in his discussion that he had hardly noticed Simon and Warwick return home. They had tiptoed around him, collecting food from the kitchen and taking it to their rooms while he conversed with his boss. By the time he had finished the call, both boys were already heavily engaged in watching TV or listening to music on headphones, their studies set aside. With the briefest of reply, a grunt from both, he had said goodnight before making his way to join June in bed. When he entered the bedroom he noticed that she was still reading.
"How is the book?" he asked, noting that she was still reading the same memoir.
"I'm about three-quarters of the way through it," she answered. "It's quite sad in a way," she continued, proceeding to give him an overview of what she had read to date. What she told him would resonate later.

The room was filled with excited voices as he and DS White entered. Apart from his usual team, there was a member of the drug squad, the backroom technical team, and several support team members, including a research adviser, a behavioural specialist, and other advisers. Brierly was always surprised how resources could be found at a moment's notice and inwardly queried why there were so many of them, given his ongoing budget battles. He wasn't even sure if all those in the room were needed, but he decided not to look a gift horse in the mouth. Policing used to be so much easier, but nowadays he and his team were obligated to engage with specialists and advisers who always seemed to require additional hangers-on, for reasons he could never fathom. Brierly thought there were now too many tellers and not enough doers; Chiefs versus Indians!

He brought the meeting to order, the room falling quiet with only the odd cough and sneeze to disturb the silence. As he looked around him, he felt the tension. The atmosphere was one of contained excitement. Things were happening, expectations were high.
"There are a number of things I want to discuss this morning, so we need to get through them as quickly as possible," he began. "Let me expand on what I mean." He stared at every face in the room in turn, increasing the tension. It was another tactic he used, something he had done many times, even in the navy, to motivate his crew members. When certain activities outside the building were required to help close a case, such as making arrests, people seemed to put more into the job. It was as if one case that was on the verge of being resolved created excitement and an increased impetus to solve other cases.
"Before we begin, however," Brierly continued, "I just want to thank the team for the work done so far. I came in early this morning and read the reports that I asked for and I want to give you my summation of where we are in respect of the matters we are investigating."
A few nods and the odd smile appeared on the faces in front of him. His acknowledgement of the work they had done to date was appreciated by them all.
"There are three matters that we are dealing with currently. At first, each appeared to be random acts, but it is now clear to me that in some way, directly or indirectly they are all linked. The reports that I referred to have solidified that view. However, there are still a few loose ends to sort out so this afternoon we need to complete our planning to ensure that we are ready to take the necessary steps tomorrow morning."
There was a ripple of anticipation throughout the group. Brierly's implication was like music to the team's ears. He continued to explain why he had formed the views that he had. "Firstly, let me start with the murder of Dave Crossley, the young student who was also dealing drugs. In my view, he was killed because he was in the wrong place at the wrong time. We know when he was murdered, and I believe I now know the why. Tomorrow I expect to arrest the who that killed him. In addition," he said, "we now know that our first victim found in the Hollybrook cemetery was Crossley's father. This was confirmed by DNA analysis as laid out in the report we received

from Dr. Atkins. From the follow-up undertaken by DC Hughes and DS White with the Crossley family, we now have a reasonable understanding of why Crossley's father was in the area. It seems he had found out where his son was studying and wanted to reconcile with him, unfortunately, it was not to be. We also know that he was murdered in similar circumstances to his son. Our investigation will continue on this one, but I am confident that tomorrow we will prove beyond doubt as to why." He explained what steps were to be taken and by whom. He was now in full flow adding, "With regards to the murders of the Millwright family, DS Track has done some excellent work and submitted a report which has found the link between that family and another. That link along with the evidence already gleaned has confirmed my suspicion as to who killed them. The reason why is still to be properly determined, but I am sure that once we arrest the individual concerned, we will eventually get to the truth. Finally, about an hour ago, I listened to an anonymous phone call that was left specifically for me. The individual who made the call was a young woman. Voice analysis was conducted overnight by our technical team," he pointed to one of the occupants in the room, a man in his late twenties dressed casually in jeans and a faux leather jacket, "and Francis there has confirmed that the caller is from this area, despite a rather poor attempt to disguise the voice and accent."
A hand went up as he was about to continue. It was DC Hughes, partially obscured by one of the advisers.
"Excuse me, Sir, do we know why the message was left for you personally?"
"I am not quite sure, Hughes. My guess is that with the murders reported in the local press and my name associated with leading the investigation was enough for the caller to make contact."
"What did the caller say, Sir?" Hughes questioned him.
Brierly smiled. Breakthroughs in cases often came from the most unlikely of sources. This was one, that allowed him to confirm his suspicion. It was the answer he had been searching for. The next steps were crucial, however, if they were to get the conviction they sought. He needed a confession even though he believed he had enough evidence to prove his case. He told the team what the anonymous caller had said and then explained his thinking as to why he was convinced the call was genuine. The room stayed silent as Brierly then outlined his thoughts about what needed to be done

next. The steps and actions to be taken. The plans were to be formalized in the next few hours and would be shared with the team by late afternoon. He shared a brief smile with White, who sensed how his boss was feeling. The electricity and energy throughout the entire team, the immediate and extended, was palpable. It was why they were all there; to finish the job. Brierly then emphasized that he wanted everyone to be ready to act before dawn, then closed the meeting by thanking everyone again for their collective efforts. As the room emptied, the sound of excited voices receding, he and White remained behind until they were alone.

"What do you think, Barry?"

Without hesitation, White said, "I think we are nearly there, Sir. Though I'm still a little confused about the voicemail message. Do you know who the caller is?"

"No, I don't, at least not yet, but I have an idea. I think DC Track has been able to give me enough to fill in the gaps in my th…."

Brierly stopped talking in mid-sentence as his mobile phone began to ring. White waited while he answered it. His boss looked at the screen to see who was calling then mouthed silently that it was DI Sutton.

"Good morning, Phil. To what do I owe the pleasure?" Brierly asked.

"I'm not sure it's such a good morning, to be honest, Jim," Sutton replied, his voice exuding softly from the speaker.

"Go on," Brierly answered, a sense of dread starting to inveigle its way throughout his body. Sutton's tone was very measured. It suggested something of concern.

"We have just found the body of Trevor Owen," Sutton replied. "In his house. Half of his head had been blown away."

Brierly stiffened. He was stunned, shocked, unbelieving. White watched as his boss seemed to become catatonic for an instant, almost frozen.

"What?" Brierly queried, suddenly recovering from his trancelike state. "When did this happen?"

"We believe it was last night looking at the scene, but we only discovered him about an hour ago. My team are combing through the place as we speak."

"Who discovered him?"

"Well, we found the body itself after we broke down the front door. I received a call from his daughter, Mary. She had tried to contact him

earlier this morning but hadn't been able to get an answer, so she contacted a neighbour who went to look for him."
"And?"
"The neighbour apparently rang the doorbell and knocked on the front door but got no answer. So she went to peer through the front window which still had the curtains partially open and saw him on the floor. Fortunately, she wasn't able to see the blood around the head and upper body that we have, but she said she could see his feet sticking beyond the edge of a couch where he was lying on the floor. That was enough for her to call the police."
"Poor woman," Brierly stated, empathizing with the neighbour, thinking how traumatic the entire scene would have been for her. "I assume no one heard anything then?" he asked.
"Well, it's a bit early to tell, though I doubt anyone did. We might get lucky, though I doubt it. Last night was cold and pretty miserable here. Most people in the immediate area were probably locked inside with their TVs on and their curtains and blinds closed. I suspect hardly anyone would have heard anything, even if the moon, a star, or even an alien had landed on top of their houses."
Brierly considered the comments to be a bit harsh, but he understood why Sutton had said what he had. It was a fact of policing that without good neighbours, and people willing to share their observations, many crimes would go unpunished, and the perpetrators never found. It was a sad fact that break-ins and burglary cases often remained unsolved, With no one injured and with limited resources the police often let the insurance company pick up the tab rather than waste its own money. Sometimes luck was on their side…an observant neighbour could often be the key. In this case, it seemed that luck was not on their side.
"So, what are you thinking, Phil? Suicide?" Brierly asked.
"Perhaps, but I don't understand the why."
"The why meaning, why now?"
"Yes, as well as what was to be gained."
"From killing oneself?"
"Yes."
Brierley considered this new development for a few seconds. In the silence, he indicated to White that they meet again in Brierly's office once he had finished the conversation. He watched his Sergeant leave the room and then quizzed Sutton again.

"Did you find the weapon?"
"Yes. It was lying next to the body."
"Type?"
"The same type we confiscated from him a short while ago, a semi-automatic Beretta 9000."
"Which indicates that he had access to several guns."
"Absolutely."
"Which again would suggest how serious he had been taking the threats against him and his family?"
"Agreed."
Throwing a curveball, Brierly said, "Unless he was the killer."
Sutton almost choked. The reaction from down the line indicating what he thought of Brierly's comment. "Are you serious, Jim?" he asked.
"No, but your reaction tells me everything Phil," Brierly said. "I think you are right. The poor man was murdered and I'm pretty sure I know by who."
The two men spoke for a little while longer, Brierly outlining his suspicions and explaining to Sutton the rationale behind his theory. The latter said that he would keep an open mind concerning Brierly's conclusions, adding that there was still the need for evidence but he also acknowledged his counterparts' reasoning. Chuckling in response, Brierly told Sutton that it was almost certain that DNA evidence would be found at the site of Trevor Owens' murder. It just needed to be gathered. Evidence that would confirm Brierly's conclusions. Sutton was still not convinced but agreed to go along with Brierly's request to look for it. It was the least he could do, especially if Brierly was right. Disconnecting the call Brierly mulled over what had been discussed. He knew that he was right....at least he believed he was. The end of the individual investigations was in sight, the killer had almost completed their mission. It would end soon. The death of Trevor Owens was part of the killer's story, like a comma in an extended sentence. Brierly realized that the full stop was only another evening away. He left the room to seek out Hammond and tell him of the latest developments. Once he had an agreement on his plan, then he would be off to court.

CHAPTER 54

They had been able to reach the front door under cover of darkness. The rain which had stayed away for a short while was back, a steady drizzle now falling. Droplets large and small attached themselves to the backs of the coats and uniforms, especially the headgear of the policemen who waited patiently in the cold for the order to make the arrest. It was not yet five am but most of them had been up for several hours having met at the police station at two, readying themselves for what was to come. With quiet resolve, two of the six policemen standing against the house wall peeled away and made their way quietly to the back door, walking through a small gate attached to one side of the building. DS White held the arrest warrant in his hand having received it the previous evening. The magistrate concerned had no problem with the request to issue it. The threat of violence and the suspicion of a murder having been committed were enough to convince her to do so. The lights inside the house were off. The police used narrow beam torches and the light from nearby streetlamps to get themselves into position. Usually, an arrest like this one would be conducted calmly. A knock on the door with a simple, "please accompany us to the station," request being made. However White had agreed with Brierly that there was a risk that the suspect may try to use others as hostages, so their approach this time was going to be much more aggressive. Tactically it would ensure that the suspect did not have any time to flee, hide or destroy any evidence. It was why everyone was required to be in place early. Everyone was at their most vulnerable while they were sleeping, and Brierly knew that in this specific case it was highly unlikely that the suspect would be anywhere else at such an early hour.

When everyone was in position, White rang the front-door bell repeatedly and hammered on the wooden panels. "Police! Open up!" he shouted, "Police!"

Within seconds a light appeared in an upstairs room, then a curtain twitched as a face looked down upon the group of men standing at the door. From inside the home sound of footsteps could be heard as somebody appeared to be moving towards the front door. White shouted again, this time more aggressively. He noticed lights coming on in the neighbouring house to the right-hand side and in another couple of bedrooms across the road. It was obvious that the commotion being made was disturbing some of the neighbour's dreams. Suddenly a porch light above White's head came on and for a second he was blinded. Then the front door opened partially and there, dressed in a blue housecoat, her hair dishevelled from having been asleep in bed stood Christine Grovedale. She blinked her eyes a few times as White started to speak with her. With just a few words having escaped his lips, she suddenly disappeared again behind the door, a cry of pain renting the air as her head smashed against an inside wall. Terence Silver had pulled her arm and flung her away from the door in his attempt to slam it shut. White realized what was happening and with brute force and support from DC Proctor, smashed a shoulder against the door sending it flying inwardly, knocking Silver and Grovedale to the ground. The policemen stumbled across the threshold barely keeping their feet as their momentum unbalanced them. Silver tried to stand up but was tackled by Proctor, whose wet clothes stuck to the exposed skin of Silver, shocking him into silence for a second.

"Terence Silver?" White began, as Proctor dragged the man up from the floor and locked a pair of handcuffs onto him. Silver looked at Grovedale from out of the corner of his eye. One side of her face was bloodied from where her head had banged against the wall. He was filled with rage and began to scream at her. He ignored Whites' caution concerning the charge being laid against him, the explanation of his right to silence, and legal representation. "Bitch!" he shouted. Anger and malice reflected in his eyes and his aggressive mouth, spittle flying as he screamed again, "Fucking Bitch!"

White finished what he needed to say, then instructed Silver to "keep quiet and get dressed!" Telling him that a house coat over the man's naked body was inadequate for the drive to the police station unless Silver wanted to add further embarrassment to his arrest. With no significant response, White arranged for himself and two of the Constables from the arrest team to help Silver change into a tracksuit and running shoes, readying him for the short trip to the station where he would be formally charged and placed into a holding cell. While White was busy with Silver, Proctor and another member of the team, took Grovedale back into the house, sitting her down at a kitchen table before attending to her wound. As they did so, they explained to her what was happening, observing how relieved she

seemed at what had taken place. They suggested at one point that she be taken to hospital for a checkup, but she said that it was unnecessary. Eventually, she was offered a policewoman to come and sit with her for the rest of the morning, to keep her company and provide any moral assistance she may need. However, with what seemed a bone of contention she declined the offer. She decided to make coffee instead, insisting that she would be okay. It was an obvious attempt to settle her nerves, to stop her hands and her body from shaking. The policemen understood how she felt. A thundering wake-up call so early in the morning, and one so unexpectedly loud and violent was not an everyday occurrence for anyone. Also from where she was sitting, she could still hear Silver shouting, swearing, and snorting occasionally, calling for his dog which had been sleeping in the utility room when the raid had begun. The dog was safely on a lead and had been properly secured, but it still reacted to Silver's snarls each time he made enough noise for the animal to hear him, barking in response to its owner's outbursts.
"Get him out of here," White ordered, as soon as Silver was properly dressed. It was now almost six am and the cold and damp of the day was like a thick black wall pressing against the front door. It would still be another ninety minutes before it started to get light. As Silver was led out of the house and placed into an unmarked police car that earlier had been parked a few hundred metres down the road, he was joined by Proctor, who sat beside him in the back seat. His huge frame and rugby physique intimidated their suspect into complete silence. The only sign of how Silver was reacting to his arrest, was an angry grimace and a flash of disbelief in his eyes. "Bitch!" he mouthed again, his face at the window as the car drove away. White stood in the open doorframe, looking outward, trying to stay dry, watching the rain splash on the body of the receding car as it disappeared from view. He turned around, walking towards the kitchen where Christine Grovedale remained seated, contemplative. With the house now effectively silent, the events of the morning over, he called the balance of the team together and repeated what he had told them a few hours earlier. They still had work to do. It was not yet over.

It took them forty minutes to find what they were looking for.
It took them a further ten minutes to find something unexpected.

CHAPTER 55

Mary Owen was beside herself. She had answered the phone when the shrill of it had woken her. After leaving her father, the previous day she had arrived back at her house, bathed for an hour, even falling asleep at one point, before ending her evening by sitting with her thoughts in the silence of her lounge as she drank a couple of glasses of wine. She had been angry with him and was even too angry to eat. She was now feeling the effects of not having done so. A headache and now heartache at the news left her feeling completely devastated, alone and scared.

She had tried to get hold of Tom before she dressed but had only been able to leave a voicemail for him, having no idea where he might be, as he wasn't answering his phone. She desperately needed to speak with him. Sutton's call, during which he had broken the news to her, had sparked cries of despair and anguish, which had rattled down the phone line. The pain and grief were coupled like twins that expelled groans and tears from her very soul. Her first reaction was disbelief and then an insistence on seeing him, but Sutton had told her to stay away. The house was a crime scene, and she would be denied access anyway. He had told her to wait for the police to contact her again, but he could not guarantee when that would be. She needed to remain calm, be patient, and if she felt unsafe to call Brierly who was the principal detective in charge of the case.

As she sat on her couch, her legs tucked underneath her, she felt numb, her head pounding not yet reacting to the paracetamol tablets she had taken earlier. She turned her head and stared out of the window at the sad and murky sky. Thick clouds hid the sun which had no chance of breaking through them. Spots of rain tapped gently onto the glass, running down the pane and accelerating as gravity took hold. She found herself in a stupor, not willing to move nor willing to act. Everything that had happened was now stacked on top of each other. Layered like a cake in the forefront of her mind. What was worse however was that now that he was gone, she had no way of telling him how she really felt. She wanted him to know that she hadn't meant what she had said the previous evening. She wanted to tell him that she loved him, that she was grateful for everything he

had done for her, that she was not angry with him anymore!
She burst into tears. Rivers ran down her cheeks and her vision blurred. Outside her window, beyond the garden, people walked along her street their heads bowed against the rain. Umbrellas twisted and bent as gusts of wind showered them with rain that occasionally became horizontal to the ground rather than vertical. Despite the irritation, none of them knew what she was experiencing. Life was continuing. It always did. Death may have visited her family and potentially destroyed it completely yet for others it was just another day. Her anger grew. Who was the bastard who did this? she asked herself. How could killing an entire family be justified? She recalled Tom saying that he would find the perpetrator and she decided to try and contact him again. She needed to know what he intended to do. Was he for real or was it all talk? If he was serious then she would join him. With everyone in the family now gone, there was only the two of them left. She picked up her mobile again dialing his number, and surprisingly he answered.

Patricia sat in the kitchen chair facing toward him. Her shivering had stopped a long time ago but the warmth of the cup she held in her hands barely compensated for the ripples of need that coursed through her body. She had slept well despite needing a hit, and the bed that he had provided, her normal one, was as comfortable as always. The last of the bacon and eggs were finished, and only a single slice of toast remained uneaten on his plate. She was tempted to reach for it, but decided not to, despite her hunger. She watched him, his back to her, as he began to stack the dishwasher.
"Are you sure you have had enough?" he asked, concern showing on his face.
"Yes, I'm fine."
With a smile he continued with his job, using a dishcloth to wipe away crumbs from the kitchen table. She continued observing him, her eyes following him above the rim of her cup. Another shiver. She needed to find her dealer or at least someone who could supply as soon as possible. Dressed as she was, she could be out of the house within minutes and into the city very shortly afterwards. The only thing she needed was money. When he eventually arrived home, she

had been able to follow him into the house, almost immediately. He had appeared to be non-plussed when she had walked up his drive only a minute or so after he had parked his car. He had been about to open the front door when she spoke to him and had almost dropped his keys at the sound of her voice. She had noticed.
Without hesitation, he had invited her in and organized dinner for her. She had not raised what she knew, as she wanted to keep it under wraps until she could maximize its value. Knowledge was power and she intended to exercise it to her advantage. It was all about looking after oneself nowadays, getting what you believed was yours rather than getting what you actually deserved.
"I know," she said suddenly, her voice monotone, her eyes downward facing, her fingers revolving the now empty cup in her hands. The response she received was as she expected. A pretence.
"Sorry?" he questioned.
She raised her head, looking him straight in the eyes, and repeated her comment.
"Sorry love, but what are you talking about?"
She smirked. His denial reaffirmed his guilt in her eyes. Even though she would say that she had no intention of telling another soul and that it would be their secret, she wanted him to feel uncomfortable so that he would always need to pay to keep her from talking to the authorities. Was it blackmail? Yes, it was, but she didn't care. Their secret would be her passageway to the bank. His bank!
Slowly, like a languid cat, she unfurled herself from her chair and stood up, stretching her limbs protractedly, revealing her flat stomach as her top rode up. He saw how emaciated she was under her clothing, her body so much thinner than one could imagine under the baggy clothes that she wore. He stared at her wishing to himself that she would do the right thing. That she would do what she had promised him many times before. Settle down, straighten herself out, get back to normal and jump off the bandwagon that she continued to ride. Without feeling a need to tell him why she launched into a partially rehearsed speech that she had compiled before they had sat down for breakfast. She began to talk about what she had seen, what she wanted in return for her silence, telling him that he had no choice but to comply with her demands. As she stood against the pantry door, she received the response that she had hoped for but it was still unexpected when it came. Agreement to all of her requests. Regular

receipt of money, her dropping out of college, and him stepping back from telling her how to live her life and with whom. On reflection she thought, it had been much easier than she had expected, and she felt proud of herself for getting through it as quickly and as successfully as she had. She relaxed, picked up her empty cup, and went to pass it to him, making a small gesture toward the dishwasher. As she did so, he suddenly appeared to react to something she hadn't seen, grabbing the wrist of her right hand and pulling her towards him. She spun, losing her balance, and started to fall, but he caught her on the second attempt. She thought initially that she had tripped but soon realized that he had grabbed her on purpose, his vice-like grip across both wrists now beginning to hurt her. She tried to kick him away but with her wrists locked inside his own hands, she found herself helpless.

Almost immediately she was frog-marched along the passageway toward the front of the house. She guessed that he was taking her back upstairs but as they reached the middle of the passage, she realized what he was going to do. Under the stairs was a small storage room. She had never been inside it before, but she had always called it the hole. Inside, it was big enough for a couple of chairs to be stacked on top of one another, several boxes of different sizes, and herself. An overhead light (the switch of which, was outside in the passageway) provided the necessary illumination when needed. He had managed to wrap an arm around her waist and had carried her towards the hole. She had tried to scream but an expert hand had covered her mouth, muffling any sound that she had attempted to make. Within seconds she was alone and in the dark, the door to the under-stair room slammed shut and locked. A padlock was also snapped into place. She had been told not to scream as it would be of no use. The room had been insulated against any noise escaping. In a panic, having experienced the highs of being in control to the depths of being a prisoner, she scrambled around in her pockets for her phone, but she couldn't find it. Instantly she remembered where it was. It was on the kitchen table where she had placed it while she told him what her demands were. With the haunting realization that she had misjudged him, she began to tremble. She had no idea what was going to happen to her, and the fear of the unknown played on her imagination. She banged on the door and screamed as loud as she could, but she only heard the dull babble of a radio being played. It was obvious that the sound outside exceeded any noise that she could make. After a while she was exhausted, giving up any attempt to find a rescuer. She fell asleep, the darkness of the room cloying, the firmness of the floor that she now curled up on, hard. Almost as bad as the pavements and park benches that she often used as a bed. When she awoke sometime later, she could see very little in the darkness that cloistered all around her For a few seconds, she was unsure where she was. She was confused. Then she remembered what had happened to her. She tried to stay calm, but in her mind's eye, the ghosts of her past came calling. Brought on by what she had gone through and her increasing need to fill her veins. She began to hallucinate. Hands began to reach out from the side of the walls, from the floor on which she cowered. She could feel them grasping at her, clawing at her clothes, her face, her body. She tried to push them away, but they kept reappearing. She could feel their presence all around her. She felt as if she was going insane and began to cry out again, but her screams went unanswered. With tears in her eyes, she collapsed into herself, sitting on the floor rocking backwards and forwards, mumbling.

She didn't see the ghostly hands that came to take her.

CHAPTER 56

Brierly held up the plastic bag that contained the knife. On the table in front of him was another, the contents - a mobile phone. Seated next to him was DS White. On the other side of the table, Trevor Silver and Duty solicitor Gerald Walker. They had been here so many times before. It was a sign that a result was imminent, at least Brierly hoped it was.

"Care to explain this?" he asked, waving the bag in front of Silver's face. The man looked straight through the plastic as if it wasn't there, his eyes fixed on Brierly. There was no response, not even a flicker of acknowledgement of the question asked. Brierly put the bag down on the table. Picking up the second bag he said, "For the record, I am showing Mr. Silver an evidence bag with a mobile phone inside. Care to comment, Sir?"

There was none.

Brierly stared back at the man. It was obvious that Silver had been briefed by Walker not to respond to anything unless the Solicitor believed it was the best thing for him to do. "Silence could harm your defence," he had told his client, to which Silver had retorted that he understood the caution that he was under. He advised Walker that he was a man with reasonable intelligence; a man who was a partner in his own business and who knew where he stood given the circumstances. Walker had been taken aback by Silver's arrogance but had remained professional. He would advise his client as he was obliged to do until Silver decided to appoint his own legal counsel. Given his client's attitude, Walker expected that request would come before the day was out, surmising that Silver's opinion of himself would also be his downfall.

Not my problem, Walker thought to himself.

Brierly sighed. He knew that he was dealing with someone who wouldn't be easy to break but he had seen this personality type before. They lacked self-awareness, they were rude, they sought to be admired, and exaggerated their abilities. Brierly realized that he should have seen the traits when he first interviewed Silver and Christine Grovedale at their home. He recalled her listening to his conversation with Silver from down the hallway at the time of the first cemetery murder. Silver gave a different impression of himself at

the time, but his now obvious arrogance was hiding an innate insecurity. That insecurity had led to the unfortunate killing of Dave Crossley.
"I'll ask you again, Mr. Silver, would you care to explain how this knife was found in your garage?"
Silver spoke for the first time, "No comment," he replied.
"Ahh, the no-comment response. Very clever," Brierly teased, smiling at White who remained passive as his role demanded. "I suppose no comment means that you have no idea?"
"No comment."
"Well let me comment for you, Mr. Silver. The knife was in your garage because you hid it there, didn't you?!"
"No comment."
"You hid it there after you killed a student by the name of Dave Crossley, didn't you?"
"No comment."
"A young man, who was in the wrong place at the wrong time!"
"No comment,"
"A young man, who was dealing drugs, but who you thought was spying on your partner. Isn't that, right?!"
Brierly noticed that Silver was starting to become agitated. It was clear that his accusations were starting to have an effect.
"What was it?" Brierly continued, "A slight to your manhood?"
The barb was intentional and Brierly knew that he had hit a nerve. Under the table he felt White react, the latter's knees giving a quick push against his own.
"No."
"No?" Brierly replied, incredulously, "No?"
"No!" Silver shouted, banging the table with his hand, causing Walker to jump slightly at the unexpected violence. Brierly waited for a full ten seconds before speaking again, watching Silver's breathing slowly subside after his outburst, noting however that the fire remained in the man's eyes. He picked up the bag containing the mobile. "On here," he said, pointing, "on your phone, Mr. Silver is video of your partner Christine Grovedale and Ms. Jill Tucker. They are having sex in a car. Jill Tucker's car." There was no response from Silver. "The video was taken on the same night that Dave Crossley was killed. Did you take the video, Mr. Silver?"
"I.."

"Did you take it to confront Christine, or was it for your personal enjoyment, Mr. Silver?"
"Inspector!" chimed in Walker, "that's an irrelevance as to why…."
"Is it?" Brierly interrupted. "I think counsellor, it is a motive. A motive that resulted in a young student being murdered."
"I don't see.."
"I do, Mr. Walker. Your client here clearly had an issue with someone else filming his partner and her lover. Is that how it happened, Mr. Silver? Is that why you had the knife?
"No."
"Of course it was, Mr. Silver. You intended to kill Christine, didn't you? I think that while you were hiding in the cemetery waiting for her to go home, Dave Crossley saw you there didn't he? He got in your way, and could have exposed you, and spoilt your plan, yes? You were so angry seeing those boys film what was happening in the car, that you lost your temper with them, didn't you? You couldn't take the embarrassment, so you sought revenge. You killed Dave Crossley in a fit of rage all because Ms. Grovedale had rejected you and had a female lover. Isn't that right?!"
White noticed that Silver had slowly, progressively, put his hands to his head, covering his ears while sinking further and further forwards in his chair, denials from his lips, tears flowing and his body shaking as Brierly laid out his case.
"I didn't…I didn't..mean..I…," Silver sobbed, his cries of despair echoing off the walls of the room. The beginning of a confession slowly tumbling from his lips.
"We know that this knife was used to kill Dave Crossley. It still has traces of his blood on it and has already been DNA tested," Brierly continued. "We believe that there is also sufficient evidence on the knife that proves it was handled by you Mr. Silver, despite an obvious but rather poor attempt to hide the fact! Ms. Grovedale has also confirmed that a similar knife was bought by you to replace this one which she noticed was missing in the knife block that you have in your kitchen. She has advised us that you told her the day after we visited you at your house, that the old one had been dropped and broken by you the previous day. Coincidence? I think not."
Walker looked towards his client who was still facing the floor, his shoulders heaving with silent sobs.
Brierly continued with his accusations, pushing toward a full

confession. He knew it would come. "So let me repeat, the film on this phone proves that you were in the vicinity of the cemetery on the night Dave Crossley was killed. We have the knife that was used. It won't take a genius to convince a jury that it was you who murdered him…so…."
"Alright! Alright!" Silver exclaimed, "yes, I killed him. The bitch was laughing at me….and so were they, those kids. Laughing at them…in the car, filming…voyeurs…watching. Watching me being humiliated…I just snapped. I couldn't take it anymore. It had been going on too long…"
Brierly winked at White, their job was almost done. Silver had given them what they wanted. And now they knew the motive; Revenge. Revenge for being rejected. Rejected as a man, something his character and personality could not accept. Brierly advised Walker that he and White would be excusing themselves for a short while and that a Constable would be brought into the room while he and his client readied themselves for the charges that were to be laid.
Walker nodded. Inwardly he felt relieved that Silver had confessed. The man had been arrogant initially but was now a parody of his former self. All the bravado that he had shown had now dissipated. He was just a shell of a man.
Once outside the interrogation room, White stopped Brierly with a tap on his boss's arm. Brierly still holding the two evidence bags turned to face him.
"Yes, Barry?"
"The knife," White said, indicating the bag. "Does it really have Silvers' fingerprints and DNA on it?"
"What do you think?" Brierly asked.
"I'm not sure, but…"
"Let's just say, it does…sort of."
"You mean?"
"That there are others on it as well. Yes, including those of Christine Grovedale."
"So?"
"So the evidence is inconclusive, but he doesn't know that," Brierly said, his head making a slight flick toward the room they had just vacated. "But we got a confession from him and that's what counts."
"I suppose so, but there is another thing I don't get."
"Which is?"

"Why didn't he dispose of the knife? Why hide it in the garage?"
"I don't know," Brierly replied honestly, "but my guess is that he wanted to use it again. I think he intended to have another go at Grovedale and maybe Jill Tucker as well. That's why he kept the film on the phone. To use it against both of them."
"You mean if he got away with Crossley's killing?"
"Yes and if he hadn't gotten so angry and started threatening Christine, he may well have done so. Remember it was only because of his increased aggression that caused her to share her concerns with Tucker."
"Do you think Grovedale knew that he was following her to the cemetery, watching and filming their liaisons?"
"I think she might of, I'm not sure," Brierly answered. "But whether she knew that his ego would be so affected and that his insecurity would result in murder, I doubt it."
White frowned. Brierly had taken a risk. It was unusual for him to do so, but it had worked. "Can I take those to the evidence room for you?" he said, pointing at Brierly's hands. Brierly handed the bags over.
"Thanks, Sergeant. I'll see you upstairs. Can you get the team together for a meeting in just short of an hour?" he asked, looking at his watch.
"Yes, of course."
"Good. I have a couple of things to check before we make our next move. I'll be with you shortly, but the next twenty-four hours will be crucial in solving the rest of these bloody riddles."

CHAPTER 57

He had been sleeping for several hours, waking to the still-dark morning. He remembered feeling drowsy and falling asleep as the night closed in. He had tried to ignore her cries and let the music from the radio drown out her screams. The sound kept him calm as well until she finally settled down. They were both exhausted by that stage. He was very worried about her now. Her physical well-being and also her state of mind. He had decided to let her go through the stages of withdrawal, as he believed she needed to. Insomnia, irritability, aches, pains, depression, cravings, hallucinations, some if not all he knew she was subject to. He had seen it so many times before during the course of his work, but with the others, he had not had such an emotional bond. This was different. This was necessary.

He was sitting in his room. The darkness enveloped him, and the tree stood before him, its branches now fewer. There were two left but only one of them was relevant now. After his recent handiwork and his pruning, there was only a single branch that needed attention. Once that had been cut off, he would put himself into the care of the state. He didn't care whether that was the hospital or a prison cell. He would have done his duty.

He walked quietly to the door; the room under the stairs. He listened for any movement but there was none. Removing the padlock and then inserting a key into the keyhole, he slowly turned it anti-clockwise until he heard the click. Inching it open, he held the door ajar by a few centimetres peering into the void, his eyes adjusting to the gloom within. He had deliberately left the lights off in the house until now, then once he was able to see her, still asleep on the floor, he reached for the switch and turned on the inside light. For a few seconds, she did not move. He could see that she was asleep but as he reached for her, she screamed in fright when his hand gripped her arm.

"It's okay," he said, his voice soft and soothing, as she tried to rub her eyes with her free hand. "I won't hurt you. You are safe here."

She squinted in his general direction, her mind still confused from the dreams and terrors she had endured over the past few hours or so.

"What do you want?" she asked. "Why did you stick me in here?"
"I just want to help you," he replied. "I've been trying for ages, but you haven't been the easiest person to deal with."
She rubbed her eyes again. She was still sleepy, but her body was racked with stiffness, and she was feeling cold. She needed to stand, but until he let her out, there was no space. She looked beyond him for a second, noting the familiar pattern of the wallpaper in the passageway, partially lit by the overhead light. She had seen it so many times before. "Can I come out, please?" she asked, trying to sound grateful if he would just consider her request.
"Yes, of course. I wanted to show you something anyway."
He withdrew backwards from the small door space and allowed her to crawl out, the light from inside casting a shadow on the floor as she did so. As she stood upright, he turned on another light in the room just to one side of her cell, on the opposite side of the passageway. She realized that except for the second, additional, light, the rest of the house on the ground floor was still in darkness.
"Are you hungry?" he asked as he followed her into the brightly lit room.
"Yes," she replied meekly. She could tell that her energy level was low, her feet seemed to drag along the floor, as she sloped ahead of him, sitting down quickly in a chair opposite the large desk.
He noticed how languid she appeared. How gaunt her face was and how her fingernails were blackened and had been bleeding. He hadn't noticed them previously, but he was glad that he could see them for himself now. Her physical state only served to add to the justification of his actions.
"I'll make you something to eat once I've shown you this," he said, picking up the tree and handing it to her.
"What is this?" she asked, tentatively, suspicion in her eyes.
"It's why you are here."
Holding the picture in her hands, she saw where the branches had been removed, scored out, large crosses in red sitting over the various boxes.
"What is it?" she asked, still not comprehending what he was alluding to.
"It's a tree. A family tree. It ends here!" he exclaimed, pointing at a box at the bottom of the diagram.
Inside was a name and a date: Mary Owen - April 15th, 1992.

CHAPTER 58

She had driven all the way to meet him in the Royal Oak pub in Havant, on Langstone High Street, opposite Langstone Harbour. It had been a difficult drive, not because of the distance or the road, but predominantly because of the weather. The rain had started to come down harder than when she had first left home, and the closer she got to the coast, the stronger the winds had become. When she finally arrived, Sweare Deep was dirty with waves that curled in anger despite their low height and depth. The mud flats and the birds in the area, Terns, Greenshanks, and Teals were agitated into a frenzy of noise and phosphorescence. She was pleased to get inside the pub, but her stomach felt like the winds outside, churning with fear and vengefulness. It had been her idea as she didn't want to wait for him to come to her, so she had agreed with him that they meet halfway.
The pub itself was only a third full. There were a few diners in the restaurant area but the majority of those brave enough to challenge the elements were in the bar. No wonder, she thought to herself, only stupid, and desperate, people came out on nights like this. Most were talking quietly amongst themselves in little groups, though occasionally a loud laugh would escape from three men who were of similar age, mid-forties, she guessed, and who were trying to chat up a young girl behind the counter who was barely out of her teens.
"What do you want to drink?" Tom asked her, once she had settled in the seat next to him. They had a booth to themselves, the closest group sat a good ten feet away, two couples, in their early twenties.
"A glass of merlot will do," she replied.
"Anything to eat?"
"No, thanks."
She watched as he walked away. He had smartened himself up, wearing new jeans, a light grey jersey, and a black overcoat. She wondered how he was really feeling. It was difficult to tell given he appeared outwardly confident and measured as he stood waiting to order their drinks. They still hadn't been able to arrange any funerals that may have brought them both some closure and there was no indication as to when they would be in a position to do so. She knew however that he was close to the edge. He had said as much when

they had spoken briefly on the phone. He had lost his entire family; his wife, and his children. She had lost a sister, and a niece and nephew. Both had lost a father figure. In Mary's eyes, the police had failed them and Tom had agreed that they both needed to do something about it before they themselves became the next victim. But where to start?

Returning from the bar, Tom sat her drink down and then placed a pint of bitter and a small whisky chaser of his own onto the table. She looked at him again, wondering. Picking up the larger glass he raised it in her direction, wished her good health, and without stopping to draw breath drank half of the beer in a single mouthful. She left her glass untouched.

"You still don't have any idea who is behind this?" she asked.

"No."

"Not even an inkling?"

"No. Why would I?"

She looked at her hands before grasping the neck of her wine glass and taking a quick sip. "Because something doesn't make sense to me," she said.

"What's that?" he replied.

She looked at the wine glass, contemplatively, staring at the light glinting off the burgundy liquid. He waited for her to continue.

"I keep thinking about the threat," she said eventually.

"What?"

"The threat. I keep wondering, why you?"

"I'm not with you," he replied, obvious annoyance in his voice. "What are you suggesting?"

"I'm not suggesting anything to be honest. I'm speculating."

"About…?"

"About why you were targeted as well. In the message that Dad received, the list of birthdates. It included my family and you, but not any of your own family."

"What do you mean?"

"Well, I'm trying to work out why your mum wasn't threatened or even targeted. Not to mention your sister."

He looked at her suspiciously. "You already know that my mother is in a home with Parkinsons disease and has been blind for years and my sister lives in the US. So whoever is behind this probably either knows that or doesn't care."

"Yes, but …"

"But what? My mother and sister are irrelevant. What is relevant is you and me. *We* are what's left of your family and my family, that's it!"

His raised voice had carried in the quietness of the pub and he suddenly realized that some of the other customers had stopped talking. Several were staring at him. He gestured to those that he could see that they should get on with their own lives and stop listening to his conversation. Annoyed he grabbed the whisky glass, spilling some of the honey-coloured liquid in his haste to take a drink. With the glass to his lips, he swallowed the entire double tot in one go, warming his throat as he did so. Placing the glass back onto the table he said, "We need to talk to the police to find out where they are up to. If they have a suspect, we should try and find out who that person is, and….." His voice trailed off. He was conscious that some of those in the pub may still be listening.

"And do what?" she asked, almost afraid to hear his answer.

"We make sure that they get what they deserve."

She stared at him, a frown on her face. Initially, she had thought that getting even or seeking revenge was the only way to recover from what had happened to the family. That the culprit should suffer in the same way that they were suffering. However, the closer the possibility, and the more he spoke of it, the less she considered it as sensible, realistic, or even logical. She knew she wasn't a vengeful person but was someone who believed that justice should prevail. Those involved needed to be caught, yes. They needed to be punished, yes. But by the police, not by vigilantes as it seemed Tom wanted them to become. He noticed her reaction, her obvious discomfort.

"You're not getting cold feet are you?" he asked.

She took another sip of her wine, biding her time, wondering now why she had suggested they meet. Her impatience had gotten the better of her. Her need to find out who was behind the killings, while natural, had begun to eat her up from the inside. After taking a deep breath, she said, "I think we should let the police do their job."

"Are you serious?"

"Yes. I know we spoke about it earlier, but I think it's crazy to try and do anything on our own. I mean what would happen if we did find the killer? What are we going to do, kill them ourselves?"

"That's the general idea," he whispered in reply.
She looked at him, wide-eyed, surprised at his candour. What had seemed a natural human reaction now seemed irresponsible, and irreconcilable with her own values. She began to stand, but he put his hand on her arm, suggesting she remain seated. Slowly, her eyes fixed on his face, she retook her seat.
"Okay," he said, "I'll make a deal with you. Instead of going to the police now, we give them five days to do what they need to. If at the end of that time they haven't arrested anyone, or they don't have any suspects then I'll go hunting....with or without you."
"And if you do go hunting, what happens if you don't find the bastard? What do we do then?"
"If that happens, then we could both be in trouble. It's pretty obvious that we are still targets. The police can't protect us forever even if they, or we, wanted them to. That's why we need to get on the front foot, otherwise, either of us could be next, ending up lying on a slab under a pathologist's knife."
Mary shivered. She understood where he was coming from but felt that what he was saying to her was nothing other than Hobson's Choice. He was going to take matters into his own hands, irrespective of what she wanted. She wondered if there was more to his anger than what was obvious. Delaying any attempt to go on the hunt for a few days was merely a flippant gesture on his part, she guessed. Standing up and putting on her coat, she said, "Is there something you know, that I don't?"
"What do you mean?"
"Nothing," she answered, "just asking."

CHAPTER 59

He had taken her to the surgery. It was easier that way. Carol would not be around to get involved and he felt that it would allow the three of them to try and find a solution. When they walked through the front door together, the receptionist recognized her immediately but decided not to comment. She allowed him to take her directly into the consulting room. It was obvious that the girl was in a bad way.

The morning was gloomy and wet, thick clouds blew in from the southeast, so low that they scraped below the tops of the few tall buildings in the city. Moresby and Canberra towers were shrouded like someone with a scarf around their face. The short walk from the car park was enough for both of them to feel the impact of the wind and the rain which seemed to seep surreptitiously into every exposed pore.

Seated together, they waited. He watched a computer monitor that showed a yellow bouncing ball travel across the screen. Very basic, but suitable for a Doctor's office. She kept her eyes closed.

He spoke the instant his son came into the room.

"She needs help," Philip Boothby said, holding his Granddaughter close to him. She appeared uninterested in what was going on around her. Her eyes appeared to be glazed over, lacking any focus. It was as if she had drifted off in a dream somewhere and had never returned.

"Don't you think I've tried?" Alan Boothby replied. "Don't you think it's time that Pat…"

"Patricia!" the older man said, interjecting. "Her name is Patricia."

Alan sighed, "Of course I know that Dad, I named her."

"Well seeing as you had that privilege, what are you going to do about the situation now then?"

"I'm not going to do anything."

"What?"

"I've done enough, Dad, and frankly I've had enough. It's up to Patricia now."

"But she's being exploited."

Alan Boothby laughed, "Exploited?! By who? If anyone is doing any exploiting, it's Patricia. She's an expert at it."

Phil Boothby could not hide his disgust, his disappointment at his son's comments. He had hoped that their face-to-face meeting would be more positive, more constructive. He was obviously wrong.
"So, you are not prepared to help?" he asked.
"Not unless Patricia agrees to go back home, get clean, and continues studying or she gets herself a steady job. If she does that then I'll do what I can to support her financially....at least until she's able to stand on her own two feet."
"Fuck off!" a small voice exclaimed. Patricia speaking for the first time. Her words were blunt, but the execution was deliberate and her message clear.
Alan looked at his father. "I haven't got time for this," he said, "You see, no matter how I try, she reacts as if the whole world is against her. If she doesn't have things go her own way, she attacks everything and anything."
"Maybe she has reason too."
"Look Dad, we are not going to go over that again are we?"
"What do you mean?"
"You know bloody w...oh just forget it," Alan Boothby said.
The older man looked at his Granddaughter. He was annoyed by the continued lack of compassion his son was showing. He had tried to move the mountain but had little success. He decided to use the one thing he had left.

Her jibe, her subtle dig, had irritated him, and overnight he had lain in bed thinking of the next steps. By the time he finally fell asleep in the early hours, before waking around 5 am. he still didn't have much of a plan, but he did have an idea. He called her before six and her irritation at being woken up so early was obvious. After a brief discussion that had partially cleared the air, she had agreed to accompany him despite believing that he was wasting their time.
They were now sitting in the car, parked outside the police station building, on the Southern-Road side. Rain lashed the windscreen, the cold seeping into the now silent car. Drops of water occasionally fell onto her neck as a strong breeze outside gusted erratically, sending little sprays of rain through the partially open back windows. With the inside of the vehicle steaming up from their breath, it was the only way to keep the windows somewhat clear without having the

engine running. She was beginning to feel uncomfortable due to sitting in the same position, the cheeks of her backside slowly becoming numb. They had been watching the comings and goings of various people, for forty-five minutes, hoping that the public, a police officer, or any of the admin staff wouldn't take a walk over to the car to see what they were doing, sitting as they were.

"I think the rain helps. Most people have got their heads down or under umbrellas," Tom Millwright said, pointing to a couple who were reaching for what appeared to be access cards from inside coat pockets. They could be seen placing lanyards around their necks, as they entered the building. Mary Owen didn't reply, she was beginning to wonder about the merit of what they were doing. He had been convincing when he had called her but now she was having second thoughts. Silently she cursed herself, wishing that she had been more alert when she had answered his call at such an ungodly hour. She was about to let him know how she felt when the words died in her throat. Tom had suddenly stiffened as if a bolt of lightning had struck him.

"There," he pointed, rubbing away some of the condensation on the lower part of the glass in front of him. "There he is, look!"

Mary sat forward in her seat as Brierly, and DC Hughes were making their way outside, running a gauntlet of people going the other way, into the building.

"That's right, it's him," she said. "What now?"

"We follow them," Millwright replied. "Let's see where they go. Maybe they'll lead us right to him?"

"Or maybe not?"

"You never know," he answered, cautiously. He was aware that his idea may come to nought, but at the same time his desire to get revenge for whoever destroyed his family was eating him up inside. He started his car and waited for Brierly and his colleague to drive off in theirs, which was parked in a reserved bay no more than thirty metres away. It seemed to take an age but eventually, they were on their way.

Millwright and Mary had no idea where they were going but they would follow at a safe distance staying as far back as possible without losing sight of them. As they did so, the rain continued to stream down, sloshing against the windscreen making it much more difficult than they imagined. A determined look spread across Tom's face as he concentrated on keeping close to Brierly's car. She could feel him tense up as he drove, noticing how his hands gripped the steering wheel, the knuckles turning white.

"What's the plan, Sir?" Hughes asked, his accent more pronounced now that they were taking action, the investigation reaching the crucial final stage.
"Well, if I'm right, it should be straightforward, Constable," Brierly replied, readying his phone for a brief call. "At least I hope so."
"Do you think that we have enough evidence, Sir? I mean from what we went through yesterday afternoon and last night, it still seems circumstantial."
"To some degree you are right, DC Hughes, but sometimes you have to go with your gut. I hope though that from the work I asked Prof. Atkins to do, we'll get a DNA match. Once we have the suspect in custody we'll get a sample and I'm pretty positive it will."
"How can you be sure, Sir?"
Brierly smiled but did not reply. He looked at the screen of his phone and scanned through his contacts list, finding what he wanted then put the phone to his ear. He called Janie Fenchurch. Hughes continued driving. After a brief conversation, Brierly stated, "Change of plan, Hughes. Our suspect is not where we expected, so here is the new address." Giving him the revised destination, he added, "…and step on it, please," effectively encouraging Hughes to put his foot down. Silently Brierly thanked Fenchurch for giving him the information she had. Mentioning to him that she had been required to cancel a meeting that morning as his suspect had declined it unexpectedly, informing her of a medical emergency. Brierly had been made aware of the scheduled meeting, which was verified by his team during their investigation, and he had decided to use the opportunity to arrest the suspect and bring the individual in for questioning.
"No problem, Sir," Hughes said, as he made a sharp left turn and headed toward the new address. He then turned on the car's headlights which flashed on and off sequentially letting other drivers know that a police vehicle was in a hurry and had right of way. As the car accelerated above the speed limit, cars and trucks ahead of them moved out of the way pulling off the road to the left and right where

they could. Brierly looked at his watch, it was just before 10:30.
"In answer to your question, DC Hughes," he said, looking out of the rain-coated side window at the dreary sky, the wet roads, and the spray from the tyres of cars that moved off the road ahead of them, "our suspect gave themselves away. A simple slip of the tongue was all it took. I should have realized at the time, but sometimes it takes something else to happen to allow the brain to link the two things. The voicemail from the anonymous young girl confirmed my suspicions."
Hughes nodded, unsure what Brierly was referring to. He took a quick glance into the rear-view mirror noting the rows of cars behind them slowly merging back into their lanes. It was like a zip closing. He noticed a car he had seen previously, reaching the front of the merging traffic just as the last of the vehicles came together.
"Just a heads up, Sir."
"Yes, Hughes?"
"I think we are being followed," he said, pointing out to Brierly which car he thought was tailing them.
Brierly looked behind him, but the spray from their own car obscured his view. He looked in the side mirror to see what his Constable was referring to. "The Vauxhall, white, relatively new model." Hughes declared, "looks like two people inside."
Brierly looked again, focusing on the car Hughes had described which seemed strangely familiar to him. "Are you sure?" he asked.
"Yes, Sir, no doubt about it."
"Okay, well thanks for letting me know. Just keep driving, we are almost there anyway," Brierly answered, considering whether to call DS White quickly and ask for backup in light of any potential issues with their stalker or to leave things alone and see what came of it if anything. Maybe Hughes was wrong? As he considered what steps to take, his own words of, 'trust your gut', came back to him as they made the penultimate right turn. The surgery would come into view shortly. He decided to wait.

"Do you think they know we are following them?" she asked, feeling more and more uncomfortable as they started to close the gap between the two cars.
"Don't know, don't care," Millwright replied, his eyes squinting

through the windscreen. The wipers were making a strange sound as the rubber slid slowly back and forth across the glass. It was going to be exceptionally cold and wet all day. Thick clouds in the south, some almost black, appeared to be readying themselves to dump even more water on the poor citizens of the area.
"But if we..."
"If we are wrong. If *you* are wrong," she repeated, "we could find ourselves in a very bad place."
Millwright laughed, a strange almost maniacal sound. "I don't care to be honest," he added. "With Gretchen and the kids gone, what do I have to live for?"
She looked at him, seeing only one side of his face. He stared straight ahead, focused on the road. Feeling uneasy, she pulled her seat belt a little bit tighter as they squirmed their way through the traffic nearing ever closer to Brierly's car.

"Why didn't you tell me?" he asked.
"Because you wouldn't listen," came the reply.
"How long have you known?"
"Not too long," Philip Boothby answered, "and anyway would you or Carol even care if I died?" he added, his voice rising slightly.
"That fucking bitch!" Patricia Boothby shouted, her voice echoing off the walls of the room. The sound penetrated through the closed door, careered down the passageway, and into the waiting room. It appeared as if she had suddenly come out of her stupor, jumping up from her seat when her grandfather had told his son of his condition and prognosis.
"Shut up!" her father shouted. "Shut up and sit down."
Chastised but disinterested, she gave her father a mouthful of abuse to which he responded in kind. His temper had reached boiling point at his daughter's continued aggression and profanity. Abruptly getting up from his chair, he went to grab her, but she was able to evade his grasp despite the relatively small room, knocking her grandfather to the floor in an attempt to reach the closed door and escape. Philip Boothby tried to stand up as Patricia clambered over his legs. He caught her on the shin and she fell against the examination table hitting her face on the metal frame of the bed. A gash opened on her

cheek and blood began flowing down her chin and neck. Putting a hand to the wound she felt the warm sticky substance on her fingers. "You bastard," she shouted at her father, who was now bent over, his arm interlocked with one of his father's arms trying to lift him from the ground. She kicked out in spite, catching her father on the knee, then as he crumpled in pain, she opened the office door. Turning to her grandfather, Patricia helped him to his feet. They could hear someone walking noisily in the passageway coming towards the room. The old man looked around as his son, still prostrate on the floor, grimaced and rubbed his leg vigorously. He noticed a small metal kidney-shaped dish on a shelf filled with several small metal instruments. He grabbed at one, stuffing it quickly into his coat pocket.

"Come on," Patricia said, grabbing the old man by his other hand, "let's get the fuck out of here!"

The voices outside in the passageway were much louder now. Several individuals, including a locum doctor, a patient, and a receptionist were all gathered together as Patricia and her grandfather suddenly burst through the office door, surprising them. The receptionist screamed in shock noticing the blood flowing down the girl's face.

"What happened? What's going on?" the locum asked, as the unlikely pair barged through the concerned triumvirate without any response.

"Out of the way!" Patricia shouted, scattering a small group of patients that had stood up from their chairs trying and see what was happening along the surgery passage. In seconds they had slammed their way through the glass doors at the surgery entrance and were out into the cold, wet, day.

Patricia stopped for a second, her arm around that of her grandfather.

She couldn't remember having arrived, suddenly unsure of where she was. "Where the fuck is the car?"

Philip Boothby stared straight ahead, not listening to what she was saying. Walking directly towards them were Brierly and DC Hughes.

He lengthened his stride as he walked off the last of the steps that led from the upper-level car park. With the lower level full, Hughes had needed to drive the car along the c-shaped road to reach a spot where

they were able to park. There was no sign at all of the car that appeared to be following them. Brierly had expected that it would be an easy arrest, a simple procedure. He was wrong. With Hughes a few paces behind, him he saw the doors to the surgery, fifty metres away, open ferociously. Two people almost fell through them in their haste, practically careering into another couple who were about to enter the building. Brierly recognized one of those who had exited. He didn't know the young woman with the older man, but his instinct gave him a clue. The pair stopped on the concrete pavement and began looking around them. From Brierly's perspective, they seemed to be unsure where to go, confused. It was as if they were lost. It was obvious, however, that they were in a hurry and extremely agitated. Arms like windmills were pointing in different directions. Brierly and Hughes closed the gap, walking Indian file between the vehicles that filled the parking area, getting to within twenty metres of them. Hughes was the first to notice the blood on the young girl's face. He began to say something, then suddenly noticed something else.
"Sir," he pointed, "look…!"

He had driven the last quarter of a mile much more slowly. When the roads had become less congested, it had been easier to see the car ahead, despite the rain, so he had taken a more conservative approach. Holding back, he had been lucky. When Brierly's car had turned into the surgery car park the lower level was full, but Millwright was presented with a gift as an SUV pulled out from a bay just as he drove into the lot. Mary pointed it out to him. The parking bay they occupied was in the third row back, facing the building and giving them a clear view of the premises and the entrance. It would be easy to see what Brierly was up to and whether the policemen came out with anyone of interest. Tom had barely parked the car when they noticed the doors to the surgery slam open nearly causing a middle-aged man and woman who were about to enter the building to be bowled over by a young girl and an old man. Watching it all unfold, Mary screamed in surprise, just as loudly as the couple in the doorway.
"Look she said," pointing to their left, noticing Brierly and his colleague breaking into a jog as they ran past Millwright's car towards

Philip Boothby and the bloodied girl. Tom Millwright's face turned white. He recognized Patricia despite her now bedraggled appearance.
"Fuck," he said under his breath. Mary looked at him quizzically.
"What is it?" she asked, her eyes now back on the scene in front of them, the two policemen were now just a few yards away from the obviously distressed pair. Millwright did not respond, his mind linking strands together, slowly realizing what he was seeing.
"It's him. That's the bastard that did this!" he shouted, opening his car door and starting to climb out. Mary was confused, calling out to him as he started to walk briskly towards the group of four now standing together at the entrance to the building. Millwright paid no attention to her shout, he walked away with clear intent. The rain has ceased for a minute and was only spitting now. As she watched Mary saw the tiny drops make little dots on the back of Tom's jacket.

"Philip Boothby, I'm arresting you for the murders of…." Brierly began before he was pushed in the back and sent sprawling. Tom Millwright had closed the gap between his car and the small group within seconds. Just as he was reciting the old man his rights, Millwright barged into him, knocking Brierly to his knees. Hughes who had been standing next to his boss, grabbed hold of Patricia pulling her away from colliding with him as Brierly fell.
"You bastard! You fucking bastard!" Millwright screamed at Boothby, his hands reaching for the old man's throat. "It was you, wasn't it? It was you who killed my family!"
Brierly dragged himself up, noticing Hughes holding Patricia around the waist, keeping his body behind her. She tried to kick out at Millwright, to get him to let go of her grandfather, but Hughes was able to hold her back.
"Mr. Millwright!" Brierly shouted in an attempt to get him to release Boothby, but the man wasn't listening. Boothby made a horrible noise as Millwright smashed a fist into his stomach. Brierly jumped onto Millwright from behind pulling the man's arms backwards in a single movement and slammed him into the surgery door.
"Stop it, for Christ's sake," Brierly shouted, turning Millwright around to face Boothby who was breathing heavily, spittle at the side of his mouth. He launched a tirade of abuse at his attacker.

"They deserved it, all of them," he said, "and it's all your fault!" He pointed a finger back at Millwright.
"What the fuck are you talking about, you stupid old man." Millwright said.
"Shut up, leave this to me," Brierly shouted at Tom, breathing hard at his unexpected exertions. He looked towards Hughes for support, but the DC still had his hands full with Patricia, who seemed dazed but was also erratic and extremely aggressive. Under the prevailing circumstances, it was obvious that they needed backup. It was difficult to handle three angry people with just the two of them. Millwright ignored Brierly's comments and began screaming at Boothby again. The old man took a handkerchief out of his pocket and wiped his mouth. Sweat and drops of rain glistened on his cheeks and forehead. It was a surreal moment which Brierly later shared with DCI Hammond. As he held Tom back, Boothby walked the three paces between them and spat in Millwright's face.
"If it wasn't for you, none of this would have happened," he said.
"What?"
"Shut up," Brierly said again, maintaining his grip on Millwright's arms.
"No!" the old man responded, "I want him to hear this," Boothby continued, his finger pointing at Tom who was still trying to break Brierly's grasp. "I saw you once selling drugs to my granddaughter here, one night in the cemetery. You were her dealer, weren't you? Weren't you?!"
Without waiting for a reply, extreme anger in his eyes and a vicious curl to his mouth, Boothby continued with his tirade. "All my life I have tried to help people get off drugs, to get off the street, and all you've done is put Patricia here back out there. A young girl's life, my granddaughter's life ruined by the likes of you! You bastard!" Boothby shouted.
"That was her decision," Millwright replied.
"No, it wasn't. It was a response to her parent's divorce, a cry for help that you took advantage of. You groomed a young girl who eventually became hooked on drugs due to your greed! You gave no thought to the consequences. You were only interested in the financial benefit to yourself and your family, but you were wrong weren't you? It affected my family too!"
"You killed my wife and kids, my family, because of that?" Millwright

asked in despair.

"No, I took my revenge because of what your family was. A group of parasites!"

"I can't…"

"It wasn't the first time that you all took advantage of others, but it will definitely be the last."

"Mr. Boothby!" Brierly said, realizing that things were getting out of control. He looked around for assistance but with the rain increasing, the immediate area was suddenly devoid of people. Even those in the surgery and car park seemed to have hidden themselves away. Ignoring Brierly completely, Boothby carried on with his invective, justifying his actions, the killing of Gretchen Millwright, Trevor Owen, and Tom's two children. His smile grew into a wicked smirk as each of his victims was mentioned. "Your family shouldn't exist and now it doesn't anymore. If only Fred Amberley had died before he killed my Grandmother, your lot wouldn't….!"

Millwright began to scream abuse at the old man, Brierly struggled to keep him under control, as he lashed out again with his feet, trying to kick the old man. Boothby laughed then without warning took out the blade that he had taken from his son's room, and slashed Millwright's throat before stabbing him in his chest.

"Christ!" Brierly shouted as Millwright crumpled in his arms, blood spurting down the front of his jacket. Hughes released Patricia and made to help his boss who screamed for him to get a doctor from inside the building. Brierly dropped to the floor trying to staunch the blood gushing from Millwright's throat, using a scarf that he had been wearing under his coat to keep his neck warm. As he did so he realized that Patricia and Philip Boothby were now free. He looked to his right just in time to see the pair of them hobble away. He suspected that they were heading to their car, but he had no idea where it was parked. As they crossed the driveway between the surgery pavement and the first row of parked vehicles, Brierly suddenly heard the roaring of an engine and the screeching of tyres. A car shot out from the third row, the engine's revs carried through the still air and the increasing rain. It was the car that had followed them. It headed towards Boothby and his granddaughter, and as it passed him, still accelerating, Brierly saw Mary Owen in the driver's seat. "No!" he shouted, his mind reeling as to the horror he was about to witness. His cry was to no avail. As his voice died, the car

smashed into its target; two people that were desperate to escape, two people limping away, almost comically running for their lives. They were five metres from safety, the full first row of cars, at the time of impact. As the car hit them, the two bodies flew up into the air, one landing with a sickening thud on the bonnet before cracking the windscreen, sliding across the car's roof, and then landing on the road behind. The other, that of Patricia, sailed like a rag dog ten metres to the left, smashing against the surgery building before coming to a stop in a bloodied heap on the pavement alongside the driveway. Both Boothby and his granddaughter were dead before they hit the ground. Mary struggled to control her vehicle. With its windscreen shattered she plowed into the first row of cars, spinning through three hundred and sixty degrees before flipping the car onto its roof. Within twenty seconds of the carnage beginning, people poured out of the surgery. Some screamed at the sight before them. Parents hurried their children back inside. Alan Boothby stopped at the surgery entrance staring at the chaos all around. He saw his father's battered body lying on the tarmac. He fell to his knees, tears streamed down his face. People spoke to him, trying to comfort him, but he didn't hear a word they said. It would take many minutes before he was able to stand and walk over to where his father lay, inert, bloodied, bent. A colleague of Boothby tried to help Brierly, who was himself covered in blood from Tom Millwright's wounds.
"It's too late," the doctor said softly, "he's gone. I'm sorry."
Brierly sighed angrily. His attempts to save the man had been in vain. He looked at his hands which were stained red. Slowly he eased himself up, hearing a cacophony of noise around him, but taking little of it in. It was like a scene from a film, but without sound. He looked for Hughes only to see him helping someone drag Mary Owen from the smashed car. Steam rose from the damaged radiator as she was laid out on the ground. Hughes raised his eyes, meeting those of his boss some twenty metres away. With a subtle shake of the head, he let Brierly know that she had not survived the crash. A broken neck was how the coroner later described what had killed her. Brierly walked towards Alan Boothby who was kneeling beside his father. Someone had brought a blanket and covered the body. Boothby pulled it partially away revealing the smashed and bloodied face of the old man. Sadness filled his eyes again. Brierly stood beside the stooping doctor, placing a hand on his shoulder. He squeezed gently.

"What a mess," he said.
"Yes," Boothby replied, his voice cracking with emotion, speaking so softly that Brierly could hardly hear him. "What a bloody mess."

Sitting in his office, Brierly could sense the silence permeating throughout his team. It was way too quiet, and it concerned him. He knew that he had a full complement of officers for a change, and they were all present and correct. It was less than forty-eight hours since the incident outside Alan Boothby's surgery. The team was collating all the necessary evidence and data for the report that would be needed both for 'upstairs' review as well as the applicable inquest. Brierly typed a few notes into his desk computer, a cup of tea, surprisingly untouched and now cold, stood on one side of the desk. He sat back, the lack of noise was unnerving. He wondered what was going on and was about to call out through his partially opened door when a hand appeared, knuckles rapping a rat-a-tat sound on the blue paint.
"Can I come in, Sir?" DS White asked.
"Sure," Brierly replied, pleased to have the opportunity to find out what was going on.
"Thank you, Sir," White replied, taking the seat opposite his boss. Brierly waited for his Sergeant to speak, attempting to hide his worry about the lack of sound outside.
"Go on then," Brierly indicated, his patience in letting White speak first, was tested by the clock. Waiting for just a few seconds was too hard for him to manage.
"Well, Sir.....Jim, I just thought I'd give you an update as to the current report on the Boothby matter from the other day. The supporting facts."
Brierly nodded, without commenting, letting White continue to speak. "We have begun compiling a timeline of events from CCTV footage taken around town. We've also been able to find some in those areas that we believe Patricia Boothby frequented. It will take us a while to check through everything, but we are making progress already."
"Good."
"In addition, we have witness statements concerning the grandfather's movements, especially now that we know he stalked the

Owens and Millwright families. We'll be following that up, but it's strange how people suddenly remember seeing his car parked in various locations, particularly on the night Gretchen was killed. Not to mention some of the staff at the shelter now recall seeing him use the computer one day, the same one that Anderson used. They had never seen that happen before, even Janie Fenchurch said that she found it unusual at the time, but he had justified it by saying he was helping Anderson learn the ropes. She hadn't questioned it any further as there was no obvious need to, especially given his position on the board and his long-standing association with the shelter."

"Which makes sense doesn't it?" Brierly replied. He knew that people's memory could often play tricks on them when asked about an activity or a certain time or date. It was even more challenging when the person whose activities you are querying was in a position of power over you, no matter the governance obligations of that particular entity. Power over others often hid corruption or manipulation in even the smallest of institutions.

"I expect we'll also have some more substantive evidence from Boothby's house after the search that was conducted by the Forensics team yesterday morning," White continued. "From the statement given by his son, it looks like the old man would never invite him to his house, always asking to meet at the doctor's place or talk on the phone. From what I hear there's plenty of stuff that the boys have seen during their search that indicates the old man's obsession."

"I don't doubt it," Brierly answered, still unsure why his team had been so quiet. He decided to put the question directly to his Sergeant.

"It's because they are still trying to work out how you knew," White said.

"Knew what?"

"That the older Boothby was the killer. I mean we know that now, given his confession, but before that?"

Brierly suddenly realized that he had been so busy over the last day and a half, managing the fallout from the deaths in the car park. With the media, print, and radio interests, along with keeping the hierarchy abreast of developments, he had completely forgotten to relay his thinking to the team. They hadn't even had a decent de-brief meeting as yet. Everyone was busy and no one was able to celebrate. There was no prosecution to be had and no conviction. No posthumous trial either.

"You're right," Brierly said, contritely. "I remember starting to tell DC Hughes but not getting into detail. I got sidetracked when he pointed out that we were being followed."

"So, are you going to tell me? Tell us?"

"Naturally."

"Well then?"

"It was when the old man mentioned if we had discovered the identity of the body in the burnt-out van."

"What about it?" White queried.

"Well, it's obvious, isn't it?"

"Is it?"

"Yes. We never released anything to the media that wasn't embargoed. So, no one was ever told that we found a dead body there."

"Which meant that only the people who attended the fire that night…the police, paramedics, forensics knew….."

"That's right. Or, someone who had been involved in the murder," interrupted Brierly, "they would have known about the victim."

"Got it," White replied, then suddenly realizing something else, said, "But Jim, wasn't the van found by that motorist, the rep…err, Shepparton?"

"Yes, that's right."

"Well, what about him, was he involved?

"That's possible, but from his statement, we know that he was away from home for the three days prior to that night. He's a rep and we've confirmed that he was in the country seeing his clients before making his way home, finding the van already destroyed when he took the shortcut. In addition, Forensics tested him, his clothing, and his car for any residue or traces of accelerant that night before allowing him to leave. All the tests were negative, so we know he couldn't have been involved."

"But maybe he said something to someone afterward, and it got back to Boothby?"

"Again, it's possible but highly unlikely, after all, he didn't know the old man, and neither did his wife. Given they live a long way from the city, the balance of probability suggested to me that there was only one suspect."

"I suppose so," White replied.

"I can tell you are thinking it was a lucky guess, Sergeant, but there was one final clincher."
"Which was?"
"The voice mail left by Patricia Boothby. She left enough detail on it, suggesting she knew who the perpetrator was."
"But she didn't say precisely who that was did she, Jim?"
"No, but she did try to use the information she had to blackmail her own father. She saw Phil Boothby bludgeon the poor victim unconscious before dragging him into the van and wanted to embarrass her own father with the information into giving her money to keep quiet about it. Which we now know he refused."
"Which you didn't know at the time."
"That's true," Brierly replied, "but sometimes Sergeant, one has to go with one's gut on these things. Philip Boothby was the only link I could see to the other murders after we were able to tie Silver to the Crossley case. Do you remember the story Mary Owen told us, about her family members?"
"Yes, sort of."
"Well, you may not recall everything but there was one name that we didn't know much about. David Warrington, the husband of Susan Amberley, the woman killed by her brother, Fred in 1927. Remember Mary didn't know what happened to him."
"So. What did?"
"Well, he was killed in 1943, but he and Susan had a daughter, Ann in 1925. Ann died tragically in 1962 but in 1948, a few years after the war, she married Wilfred Boothby."
"Philip Boothby's dad?"
"Yes. Philip Boothby was born in 1955. His son Alan was born in 1980."
"So," White said, "the Boothby's were descended from the Amberley's? The same lineage as the present-day Owen family."
"Yes. The team did a great job in connecting those dots. It's why Philip Boothby was so determined to end their line. With Patricia's drug problem being fed by Tom Millwright, Phil Boothby lost his mind somewhat. All his adult life he was trying to keep people off drugs, Trying to get them clean. Which is why he was so passionate about the shelter and it remaining drug-free. He loved his granddaughter so much that when he knew she was back on the streets it was enough for him to kill for her."

"Is that all? Was there anything else that pointed to him?"
"There was one other thing that tied in with what I just said. It bothered me for a while until I narrowed down the fact that it was the old man who killed Gretchen Millwright, her kids, and Dave Crossley's father."
"What was that?" White asked, curiously.
"The marks on the fingers, on the ring fingers."
"What about them?"
"They weren't just random cuts. They were done in a specific way. I only worked it out once we knew of the family links."
"So what were they?"
Brierly took a few seconds before answering. "They were stars, cut into the fingers. Everyone one of the cuts was the same. That's what roused my curiosity. Atkins' report had spelt it out but it took me a while to understand the meaning."
"Stars? I still don't get it." White quizzed. The debate the team had been having quietly outside had not considered anything that Brierly was now saying. It seems they had all missed the clues.
"Yes, stars," Brierly stated. "The star of the shipping company that owned the Titanic. The White Star Line. Philip Boothby was telling us where this whole thing started and I never saw it until it was way too late."
"And what about the other victim…in the van. Who was he?"
Brierly put his hands together on the surface of his desk, interlocking his fingers. He looked directly into White's face, and sighed outwardly, a feeling of sadness overcoming him. "We don't know yet who that was. We may never find out. It could be a traveller. It could be anyone. We know it's a man, a son, maybe a father, but whose? Let's hope we can find out at some point otherwise he'll just become a Joe Bloggs or a John Smith….Maybe nobody cares anyway."
"Sad isn't it?" White said.
"Indeed….families hey?" Brierly replied. "Families."

EPILOGUE

The funerals of the Millwright and Owen families took place three weeks after the deaths of Tom and Mary. Ironically they were not buried, but cremated, leaving no lasting legacy such as a gravestone. Their ashes were scattered in the sea from off the Palace pier in Brighton. It was a decision taken by Brierly after it was established that there were no other family members alive. He deemed it was an appropriate measure given how a relative from the sinking of the Titanic who had passed on a keepsake hoping to be remembered in his family's heart, had gone down with the ship. Given his own background of being at sea over many years, he guessed how the sailor would have felt knowing that he would never see his loved ones again. The attempt to have a little part of him live on had turned out much different from what Brierly guessed the sailor would have expected. When Brierly finally discovered the back story and verified the man's legacy, the ring which caused so much pain and death over four generations, it became obvious to him how things should end. His suggestion to close the circle and return the family to where it all started, seemed appropriate.
The coroner was satisfied with the report that Brierly's team compiled. The killings of the children and Gretchen were ultimately confirmed through evidence found at Philip Boothby's home after subsequent investigation at the old man's home. A paper tree, a family tree showing the various familial branches from 1865 onwards, surveillance photographs taken over months, as well as draft copies of the threatening letters sent to Trevor Owen were found on Boothby's computer. The verbal confession made outside the surgery and the photos taken as he followed the Owen and Millwright families were more than enough to convince the coroner of the intent and guilt of the old man.

Patricia Boothby and her grandfather were buried in the Millbrook cemetery. The only attendees, apart from the undertakers who acted as pallbearers and a rather sad-looking celebrant, were Alan Boothby, his ex-wife Anneline and DI Jim Brierly. Carol Boothby refused to attend, telling her husband that as his father had no time for her in life, she had no time for him in death. It surprised Brierly that no ex-councillors or anyone from the homeless shelter came to pay their respects to the deceased. He understood that many would have been horrified by what Philip Boothby had done and likewise would have little awareness of his granddaughter's problems or her attitude to others, but he rationalized it within himself eventually. The difference between the family relationship and those of their friends and acquaintances and how they interact with each other was stark. Blood was always thicker than water and bloodlines were often a cause of conflict. A friend could walk away from an issue, families however often lived with it, sometimes for years until things were either resolved or remained broken forever. On that basis alone, he realized why there were so few mourners standing at the graveside as grandfather and granddaughter were laid to rest next to each other.

Brierly kept the Star Walk app on his phone for another month. He battled with its complexity, enlisting his sons to help him in trying to improve his understanding of it. He gave up eventually, reverting to his magazines.
"I'm sure it's very clever," he said to June, "but it's just too involved."
"Was it of no use at all?" she asked.
"To be honest with you, it was very useful, but not in the way that you would think."
"Oh? In what way then?"
Brierly took a few seconds to gather his thoughts before explaining to her how the names of stars, planets, asteroids, and comets originated.
"It was this that led me to understand a bit more about families and how they interact. The ancient Greeks and Romans had their fair share of wars and fights across their empires and they named the objects in the sky based on what they knew at the time. They believed that the Gods delivered divine justice from above…so they created myths and legends about the stars and other celestial objects that fit with their narrative."
"When in reality what was happening around them were typical human frailties?" she questioned.
"Yes, those of greed, hatred, and jealousy."
"So not much has changed then," June stated matter of factly.

"No, and I doubt it ever will. No matter what the stars say."
"I suppose," she added, reaching for her book.
"Aren't you nearly finished with that?" he asked, pointing to the cover, a picture of the actress Pauline Collins on it.
"Yes, just a few pages left."
"And?"
"Well, it's funny in a way, as it's also about family, but far more positive. A lovely story. You should read it sometime. It's the total opposite to what you were talking about."
"Maybe I will," he answered.
She smiled at him before asking, "So why do you want to get rid of it, the app I mean? If it was useful."
"It's the weather really, especially if it's a good summer. When we get to the longer nights, it will be almost impossible to see anything. With our extended days, especially with daylight saving it will be too late in the evening before it gets dark enough. I'll be in bed by then."
"Fair enough."
"And in the winter, like now, the sky is either covered with clouds, it's raining or what is happening out there is either too low on the horizon or is happening during my bedtime."
June looked at her husband, a loving smile on her face. She knew him well enough to recognize that he would continue to be fascinated with the heavens and would likely revert to the theoretical and the use of his imagination rather than relying on a tool that told him when and where to look. Reading his magazines, and scanning the night sky when he could, but staying out of the digital realm was his go. Magazines, paper journals, and books would work just fine.
"I'll tell you what though," she said.
"What?" he asked.
"It's my bedtime too," she pointed at her watch. "Give me five minutes to finish these last couple of pages, and maybe we can spend a bit of time contemplating the heavens…if you know what I mean."
A grin spread across Brierly's face, "I know what you mean," he said.

ABOUT THE AUTHOR

Eric Horridge was born in Manchester. A former semi-professional football player with degrees in Commerce, and an MBA, he has had extensive experience in business including roles as CFO and CEO within the Technology sector.

After such a successful period in his life, he decided to turn his hand to writing fiction.

Damaged is his second novel using the Saul Friedmann moniker

The author understands and accepts that all extracts or references used in this book are in the public domain.

Printed in Great Britain
by Amazon